A CANDLE FOR JUDAS

David Fraser, biogapher of *Alanbrooke*, historian of the British Army with *And We Shall Shock Them*, social commentator in *The Christian Watt Papers* and novelist with *August 1988* and the *Treason in Arms* series, was once one of Britain's most senior generals. He is married, has five children and lives in Hampshire.

A Candle for Judas completes the *Treason in Arms* series, which depicts the turbulent and dangerous period in Europe from the First World War to the aftermath of the Second. The first four volumes are:

The Killing Times
The Dragon's Teeth
A Kiss for the Enemy
The Seiz

Books by David Fraser

ALANBROOKE
AND WE SHALL SHOCK THEM
THE CHRISTIAN WATT PAPERS
AUGUST 1988

The Treason in Arms series:

THE KILLING TIMES
THE DRAGON'S TEETH
A KISS FOR THE ENEMY
THE SEIZURE
A CANDLE FOR JUDAS

DAVID FRASER

A Candle for Judas

[illegible]

27th December, 2004
– 1st January, 2005.
Humewood Hotel,
Port Elizabeth.
South Africa.

FONTANA/Collins

First published in Great Britain by
William Collins Sons & Co. Ltd 1989
First published in Fontana Paperbacks 1989

Printed and bound in Great Britain by
William Collins Sons & Co. Ltd, Glasgow

1

It was in a church that John Tranter saw him first. The church at Varnas is Romanesque, small, with origins in the tenth century (according to the description in faded ink pinned up near the door by a previous curé). It is beautiful, with its rounded arches and alternating rose-coloured and grey stones at the curves of each arch. It is also dirty, and sadly disused. Like most churches of Provence its cool darkness offers refreshing contrast to the fierce brilliance of the day. On this July afternoon in 1978, however, John Tranter had sought sanctuary not from heat or harsh light but from rain. He had been shopping and was caught by an afternoon storm rolling off the Vaucluse plateau, a storm which would, with luck, not last long, and after which he could walk back to his lodging at the little village of Les Manottes, not two kilometres from Varnas.

John moved into the church in a practised way – it had several times provided him with shelter from something or other, and as often as not he had it to himself. He liked it for its peace as well as for its convenience. He knew it well. Sometimes a shuffling old woman would pass him on her way out or in, muttering and wobbling towards some act of devotion. Generally, he was alone.

But not on this occasion. John saw the man as soon as he, himself, sat down near the door (for there would be at least five minutes of tempest, probably ten). The man was sitting near the front of the nave, very still, apparently gazing at the altar (of no artistic interest, as it happens) with an intentness, an immobility which yet did not, somehow, suggest prayer.

Nor did the man's back, the rather awkward squat on the uncomfortable little chair, imply familiarity. This one did not appear at home. The rear view did not signal piety. The man looked – if a back seated some distance away in semi-darkness looks anything – as if not so much absorbed as detached. Almost as if dead.

John Tranter was a painter – of indifferent talent, he had come to acknowledge, but uninterested in doing anything else. His eyes were his trade. The visual impression the man made was not dramatic – there was nothing particularly arresting in the presence of a stranger in Varnas church, especially during a storm – but it was definite. Had John been attempting, with whatever lack of success, to paint a man absorbed in religious exercise or in artistic contemplation, that back would not have filled the mind's eye. Had he on the other hand (improbably) sought to depict a figure struck lifeless by some awful visitation or spasm, he thought he could have had worse models. They sat for a little at their separate ends of the church. John thought the downpour was stopping.

Suddenly the man got up, moved – rather blundering – into the aisle, and without hesitation or genuflexion walked towards the door. He passed John without a glance. His front view exactly corresponded to the impression his back had made and John felt a touch of satisfaction. The stranger looked exhausted, drained, incapable of response – a great, dark, pale man whose gaze seemed more unseeing than that of the naturally blind. But John also noticed, with a shock, for it was unexpected, that he was looking at an expression of remarkable beauty. The face, high-cheekboned, severe, held brown eyes of great gentleness. There was a look of unnatural, exaggerated tension, like a figure painted by El Greco. The features were still, but not serene. There was magnetism and much disquiet. A cold wave of unhappiness seemed to wash behind him – whatever comfort he had sought in Varnas church he had surely not found it.

Then, as the man's footsteps echoed on the stone floor

between John and the exit, as John waited to hear the creaking sound of the door swinging as the other left, he became aware of something unexpected. The man appeared to be talking to himself, having paused somewhere behind. John looked round. Talking – but not to himself! A figure identifiable as the curé had put in a surprise appearance from one of the side-chapels and the stranger had accosted him. He did not speak in a low voice and John listened. The man's French was grammatical but halting, his accent that of an Englishman. The words were peculiar, and the curé was responding with disapproving shrugs.

'I believe your Church, Father, teaches that Judas Iscariot is of all men the most nearly certain to be damned, so great was his offence. Don't you think that prayers should be said for him now, poor man? May it not be, Father, that enough time has gone by for a forgiveness to be shown to Judas, even a candle lit, a Mass said now and then? Is not that reasonable, Father?'

John could not hear the priest's reply, but saw him move uneasily away and guessed he suspected this unusual tourist of being English, heretical and unattractively insane.

John Tranter's father and mother had come to live abroad after his father's retirement from the civil service in 1956. This retirement was premature. A retrenchment, as periodically occurred, led to the offer of fairly generous additional gratuities to middle-grade men prepared to leave on pension before their time. Mr Tranter's prospects (although he seldom spoke of them, and always indirectly) were certainly not glowing. The gratuity, in aggregate, composed a tempting sum. Tranter senior was not in the least well off but he had inherited a small house in Wimbledon (and little else) from his own father, and values had risen. He reckoned that by selling this and investing his gratuity he could afford to buy a modest home in France or Spain, and live quite comfortably off his pension and off the dividends from gratuity and invested balance of sale price of the Wimbledon house (tax rebated to those domiciled abroad). John's mother liked the sun and spoke reasonable French. His father's French was and remained appalling, but the plan was adopted and the Tranter parents moved to a small, ugly modern house about a mile from the Mediterranean coast in the district of France called the Roussillon, at the eastern extremity of the Pyrenees.

In retrospect John always thought this emigration surprising. His father was intensely, narrowly English; had travelled in Europe on infrequent holidays, with suspicion, and, in the Second World War, had visited Italy as a soldier with, as far as could be made out, no very agreeable memories as residue. John was born in 1940 and was sixteen when the decision was made to leave England. It was true that life was still cheaper in parts of France and in Spain in 1956 than it shortly became; but Mr Tranter had been earning a respectable salary in the civil service, and, even retiring when he did, was only forty-one and could, like most men in such circumstances, hope for some sort of a second career, helped by gratuity and pension. Instead, in the prime of life, he decided to live in France on a small income and do absolutely nothing. He said, when questioned by friends (very few) or relatives (equally few and, without exception, unloved), 'We went into it.' He managed to convey by this a process of exhaustive analysis, helped by data not available to all.

John's mother tagged along, not unhappily. She came from a Sussex family, the Patersons, a cut above the Tranters, at least in recent times. The Patersons had owned land, lived in large houses, were part of what would later be called the 'establishment' of the county. One cousin, Hilda, had married into another large landed family, the Marvells; and cousin Hilda Marvell was fond of John's mother and had the Tranters – generally John and his mother, with father declaring firmly that he 'couldn't get away' – to stay at her home, Bargate, on several occasions. John found Bargate grand and beautiful and his cousins kind; but his father made plain, with an undertone of disapproval, that there was and would remain a mighty difference between Bargate and any world the Tranters were likely to inhabit. Bargate remained something of an enchanted castle in John's young imagination; but when he was thirteen Hilda Marvell died and he never went there again. All that was before the emigration.

John came to believe that the real explanation of his father's move to France lay in unacknowledged but profound laziness. Mr Tranter's character, upbringing and previous career condemned this as a sin – almost the most contemptible of sins. His secret taste, however, was for a life of simple, unluxurious inactivity. He liked to sit in the sun and do about one undemanding task in the day. With so desperate a predilection he had, of course, to live abroad to indulge it.

The move to the Roussillon came at a slightly awkward time in John's own education – the run-up to the possibility of entry to a British university. He was attending as a day boy a good local school in the southern suburbs of London, and a sudden transition to any sort of 'boarding' would have been difficult. His parents, who were loyal to him and did their duty in an undemonstrative way, contemplated deferring the flight to the Mediterranean until their son was at a later stage, but decided against this. John's father was sure (mistakenly) that the price he could get for the Wimbledon house represented a false property boom which would collapse (in fact John later learned that the house changed hands in 1976 for a sum exactly ten times that which the Tranters received). Mr Tranter also thought, more accurately, that prices abroad would rise. 'We went into it.' The die was cast. John continued at his school in London and lodged in term time with a dull widowed aunt by marriage. Holidays were spent in the Roussillon and John learned, by his own determination and some sensible initiatives by his mother, to speak French idiomatically and with enjoyment. When examinations came he failed them all.

The Tranter parents took this well, although John's father

wondered without acrimony how his son proposed to earn his living. John did not suppose his father feared his own idleness would be reborn in the next generation, because it was clear Mr Tranter never saw himself as idle – indeed, each day he gave a strong impression of being rather over-extended and short of time. But it was recognized that the family budget would not cover John after the age of twenty.

John had some facility at 'Art' at school. He liked drawing. He enjoyed paint. He also responded warmly to colour, the sort of strong colour which only the sun and the south produce. It would be absurd to pretend that he felt a divine creative impulse; but he preferred painting to doing anything else and it was, he thought, surely possible – just – that he could exist by it. He went to art school in Aix-en-Provence. Three years and a modest diploma later he started knocking on doors in London. He realized that his talent was mediocre, but that he had to live; and the British are more generous toward mediocrity and more tolerant of it than the French. John got a job in the design department of a large advertising company. It was not the life dreamed of at Aix, but it was not bad. By living economically – and, on the whole, dully – in London he saved enough to visit his parents and the Roussillon for one blissful summer holiday each year. He travelled widely in France: it was his sole luxury, and each year he disliked more the return. He rose – slowly – in the peculiar hierarchy of the world of commercial design. He had his niche and a modest salary. He loved a little, and did not marry at all. He liked girls but feared domesticity. He had no hankering for fatherhood.

Then – John was thirty-four – both parents died. The Tranters were a quiet family, but there was no unkindness in it and the shock was sharp. Both father and mother had been seized with a severe form of food poisoning. Medical attention was, at that time, less reliable than in Britain (or so Mr Tranter had believed, recounting with grim relish many horror stories about the local practitioners). Whether something might have been done had his parents acted more urgently or been treated more wisely, John never determined. His father was only fifty-nine, his mother a year older.

Clearing up the estate was not difficult. On the whole, despite the care with which, allegedly, he 'went into it', John's father was an unwise investor. In order to obtain the best return on his money in an age when inflation was already beginning to bite, he had bought high-yielding gilt-edged securities whose value had most certainly not increased with time. The house in Roussillon was a decent asset, but some charmless and too adjacent recent building had done little for it. Mr Tranter had also, it was clear, had to dip deep into his capital to keep afloat – John was rather glad of this and hoped his father had felt no compunction. Meanwhile there were significant debts and overdrafts. When all was finished (John immediately put the house on the market and sold it) there was left just under £40,000. It was, in 1974, a reasonable inheritance for a man of John's age; it did not seem likely, however, to bring a revolutionary change to his style of life.

Or might it?

It was September, 1974. John, also, bolted. Like his father before him he did his sums, and went into it. He was advised that £40,000 could be invested to show about ten per cent, with some restrained hope of preserving, by growth, the value of the capital (this proved absurdly optimistic). After establishing domicile abroad it was possible to escape British income tax on investments: the Tranter fortune would thus bring, net, just about £4,000 per annum (John also had a few savings of his own).

Fortunately, John had – and desired – few tangible possessions. He had parted with his parents' house and furniture without a pang. He needed a roof, somewhere to paint, enough money for one decent meal a day and sufficient cheap wine. He also needed to be able to buy paint and canvas (of ever-increasing cost) with a margin for travel (he did not intend much), postage and telephone (to whom?), and clothes (wardrobe was already adequate, and clothes in the south were a negligible item). The whole thing depended on finding a decent room; although frugal and with simple tastes, John disliked anything sordid. He knew that he could eat and drink for the equivalent of less than four pounds a day. But a room – and somewhere to paint – was different.

In time, however, John found it. Mme Blanchard was the sixty-year-old widow of a professor of art at Aix. Two introductions led John to her and to Les Manottes, where he took a room at the top of a little house from which the professor previously contemplated his and Cézanne's beloved Provence.

John was fair-haired, stocky, thirty-four years old, with an attractively ugly face and a thorough grasp of conversational French. Mme Blanchard expected, and received, an honest ration of conversation. She clearly felt, through John's efforts, that she was in touch with the world her late husband adorned. John made a firm compact – he always supped at the little café, except on Mondays. He needed only one meal a day, and coffee in the morning was produced by Mme Blanchard. At midday he drank a glass of wine and ate some bread and some fruit. He also had, chez Blanchard, a disused stable as studio (windows glazed by the professor, who entertained promising pupils there), well lit, excellent in summer although challenging in winter (oil stove: ineffective).

Six hundred pounds per year.

After food and wine, this left John (in theory) about £2,000 per year for paint, canvases, travel and 'margin'. In 1975 this appeared riches. In theory, too, this was a temporary budget until sale of pictures made the calculation less constraining. In fact, with the optimism a bachelor of thirty-four can still experience, John decided that he would, come what may, 'manage' – and draw on capital if in grievous debt. A few years like that would surely end in glory. The whole thing made return to something like the commercial art studio, with its secure, salaried frustrations, unthinkable. John had, at first, told himself he was making calculations, weighing the pros and cons. There was little of that – instinct was gloriously dominant. He would be free, sufficiently fed, respectably housed, as near solvent as made little difference, and pass his days in doing what he liked doing – the *only* thing he liked doing. In 1977 he sold two pictures – one for less than the cost of paint and canvas, the other for fifteen hundred francs. That, he knew, was but a beginning.

Life, therefore, became extraordinarily free from stress for John Tranter. In every small town and many villages in Provence there are people who paint, generally doing other part-time, unskilled jobs to feed themselves, but painting as a compulsive, primary activity. Few have much talent. All need to paint to feel alive. John joined their fraternity without difficulty. His student time at Aix gave him an entrée. He did not lack casual friends, although he was older than most and had, of course, the taints of English blood (in the most chauvinist of all countries) and a past life of compromising salaried security. But after a little he gained enough acceptance seldom to be lonely; and he was, by nature, a solitary, a man who liked silence. Now and then he missed his own kind, if they existed. He sometimes talked in his imagination to reasonably well-informed folk of British blood and background, whose inward thoughts he could share a little. But by and large he was happy among the quick, cynical Latins who surrounded his hours with advice, criticism, and, in time, a certain measure of affection. He was not sure whether this was enough in life: to paint in the sun, to drink wine, to feel free, cheerful and not unloved. But he told himself that he was by no means idle. One dealer had shown particular sympathetic interest early in 1978 and a modest exhibition might, he managed to believe, not be far away.

Then, on that July afternoon, John saw the man, the tall, unhappy, somehow unforgettable man in the church at Varnas. And after that nothing was the same.

*

Three evenings after that July storm in Varnas, John was sitting in the café at Les Manottes. The man passed the café front, and was instantly recognized. Then he retraced his steps and came to John's table. The large, pale face, handsome and disturbing, was expressionless. The man pulled out a chair.

'Mind if I join you?' It was perfunctory. He intended to do so.

'Please do. You knew I was English?' John said, smiling. He had been reading a Provençal paper. He did not, he thought, look particularly British. Nor did he fake Latinity, or the sort of outer appearance expected of the artist by some. A nondescript exterior. The man looked at him with a grave, not ill-mannered disinterest.

'I knew you were English. I know your name – John Tranter. You are a painter, and you live in lodgings here, and have for a few years. I'm at the Auberge in Varnas, and they told me of you when I asked if any English people live here permanently.'

The Auberge in Varnas was not cheap.

John nodded. 'Have you been here long?'

'I arrived last Tuesday.' (John had seen him in the church on Saturday.) The man added, 'I haven't decided how long to stay. Probably a few weeks. I really like heat, unlike most Englishmen.'

John could not place him – taking a holiday by himself, in the July heat of Provence, seeming so solitary, so detached, so sad. He had apparently sought John's company – Les Manottes was not a natural evening visit for a guest at the Auberge de Varnas. He must be well off, yet without any absorbing interests or resources. Furthermore, he knew John's name and John did not know his. As if answering the last, unspoken point, the man said, 'My name is Simon Marlow.'

He ordered a *citron pressé*, in correct but limping French. John tried a question.

'You know Provence?'

The *citron pressé* arrived and they sat in silence for a moment or two. Then Marlow shook his head. His next remark was delivered in the same flat, neutral, unimportant tone with which he had given his name.

'I'm dying.'

John said, 'I'm sorry.' He was indeed. First, it is hard to get on terms with a person, even a stranger, who knows his days are numbered and has faced the fact. So many of the small conventions of conversation are linked to the pretence that a limitless future extends before us all. Second, John was appalled at the possibility that Marlow might crush his liberty, destroy his peace by drawing him (accosted for the purpose) as an unwilling companion into that private place where Marlow himself communed with imminent death. John was suddenly a visitor to a condemned cell, the prisoner saying, beseeching, 'Don't leave me!', the warder nodding, 'You're staying here too!' This was entirely selfish, John realized, but he knew that it was probably dominant. Third, John pitied Marlow. He remembered the sight of that back in the church.

'I'm sorry.'

Marlow was about John's age, dying at not much more than forty, he judged. It did not occur to John to doubt him.

'One gets used to it. I haven't long. Meanwhile, I shall go where I feel inclined, do what I want to do.'

Any conventional gambit of conversation was bound to be inane. It didn't matter. John murmured, 'Perhaps you'll be happy here, in Provence.'

Throughout their acquaintance, Marlow never gave the slightest impression of being concerned about what John did, said or thought. He was invariably courteous, and he put any remarks of his companion into what appeared to be a machine, producing an intelligent response. Talking to him – in the sense of give-and-take – was indeed, John found, like communication with a well-designed machine. Now he said, 'One takes happiness or the reverse about with one. It's not much to do with external circumstances or places. Do you generally eat here?'

John said he did. Except on Mondays.

'Would you have dinner with me at Varnas, tomorrow evening? At the Auberge?'

And so began for John Tranter a long series of evenings with Simon Marlow. John thought of him always like that – 'Simon Marlow', or 'Marlow'. They never grew to anything like intimacy. 'Simon' was difficult – John tried sometimes to say it, to practise a sort of familiarity consistent with knowing, as he came to know, so much about the man, but it didn't work. For his part, Marlow hardly used John's name. He was always considerate; as a host, generous. But it was a mechanical generosity, a purely instinctive consideration. Simon Marlow was imprisoned in his private world of memory, self-examination and pain. To an extent John's first, egoistic concern was justified. Marlow wanted John to join him for a little in his prison. But he did not wish this because he needed a companion only as one who could hear and forget – on the contrary, he needed to record, and preferred the ear of a stranger to pen, paper, dictaphone or friend, if, indeed, he had a friend. It was apparent to John after that first evening, after he heard the opening, curious passages of the other's story, that he was condemned to listen until what instinct suggested could be the unnerving end.

As he listened, evening after evening, John discovered that Marlow's ability to paint a scene was exceptionally good. His recollection of events, sensations, processes of thought was extraordinarily detailed. He spoke meticulously, with a curiously old-fashioned exactness of phrase, as if he was relating to John events, or describing to John people, on which he had reflected so long and so carefully that he could talk as if reciting an analysis of happening or person rather than producing an impression. And when he described conversations he did so in a way which convinced John that he could, as he spoke, hear those long-ago voices; and was using again the words that had been used.

Letters he often recited, as if reading aloud. He was always accompanied by a briefcase in which he had put together, as he expressed it, 'a few documents to illumine the story'. Sometimes he would hand John a piece of paper.

'Here's the letter. Read it.'

This was often impossible because of poor light, and Marlow would say, 'Well, it said something like this,' and on the few occasions when John had been persuaded thereafter to look at the letter itself, its contents, as far as he could judge, had been recited almost without slip by Marlow. The man's power of recall was remarkable.

They dined, on average, three times a week together (very well: food at the Auberge was excellent and Marlow was punctilious in seeing that John had what he wanted. He, himself, ate little and drank very moderately. He was a rich man). During these dinners Simon Marlow never said anything like, 'I don't know why I'm telling you, a stranger, all this', or, 'I'm afraid this is all rather boring, rather personal, rather confidential'. He talked in his gentle, dispassionate voice, of private dealings, intimate emotions, without the least restraint, embarrassment or self-consciousness – still less remorse. He talked objectively and clearly. He conveyed, ill though he was, a certain inner force, a sense of power. He showed not the slightest interest in John's reactions. John's presence merely reflected the fact that, like most people, Marlow could not comfortably or satisfyingly talk to himself, and that he wanted someone to know, and perhaps remember, his story.

Being a man of good manners he naturally, however, apologized for the imposition. He said, after their first dinner (during which he made perfunctory enquiries about John's life and painting), 'I want to talk about myself, it helps me.

You're easy to talk to. It's easier to a stranger. It will take an hour or so. Then I hope you'll return and let me resume on another evening. It will be a great kindness.' John nodded. Then they talked, on each occasion, in the half-darkness of the garden at the Auberge de Varnas, over coffee and a bottle of Luberon wine which Marlow sensibly ordered every time so that John could help himself (rarely Marlow) without the intrusions of the patron or waiter. John seldom put in a word or question, but, if he did, his host considered it and answered very exactly, making a point clearer. Marlow was deprecatory about his physical state. His only indication, ever, of some concern that his story might be wearisome was when he referred again, before he started talking at their first dinner together, to the seriousness of his condition. It appeared that he had had more than one coronary attack. An artery behind his heart was diseased and had led to it. 'Apparently,' Marlow said, 'it's a remarkably awkward place. That's why they can't operate – or why they doubt an operation's success. And I would prefer to leave things. I don't mind the danger of an operation. It's just that I'd prefer to go at leisure and in my own way.'

It seemed that this angina was, however, getting worse with some rapidity, and as their evenings together extended and John noted the other's slowness of movement, fatigue, he was not surprised that a leading London heart specialist had told Marlow his chances of a further attack within the year must be reckoned as very high; and that he was likely to deteriorate fast. Marlow spoke of this with his usual concision and economy of words, with no trace of self-pity. John could find no possible comment to make.

Each evening they were together, Simon Marlow finished with roughly the same words: 'I'm tired. I expect you are, too. Do come back. Shall we say . . . ?' (He would name a day.) 'And thank you.'

And John said, always, 'Thank you,' and looked at the other in silence for a moment. Marlow would lift a gentle, exhausted hand in a gesture of dismissal, farewell – it could even be imagined of friendship as the evenings continued. Then John would walk back to Les Manottes.

2

'My father,' said Marlow, on that first evening, 'was killed in the battle to take Rome, in 1944. I never knew him, of course. I was three years old, and he'd been abroad since the summer before, 1943, when the British and Americans invaded Sicily. He met my mother in Gloucestershire, where he was stationed and where she lived. When they married, in 1940, she found a cottage in our village, Penterton, and he came there sometimes, for leave. I believe he was a gifted mechanic, a quality he has in no way transmitted to me. He was an officer in some engineering branch of the Army, and my mother always spoke with awe of his intelligence. She was practical, without intellectual pretensions. He must have been talented, quick-witted and, I suspect, impatient. They had little married life together. After his death my mother 'coped' with courage, and of course knew everybody in the neighbourhood. Her own mother was still alive – and also a widow, my grandfather was killed in the First World War – and I knew my grandmother well until she died in 1960. She was a disagreeable woman, but I expect that for my mother at that time a disagreeable parent was better than none at all.

I am sure my mother's family (she had several aunts, uncles and cousins, although, like me, she was an only child) thought she'd married beneath her. Her father was a solicitor in the local town who had joined the Army in 1914 and been killed. They were well-established people in Gloucestershire although there wasn't much money. My father came from the Midlands, somewhere, and my mother seemed entirely vague about his origins. She said he was an orphan and I suspect she'd never met any relation of his. I once heard my grandmother refer to my father and say, 'Of course we knew nothing about him,' in a disdainful way. He had appeared, wafted by the war to Gloucestershire, had married my mother, sired me, got killed, left her without any money; and that was that. I wish I'd known him.

I was very well and lovingly brought up by my mother, but the prevailing impression, quickly taken in whatever one's youth, was of shortage of money. My mother 'managed' pretty well, I think. She had something from her family, but was always hard up until my grandmother died and she inherited a reasonable sum. She used to work in the county library for a small salary, and that, together with whatever was later done for war widows and a pittance from her own father's money, kept us going. Appearances were, of course, important, which placed further strain on her. My mother was an educated woman, and some of her friends were well off. Poverty in those circumstances carried additional penalties. In practical terms we were adequately fed and the cottage wasn't bad, but there was nothing in hand. The only thing which would ultimately ease my mother's circumstances was my grandmother's death; and she probably felt guilty about this indubitable fact. Whatever her relations thought of my father, they never did anything – or showed any family feeling – for my mother. They visited seldom and left swiftly. They played no part in my life. My mother did everything. Apart from her I was alone.

Soon after the war ended I started going to school in the next village, a much bigger place. I went by bus. Then, in 1952, I went to the nearest grammar school. It was excellent – admirable teaching. They had no boarders though, and Penterton was fairly near; so, again, I travelled by bus, with children from the grammar school and from others. This was a nuisance because the bus was dominated by one or two particularly unpleasant boys, with a jealous loathing of the grammar school, and the journeys were often a nightmare. I was not a good mixer. I had a few schoolfriends, but none of them lived near Penterton. I was quiet, something of a loner, a target, naturally. I did not learn, at that school, to love my fellow men. The bus played too large a part in the hopes and fears of the day. I lived very much in the world of my own imagination – a world in which, very often, our circumstances would suddenly be altered by some miracle for the better, my mother's anxieties dispelled, myself successful and honoured, life heroically transformed. Meanwhile unheroic life went uneventfully on. Food rationing was ended in 1952 – a milestone of memory still. In the following year – I was twelve – I actually won a school history prize.

It was soon after my twelfth birthday that I first witnessed hatred.

It was during the summer holidays – the summer of 1953. I enjoyed them in a desultory sort of way – we never, of course, went away; but it was pleasant being idle among the Cotswold fields, walking in the woods without hurry, reading a good deal, fishing in a small stream where, by custom, anybody in the village was free to take anything he could with rod and line, whatever the bait. There were two particular acquaintances in the village who were, I suppose, the nearest I had to friends. Neither went to the grammar school, and they were both quick to suspect and deride any airs of superiority I might assume. But they had little to complain of on that score, and as companions in the ordinary pursuits of a country summer they did well enough. They were easy and light-hearted. I don't know what became of them later. They were called Bob and Mick. They called me Si.

One day I met Mick by arrangement, as usual outside the village shop and post office, about one hundred yards from our home. Bob was also due, but didn't appear. After a few minutes Mick said, 'There's Bob. What's got into him?' Bob was running towards us, pointing behind him, out of breath, trying to shout a message as well as get his wind. He lived at the far end of the village, in one of a pair of cottages on the road to Stroud.

'Ease off, Bob,' said Mick. 'What's the hurry?'

Bob, gasping, gave us, 'Come on – Boshy. He's been swearing at them. Broken his windows. Bloody funny –' He turned, gesturing to us to follow, and went off in the direction whence he'd come at a steady gallop. Mick, who was swift, soon caught him up. I, who was extremely slow, lagged well behind.

Oddly enough I had only once seen the man the village called 'Boshy', and that only at some distance and with unease. He had been five years in the neighbourhood and lived by himself in a cottage set back from the lane and overhung with trees. It was said he had bought it, though how was the subject of much suspicion. It looked indescribably filthy, with grubby glass in the windows, peeling paintwork, rotted wood, and tiles which always seemed to have just fallen off lying in the untended garden. It was a terrible-looking place, no decent man's habitation. I had spoken of it once to my mother – 'Who's this man they call Boshy? Some sort of gypsy or tramp?' – because although the cottage, which was not small and was set in a large garden of nettle and thistle, could hardly belong to a tramp, I associated it with the sort of squalor and poverty the word 'tramp' evoked.

My mother said, 'No, I don't think so, I believe he's an educated man but I'm afraid he's not quite right in the head, poor thing. He swears at people. Everyone here seems to hate him. He's completely on his own. And they say awful things about him. I'm sure they're not all true.'

'What sort of things?'

My mother was vague on this. Much later I learned that Boshy was alleged to have made an indecent advance to an eleven-year-old girl in the village (this was entirely without foundation but was enjoyably believed). This, his appearance, his dirt and his rumoured wealth had set up around him a network of gossip and suspicion. Boshy had, apparently, reacted violently and had on one occasion pursued two boys, who had stood in the lane shouting insults, with a garden fork. The village policeman had been invoked ('to have a word') and had aroused temporary unpopularity and perplexity by referring after the interview to a 'decent-spoken enough man'. The village had, with determination, erected Boshy into an object of hatred and they were going to keep it that way.

My mother said, 'I think it's best not to have anything to do with the man – he doesn't want anything to do with anyone else. I'm afraid he's got a wicked temper. He was really awful to Mr Agnew' (the vicar, an agreeable, idle person, tolerated without enthusiasm by largely godless Penterton).

'But don't join in rudeness and baiting of the poor old creature,' my mother had added.

I pounded along behind Bob and Mick. When we came round the corner beyond which was Boshy's cottage we heard a number of voices shouting, and when I finally came up with the others there were about seven youths standing in what passed for Boshy's garden. Everyone was yelling. I looked at the cottage. All but one of the windows were broken. As I arrived one of the group (they were older than us, sixteen- and seventeen-year-olds) threw a stone at the unbroken window and missed.

Then I saw Boshy. He was making no gestures of defiance, neither beating retreat, organizing defence, nor counter-attacking. I saw him sitting in the lower room; through the by now paneless window one could see clearly into the back of the room, which must have been fifteen yards away. He appeared motionless, not looking in our direction. The same boy as before threw another inaccurate stone.

I said, 'What's he done?'

This aroused hostility. The stone-throwing boy, son of a man who went daily to work in Stroud, shouted, 'What's 'e done? 'Ear that? Kid 'ere wants to know what 'e's done!' There was a lot of aggression in the air. Bob, rather courageously, said, 'We've just run here. Give us a bit of the gen,' thus implying that our status as co-belligerents need not be questioned.

A lot of voices now chimed.

'Swore like filth at Bill 'ere.'

'Then come out when Bill stopped, yelled, and tried to go for him –'

'Filthy old bugger.'

''Ere, Fred, see if you can knock a tile or two off –'

Laughter and cheers greeted this suggestion, and a boy hurled a stone at Boshy's roof, without, needless to say, any very dramatic effect.

At that moment the affray was broken up by the wholly unexpected appearance on his bicycle, from the Stroud direction, of Police Constable Crabbett. I never learned why this happened. If word had spread in the village he would have come thence, from the other way. I think it was coincidence – a lucky one for Boshy. A lucky one, as it happened, for me. Crabbett was the old-fashioned sort of policeman who looked the part and said predictable things. Now he said, 'What's going on here?'

This was entirely clear. Crabbett took in the scene sternly, nodded once or twice when Bill explained that Boshy had tried to assault him (this sounded unconvincing when recounted by the principal) and listened impassively as red-faced Fred explained why he had been throwing stones at a citizen's roof as Crabbett arrived. Crabbett knew them all. He also knew me. He took in Mick and Bob, and assessed things accurately. He nodded in the direction of us three.

'What's these lads doing here? Been with you all along have they?'

Bill did the decent thing.

'No, they've only just turned up, Mr Crabbett, honest. Just before you come.'

Crabbett accepted this and said to us, 'Off with the three of you and no hanging about.' Then he said to our elders, all familiar to him, 'Breaking windows is no joke, my lads. I'll see you at the station in ten minutes.' The station was Crabbett's cottage. He bicycled off, and a gloomy little procession, ferocity much abated, straggled back towards the village. I had for the first time seen, and smelled, hatred. Those boys were, for a little, capable of great violence and cruelty. Now there was only shame. We shared it.

Before we trudged off, I looked once more towards Boshy's window. One could discern him still. My eyes were always excellent and I could see, to my deep disturbance, that his upper body (he must have been sitting, as I later discovered, on his bed, which was downstairs) was shaking. A sort of convulsion seemed to be gripping him. I looked harder, worried, appalled. There was no doubt about it. Boshy was crying.

Two hours later I did something of which I am still proud – in fact I think it is almost the only thing in my record of which I am proud, since I know it to have been disinterested. It was also, though I could not know it, the action which transformed my life. Bob and Mick had gone off on some ploy and I had dropped out.

I returned to Boshy's cottage.

I went to the door and tapped on it. I heard movement and I knew he was there. He was seldom anywhere else.

After a bit the door opened a little and Boshy's head appeared in the crack. I had never seen him at close quarters, and was bound to confess to myself that he looked as bad as painted. He was filthy, and his hair – and a straggly grey beard – cannot have been cut for years. He was wearing corduroy trousers, and a stained and torn cardigan. He didn't seem to be wearing a shirt, and there was a lot of grey hair on the chest as well as on most of his face. But his teeth, I noticed, were clean.

'What do you want?'

I had prepared this.

'I just wanted to say, sir, that two friends and me were

outside the cottage, although we didn't throw stones and break your windows because we arrived too late – I mean, we didn't know about it. And I'm very sorry it happened and I'm sure the others would be too. They just got excited and angry and I think if they were with me they'd apologize too. That's all, sir. I'm very sorry.'

Boshy looked at me for a bit in silence. Then he said, 'What's your name?'

'Simon Marlow.'

'Do you live here?'

'Yes, in the village, in the house with a yellow-painted door on the left, four houses beyond the shop. With my mother.'

Boshy turned away from me. Then he said over his shoulder, 'Come in.'

This was tricky. My mother ran me on a loose rein, but something told me that getting on to visiting terms with Boshy might go down badly. There was also my reputation, such as it was, in the village. I had already drawn heavily on my limited stock of courage by returning to the cottage and tapping on Boshy's door. I did not fancy sharing his fate as possible victim of some village pogrom.

All boys are curious, however. I stepped in. The windows were broken and the room utterly wretched. A bed and a few upright chairs apparently furnished it, although there were one or two pieces against the inner wall, in the shadows. Boshy grinned.

'Not much, is it. And not helped by your friends' attentions. We'll go in here.'

He led the way through a door into what I supposed must be the kitchen of the cottage. So it was, and the largest room in it. But Boshy did little cooking, and did it on a small stove in the room where he slept. The room we now entered had a sink, but otherwise no trace of a kitchen. I stood amazed.

Every wall was covered from floor to ceiling with bookshelves. And every bookshelf was full. On a table – the kitchen table – in the middle of the room were more piles of books.

Others were stacked on the floor. There was one chair, the sort of chair a man sits on behind a desk. Boshy gestured to it.

'Sit down.'

'I shouldn't stay, sir. I'm afraid my mother's expecting me.'

'Sit down.'

But he smiled as he said it, and the smile was extraordinarily and pathetically endearing. There was nothing wolfish or lunatic in it. I look back on it now. It was a sweet smile. I sat.

Boshy perched on the table, moving two piles of books to make a place.

'I've got a lot of books, haven't I? Do you like reading?'

'Very much. I don't think I've ever seen so many books except in the library at school – or the library where my mother works.'

He looked interested at this and said, 'Your mother works in a library?'

I told him about it. Then I found myself telling him about school. He listened – he was a marvellous listener – and to my (later) amazement I found myself telling him a great deal – hopes, fears, characteristics of masters. Boshy responded with enormous, astonishing understanding. He spoke in his deep, musical voice of school and what being at it was like, of the sort of subjects which had already touched my imagination. Each time I tentatively mentioned something I'd read or heard of, something which seemed to promise new adventures of the mind, new voyages of discovery, he responded with exactly the words, the phrases which assured me that I was on the right track. I quoted – I had an excellent memory – a line from a piece we'd had to learn from *The Oxford Book of English Prose*. He instantly capped the quotation. Time raced by. How could the village hate this man?

'And you're learning history?'

'Oh, of course, but I like history – I got the history prize for my year, actually. I like Latin, too. We're keen on it at my school.'

'I didn't know Latin was taught so thoroughly at grammar schools.'

I was rather stung by this. It sounded patronizing and snobbish – and it was being uttered by a dirty old scarecrow. My school was, as it happened, among the best in the West Country, of any type.

'We sent two classical scholars to Oxford last year.'

He said, 'Did you indeed?' I looked at my watch. I'd spent forty minutes with Boshy! I got up.

'I must be going, sir. As I said at the beginning, I'm really sorry –'

Boshy said quietly, 'I hope you'll come again, Marlow. I've some books here I think you'll enjoy.'

I muttered something. Then Boshy said (I'd never before heard the expression, which struck me as so absurd and peculiar as to be slightly mad; later I realized it was mechanical good manners, born of habit), 'I expect you can find your own way out.'

He took up a book. As I moved towards the door into the awful front room where he slept, he said gently, 'Thank you for your visit. It has delighted me and was good of you.'

I told my mother at once. As I anticipated, she was concerned. She told me she was glad I had returned to apologize – 'Nothing,' she said, 'is worse than being one of a gang that turns on someone like that. Gangs are beastly things, and everyone behaves worse than each would individually. Don't forget that.'

But my mother did not care for the invitation to pay another call on Boshy. I had mixed feelings myself. There was a certain natural timidity at being seen as on terms with an object of village distrust. I thought I could with skill defuse this. (Later I was justified in my assumption. I was disingenuous, and let it be known through Bob and Mick that everybody seemed scared of Boshy, while I had walked up, bold as brass, and asked to see round the cottage. I turned what could have been guilt by association into an act of bravado, and this came to be accepted. After the stone-throwing, the hatred of Boshy anyway quietened a bit.)

My other reservation was not dissimilar to my mother's, I later appreciated. She had, of course, heard the stories about the eleven-year-old, and saw me as a possible victim of assault.

Now she said, 'I think he may be a little peculiar, Simon, my dear. I think it would be wiser to be polite but keep your distance.'

'But Mum, he's got a fantastic collection of books, and he's really interesting. He'll lend me books. He's more interesting than anyone else here.'

'I'm sure he's an educated man, and not bad. He's a recluse – someone who's decided to be entirely alone. People like that sometimes get a little odd in the head, you know. It comes from having only themselves to talk to. And a village – any small community – generally distrusts anyone out of the ordinary. People resent what they don't understand. It's a short step from that to making up tales and believing them. But even so –'

I said I thought I should, in politeness, call once more on Boshy. My mother was silent, dubious. She said, 'Do you know why people give him that silly name?'

I didn't.

'It's from *Boche*: German. People have got an idea that he's German, or of German origin. That was the start of it, when he first came here, and as nobody knows him, of course, nobody does anything but refer to him by the nickname. I feel quite ashamed, but I don't even know his real name.'

This added, remarkably, to Boshy's mystique. A dirty, nameless enchanter from none knew where.

'Can I go?'

My mother told me she'd like to think about it. Next day, however, she brought the subject up herself in the evening. I had spent happy hours fishing with Mick.

'By the way, Simon, I found out your Boshy's name. I got

it at the post office, from Mrs Wright. It's Kinzel. He's Mr Henry Kinzel.'

'Is that a German name?'

'Yes, I think it is. But of course he was brought up in this country. His family have been here for three generations; his great-grandfather married an English girl and came to work in London. He's entirely British now.'

I looked at my mother in astonishment.

'Mum, surely Mrs Wright didn't know all that?'

'No,' said my mother sedately, 'I thought I'd call on Mr Kinzel myself. I thought as he'd been kind enough to ask you to see him and borrow books and so forth I'd better introduce myself. So I called on him.'

My mother loathed dirt, untidiness, squalor with a deadly loathing. My imagination simply failed to picture her in Boshy's front room. I remained silent.

'I agree with you, he's very nice, really, if one gets behind the awful appearance and the way he's let himself go. He must have had some dreadful disappointment and tragedy in his life, I'm sure. The cottage is – well, you've seen it, Simon, and I can't think of you there without a shudder.'

But my mother had established a line of communication with Boshy. She had, I gathered, told him that she understood her son had called to apologize – 'quite right, too' – for some hooliganism by others. She had been told by me of Boshy's invitation to return for a visit, and had thought, in those circumstances, that the mother of a twelve-year-old should make acquaintance first.

Boshy, clearly, had understood her perfectly. He had, it appeared, been charming. He had told her that he saw few people and that my visit – and now hers – had been a delight. He had apologized for what he called the 'simplicity' of his surroundings.

'Simplicity,' said my mother. 'I really think he's one of those men who don't *notice* dirt. I don't think he *cares*. One thing – every piece of furniture was good. Little enough of it, unpolished, two chairs broken – but good. Curtains were dreadful, of course – bought with the cottage. Do you know another thing which impressed me?'

My mother told me the windows had already been repaired.

'Already! That means he must have gone to a telephone box – for there's certainly no telephone – and got someone like Wentworth out from Stroud, *and straight away*! It certainly wasn't done by Hickson' (a local builder).

My mother was puzzled, and how not, by the contrast between the lordly way in which Boshy apparently demanded instant services of this kind and the impoverished character of his way of life. She had, however, presumably been satisfied (I still do not know why, although she was entirely right) that Boshy had no illicit designs upon me. I received permission for another call, and each was succeeded by another, arranged on parting.

Thus began my friendship with Henry Kinzel. It lasted through that summer holidays – only until the autumn. But what a summer! We talked of everything, he and I. I was twelve, he sixty-five, as I learned later. Every time I went to the cottage – it had the plain name of 'Potters', I suppose from some earlier artisan inhabitant – every time I went to Potters I came away enriched. Boshy opened doors. He piled my arms high with books, and then used to say, 'Too many, those must wait, so you must come soon or they'll grow impatient.' He never offered me food or tea – it wasn't that sort of friendship. He generally, I thought, made some effort to make the front room, his bed and living room, a little less unsightly before I arrived, so that when I passed through it, as I had to in order to reach the kitchen, I never received as revolting an impression as on my first visit. But Boshy had little sensibility over such matters. Whatever he had inherited from German ancestors it was not a love of order. I came not to care. Once I said, 'Mr Kinzel,' (I always called him 'Mr Kinzel', and he had said at the beginning, 'So you know my name!') 'Mr Kinzel, does any woman come in and help you, clean and so forth? There are several people in the village who might, my mother knows them, would you like . . . ?' and he had answered, impatiently, 'No, no, there's nothing to be done here, one man, one bed, one plate, one floor – absurd to get anybody in; and I prefer my own company.'

That was that. On the other hand, on my second visit, he said to me, 'Your mother is a very charming lady, Simon.'

'Yes, she is.'

'She came and inspected me. I am surprised I passed. I expect it was because she is not only charming, but intelligent and good-hearted.'

He said this, or something like it about my mother on more than one occasion. I wondered – without relish – whether we ought to invite him to our house some time. One could not envisage Boshy anywhere except among his books and dirt. Once, after another encomium on my mother – 'intelligent and good-hearted' – he added, 'as you are, Simon.'

'I may be intelligent. I hope so. I don't think I'm good-hearted.'

He did not pooh-pooh this.

'No? Well, it's a mistake to be too good-hearted, if by that we mean too trusting. The world should not be too much trusted. It is full of betrayers. Most of us meet at least one in life. If excessively good-hearted, we pay for it.'

Boshy could always surprise one. His conversation was unlike any other I knew. On one occasion, he said to me, 'Do you hate those who killed your father?'

'I don't think particularly. I suppose it would be different if they'd killed him because they wanted him, personally, dead. As it was, I suppose they simply did what they were told to do. I don't expect anybody knew they'd killed him, anyway. I believe he was killed by a mine.' (He was – and in a very brave action, lifting mines during the crossing of the Rapido river, as I later discovered.)

Boshy said, 'A sensible answer.' Later he said, 'One has a small store of hatred. Very few people have more than a little. Parsons tell us we should have none. But most of us have a little. It can be deadly, and effective, if it's concentrated and used only when and where it really matters. Never say, "I hate" a tribe, or a race, or an institution. It can't be true. One may find some people antipathetic, and be led to injustice, even mindless cruelty towards them on that account. But that's not hatred. Hatred is real force. Think of it as a small stock of deadly poison which can be used only in extremity, against an enemy who really deserves it.'

'Mr Kinzel, can hatred ever be justified, in that way? Aren't we told to love people who injure us? "As we forgive them that trespass against us", and so forth?'

'You love your mother.'

'Yes.'

'Someone does her a frightful hurt – perhaps of mind as well as body – and gloats over it. Enjoys it. Goes on enjoying it. Are you going to love them?'

It was the sort of thing even twelve-year-olds asked themselves when faced in chapel with the imperatives of religion. I was silent.

'Or are you going to plan to hurt the perpetrator as he or she has hurt – pay them in their own coin, go on paying, let them know who it is that exacts the penalty? Revenge?'

'Yes, I think so.'

Boshy sighed. 'One might, I imagine, rise above that. Or would it, perhaps, be falling below it? Anyway, to maintain one's purpose in revenge, hatred, real hatred, has to be cultivated. It's what it's for.'

I was struggling a bit.

'I suppose that leads to blood feuds and so forth, though, doesn't it? I mean, I feel just like you say, but where does forgiveness come in?'

'Where indeed, Simon? Where indeed?''

*

Marlow was quiet for a long time after telling of these exchanges with Kinzel. He said, 'I think we're both probably tired. More wine?'

'No, thank you.'

'I never offered you a cigar. Do you smoke?' And when John shook his head, 'I used to – very heavily indeed. But I don't care for it now – haven't for a year or two. You'll come again? I must try to be Scheherazade – bring you back for more each time by the inconclusive note I strike at the end!'

John walked back to Les Manottes with an excellent dinner and most of a bottle of Luberon wine in his belly; and in his head a vivid picture of young Simon Marlow talking of the nature of hatred and the passion of revenge to an ageing, cultivated grotesque in a Gloucestershire kitchen, a quarter-century ago.

3

Mme Blanchard knew a good deal already. Although a most discreet and respectable woman, she made it her business to be well informed.

'You were very late last night, John.'

'I was dining with an Englishman, madame. At the Auberge de Varnas. We talked late.'

'I have heard of that Englishman. I have also seen him once. *Il est vraiment beau*! You know he is very ill?'

'I rather believe so.'

'I know so. He is also rich, I think.'

'Well, he gave me a very good dinner and I'm going again on Thursday.'

'He is rich. He stays at the Auberge, where they charge ridiculous prices as all the world knows. He asks if he can stay "indefinitely". *Indefinitely!* At those prices! Of course they agreed – they keep him even until the quiet season, when prices are lower, but *his* prices won't be, I assure you! And he is content! You know why? He's very ill.'

John thought of Marlow's unseeing gaze, of his back in Varnas church, of his low, courteous voice, of his handsome, haunted face, of a boy returning to apologize to an old, dirty, lonely man, sobbing by himself in an English cottage.

'It is well known,' said Mme Blanchard, 'that Dr Pelegrin has had long conversations with him, and has visited the Auberge regularly. And listen, John, if he were to become *gravely* ill – you understand? – they would *not* keep him at the Auberge. Of course not. Naturally, an hotel cannot be a hospital. But he would be turned out *instantly* – without ceremony. Without sympathy. I know that woman!'

'We never,' said Marlow, 'pictured Boshy – I couldn't think of him by any other name, privately – except in his cottage or walking to the village shop. He'd once been seen on the bus to Stroud. He never spoke to me of his routine or arrangements – it simply wasn't the sort of thing we talked about. So I was surprised one evening when my mother said to me, 'Perhaps it's your good influence, Simon, but Mr Kinzel has tidied himself up a lot. I saw him this morning leaving the shop in a suit, a town suit, and looking quite smart – tie, shirt and so forth. Of course, the hair and the beard . . .'

Boshy in a suit! My mother continued. 'What's more, he's breaking out of seclusion. Stewart's taxi took him to the station. He must have caught the nine-fifty to London. *And* the taxi collected him off the seven-fifteen. Stewart's taxi! You can imagine how they're all talking about that! I worry, because the next thing will be wicked people, sure that he's got huge sums of money in the cottage, coming and breaking in and attacking him. One reads of it all the time. People living like that on their own.'

Next time I visited Potters, I said, 'I hope the cottage is safe and locked when you're out, Mr Kinzel. It would be an awful thing if anyone stole some of your books.'

'What would people want with my books?' said Boshy. 'There are no first editions, no objects of real value here, nothing to get a crook dealer excited. If people rob to read I wish them luck.'

I remember on another occasion opening a book of Boshy's and seeing a photograph, inserted no doubt as a marker, fall out. It was an old photograph, brown in tone and backed with card, stiff, but a snapshot, clearly; not a studio portrait, although a snapshot which someone had taken trouble to mount and preserve.

The photograph was of two men in Army uniform –

obviously field service uniform which I, who knew nothing of such things, thought more reminiscent of the earlier war we were taught about, the war of 1914, than the war of my own childhood in which my father had fallen. The two men – I knew they were officers; they wore leather belts and that cross-piece over the shoulder, and both wore what looked like leggings and riding breeches – were smiling broadly. They looked happy. Their peaked caps were both set at an angle. I saw Boshy peering at me.

'Was this taken in the war, Mr Kinzel?'

Boshy held out his hand for the photograph, gently. He stared at it silently for a long minute.

'Yes. In the war. The other war, you know, the first one.'

'Were they friends of yours?'

He looked at me distantly, as if for a moment mindless of who I was. Then he tapped the photrograph.

'That's me.' His grubby forefinger jabbed the obviously older of the two smiling officers, a handsome, rather dapper figure with a small moustache. I had the wit to disguise my astonishment but Boshy would have been unmoved in any case. For a while he couldn't put the photograph down. He stood gazing at it, face expressionless. I sensed that it was opening a window through which he seldom looked now. The silence grew a little difficult and I felt the need to blurt something out, to break it. I said, 'And the other officer?' And Boshy said, 'He was killed. The photograph was taken in 'seventeen, in the Salient, the Ypres Salient. I remember that . . .' He seemed to be struggling for something, and his voice sounded more animated than usual, as if the memory summoned by the photograph brought to life feelings long asleep. 'He was killed, Simon, yes, I remember clearly, he was killed the very next week. The very next time we went up.'

'Went up?'

'Into the line. We were in rest billets when the photograph was taken, you see. One went up for three days, then back, reserve, rest, train. Then up again.' It meant little to me, and Boshy smiled his very sweet smile and said, 'Yesterday's wars are today's bores, Simon. I've talked enough.'

I didn't particularly want to listen to military reminiscence, though the image of Boshy as a smart, well-groomed officer certainly had power to shake me. Out of politeness I said, 'What was his name, Mr Kinzel? The one with you?'

Boshy had his back to me by now, stowing the photograph away somewhere else among the books. He took time to answer and then said, 'Name? I can't remember.' He shuffled away. I knew it was untrue, and realized, with a certain muddled disturbance in my own childish heart, that he couldn't bear to talk of it any more. I never learned the officer's name.

I think it was probably on the same occasion that Boshy suddenly said, as he was hunting a book for me, 'I've got indigestion!' and sat down quickly on the table, shutting his eyes and putting his left hand on his breast. It seemed surprising because I never saw him eat or heard him mention food or give evidence of preparing it. Perhaps, I thought, that was the indigestion's cause. I remember that he was holding, to show me, a particularly beautiful illustrated book. He dropped it and I picked it up, rather scared. It had fallen open and I saw that it had been produced by a German publishing house, Fischer & Premnitz. When he had recovered, Boshy nodded to the book. He was still speaking in short, gasping spurts.

'Look at it! It's beautiful! The publishers, old friends of each other, came together late in life – publish a few books of that sort of quality. I used to know one of them, long ago. The other spent years in America. Only in recent years returned to Germany.'

I fingered the book carefully. It was a joy to hold. I heard in Boshy's breathless voice his tenderness for beauty, his sense of community with men, of whatever nation, who, like him, treasured the European heritage. It gave him pleasure to have known one of these two old men who had joined forces at last to produce books like that. I could not, of course, articulate any of this to myself, but when I look back I know all of it and more was there. That was Boshy. And that, unforgettably, was Potters.

The autumn term began and passed quickly. I worked hard, in the evenings and at weekends, as well as in school. It was tacitly accepted by all that visits to Potters were for the holidays.

Then, one evening, I came home by the awful Penterton bus, and immediately I walked into the house I knew perfectly well what had happened. My mother came and put an arm round my shoulders. She needed to say little.

'I think, Simon, you've known.' I heard the words, '. . . ill for some time, poor man'. I sobbed, as she knew I would.

Boshy's funeral was undertaken by Mr Agnew. I was at school, but my mother went as she appreciated that I wished. She told me that nobody else from the village attended. It would have been humbug had they done so, but it was mildly surprising, because there was in our village, as in most, a hard core of compulsive funeral devotees. There were, my mother said, one or two strangers, middle-aged or elderly men, who had travelled from London and disappeared immediately the service was over. A 'For Sale' board was set up at Potters a few weeks later. I hated passing it. I missed Boshy enormously – his smile, his quiet voice, the way he understood what I thought and how I felt, his trick of telling a boy fascinating snippets of information without seeming to lecture. Even my mother couldn't appreciate what I'd lost, and I kept my sadness in a small private place inside me until it should fade.

The two letters arrived by a Saturday morning post six weeks after Boshy's funeral. I was at home. My mother was silent for so long and appeared to be re-reading the first one so many times before even opening the second that I thought something must be wrong. We were at breakfast in the kitchen, and I clattered my eggspoon on the plate ostentatiously and pushed my chair back in a way which squeaked and generally drew admonition. No reaction. After several more minutes, my mother said, without much conviction, 'There must have been some sort of muddle over names and addresses, I suppose.'

'What's up, Mum?'

She seemed unwilling to say.

'Oh, it's nothing, some mistake – something meant for somebody else.'

But she looked at me in a way which made me sure the mistake and the muddle concerned me in some way, and I was curious.

'What sort of mistake? They've got your name right on the envelope.' The letter which had taken my mother so long to absorb appeared, too, to be quite short, as I squinted at it beside her plate. But my mother said, 'Just a minute, darling,' showing no inclination to share the mistake with me, and appeared engrossed in the contents of the second envelope. I got up and manoeuvred myself to her side of the table in an offhand way, thus getting a look at the first epistle.

It was printed, with certain words filled in in ink. The words which stood out, in the latter category, were my names – Simon Marlow. I also saw a date: 1954. I was able to make out the address of the top of the communication, since it was in block letters, as were three words above it:

FINAL ENTRANCE FORM

ETON COLLEGE
WINDSOR

and I could see that my mother's name followed a printed 'Dear . . .' It was no time for discretion.

'What on earth's this, Mum?'

My mother was deep in the second letter and didn't answer, so I focussed on the document from Eton College, Windsor.

'It is now possible,' it ran, 'to reserve for your boy' – and here 'Simon Marlow' was inked in – 'a definite vacancy at Eton in the year 1954, subject to the conditions set out below.' There followed some lines about the completion of a form and the remittance of an entrance fee. The letter ended 'Yours sincerely, Francis Betteridge'.

'Mum, what on *earth* . . . ?'

My mother, with rare impatience, said, 'Simon, *will* you be quiet and let me finish reading.' After what seemed an hour she finished the second letter and pushed it towards me.

'I can to this day,' said Marlow, 'remember every word of that letter.' He started intoning, and John found himself believing that he did, indeed, recall the exact text of that letter long ago. Then he stopped, and held out to John a sheet of paper.

'Here, read it.'

Dear Madam,

We have been instructed by our late and esteemed client Mr Henry Kinzel to communicate with you in connexion with your son. Mr Kinzel some months ago visited Eton College and made certain enquiries and arrangements. He then informed us that he had succeeded in getting a provisional place at Eton for your son, Simon Marlow, in 1954. We understand this to be likely in the Michaelmas term, beginning in September. Our client informed us that he proposed to discuss this matter with yourself in the forthcoming Christmas holidays. Meanwhile, he made very complete arrangements with ourselves for the payment of fees, when and if they arise as a result of your being content with Mr Kinzel's proposal and your son taking up the place. We have also been instructed to make available to you, in that case, a sum sufficient to cover such extra expenses as clothing, sports, subscriptions and so forth during Simon's school period. I or one of my colleagues will be glad to discuss these arrangements with you in further detail at your request, and you may find it convenient if one of us call on you in Gloucestershire, or, alternatively, you may prefer to visit us here.

It was Mr Kinzel's intention, as I have said above, to discuss this with you in the winter months. However, he also made explicit provision for the matter in the event of his death. I am, therefore, in a position to assure you that Mr Kinzel's will provides for the above arrangements. Our client also left instructions that should he die before the end of the current year, we should correspond with you in the sense of this letter. I look forward, therefore, to hearing your wishes in the matter, and remain, dear madam,

Yours faithfully,
Jacob Austin

Marlow held out his hand and took the letter back. He said, 'As you can see, the paper was headed "Barker, Austin and Tyrrell" at an address (which meant nothing to me) in Lincoln's Inn Fields.

After what seemed another hour, my mother said, 'I don't know what to think. I don't know what to do.'

She talked then, sensibly, about the fact that if I went to Eton other boys would have, and would feel they had, grander home circumstances and broader expectations than my own (in fact my mother somewhat exaggerated this, but the apprehension was reasonable). She did not want to separate me from those among whom I would have to compete in life by a barrier of resentment or inverted snobbery. She hated the idea of losing me to boarding school. She feared, in spite of the assurances of Barker, Austin and Tyrrell, that there would be hidden expenses she could not meet, terrible embarrassments, hateful exposures. Against this there struggled her desire to do 'the best' for me. Her own values were conventional and conservative, and she probably equated an education at Eton with 'the best' without any particular experience or knowledge of it. On one matter, of course, she was proudly assured.

'You'd certainly be as well prepared, as well spoken and as well mannered as any boy, I know that.'

And better than many! I could have answered, had I known what I know now. It was true – my schooling had been excellent, and the Common Entrance exam held few anxieties for me. My mother was an old-fashioned stickler for the small observances of good manners, and my speech (to my frequent embarrassment) was what was generally called 'posh talk' at the grammar school, although mixed, as protective colouring, with a number of phrases and inflexions which I generally shed at home and could, if necessary, at Eton (unnecessarily, I discovered: they went down very well and were a source of much mirthful pleasure).

'I wish I knew what to do,' said my mother again.

And so I went to Eton.

I was, of course, terrified at first. I had never been away from home, whereas other new boys arrived from preparatory boarding schools. Many of them knew each other. Everybody knew somebody. Nobody, like me, knew nobody. It seemed to me that the other new boys were bonded together to my total exclusion. They all seemed to have relations.

'I've got a cousin at Walton's' (another house).

'He was at my private' (preparatory school).

'When my father was here, before the war of course, you wore a top hat all the time, except in the evening. People in Pop had sealing wax on the brims of theirs.'

This talk was not for me. My housemaster ('my tutor' we called him. It was the Eton way) was a man called Francis Betteridge, and I owe him much. From my first day he came to my room after prayers in the evening, as he did every day to every boy, and chatted for a little, often joked (rather feebly), saw a book on the table and spoke about it, or just said, 'All well, Simon?' He always used our christian names on those occasions. It would have been difficult for any small boy to be profoundly anxious or unhappy without Betteridge's sensible eye discerning the fact without a word passing. He was a classicist. He knew something of my background. From the beginning he was a friend. He was also (he did not tell me this until I had been at Eton about a year) a friend of Boshy, although, of course, much younger. I suppose Boshy had visited him and managed with his help the difficult business of getting a place for so late an entry.

I knew no Greek. This excluded me from the more academically gifted sections of each block as I went up the school, but I did well enough. My Latin was better than adequate, my other subjects the same. I excelled at history. I did not shine at games, but played an undistinguished game of football for my House eleven – Eton football, an enjoyable if peculiar game. At that time Association football was played only by a handful of particularly skilful boys in the spring term, a practice which has, I understand, now been changed, as breeding an undesirable isolation from other schools. I don't think we minded that isolation, but perhaps it was bad for us. Eton was large – over a thousand boys – and we needed nothing in the way of competition or society outside its own enchanted confines. For, from the first, I loved it. I was, as I have said, terrified by the size, strangeness and loneliness. But I loved it. I loved its beauty, I loved its tolerance – it was a very tolerant community, exerting little regimentation provided one obeyed certain fairly easy-going conventions – and I loved, above all, the sense of independence and adulthood which pervaded one's life even when only thirteen years old. Eton, at that time, was one of the few English institutions left which actually believed in liberty, in practice as well as with verbal profession. One was, on the whole, left to sink or swim. There was very little bullying. One was beaten with a cane for behaviour which was regarded as particularly vicious or anti-social, but by the time I was there this was infrequent, and generally regarded as a brisk and sensible – albeit painful – way of dealing with the difficult question of punishment and sanctions. One was sometimes conscious of arrogance, of course. A boy whose family possessed great wealth, or huge estates, would make some remark which left one in resentful silence: 'Well, at home, who'd even learned how to lay a fire or clean a shoe, I ask you? I must say, when I started fagging I thought, my father's paying a hell of a lot to get me trained as a footman.'

Yet Eton was a great leveller, and within the school anybody giving himself airs, or flaunting with insolence the size of his family's possessions or the length of his pedigree, was generally put down very properly and effectively. Nevertheless, there were moments when I felt a gulf between at least the better off among my friends, those who could look at the future without anxiety, and myself, conscious of no support but my wits. I told myself that my situation was how it should be – and in an increasingly egalitarian world how it more and more would be. I took some pride, now and then, in saying, 'My father was killed, and left my mother with pretty well nothing. I've got nothing nor ever will have, but what I earn.'

In fact, I suppose I became a bit of a prig, but it was a defensive priggishness. I would have been repelled at any thought that I could appear ashamed of a humble background. It would have been a betrayal. But the small snobberies and insensitivities of boyhood sometimes grated.

'You come from Gloucestershire, Marlow,' a boy said. 'I expect you know the—' He named a family well known in the county for its riches. I believe my grandfather's firm once acted for them.

'No, I don't know them.'

'Oh! They're having a party and I'm staying down there at the beginning of the holidays for it. I thought maybe you'd be there.'

I shook my head. Half the school, at times, appeared to live in Gloucestershire, but not one knew me. I told myself that it was necessary never to mind this, never to let any bitterness or absurd sense of injury take root. As the years at Eton passed, and I achieved a few modest successes, I told myself that I was indeed fortunate to be there, that I must, at all costs, count my blessings.

Boshy's provisions meant that I had, while at Eton, a generous allowance which enabled me, within reasonable limits, to carry out any pursuits open to us and to clothe myself without burden to my mother. She, herself, worried quietly from time to time. I reassured her.

'I hope Eton won't spoil you for life, Simon darling. You haven't many friends round here and I don't seem to know any of your schoolfriends – I suppose, I don't know . . .' Mother was too proud to say, I suppose we're not grand enough for your friends, but she meant it.

'Mum, I've got very good friends. Not many live near here, that's all.'

'I know the house is awfully small, no room to have someone to stay, I worry about that . . .'

I could handle that one.

'Mum, don't get the idea that my friends all live in huge houses, with servants and things – they don't, not now. Lots are just like us – without fathers, mothers living in a pretty small way and so forth. I *promise* that's how life is now, you've got it all wrong, Mum.'

But she had not got it completely wrong, and, however unworthily, there lay in my heart a seed of envy from which much would grow. One day, I told myself with obsessive determination, I, too, would have the sort of possessions which make the world glad to claim a man's acquaintance.

It was in the summer of 1956, when I had been two years at Eton, that I first became a friend of Harry Wrench. He was not in my house, although of the same age and in what Eton called the same 'block', or scholastic generation. He studied different subjects, was worse than me at some things and easily my superior in others, so that we were seldom in the same class. We found each other by accident. One day we were both mounting the staircase that runs up to the ante-chapel of

Eton College Chapel. There was the usual close pack of boys surging up the ancient oak-banistered stairway. I was humming an air which was refusing to leave my head. I had heard it on the radio and succumbed to it, although I didn't know its provenance and I was not musical in any formal sense: I did not learn music at school. I pushed up in the crowd, humming away.

I reached the end of a bar, and a very tuneful voice on the stair below me immediately took up the melody and hummed away with greater energy and skill than I. I looked down with a smile. It was Harry Wrench. He smiled back with a sort of joy. I said, 'What *is* that?'

'Oh, it's a Mozart piano concerto, I forget the number, second movement.'

'I love it.'

After chapel we found ourselves downstairs again, and talking like old acquaintances. This tiny incident began our friendship.

Harry Wrench was interested in all things and amused by most of them. A dark-haired, rather swarthy boy, he had a delightful, warm-hearted laugh, and I think in many ways he taught me how to laugh as well. I had been, until then, serious, rather solemn, undoubtedly priggish and, of course, insecure. Harry made me see the funny side of things. He introduced a vivid element to life. He was not academically brilliant and was rather indolent, but he had natural taste and talent. He loved the English language. He rolled it round the tongue with surprising relish for a fifteen-year-old. He also had a great sense of drama. Harry was much better at games than I but (again, unusually for a boy) he was remarkably uncompetitive and often decried – it was not affectation, I think – the great part played by the athletic prowess of a house or individual in Eton's values.

'As if it really matters!' Harry would say.

'Well, I think it does to some extent. Life would be pretty dull if one approached it in a spirit of "I don't care who wins".

While one's competing one's surely got to care like hell!'

'Then I suppose we're meant to carry the same spirit on later, are we? Into business! Into politics! "My side, my company, my party, my country is *right* and down with the opposition!"'

'Yes, all right, you make it sound absurd, but how else can one succeed – whatever one's doing?'

We were walking along the banks of the river, opposite 'Fellows Eyot'. Harry had been reading of the seventeenth century in English history, and someone had quoted to him Cromwell's exasperated injunction, 'I pray ye, in the bowels of Christ, consider that ye may be wrong.' Now he quoted it to me.

'I think that's a splendid saying, and needs uttering all the time.'

It was a lovely autumn afternoon.

'I don't think it helps much if one's trying to win a house match. Or an election. Or a war. And I don't know that Cromwell himself suffered from much doubt as to who was on the right side, whatever he said to other people!'

But Harry simply quoted Cromwell again, with huge enjoyment.

In considering such matters as the drive of patriotism, the fervour of partisanship, we were at that moment being not precocious but topical. The previous months had been dominated by the Suez crisis. Boys at Eton listened to the radio news bulletins, read the papers, reflected or in some cases rebelled against the parental attitudes they heard at home, and in the overwhelming majority of cases were initially proud and delighted that Britain appeared ready and able to assert its will by force of arms. The years since 1945 had been marked by a certain frustration. There had been military tasks – in Malaya, in Kenya, above all in Korea – in which fathers and elder brothers had been engaged, which touched here and there the life of the school. But Suez was different. Here was a prime minister exhorting the country in terms like those (if our parents were to be believed) with which Churchill had stimulated England. Every generation which succeeds one tested by a major war feels a certain deprivation. A man likes to believe he can face the same challenges as his father with no less vigour. Like man, like boy. Eton, for the most part, supported Suez, and shared the national mood of confused humiliation when it became clear that the entire undertaking had misfired. My own feelings were with the majority.

Harry's were not. From the start he had stood out, with unpopular obduracy.

'Wrench, you don't seriously support Gaitskell? He's been a bloody traitor. My father says that it was people like him who encouraged the Americans to let us down – the Yanks reckoned we were a divided nation.'

'Wrench, my mother lives in France now and you ought to *hear* what the French think of us! They think we ran out. The *French* think that! They look down on us. On *us*! After Dunkirk and so on!'

'Wrench, it's obvious you've never been in Egypt or anywhere like that' (this was an older boy who assumed some authority since his father had once served in the High Commission in Khartoum). 'If you had, you'd know that the Egyptians have *no* hope of running the canal properly, and the *only* hope for the whole world's trade and so forth *was* to take it back and run it properly ourselves, through the Suez Canal Company. You'd also know that the Egyptians, or most of the so-called officers, were utterly pro-German in the war, waiting to stab us in the back if Rommel won just one more battle. Those are the people you're defending, it appears!'

Harry used to fight back with a good deal of spirit, using tactics, on occasion, of unconventional daring.

'Well, wouldn't you have been?'

'Been what?'

'Pro-German. As an Egyptian officer. What did they ever get from us except rudeness and contempt?'

'But good God, Wrench, what do you think they'd have

got from the Germans? They'd have probably put them all in gas chambers as "inferior human beings". Which most of them are, incidentally.'

'I don't think,' Harry said loftily, 'there's the remotest likelihood that what you suggest would have happened. Not the remotest.'

He and I grew very close during those autumn weeks. I even came nearer to his point of view. He was by no means a compulsively rebellious or unpatriotic boy, but he loathed what he thought was unfairness – the inability to see things from another's standpoint. I think he was born like that.

One day Harry said, 'The village you live in is called Penterton isn't it?'

'Yes, Penterton, Glos.'

'It's funny, I heard the fag-end of something my mother and father were saying to each other, and they mentioned it. My mother said, "Where did he go? Do we know?" and my father said, "A place called Penterton, I believe." I don't know who they were talking about.'

Nor did I, but it was highly unlikely that whoever it was knew or was known by us. For one thing (for me) clouded our friendship. Harry's family was undoubtedly rich. In fact, I suspected – although certainly not from words of Harry's – that his father was very rich indeed. We talked, of course, about our families as we became closer, exploring together what we thought about life, Eton and the world. I was, as usual, aggressively frank about my own circumstances.

'I envy you living in a village,' said Harry. 'We live in London.'

The Wrench family did indeed live in London. In a large house in Eaton Square, one of the few, even then, remaining as one family's habitation. Not that I knew this, or that Eaton Square conveyed anything to my mind. London was a closed book to me. Harry's references to his home, however, led me to envisage a big house, supported by a number of servants; and in this I was right. A Filipino couple, a large number of 'dailies' and a chauffeur supplied by Mr Wrench's company kept (with some difficulty) the house in Eaton Square going.

'Sometimes we take a house for the summer holidays or something like that. For the last four years we've taken a place in Scotland, really lovely, three miles from anywhere, shooting, stalking, fishing, *tremendous* fun. But it would be more fun if it were home. Home's always been London. My father works enormously hard and I know he couldn't bear to live far away from his office.'

'What exactly does your father do?' I knew that Mr Wrench was 'in business'. Harry referred to 'my father's company' or sometimes, again, I heard 'one of my father's companies'. Wrench senior seemed to travel a good deal. There had been fewer references to Harry's mother, the reported conversation about Penterton being a rare one. But his father was often on Harry's lips, and was frequently quoted. Harry was rather vague about Mr Wrench's activities. I gathered that he had started in humble circumstances – Harry once said that his parents 'said they'd hardly got two sixpences when they got married', but that in about 1930 there had been exciting developments. 'My father says,' Harry told me, 'that when everybody was going downhill, 1931, the Depression and all that, it was possible to keep one's head, and what he calls "read the signs of the times rightly", and come out of it all pretty well. I think his business really got going then – he bought a lot of other people's concerns which they didn't believe in and couldn't run any more, and put them in good shape and so on. And we bought the lease of our house about then – 1934. Things didn't cost a great deal at that time. It was far too big at first, of course, because there was only my elder sister – six years older than me – until I was born in 1941 and my younger sister a year and a half later. We're very well spaced, aren't we! Then the house filled up a bit, with nannies and so forth. And my father had to do a lot of entertaining, to do with his business. Still does.' It was all a long way from life at Penterton.

'You must come and stay in London, Simon.' I wasn't keen on this. I was proud.

'It's a bit difficult. My mother very much depends on my being there. I'm all she's got, really.'

'Well she can spare you for a night or two, can't she?'

But I always hedged, and although I was dazzled by the visions of Harry's world which his talk so easily and unconsciously projected, both dazzled and drawn, I could not bear the possibility of feeling inferior status. I was not only impoverished but inwardly insecure. Harry didn't, of course, fully understand this. Feeling his way, he once said, 'I know what you think, although you may hate me for saying it. You think we're well off and live in a big house and that if you stay with us you'll feel out of place, and that makes you resentful. You couldn't be more wrong. First of all, as I told you, my parents used not to have a bean. My father likes people who, as he says, "make their own way". And we've lots of friends who have nothing – there's a friend of my mother's called Branson, Charlie Branson, who apparently got through about three fortunes when he was young and is absolutely *broke*. When he comes to Eaton Square he just leaves the taxi outside until the man rings the bell and then the butler pays him – Charlie never has any money. And he's *always* at home, practically lives with us. You've got more money than he has, just out of your allowance here, I bet! I'm saying this not because I think of money all the time, but because you seem to. And it just doesn't matter. If we've got some – a good deal – it means we can help our friends.'

I could imagine Charlie Branson, and was unmoved by his allegedly splendid example of unselfconscious poverty amid affluence. Sponger!

'Well, you're very kind, Harry, but honestly . . .' And we would talk of other things. Very occasionally, this line of conversation threatened our friendship. I would reject some offer or counter some remark with sarcasm touched with jealousy. The chip on my shoulder would obtrude and hurt us both. 'Oh, you spoil *everything*,' Harry would say, angrily. 'And what have you got against the world? You're cleverer than most people, and you're the best-looking chap anyone's ever seen, when you're not looking sulky!' He was half irritated, half consolatory on such occasions, youth merging into manhood in both of us, the awkward age. But for friends from very different traditions we did well enough.

The years at Eton passed, each year different, each month bringing new perspectives. A nervous, rather overgrown child when I first went there, I was to leave five years later with at least some of the appearance and character of a man. During these years I thought surprisingly little of Boshy, and of the extraordinary munificence which had, wisely or not, given these privileges to me. Sometimes my mother said, 'It really was a wonderful thing of Mr Kinzel, after just that short acquaintance. I *wish* I'd known him better.'

'He was super, Mum. People here hated him and not a soul knew him. He was super.'

'So you say. Well, I think to give a new young friend a wonderful education like this – not that you wouldn't have done very well at the grammar school, I know you would . . .'

For my mother was often, still, uneasy and uncertain about my future and felt, despite my half-hearted assurances, that I might be somehow spoilt for the sort of career which might be open to me. My own disquiet was different. I was becoming, quite simply, resentful of the good fortune of some of my schoolfriends. I despised this in myself, but I recognized it. I suspected that, at least while young, I would in the future be excluded from many an enchanted experience because I was too 'dim', too unconnected, too poor.

To my mother I adopted Harry's line, without believing it. If she said, 'I suppose most of the boys have – ?' I would cut her short and say, '*Please* shut up, Mum, about what other boys have! It makes no difference what anyone has, and nobody's got as good a home as I have! There are rich boys and poor boys and it just makes no difference! Times are different now, Mum! Really!'

'What about going to the university?'

This was before the days when further education was conceived as the divinely bestowed right of all, regardless of circumstances and almost regardless of ability.

'Well, I'd like to, of course. I might easily try for an exhibition, my tutor says. I might have a chance. That would help.'

But during the spring term of 1959, I received a letter, addressed to me at Eton. It was signed 'Jacob Austin'.

My mother had had dealings with Mr Austin when my entry to Eton was originally arranged, and had described him as 'very nice'. His firm had paid my allowance, which generously covered my extra expenses and holidays; as well as paying, direct, the Eton fees. Once my mother read a letter in the holidays and said, 'He really *is* very nice, Mr Austin.'

Mr Austin had written to ask whether, in view of the rise in the cost of living, my mother and I found my allowance (paid, as it was, to my mother) to be adequate. He would, he said, be entirely prepared to discuss an increase with 'our late client's trustees', should my mother express the desire. Being my mother, she at once wrote back to say that the allowance was very adequate indeed – generous, in fact.

'He really is *very* nice.'

Mr Austin's letter to me said that he hoped I was well. It was written in a less formal style than the communications to my mother, but was still very precise. Beginning 'My dear Simon', after some preamble it ran –'

Marlow extended the letter to John, who shook his head. The light was poor. Marlow pretended to read, although John knew that he had the letter's text by heart.

'I expect you are considering your future carefully, and no doubt discussions of it with your housemaster and tutor will become more frequent as your time at Eton draws towards its close. I think it would be a good thing if you and I had a talk. In particular, I am sure that you will have wondered about the possibilities of a university career.

This letter is to say that my late friend and client Henry Kinzel, who was, as you know, anxious to give you the education you are now enjoying (I hope that is the right word, added Mr Austin in brackets, with a rare attempt at jocularity), also made provision for you to continue to university should you qualify and desire. In making your plans or resolving what challenges to accept, therefore, you should not feel too inhibited by material considerations. I suggest that you get leave to come and see me in London before the end of this term, and I have written to Mr Betteridge, with whom I am acquainted.

Yours sincerely,
Jacob Austin

Oddly enough, it had never occurred to me that Boshy might have done this. The arrangements he had already made were so generous that my mother and I had, quite unaffectedly, taken them for granted as standing entirely on their own. Following a lordly impulse, Boshy had, so to speak, left me a legacy of an Eton education, and that was that. Now he seemed to be hovering like some tutelary deity over my entire future. And at this time, I confess, there stirred some curiosity as to whether his benefactions might – just possibly – reach beyond university and into life itself. For the old scarecrow Boshy must have been, as the village had always rumoured, a man of substantial means.

I told Harry that I hoped to try for Oxford. His own future was assured. He was due to go, that October, to Magdalen. We had both decided to apply for deferment of national service until after university – although we learned, with oddly mixed feelings, that this probably meant not doing it at all since it was the government's proposal shortly to abolish the system. It was with a light heart that I got an afternoon's London leave and called, by appointment, on Mr Austin in Lincoln's Inn Fields. I was disappointed in his office, which was dark and dusty with large numbers of books in cases showing no signs of use. Mr Austin himself was a shy man of, I suppose, about sixty, with a slight stutter and very penetrating pale blue eyes.

Mr Austin told me the terms. Twelve hundred a year until I obtained a degree, or for four years, whichever was the shorter. This was, in those days, princely. I was, I expect, ungracious in the way that grateful and embarrassed young men can seem ungracious. But Mr Austin was affable and understanding. He questioned me closely about my time at Eton – my tastes, my ambitions, my acquaintances. We had tea and fruitcake on a table in his office. We made friends. Towards the end of my visit he said, 'I think, Simon, it would be a good thing to keep in touch. Would you let me know if your Oxford career looks like starting – as we both hope? Then we can meet again and talk about the details of your allowance and so forth. I want to help in any way I can, as well as professionally. I was very fond of Henry Kinzel.'

Boshy's name had not, until then, come up in the conversation at all – every reference by Mr Austin had simply been to 'our instructions'. I felt ashamed. I said, 'I don't know why he's done so much for me. I thought he was a marvellous man – you could talk to him as to nobody else – but I only knew him for a few months. Yet he's done all this – and now the chance of university! And he was so unhappy. So alone, it seems. I was very young, of course, but it really got me.'

Mr Austin said, 'He had a difficult life. He decided that he was extremely poor after a – a setback in life. You saw him at Penterton at that stage. But of course, the pendulum swung, other things accrued to him which he had not anticipated, and he died not poor at all, not at all. But he suffered. He and I were close friends at one time.'

I got up to go.

'I must catch my train, sir.'

'I'm glad of this talk, Simon. And perhaps our next one might be at Oxford. If you get there – and I'm sure you will – I shall come up and visit you. I am a Magdalen man, and I take any opportunity to go back. I love it.'

I knew nothing of Oxford colleges. I looked forward, now, to discovering more.

'Magdalen, sir? My closest friend is hoping to go there.'

'Excellent, it is a delightful college – and who is that?'

'His name's Harry Wrench.'

Mr Austin did not simply nod perfunctorily, but inclined his head, then straightened it and cocked it on one side with a frown and a faraway look in the eyes.

'Wrench?'

'Yes, Harry Wrench. He's a splendid chap. They live in London.'

'Very probably,' said Mr Austin, obscurely, and without a smile. There was a touch of frost in the air, unexplained. I left.'

4

'I went up to Pembroke,' said Marlow. 'Pembroke College, Oxford. I went up in October 1959, and read history. I made more friends than at Eton – I felt less isolated by my circumstances, of course; there were plenty of people with poor or undistinguished backgrounds.'

John said, 'Yours was, from what you've told me of your discussion with the lawyer, hardly poor!'

'No. I had enough money. But I felt, still, something of a changeling, an interloper. Unnecessary, but I felt it. I suppose because I was to some extent, as an Etonian, sailing under false colours. These complexes, these insecurities may be absurd, are probably reprehensible. Nevertheless, they matter when one is nineteen.'

'And later,' said John. 'And later.'

Their next session at the Auberge de Varnas had begun unusually in that Marlow did not wait, as he generally did, until he could talk without interruption in the warm darkness of the garden, but started to take up the tale immediately they sat down to dine. John noticed that for some reason Marlow seemed in a hurry, as if there were less time than he had thought and none to waste. He had already remarked in his host a certain breathlessness. That evening it seemed more pronounced. Marlow smiled and said, 'Yes, and later, as you say.'

John gathered that Marlow's university career had gone 'quite well'. In fact, as later appeared, he had been more distinguished than those words implied. He had shone in the history Schools and ultimately achieved a first. John came to realize that Marlow's story was comprehensible only if one remembered that it was about a man exceptionally gifted, and recognized by others as so being. He used, nevertheless, a different tone and slighter emphasis in speaking of this period from that with which he spoke of his schooldays, although it might have been supposed that his Oxford experiences would be more congenial and more formative of the man. Yet Marlow seemed less marked by them. The sense of lacking opportunities which others enjoyed had burned itself into his mind at Eton, and while Oxford did little to diminish that sense it did not at all exacerbate it. From offhand remarks, John got the impression of an undergraduate still aching for recognition, acceptance – and, perhaps, the possibility of riches. There can be many different spurs to ambition. Marlow's spur was, it seemed, a determination to excel, to compel acceptance in the eyes of those same thoughtless inheritors of superior wealth whose values and abilities he so often derided with equal disdain. John noticed that whereas Marlow's references to more fortunate boys at Eton had generally been generous, his acknowledgement of his own schoolboy envy, frank, self-critical and humorous, now, as his story went on, he spoke more sharply about those whose futures were assured by good luck alone. It was as if he could in retrospect tolerate, even smile at, the small, thoughtless snobberies of boyhood; but found it less easy to bear if these hardened later into bland acceptance by the undeserving of their gilded lot.

But Marlow's narrative of university days came alive when he spoke of the Wrench family. By then they were sitting in the garden of the Auberge. Harry Wrench had, he said, remained a close friend – John got the impression of perhaps his only really close friend. He quoted Harry Wrench often as his story went on. 'Harry used to call it . . .', 'Harry's view of that was caustic . . .'. Sometimes he said, 'I'll never forget Harry's laughter', in a voice which implied that death or desertion or something else had ended this friendship now.

But the voice, not quite steady, also made clear to John that the friendship had been deep.

It was at about the end of Marlow's first year at Oxford that he met Mr Wrench senior. John noted that he seemed to have difficulty coming to that point. He described how he had agreed to join a Wrench family skiing party in the Easter vacation of 1961. Harry had said, 'You'd better meet the family before being cooped up with them in an hotel at Zermatt,' and Marlow had stayed a few nights with the Wrenches in London after Christmas.

It seemed curious, John thought, that so close a friend had not until then met his friend's family; he put it down to Marlow's obsession with inequality. Even so it was peculiar, particularly since the picture formed of Harry Wrench was of one with sufficient charm and influence to brush such complexes aside. It was almost as if Marlow had put off as long as possible, from whatever conscious or subconscious motive, an encounter he feared.

'I met Julius Wrench at Harry's home, when he returned from his office in the City,' said Marlow. 'He could be felt immediately he entered the house. Harry heard the front door close behind him, one of those huge, echoing sounds made by London front doors in times past, when they opened into deep halls, great, heavy, secure doors of glass and iron and brass. Then there was always the smaller, but rather resonant, rattling of the inner door opening and shutting, the glass-panelled door which separated the entrance hall from the inner hall off which opened, in the Wrench house, the enormous dining room and a sitting room used by Harry, his sister and their friends; and at the end of which was a swing door communicating with pantry and various other cells. Now we heard both sounds in succession. I think I came to know Julius Wrench's particular door-sounds and recognized them as clearly as any of the family.

'There's my father,' said Harry. He jumped up (we were

sitting, talking, in the downstairs sitting room) and went into the hall saying, 'I've got Simon here, Daddy. You know – who's coming to Switzerland with us.'

'Good!' I heard his father say.'Good!' And he followed Harry back into the room.

Julius Wrench was at that time fifty-eight years old. He looked younger. He was extremely handsome, with a broad forehead, a large nose, and black hair only just beginning to grey. He wore a dark suit and in his shirt, tie, handkerchief and all appurtenances I was conscious, in an inexact sort of way, of silk, fastidiousness and expense. He had a slightly drawling voice, and his turn of phrase was such as to appear a little bored and mildly to mock whatever he mentioned. This was intriguing and subtly flattering, in that he accompanied remarks with a half-smile as if to include one as a fellow spirit in the mockery. 'This is all a little absurd,' Julius Wrench's smile implied, 'and we well-informed men of the world understand why.'

He shook my hand and said, 'Are you at Magdalen too?'

'No, I'm at Pembroke.'

He nodded in an uninterested sort of way, murmuring, 'I was at the other place,' but I noticed that he kept his eyes on me and that they were very penetrating.

'I gather you're joining us at Easter at Zermatt. I hope it'll be fun – you probably know it well. We've never been to that bit of the Alps before – we've been loyal to the Tyrol.'

Harry must, I thought, have been particularly uncommunicative about me if his father supposed I might know Zermatt well. It was more likely, I guessed, that Wrench *père* was putting me in my place a little. I was quite wrong, of course. Julius always said things like that to anyone, as if anxious to disarm in advance any knowledgeable response which could put him one down in a conversational exchange.

'No, I've never been skiing.'

'Ah! Well, try not to break a leg, these places are unbelievably boring if one is in plaster. Is Mummy in, Harry?'

Harry said, 'Yes,' and Julius disappeared, saying, 'See you at dinner, I suppose, or are you both going out?' but not pausing for the reply. We heard his foot on the stairs, which led from the hall to the large double drawing room on the first floor.

Mrs Wrench was a charming woman. She was still very attractive, very lively, full of warmth and friendliness. She adored Harry and spoiled him. She was instantly agreeable to me and had the gift – which her husband seemed actively to suppress in himself, if he ever felt it – of being interested in other people's lives. She was inquisitive, but in a wholly delightful way, about every aspect of Oxford. We soon talked as intimate friends.

'And have you any ideas of what to do when you finish, Simon? I suppose you'll take a degree?'

I hoped so. 'But I've no definite ideas thereafter.'

'Do you feel drawn to nothing – or repelled, perhaps, by anything?'

Like most young men I felt that my contribution to life should transcend routine, be marked by variety, adventure, sudden rather than long-deferred success. I found Mrs Wrench particularly easy to talk to. She had a wonderful talent for bridging generations.

'My elder daughter married a diplomat, you know.' I did know. Harry had talked little of this elder sister, six years his senior and now with a husband stationed in Cambodia. She sounded intelligent and rather formidable. 'I think that's a rewarding life if one's the right sort of person. One would, I suppose, have to find recompense in the interest of the work. One would have to feel sufficiently absorbed. It's not a very well-paid profession.'

I supposed not.

'Anyway, Simon, we must find the right thing for you. I

know from Harry about your promise – I'm so glad you're friends.'

I was deprecatory but enchanted. Half resisting, I felt drawn into her family. Her grey eyes were very gentle. But I could not talk about my aspirations except when alone with her.

At dinner in Eaton Square that first night there were only the four of us, but it was Julius's presence that dominated. Both his wife and son turned every remark towards him, inviting contradiction, response or approval. He never showed animation. He threw remarks back at them in his rather bored, drawling, mildly affected voice, making fun of what had been said or capping an observation with another, worldly-wise, sometimes outrageous. And all the time his eyes were sharp, his mind active, his guard never for an instant lowered. In material things he was ever-generous. In the giving of himself he was careful in the extreme.

Our holiday in Zermatt was, of course, memorable because I had never done that sort of thing before and was intoxicated by the beauty of the place as well as the challenge of the activity. We were fortunate in snow conditions. The Easter vacation, provided one went early and to a sufficiently high resort, was the most agreeable time for skiing, with splendid sun and the sense that every hour must be used before the snow melted. We were a large party – the Wrench parents and another couple of about the same age, together with two Magdalen friends of Harry's and, to a much lesser extent, mine. There were three girls. Harry's younger sister Miranda had two friends of about the same age, eighteen. Apart from the young Wrenches, who were both adept, the rest of us younger people were in various stages of unskilled apprenticeship, and alternated between terror and recklessness. It was all great fun. The older Wrench generation had skied from youth and although Mrs Wrench was over fifty and her husband nearer sixty they both performed with skill and enjoyment. It was clear that Miranda adored Harry. She looked with tolerance on me as Harry's friend, but it was tolerance touched with jealousy. She was, at that time, a pretty, slightly plump girl, dark like her brother, with a quick and delightful laugh echoing his and with grey eyes which compared, as yet less seductively, with those of Mrs Wrench. But Miranda was sharp of eye and sense. Like her father she missed little.

Harry and Miranda were always meeting people on the slopes whom they had met in other resorts, other years. It was most peculiar, I remember – in spite of the immensity of the Alps, acquaintances were always, without arrangement, bumping into each other. I bumped into plenty of people, but unlike the Wrenches I never knew them. One evening Harry said, 'Franzi's here. Franzi Langenbach. The one we met at Wengen three years ago – you know, I told you he'd come to see us in London in the summer, summer 'fifty-eight.'

'Of course I remember Franzi,' said Miranda. 'How is he?'

'Rather serious. Not smiling as much as usual. Skiing brilliantly, as ever.'

'What's he doing now?'

'University. Somewhere in Germany. Thinks he wants to be a doctor.'

'Simon ought to meet him,' Miranda said. 'He's a dear.'

Later that evening, Franzi Langenbach joined us. I remember it for two reasons – one because of a strange crossing of the course of his life with Miranda's years afterwards, and secondly because it was the evening we were joined by Julius. We had already been at Zermatt several days. Julius was detained in London.

Franzi Langenbach was a charming, particularly good-looking, tall young man with beautiful manners and a delightful smile which now and then lit up a rather serious face. When Julius appeared – unexpectedly, having walked from the station off a late train – Franzi was on his feet, bowing, before the rest of us had realized who had just arrived. Franzi knew Julius from encounters in both Austria and London, it appeared. And Julius, unusually, made it perfectly clear that he remembered him.

'Franzi Langenbach! Nice to see you.''

John Tranter interrupted. 'Franzi Langenbach – is that the one who, a few years ago . . . ?'

'Yes, that one.'

'The one who was kidnapped – terrorists . . . ?'

'Precisely. I got to know him well much later. He was often in England – he often went to friends of his, the Rudbergs, who had a place called Bargate in Sussex. But to return to our skiing holiday –'

John said, 'I know Bargate – it's the first point at which your story has touched anywhere or anybody familiar to me. Bargate belonged to the Marvells, who are cousins of mine. Marcia Rudberg was a Marvell – her mother was called Paterson. So was mine.'

'And you know the place?'

'It has always haunted me. I visited it often as a boy. I don't know my cousin Marcia or the man she's married.'

Marlow said, 'The Rudbergs were very, very good to me at one point, much later in my life. I first used to hear of them from Franzi. You see, Franzi was almost an adopted son of the house – of Bargate – because he was actually the son of Anthony Marvell, the illegitimate son of Anthony Marvell, Marcia's brother. Your cousin. He is called Langenbach but his real father was Anthony Marvell.'

'My cousin Anthony was killed in a car smash in 1958.'

'Just so. With Franzi driving. I learned the whole story from Harry Wrench.'

John was fascinated, indeed electrified, by the coincidence. He said, 'Well, in that case, Langenbach is a cousin of mine. I wonder if my mother knew about this? She died in 1974. She never mentioned it. And Franzi Langenbach was certainly in the news a few years earlier. I think she'd have said something.'

'He was indeed. Perhaps your mother never knew he was really a Marvell. Perhaps she didn't care to refer to it. Our parents' generation had more reticence than our own. Franzi Langenbach is now a famous surgeon. As all the world knows.'

'Did he play a part in your story?'

'No,' said Marlow, with an unexplained sigh, 'not at all in mine. But in someone else's, so that his name rather than he returned to me much later. I'll probably get to that and you've touched on it yourself. Certainly I associated him with Bargate – how curious that you know it. And Bargate meant a lot to me once. Much, much later Franzi Langenbach somewhat idealized England and the English, I recall. It is strange that he has come to my mind, introduced Bargate into our talks, and, as it were, discovered a link between us. Yes, strange.'

But, John recognized, Marlow did not find the circumstance particularly interesting, and wished to return to the orderly chronicle he was setting out. He wished to return to Zermatt.

'Julius was sufficiently experienced on the slopes, and naturally athletic, to be able to take only a week and immediately enjoy it. As usual, when he appeared it changed us all. We all deferred to him a little. His cool, bored eyes dissected us on his first evening.

'Nothing broken yet, it seems! And no quarrels!'

I can't say I knew him better at the end of that week. He had a habit of seldom using one's name, and even of appearing to forget it. It would have been rude and upsetting to one as thin-skinned as me, had I not begun to appreciate it was all part of the defensive armour which Julius Wrench assumed in all the small dealings of life. It was as if he felt that to appear certain of another's name implied the compliment – as yet undeserved – of his or her being sufficiently important to be remembered. This could have been odious, but I was already learning that to Julius no dealings were so small as to be excluded from the principles of ruthless competition which governed life.

In the bar one evening, Harry and I were for a moment alone. He said, 'My father's taken to you a lot, Simon. I'm so glad – he has strong likes and dislikes and can be devastating about people!'

I was surprised at the information that Julius Wrench had 'taken' to me. I had seen absolutely no evidence of it. I was also rather ashamed of myself for feeling so gratified. But something, after all, must have impelled Harry to pass this on.

'We've hardly talked to each other out here, your father and I.'

'Oh, he's very shrewd, you know. You don't think he's taking people in, he has that offhand way, but he doesn't miss a thing. He always has people completely sized up, even though he doesn't seem to have exchanged a word with them, or even to know their names.'

I could, by now, believe this.

'Well, I'm honoured!'

'In fact, he told me that he wants to know you better, that when we're back in England you and I might lunch with him in the City now and then. When you're in London – and you ought to spend more time there, Simon – you can always stay with us. My mother's potty about you. She said to me last night, "I think Simon's the best-looking young man I've ever seen – except your father of course."'

Marlow would quote remarks of that complimentary kind made about his looks or his intelligence without the slightest embarrassment, still less smugness or conceit. It somehow reinforced the impression of exact, objective truthfulness, of an accurate, impartial record. He continued with his response to Harry Wrench.

"'If I stay at Eaton Square I can see your father there,

anyway. It's kind of him to suggest lunch in the City, but I would have thought the aim of getting to know me better would be already met if I were staying under his roof.'

'Don't be pompous,' said Harry. 'You know very well that people always behave differently to others when they're with their family, even my father. One can only get to know people if one meets them away from one's relations, and I expect that goes for him too.'

'But you're included in the invitation!'

'I don't count. Anyway, I've lunched with my father and I can tell you we'll get a good one!' Others joined us. I felt a certain surreptitious glow.

When I went down to Penterton after the Zermatt holiday I was struck – and it gave me a sense of guilt – with how much older, rather suddenly, my mother seemed. I had been surrounded by good health, good looks, sun, snow, uninhibited enjoyment. I had been able to savour this without much sense of obligation. Harry had said, 'We all pay our whack. It'll cost you,' and he named a sum which should have been well within my means on Boshy's allowance, 'including journey, hotel and everything except drinks'. I suspected then and established later that the Wrenches, in fact, subsidized the party to a considerable extent. I had been living at a high level. My mother, on the contrary, was existing; uncomplainingly, thriftily, existing. Her enjoyments, beyond seeing me, were few. For her, no holidays in the sun, no comfortable hotels, no *après-ski*. She looked tired. I felt compunction.

'Mum, don't you think, in the summer, we might go away somewhere together, for a little break?'

'Darling, where on earth would we go? And how could we afford it? I know your allowance from kind Mr Kinzel is quite generous, but I'm sure you use every penny at Oxford, and more. I'm quite surprised you managed to go to Zermatt on it, and I'm sure it's not enough to take us both somewhere. Nor is it meant for that. And, as you know, I just about manage for myself and the cottage, but without much in hand. No, darling boy, it's a lovely idea but we'll wait until you start making a fortune.'

I persisted. 'I'll get a holiday job for the first few weeks, make a load of money doing something really academic like working on a building site, and then we'll spend it in a fortnight in the latter part of the vacation.'

My mother laughed indulgently but her eyes gleamed. It was, indeed, a lovely idea. Unfortunately, it depended upon my getting that holiday job – depended, indeed, rather more than my mother could estimate because, as happens only too easily, I became seriously overspent during that summer term, and had little enough left to exist on, let alone take my mother abroad for the holiday of her life.

Towards the end of term Harry said to me, 'Come to London at the beginning of the vacation, in July. We're going to have a party – a small party – for me, and some tiny tots for Miranda. And my father hasn't forgotten that you're going to lunch with him.' He named a few days. 'I'm sure a little London won't do you any harm.'

'I'd rather got in mind to get a holiday job. Make some money.'

'But Simon, you need a break. You've been working *very* hard, everyone knows that. You must have some relaxation.'

It was true that I had been working hard. 'I don't mean a job needing mind. One needing muscle. They're the best paid, anyway. I can entirely relax the mind wielding a pick or driving a bulldozer.'

'You wouldn't be any good at either,' said Harry, unkindly but not altogether unfairly. 'Anyway, why do you need to make money so much? Don't do your poor relation act, Simon, I'm tired of it, and you have unwisely told me the size of your allowance which, as we all know, compares *very* favourably with that of a number of our friends.' This, too, was true. 'So I suggest,' said Harry, 'that you defer taking up your pick, climb down from your bulldozer, and stay with us for a little in London. Furthermore, we're going to Scotland in September – my father, I'm delighted to say, has again taken that place in Argyllshire I've told you about. It's pure heaven – and we were *all* hoping you'd come up there as well.'

The Wrench family undoubtedly exerted a fascination over me. I held out.

'I'm hoping to take my mother abroad for a bit.'

'Well, there's plenty of time for that,' said Harry seriously, '*plenty* of time. The long vacation really is long. Everything can be fitted in, and leave lots of time for you to play with your bulldozer as well.'

So it was that I became pledged to some days at Eaton Square in July 1961 and to three weeks in the Highlands in September. And somehow between these fixtures my money-spinning job on the roads was squeezed into the future, while my Oxford debts cast a disagreeable shadow. I could, I knew, 'get straight' with a period of retrenchment, and get straighter quicker if I found profitable work to do. But my few rather half-hearted enquiries came to nothing. My mother never said a word to me. She pretended to like the idea of my going to Scotland, although these excursions did, I know, give her the recurring sense that she had lost me. To our holiday abroad together she never referred. She thought me extravagant, of course, and it perturbed her. But I let her know, carefully but not inaccurately, how well my Oxford career was going academically. I was able to imply to her, without excessive vanity, that I was thought 'promising' – somebody for whom the future could hold glittering prizes. I know she felt from this it was all proving to be worth while.

My visit to Eaton Square that July was marked for me not by the 'small party' for Harry and Miranda (of which I have little recollection) but by my lunch with Julius Wrench, which I recall exactly; and by a second visit to Mr Austin.

Julius gave me lunch in a small dining room on the same floor as his office. Harry had some other engagement and we were alone, to my considerable surprise. Lunch consisted of half a Charentais melon, some delicious cold salmon whose northern origins Julius mentioned in his offhand, knowing way, and raspberries. Accompanied by a very cold Moselle, it was delicious. I had never had an intimate conversation with him before, and this became one. After we had disposed of the melon and he had established that I was taking my degree seriously at Oxford (I guessed that Harry had praised my abilities with the immoderation of youthful friendship, and that he wanted to form his own opinion), Julius said, 'What sort of thing have you in mind when you go down, next summer?'

'I don't know. I don't think I want to undergo a long stretch of professional training. I'm too impatient. I'm not drawn to anything like the Diplomatic –'

'The academic world?'

'Good God, no! I think –' I hesitated; it took something for me to get it out. 'I think I want to make money.'

We ate our salmon. Julius said, 'I gather you've never had much – an allowance, but not much behind it.' It was perfectly true, but to my sensitive ears sounded with a casual brutality.

'Yes, that's so, my father was killed in the war, my mother's always been hard up.' Naturally, I did not mention Kinzel. Nor ever had to Harry. Obscurely, I probably felt that recognition to others of this unrelated benefactor could somehow diminish my mother in their eyes.

'You probably won't find it easy to accumulate capital from scratch. A few buccaneers do it, and you read about them. They make headlines. A few last. A surprising number don't. It's harder now than it used to be. The sensible thing is to join something with fair prospects of working up to a good salary if you do well.'

I did not think this was the path Julius Wrench himself had trod. He had been a 'buccaneer' once, I guessed. He had married, as Harry used to report, without 'two sixpences', and now he lived in Eaton Square and took places in Scotland. He had not been content with a good wage. He had taken chances, unsheathed his sword, gone for the dangerous way, to the top. Once, Harry had told me, his father had been hell-bent on a political career. That ambition had been overtaken, quite early, by the urge to make money, the throb of risk-taking, swift calculation, accumulation. Not, I guessed, accompanied by too many scruples. Now he liked steady, intelligent young men who would dutifully climb the salaried ladder. I nodded several times and he watched me with his half-smile.

'You'd better join us one day. Not at first. Do something else first.'

'I'm not quite clear –'

He preferred to drop an idea like a stone into a pool and watch ripples spread, rather than talk or offer with precision.

'I think you'd find it quite interesting. As to how well you got on, money and so forth, it would really be up to you. But if you'd like to think about it, I'll get you to meet Bill Barnett – he really runs things – and have a chat some time next spring; or earlier if you like.'

I thought of him now as Julius, but he wasn't easy to address as such. I generally avoided it, and I felt him feeling me avoiding it with detached amusement.

'I'm not really clear what your – er – business is?'

'Oh, we've got a lot of irons in the fire now. We're basically property, but we've got one or two manufacturing companies. We've got a bank too, although I don't think that's going on for ever. Things like that.'

Things like that. 'It's very kind of you.'

He dismissed this. 'Well, think about it,' he said. 'You might easily find it interesting, and we pay people rather well, better than most companies, I gather.'

My visit to Mr Austin took place the next day. I was flattered by Julius's proposal, vague though it was. I was young and confident enough to be sure that many employers would in time be avid for my services, but it was agreeable that one so obviously successful, one who by now knew me adequately, should suggest I might one day join his concern. Furthermore, I was still enchanted by the world of affluence which the Wrenches inhabited but had not inherited. By joining Julius, I had the feeling that I would be connecting myself, by some kind of transmission wire, to a powerful generator of the same sort of success. I thought it likely that I might ultimately take up his offer. Furthermore, I was bound to Harry and his family by affectionate feelings in which calculation played only a small part. I did not relish them seeing me as the young man who had spurned a Wrench offer of place and possibilities; as a young man who 'thought he knew best'.

But the nature of the suggestion had been that I should look about me, that I should do something else first; and perhaps for good. Provided that the idea did not die in the Wrench mind in the mean time, this might be as good a way to leave things as any. I felt light-hearted, already a man with several avenues opening before my ambitious tread: Marlow in demand.

I had applied to see Mr Austin, ostensibly to let him know how I was getting on. He had asked me to keep in touch. We again had tea and fruitcake in Lincoln's Inn Fields. After a brisk résumé of my Oxford career, I said, 'I haven't yet come to any decision about what to try for when I come down. It's a year away and one can change, I expect. Just at the moment, I've got no ambition for any particular career.'

'But you have, I expect,' said Mr Austin, 'got ambition.'

'I think I'd like to make rather a lot of money.' I felt, as I said it, naïve, youthful, more than a little vulgar. My earlier ebullience and optimism seemed merely silly. I accompanied the remark with a smile as if mocking myself. Mr Austin took it entirely seriously.

'That is very understandable. With few exceptions, however, men I have known who have made a lot of money – from scratch, so to speak – have done it by serving rigorous apprenticeships, enduring comparative poverty with patience at first, and then, by sheer hard work, excelling in a competitive world. Training, application, patience, stamina –'

'And some luck, I suppose.'

Mr Austin conceded this, although he did not really approve of luck. 'Oh, certainly, things can go right or wrong for any man at the crucial moment.'

I did not yet want to discuss with him the Wrench proposition. After an extended homily on how to achieve success, incorporating several cautionary tales, Mr Austin said, 'Of course my late friend – and yours – Henry Kinzel is a case in point. And I think, Simon, we should talk about him for a little.'

'Henry Kinzel,' said Mr Austin, 'made a very great deal of money. He inherited a small business from his father, or, to be more exact, he inherited a majority shareholding in a small private investment company which his family had formed. He transformed it. He came back from the war – the First World War I'm talking about, naturally – where he had, I believe, served with considerable distinction . . .'

I remembered the photograph and nodded. It seemed a long while ago, now, that a smart, smiling, handsome and youngish officer in uniform had looked at me from a brown-tinted card in the squalid atmosphere of Potters. Mr Austin was talking away.

'A temporary commission, of course. Before the war he dabbled in publishing, in many things. But after he came back, having survived the entire war on the Western Front, he devoted himself to the family business. He had great flair. He was trusted, and he expanded his business many times over. I should explain that I had nothing to do with it myself. Our friendship, although it covered many aspects of his life since I was his personal lawyer for very many years, never extended to his own business. He kept that separate. He may have been unwise to do so, but he did.

'He was trusted, and it was in his nature to trust others. He evoked the best in people, with his charm, his culture, his natural friendliness.' I thought of Boshy, windows broken, dirt-encrusted cottage floor, stone-throwing youths and hostile village.

'Then,' said Mr Austin, 'an awful moment came. He was, I gather, betrayed – or so he felt it. He found himself, in effect, ousted from his own business. I think that in the process of expansion – this is not a world in which I have made myself an expert, I may say – he had lost control; and at a crucial moment this loss of control was turned against him, and he was ousted.'

'When was this?'

Mr Austin mentioned a date which must have been about two years before Boshy came to Penterton.

'Regrettably, poor Henry took this – this displacement – particularly hard. He felt a victim of treachery, of treason; felt, too, that by misjudgement he had lost what his family had built up – which was, I suppose, true. He had, furthermore, devoted his own life and considerable talents to the business. He was being robbed, so to speak, not only of property but of his creation, his offspring,' said Mr Austin, with a rare lapse into imagery. 'I never knew the details. Nor, although one heard rumours, did he confide to me about the particular people he felt had done him down. He went slightly insane. We have to face that fact. He recovered, but for a while he was out of his mind.'

'But as well as losing control of his company or whatever it was, did he lose his money?'

'Regrettably, yes. I'm afraid that – again, I know no details – Henry tried certain desperate devices, certain very expensive gambles, which might have turned the tables, so to speak. He kept within the law,' said Mr Austin severely, looking at me as if I had just preferred a charge against Boshy, 'but he was entirely unsuccessful. He might have been perfectly comfortably off, although no longer controlling what he had created. Instead he chose to fight, and in the process beggared himself. And I mean beggared, Simon. He went bankrupt.'

My silence conveyed the obvious question and Mr Austin proceeded to deal with it. 'Then, not long before his sad death, he was proved heir to a distant cousin – a woman of substantial wealth whom he had not seen since they were both quite young. It was remarkable to him. You have spoken of luck. This was, indeed, a stroke of luck: for poor Henry had entirely given up any thought of recovering his fortunes, or, I am afraid, obtaining his discharge. He was a broken man, and although his mind had mended his will had not. Nor, as we now know, was his body fit. He sat in this room and heard that he had, once again, inherited a very considerable fortune. He was utterly astounded. He said, "Why has she done this for me? Had she no one else? Ah, poor creature, had she no one else?" Apparently this cousin and he had been very fond of each other long ago. She had married another. No children. They never met in later years. He said again, "Poor girl. Me, of all people! To leave her money to me!" Then his first thought was to re-enter the battle against those who had injured him.'

Poor Boshy.

'I dissuaded him. I said to him, "Henry, I know little of your past business, but I am perfectly sure that if you embark on that sort of line again, you will make an unhappy fool of yourself." My task was, I am afraid, made easier – I recognize this now – by his suspicion that all was not well within him.'

Poor Boshy.

'I have, of course, a reason for mentioning all this to you, Simon,' Mr Austin said. 'It was at that time that Henry decided to make some arrangements in your own favour.'

'For which I can never now thank him. Which I hugely appreciate. An unbelievable start to life.' I meant all this, of course. But my heart was beating faster.

'These arrangements have, as you say, Simon, been already of considerable benefit to you,' said Mr Austin sternly, 'and, as I told you, will continue until the end of your university career.'

He took off his spectacles and polished them.

'Whatever happens, this will, as I know Henry hoped, have laid a sound foundation for a career. It is splendid to hear that your hopes of a good degree are not undimmed. Whatever people say, a good degree shows evidence of a good mind, and the world needs good minds.'

More spectacle-polishing.

'I am sure that your future will justify what Henry has done for you.'

Spectacles replaced on nose after careful appraisal of lenses.

'I should tell you that Henry also made certain rather peculiar provisions. Very peculiar indeed, in fact. I advised against them.'

Thank you for nothing.

'In brief,' said Mr Austin, 'Henry Kinzel made you a possible beneficiary of his estate upon – and only upon – certain very stringent conditions. And he laid certain duties upon his executors, of whom I am the principal, in respect of these conditions. He also gave strict instructions that you should be told of the details of these conditions only upon your twenty-fifth birthday. I think that takes us to 1966, does it not?'

'Yes.'

'I should tell you, Simon,' said Mr Austin, standing up, 'that it would be unwise to count on this. I could, of course, have said nothing until next year when you are twenty-one, and I shall tell you more – tell you what I can. But I am sure that you will reflect on it very sensibly and that there is no harm in being forewarned. You should not count on it. Henry's conditions were – peculiar – and I cannot extend to you much hope you will be in a position to satisfy them.'

I tried to sound offhand. 'I'd better call again on my twenty-fifth birthday in four years' time! It's in March.'

'That will be delightful, but it will not be specifically necessary,' said Mr Austin with something not entirely unlike a smile. 'In the circumstances I consider that we should write to you when you become twenty-one. You will, therefore, receive a letter. In due course.'

I left Lincoln's Inn Fields.

5

'I have little recollection of that winter,' said Marlow, 'or of anything else between that interview with Mr Austin and the arrival of his letter, which took place on the day after my twenty-first birthday, on the twelfth of March, 1962. The letter was a disappointment. It was so inconclusive. At that stage the whole thing was like a treasure hunt of the kind where one is led frustratingly from clue to clue. I was surprised at Boshy having devised that sort of tantalization, but I think that it probably owed more to Mr Austin. Although well disposed towards me, he disapproved of the whole business and showed it by spinning things out as much as possible; by a very extended interpretation of his instructions.

The letter told me that I was the beneficiary of a trust established under the late Mr Kinzel's will, on conditions; and that if I were prepared to accept these I would, at the age of twenty-five, receive from this trust a certain income until the age of thirty, and be sole possessor of capital from the terminated trust thereafter (having, it appeared, satisfied further provisions). There was then a certain amount about the trust itself (needless to say, the first named trustee was Mr Austin), although there was no indication whatsoever of its approximate size.

There were then, however, some most disturbing and unsatisfactory sentences. I was warned of this, of course, but had still hoped for some more definite hints.'

Again Marlow rummaged in his briefcase and produced a letter. John waved it away.

'Give me the gist.'

Marlow nodded and pretended to read, although once again John knew he had every word by heart.

'The conditions under which you are to become the beneficiary of the trust in question are simple to state, but unfortunately involve a further period of delay and uncertainty.

The first condition which you need to satisfy from our point of view is to produce from a particular named individual a signed letter to the effect that you have agreed to do what the late Mr Henry Kinzel required. That will enable us to pay you after your twenty-fifth birthday the income from the trust to which I have referred. We shall then require a further letter, from the same individual, confirming that you have completed the task Mr Kinzel stipulated. Upon production of that second letter at any time after your twenty-fifth birthday and before your thirtieth, we shall be empowered to treat you as a beneficiary in the terms of this letter. There are provisions for the trust funds to be applied differently should you either decline to accept the conditions or fail to produce the second letter before you attain the age of thirty.

The particuliar named individual is Mr Waldo Price. Mr Price knows of these arrangements and we have been in touch with him. He will make contact with you in due course, and will, presumably, be able to acquaint you with the conditions under which he will furnish you with the letters referred to above. We must tell you that we, ourselves, have no knowledge whatsoever of those conditions.

We must, however, also tell you that Mr Price has informed us he cannot receive any communication from you, nor see you, nor inform you of what may be expected of you until after the end of the next financial year but three – that is until April 1966 – by which time you will have attained the age of twenty-five. Until about that time Mr

> Price plans to be abroad, and has told us that he has no mandate to discuss matters with you before then. In about four years' time, therefore, we shall, unless something arises to force us to vary these arrangements, communicate with you again and inform you of Mr Price's address, and by that time he may have written himself.

The letter is signed 'Jacob Austin'. As you have heard, it is purely formal in expression. Below his signature, however, Mr Austin has written neatly in ink:

> This is all rather over-full of suspense. As I explained, HK's instructions were peculiar. I remind you of what I said in London last year – do not count on any of this. I also suggest you do *not* discuss it with others. Best wishes. JA.

It was, of course, impossible not to dwell a good deal on so mysterious and remarkable an arrangement. I told myself that Mr Austin was right to warn me against any expectations. I should probably find from the strange Mr Waldo Price that Boshy had set me some extraordinary and impossible task. I could not imagine what it would be. I cast my mind back to our conversations together at Potters long ago, when I had been twelve years old. What clue to Boshy's (slightly crazed) intentions lay in those distant exchanges? He had, I reflected, been a man of great sensitivity and casual learning. He had obviously taken to me, and given full rein to an impulse of reckless generosity when his circumstances had suddenly improved. But what vicarious fulfilment *post mortem* did he expect my career now to provide?

I had one deep, uneasy feeling. Boshy had relished my enjoyment of the English language. He had liked quoting to me, and appreciated my hesitant quoting back. He might, I thought, have seen in me a man of letters, even an academic. There was, I guessed, a very fair chance that Mr Waldo Price would tell me that the benefits of Boshy's fortune awaited me, and only awaited me, if I secured a fellowship or published a book of scholarly renown. I did not welcome this prospect; in fact, I thought it put me out of court. Furthermore, how was I to respond to this contingency? For years before meeting Mr Price I would have to start earning my living; immediately on going down from Oxford, it had been made clear by Mr Austin, my present allowance would cease. I had, therefore, decisions soon to make and bread to win. And it would be, thereafter, all the harder to leave the office of some employer and patron, leave in pursuit of academic laurels of unknown character. For I was, by now, pretty well certain that this was what Boshy had in store for me. I felt, irritably, that Waldo Price was interpreting his instructions most improperly in deferring our meeting until 1966. Somebody must have failed to do their homework about the dates of birthdays, university examinations and the like; or else was hopelessly unimaginative about the need of young men to earn a living wage. The error might have been Boshy's – poor old man, couldn't think of everything, I said to myself, gratitude already being driven out by nail-biting anxiety. It might have been Mr Austin's (although he had professed disapproval of these complex designs). It might be – almost certainly was – that of Mr Waldo Price. He surely had a human duty to give me enough advance information to help me prepare myself for whatever opportunities Boshy's mind had devised – or give me fair warning that they were minimal. Meanwhile, there seemed nothing to be done.

I tried to find Waldo Price in books of reference. I thought this might give me a clue. This man was going to be arbiter of my fate. On his affirmation I would – or would not – come into my inheritance. I must find out about him. The greatest living expert on – what? A relation or long-ago associate of Henry Kinzel? A philosopher-priest who would put me through some sort of extraordinary tests of virtue or courage, as in the *Morte d'Arthur*? My imagination ranged. It returned to the innate probability that academic distinction was to be my password, my talisman. It was a most unwelcome probability. And in none of Oxford's readily accessible reference books, academic, literary, social or other, could I find the name of Waldo Price.

Then there was the matter of how much all this mattered – of how great was the prize. In his last talk with me Mr Austin had referred to a 'very considerable' fortune inherited by Boshy at the end of his life, from the remote female cousin. On the other hand he referred to my possibly becoming *a* beneficiary; not the sole beneficiary. And in the formal letter there was reference to 'a trust set up under the late Mr Henry Kinzel's will'. No indication, there, of proportions and size. So I could be in danger of tormenting myself for some very small sum.

But I did not think so. I allowed myself to hope. Boshy's provisions for my education so far (from the same trust? Surely not. I did not know much about these things) was generous and arguably implied a capital sum ultimately, and an income in the mean time, of significant scale. I talked to my tutors (I had two) about Mr Waldo Price. Neither had ever heard the name. I did my best to put the matter out of my mind. The effort was indifferent at first, but improved. A year is a long time in a young man's life, and as months slipped by and I concentrated on my immediate future I found that Mr Austin, Boshy, Waldo Price *et al.* gradually slipped into a separate part of my mind that I did not perpetually inspect. And, to my own surprise, but not, apparently, to that of others, I achieved First Class Honours when I took my degree in that summer of 1962.

I had, of course, not spent every waking hour reading for History Schools or bothering about my strange and uncertain legacy. I had also reflected a good deal on the suggestion made to me by Julius Wrench. 'I'll get you to meet Bill Barnett,' he had said, and in the Easter vacation he did so. Barnett, I immediately thought, was an unpleasant man. I never changed this opinion. He had made himself useful to Julius over so many years and in so many different circumstances that the links between them were of the kind neither could break, although it was hard to believe they were bonds of friendship. He was red-faced, smooth-tongued to anyone on his approximate level, rude to subordinates unless he thought they could make trouble for him, and sycophantic to Julius, whom he feared. Bill Barnett was about forty-five at that time. His life was said to be poisoned by jealousy of an older brother, Freddie Barnett, an unintelligent, gregarious alcoholic who lived on some extensive family acres in Lincolnshire and did nothing very much. I knew nothing of such things until much later – certainly Barnett had no need of a silver spoon, little justification to feel a younger son's complex. He was highly efficient. He knew how to delegate, he worked as hard as he drank, and he thought fast. Julius's head office was just off Covent Garden, and when I first, by arrangement, called there on Barnett he was unconvincingly effusive. He had had the word.

'Julius tells me you might one day be applying to join us? That would, I think, be rather a good thing. We're at quite an exciting stage of development . . .' He talked about the company.

It was a large holding company, entirely created in its present form by Julius Wrench. Apart from reading the financial and business columns of the Sunday newspapers, I had acquired little knowledge of this world. I enjoyed Barnett's talk. He was not difficult to see through, at one level – flashy, talking to impress. I felt a certain smug pleasure that at the age of twenty-one I could see further into him than he, I thought, could into me. He seemed to suppose I was taken in by his over-friendliness; I believed it to be as false as it was, and knew that he, a bully by nature, was being flatteringly nice to me because so instructed. But at another level I at once recognized Barnett was sharp – as sharp in a different way as his master. If I queried something he said, or referred to some matter in the economic news on which I had acquired enough smattering of jargon to formulate a question, his answers were rapid, authoritative and extremely clear. Barnett was unpleasant but he was formidable.

But I was intrigued by the organization. I wanted to belong to something like that – and particularly to that. I could see myself gaining the confidence of financiers, managers of huge investment funds, Julius's own colleagues:

'Marlow's got real flair. He can see quicker than anybody in the office when there's a deal to be put together, or when there isn't.'

'I think we should let Marlow handle the actual negotiation. There's nobody better.'

And a little later, perhaps, Julius's own recognition:

'Simon, you've not only got the hang of things quicker than I could have believed, you've done a lot of very profitable business for us. I think it would be right that you should have a stake in the business, beyond your salary. Small to start with, of course – I had in mind a share option . . .'

It would not, surely, take long to get a foot on that ladder which Julius himself had manifestly climbed so fast and high. I came back to earth. Barnett was talking about training. It sounded dull, and there would be at least three months of it. Thereafter, 'We'd see where best to fit you in. I'm particularly looking for one or two of your generation.' He also spoke of starting salary, in an offhand way as if he doubted my being interested in such an irrelevance. It sounded rather small.

'After that, of course, it's largely up to you.' What did that mean? Anyway, I was caught. If others had succeeded young, so would I. And surely I was, and would be regarded as, closer to the family than most apprentices?

Julius, however, had spoken of joining the company 'one day'. He appeared to think, and very sensibly, that I should first learn something of a wider world. Nevertheless, a few days after my meeting with Barnett I had a letter from Julius, typewritten from the office but, I could tell, dictated by himself. I was too young to understand and be impressed by so much trouble taken over so unimportant a matter. I have the letter here.'

Once again he offered a piece of paper to John who glanced at it perfunctorily.

Dear Simon,

I gather you had a talk with Bill Barnett, and he told you a little about us. I believe, however, that you should try for something else further afield for a bit quite soon after Oxford. Then, if you and we were still of the same mind, we might be able to offer you something rather more interesting in a few years' time.

You have probably been contacted by talent scouts in your time at Oxford. If, however, you would like to join us for a *short* while – say a year – immediately on coming down, I think we could then put you in touch with some possibilities, perhaps abroad. That way, if you wanted, you could see something of our work here, and possibly return to it one day – there being no obligation on either side.

If this attracts you at all, ring up Bill Barnett, who will be expecting to hear.

Yours sincerely,
Julius Wrench

John handed the paper back.

'And I did,' said Marlow. 'I did indeed ring up. And, of course, they took me on. My first six months with Wrench Holdings were spent learning something of the business and doing an incredible amount of reading. I started in September 1962.

I was attached to various departments in turn and 'shadowed' each desk within them from high to low. They took great trouble with me and with all who joined them.

Then I was given a job on the books of one of the Wrench property companies. I had not realized, in my ignorance, how much British property was in demand with certain foreign individuals and institutions. My mentor in the company was by profession a solicitor, Vivien Baker. He spoke, I remember, extremely fast on all occasions and with a slight stutter.

'There are a good many legal pitfalls, t-tax matters, currency matters which come into this side, M-Marlow. I used to advise the whole group on them, until, recently, Julius asked me to run this particular company from all p-points of view. There's rather too much to do, as it happens.' But I guessed his salary was fat. I worked very hard and learned, I think, fast. The property company in which I worked was largely, albeit indirectly, funded by overseas investors in Wrench Holdings. Since it was a wholly owned subsidiary of the holding company, of course, these investors could now only acquire shares in the parent – in Wrench Holdings itself. 'But earlier,' said Baker, 'f-foreigners held a large stake in this particular company. It's rationalized now. They've done pretty w-well.' I nodded, without understanding much.

Time went by rapidly. I shared a small flat in South Kensington with an Oxford friend, James Todd, who was reading for the Bar. My salary enabled me to live – precariously.

I found, to my relief, that I was giving very little thought to possible largess from the Kinzel estate. I had reconciled myself to the thought that this was unlikely to be significant – and was probably hedged about by insane conditions. I told myself, with what I reckoned was increased maturity, that living with 'expectations' would only serve to distract me from the pursuit of excellence and success by my own efforts. I was determined not to harry Mr Austin, who had indicated that only April 1966 could bring me another letter about the mysterious Mr Waldo Price. I had written to Mr Austin, of course, telling him of my joining Wrench Holdings, and of my address. He knew what I was doing and where to find me. He also knew I planned to get another job after an apprenticeship with Wrench. He would, I imagined, answer. I found myself looking at the mail with a touch of unwise anxiety, but on the whole I kept pretty cool. This was as well, since when a letter did arrive from Mr Austin it was as frustrating as could be:

> Dear Simon,
> Thank you for your information about your movements. This is to say that the arrangements we described in our letter of 12 March 1962, affecting Mr Waldo Price, still stand. Mr Price has recently confirmed that he does not now intend to be in this country until 1966 and will communicate with us later. As you know, no attempt should be made to contact Mr Price before his return.
>
> Yours sincerely,
> Jacob Austin

Mr Waldo Price and Boshy's legacy were both, I thought, separate parts of one mirage, which would fade into the future as each year approached and passed.

But if 1963 brought no inheritance it gave me a new job. One day in March I went into the office to hear that Julius Wrench himself wanted to see me. I had hardly met Julius since joining the company. He was spoken about with a good deal of awe; I think in most cases it was fear. I had, curiously enough, seen comparatively little of the Wrench family during the last six months. This was because Harry was abroad – he had been sent to New York, to learn the business of merchant banking at a famous house on Wall Street. It was probable that he would stay there for several years. Mrs Wrench had said, 'You must come and see us often, Simon. Don't lose yourself just because Harry's away. We shall need you more than ever.' But it was not easy to treat myself as a surrogate son of the family. Our friendship had not reached that level, although at times it had seemed to promise it. I had dined with them at Eaton Square on one occasion – a large party before a dance, a rather expensive irrelevance for them, as it happened, because Miranda, whose party it was planned to be, had developed influenza the day before and was in bed upstairs throughout the evening. I missed Harry.

Julius looked at me with his penetrating eyes and the familiar bored, ironic half-smile when I entered his office.

'How are you getting on, Simon? I'm afraid I've not seen as much of you as I'd have liked. Things have been rather hectic.'

He was extraordinary – affected yet flattering – in his way of implying that we were all on the same level, my time as valuable as his. I said I was enjoying life and finding it intensely interesting. He then spoke about the company in which I was toiling – again, by implication, as to one who was virtually running the show.

'It's gone rather well, lately. People are quite keen. I only hope they're right.'

Suddenly he said, in his drawling voice, 'Would you like to work for me for a bit? I need a new assistant in here; Andrew is going. I think you'll find it rather interesting. I don't think you ought to be here more than another six months. I gather you're picking things up pretty well, but, as I told you, I believe you ought to see more of the world.' I thought so too. 'As a matter of fact, I've got a Chinese friend coming here quite soon whom you might meet. He does a lot of business with us – operations in Malaya, Singapore, Borneo. It's possible you might join them for a bit.'

This was heady stuff.

I had no idea what went on in Julius's outer office, where two assistants, men who appeared alarmingly knowing, worked, while two decorative secretaries looked supercilious in an adjoining room. Of course I muttered my sense of honour and gratitude. I could not imagine that anything but family friendship lay behind this remarkable, temporary promotion. Julius made it slightly less bizarre, however, by saying, 'I think you'd learn a good deal. Probably best anyway not to do it for too long. Rex will show you the form.' (I did not know which of the two who had inspected me on arrival outside the shrine was Rex, and which the departing Andrew.) And so I began to work for a while in close if humble relationship with the Emperor himself.

Julius's motive may, as I imagined, have been purely one of friendly patronage, but from the start I think I earned my salary in my new position. It lasted seven months. I was a learner, on sufferance. I knew, of course, much too little about life in general and Wrench Holdings in particular. This caused some jealousy, as I could easily discern. But I had, I think, enough sense to disarm this by being helpful to all and by never seeking to appear as Julius's confidant, one with his ear. That, I knew well, would bring retribution one day. With Julius himself I was, I believe, quick, efficient and thoughtful. I learned a great deal of the business. Although I was careful to seem to others the humble and not particularly well-informed subordinate, I found that Julius did, in fact, begin to talk to me very freely about the affairs of the company. He probably found this relaxing – even helpful. Like every large concern handling major matters or large sums of money, there was plenty of intrigue and self-seeking in Wrench Holdings; plenty of place-men looking for a receptive ear at court. Julius, I expect, liked having me to talk to simply because I was so junior, so ignorant and so unimportant that I could – anyway as yet – never challenge him or conspire with any palace revolution. He felt secure with a child like me.

Julius also showed, to my surprise, a considerable flair for exposition. If I did not understand some matter I found that I could always say so, and that he would look at me for a moment and then say, 'Right. Sit down, Simon,' in his drawling voice. Then his tone would change and become crisp, his choice of words economic and supremely lucid. He could explain an issue quicker and more convincingly than any man I knew. This was undoubtedly because his mind itself was uncluttered by needless baggage, was clear, rapid and incisive. I was touched by the trouble he took with me.

I remember once, for instance, bringing to him the list of contributions, political, charitable or cultural, which the company made and reviewed annually. This list had to go to Julius himself, and although it was, of course, approved by the Board it was his very personal construction. Rather boldly I said, 'Is there ever any problem about this list? I've not been told to talk to anyone but you about it. Is it ever challenged, within the company?'

He looked at me rather speculatively.

'What makes you ask that?'

'I imagined some of the recipients might be thought, by some, to be a bit – questionable.'

Julius considered.

'Some are frankly political. We make a large contribution to the Conservative Party. Is that what you mean?'

'No, I mean –' and I cited a number of organizations on the list which were far from dear, I imagined, to the Conservative Party. Organizations on what might, perhaps generously, be described as the liberal-left of politics or sociology. I was surprised to see them as beneficiaries of some very handsome gifts from Wrench Holdings.

Julius said, 'Ah! You see my – our – policy has always been to be as objective and even-handed as possible in these matters. You may think that supporting those people is inconsistent with supporting the Conservative Party. I don't agree. Our contributions signify that we are concerned with our interests, on the one hand, but concerned with certain social and international issues we don't think should be an anti-Conservative monopoly on the other. In most cases the recipients are – grateful.' He wore his mocking half-smile, but his tone was serious.

'When I came down from Cambridge,' he added, 'I was mad keen to get into politics. It was a phase – it lasted about three years. I went into business, at first in America, to make enough money for an independent political career and I found it so much fun that the political career never started.' Julius smiled, reminiscently perhaps. I was humbled by such flattering confidences and would have done anything for him at that moment.

He looked out of the window. 'But the answer to your first question is "No". My colleagues are, I know, content to leave this to me. Contributions show on the Holdings balance sheet. Only the main Board are concerned. We're a big show, now, and I think people expect us to exercise a certain amount of – patronage.'

It was also, of course, true that Wrench Holdings was munificent to many entirely uncontentious charities. In such matters Julius never showed impatience with my questions. Nobody else asked them and he liked, at times, to justify things to himself aloud, with myself listening. That is how it appeared. I enjoyed this, and as the months passed we became closer. He was an autocrat, quietly sharing power with none. I thought that something almost like affection showed at times; but he was a hard man.

On another occasion, I had to prepare a folder and mentioned a small company specializing in a particular line of overseas property. 'How did we come to acquire this? It seems rather a mess, and when I asked Jackson' – that particular company secretary – 'he laughed.'

'It *is* rather a mess. It always was. At the time – just after the war, fifteen, sixteen years ago – I was picking up companies so hard and fast I barely had time to digest. A few of them fought me, most unwisely. That company was typical of the sort of futile condition into which some boards had allowed their companies to drift, cushioned by wartime government and controls. In almost all cases we then cleaned things up, rationalized, sold off buildings, got rid of useless people. In that particular instance there were special circumstances – legal difficulties – and I agreed to go slowly, and I did. I suppose we all liked to look at it sometimes, to remind ourselves of the sort of transition we'd achieved for the rest of the group. I wasn't in a great hurry. But it's going to be sorted out now. I can't be bothered to keep it unreconstructed simply as an object-lesson! And we do,' he said, with the quizzical half-smile, 'have shareholders, Simon! They could, very reasonably, ask why we aren't taking a harder line. They never have. But from next year they won't have the chance. You were quite right to notice it.'

Julius, to me, was kind. I came, more and more, to admire his clarity and speed of perception. I also, increasingly, watched his ruthlessness. I was in the room, once, when Barnett – not a natural pleader for mercy – spoke to Julius of an associate who had made a misjudgement. I did not know the man. I imagined he had somehow (it cannot have been easy) persuaded Barnett to 'put in a word'.

'He's pretty desperate, Julius. He's in very deep himself, you know. This will break him.'

'He deserves it,' said Julius in his unmoved drawl. 'He thought he was richer than he is, and cleverer. He started with very little and he's overreached himself. I've little patience with people who have insufficient capital and act out a dream that it's larger than it is. Now he'll pay. What's wrong with that, Bill?'

'I'm afraid he's suicidal.'

'Well, that's not my problem. I hope he'll see a good psychiatrist.'

'You don't think we might, just on this occasion . . . ?' said Barnett, voice not quite steady.

'No, I don't. Not on this nor any occasion. Don't be silly, Bill.' Julius was totally relaxed, entirely calm. His steady, penetrating gaze certainly conveyed to Barnett what I could feel was impatient contempt. No more was said.

One day towards the end of the summer, Julius said, 'You haven't been to Eaton Square for some time, Simon. Viola hoped you could have supper with us next Wednesday. Just us and Miranda and Harry. He's coming over for two weeks from New York.' I was overjoyed.'

'It was on that evening,' said Marlow, 'that I first fell in love with Miranda.' He spoke now even more quietly, frowning a little, with great precision.

Marlow had never talked, in telling his tale, of the state of his heart. He certainly did not impress John as a cold fish; rather the reverse. But although he described his feelings, his reactions to past events, his motives, with great clarity and with an almost clinical objectivity, a certain reserve hung about him and John could not imagine him indulging in emotional, still less salacious, confidences. Now he said in a very matter-of-fact way, 'I fell in love with Miranda,' but John was perfectly sure, from the impression he now had of Simon Marlow from their curious evening sessions, that he had really, profoundly and no doubt painfully, fallen in love. John had, as yet, no picture in his mind of Miranda, and it was only later that one formed. Harry, on the other hand, he could see clearly – charming, light-hearted, impulsive and independent of mind. Miranda had hitherto appeared in Marlow's story only as a plumply pretty girl with grey eyes on the snow slopes at Zermatt. Marlow did not attempt physical description, beyond saying, 'She was by now beautiful. She was just twenty. She had the loveliest skin and the liveliest eyes I ever knew.' John certainly did not ask him more. On later occasions, with conscious efforts at bringing her before the eyes, he painted a picture of Miranda in his mind, could see her as dark, slender, perhaps smouldering a little. He enjoyed the picture, such as it was.

'Mrs Wrench asked me to call her "Viola" that evening,'

said Marlow, 'told me I was a stranger, where had I been and so forth. She whispered to me that 'Julius thought the world of me'. Then Harry appeared – like all our generation he was clearly changing every month, growing and expanding with experience. But to me he was the same as ever. To all of us he was keen to explain what the United States was all about. Julius, who knew New York and San Francisco almost as well as London, listened with ironic patience. His reactions were gentle, his voice amused:

'How much I wish I'd known all this before!'

Harry chuckled. He was impossible to snub or to provoke.

'I'm sure you do, Father. I can see how much I'm teaching you.' Then he resumed. Miranda said little. I cannot possibly express the sensation she produced in me. It was not simply physical attraction, however powerful. Nor was it a meeting of minds, hearts, interests, since we barely spoke to each other. It was as if some stunning and alarming electromagnetic force ran between us. It was elemental. Once I thought I saw her glancing at me with a private, conspiratorial look. But I dared not hope so, and I looked everywhere but at her. I was terrified of showing the impression being made by her on me. I fooled myself that nobody noticed. When we had a word after dinner I was deliberately offhand. I asked her to some party, playing down its likely enjoyment, keeping my voice steady with difficulty. She declined. I was heart-broken, frustrated. Here she was – sister of my closest friend, living in a house where I was admitted as one of the family. Yet she seemed inaccessible. Before I left, Mrs Wrench suggested another visit, another supper before Harry flew back to New York. I accepted in an offhand way.

'Well,' I said to Miranda, 'I might see you on Monday, I suppose.'

'You might.'

We had hardly exchanged a word all evening, but I was, I

knew from that moment, seriously, terrifyingly in love. It can come at any age or never. It came to me then.'

John uttered a rare interruption.

'Surely – it's coming back to me – Miranda Wrench? You talked earlier of a Langenbach, a kidnapping a few years ago. Wasn't Miranda Wrench the name of the woman also mixed up in it?'

'Yes. Mixed up in it. That is so.'

Then silence. John wondered if he should not have held his tongue.

Marlow soon thereafter showed how tired he was, and John left him, as usual making arrangements for another visit. The evening had been a long one, but John felt that Marlow had broken some surface of ice, difficult to approach, in talking of the Wrench family, of his strengthening ties with them, and of Miranda. Once managed, he seemed anxious to resume his story as soon as possible, and pressed John to come only two nights later.

And two nights later he resumed, as on the previous occasion, immediately they sat down to dinner. As ever, Marlow made no apology, gave no word of even formal recognition that his own account of his life might be wearisome to another. He started by saying, 'Last dinner together I told you how I met Harry again, and saw Miranda as if it were for the first time,' and then went on to describe his next visit to the Wrench household in Eaton Square, a long week later. He talked again about Mrs Wrench, and John thought his heart had been more taken with her, fifty though she may have been, than he had admitted or perhaps fully understood. Viola Wrench was clearly a woman with great charm for the young; of ageless sympathy, John guessed. Marlow had referred earlier to the beauty of her eyes. John thought that he had once said they were, too, Miranda's eyes – described as the liveliest ever known.

'I was lucky,' said Marlow, 'on that evening I arrived early for supper, and only Miranda was there. Harry and his mother had been to some function and had agreed to meet Julius there before returning home. Miranda was alone. We sat and – and talked. I couldn't say anything wise, or sophisticated, or even sensible. I couldn't, in fact, keep my voice calm. But from the first moment, when she said, 'I didn't know how to reach you, Simon, to warn you that we're not likely to have supper until nine o'clock; Mummy, Daddy and Harry are going to be late' (it was quarter to eight), from that first moment the time raced and I extravagantly hoped. This extraordinary current was running between us. We sat in the sitting room off the hall, downstairs. She knew perfectly well what I was feeling – no simple desire but the sort of high tension that is unmistakable in man or woman, met now and then in a lifetime. When we looked at each other, and when at last she did not look away but held my gaze for a long time, I knew she knew. It was twenty times as potent as any fumbling embraces could be. I could find no words. I thought I didn't need to. We were together, alone, for only half an hour, but it brought certainty. I said her name very softly, several times, and at last she said, 'Simon'; and our hands touched and we were both trembling, both frightened. I can't put it into words, even now. It was as if we were one human being, different parts of one creature, separated but suddenly re-united. I know it sounds absurd. I can only tell you . . . '

Marlow was silent for a little as if needing to recover, and when he continued it was in his usual, rather slow voice, calmer.

'Then the family arrived and the presence of Julius, as ever, dominated. He talked of plans for taking a new place in Scotland the following year. He couldn't entirely keep the satisfaction out of his voice as he spoke of it – leased from a duke's estates, it had a high sporting reputation. Julius, I knew, liked the fruits of his success, languid about them though he always affected to be. But I was perceiving ever more clearly that the world's opinion – the powerful, fashionable, "knowing" world wherein he had won his spurs – mattered to him hugely. And he liked to be able to dispense hospitality – especially sporting hospitality and especially to foreigners in search of British traditional pursuits. I was on the fringes of his world, an unimportant and unnoticed young extra in the cast of those he loved to entertain so generously.

'The Bartholomews are coming over, I hope,' Julius said, casually, referring to an immensely rich American family with whom Wrench Holdings did much business. 'We might get them north for a few days. I think they'd enjoy it.' He spoke other names – big names. His eyes sparkled.

That evening I learned, with a shock, that the house at Eaton Square was to be sold. Julius might have mentioned this to me at the office but had not.

'It makes no sense now,' he said in his bored voice. The family had by now reluctantly come to terms with the idea.

'Nobody much lives here, in these houses, nor can, these days. They're all embassies or disguised businesses of one sort or another. We've lived on an expiring lease, and now I've got to decide whether to renew. It makes no sense. We'll be much more comfortable in a flat.'

It was hard to picture Viola anywhere else. We resent it when people desert the frame in which we first discovered them. They rob us of something precious by acts they mistakenly think purely their own business. I said, 'How very sad.'

'Anyway, Harry's based in New York and likely to be there for some time. And I expect he'll look for something on his own when he ultimately comes back. And Miranda will be marrying.'

I said nothing to this, but blushed. A distressing habit of youth, still not discarded. Miranda raised her eyebrows.

'Oh yes, darling,' said Viola, 'I somehow doubt if that moment is very many years away. We have to be realistic.'

'You might look out in New York for some appropriate

millionaire or his heir, Harry,' said Julius with his half-smile. And, for a moment, I thought there was a certain menace in the room. Yet when I went home from Eaton Square that night I felt giddy and sick with emotion. I couldn't sleep. Miranda's voice was in my ears, Miranda's face came between me and every surface on which my eyes fell.

6

'It was only two days after this dinner with the Wrenches,' Marlow continued, 'this terrifying awareness of the impact of Miranda, that Julius threw a letter at me in the office which had arrived marked very personally for him and which neither I nor a secretary had opened or seen. It was from Malaya, from Mr Ling: Ling Kuo Seng, but to Julius and others 'Jimmy Ling'. It said that he looked forward to his visit to London in August, and proposed luncheon followed by a talk on the first of several days previously telephoned out to Singapore by Julius's secretary.

'Jimmy Ling hates the telephone and has a perverse belief in the speed of mails simply because they're now carried in aircraft,' said Julius. 'He's going to be here next week. I'm going to talk to him about you, Simon. He's got a big show in that part of the world and if he could fit you in you'd get a mighty good start. Not only start – you could end up a Far East hand, and stay on.'

'I've had a mighty good start here.'

'Yes,' said Julius, 'but as I told you, this ought to be regarded as a little bit of training. You must get wider experience. Then, perhaps, you'll come back one day.' I was oversensitive at that moment. I could see Miranda's expression mirrored in every letter I read or wrote. I feared everything, and very particularly that the Wrench antennae were sensitive too, and that they thought me better in South-East Asia for a while. I imagined I detected an unfamiliar roughness in Julius's tone, in his '*perhaps* you'll come back'. I had been ten months learning the trade with Wrench Holdings. I felt at home.

'I take it you'd like the chance of a change?' said Julius.

I knew I must not hesitate. I knew, besides, that in practical terms he was entirely right. My progress was still only that of an intelligent youth, a friend of the family, an agreeable, unformed apprentice. I had to strike out on my own. I knew it and hated it. I had fallen in love a matter of days before, and now I was probably going half-way across the world for several years.

'Of course – it's a wonderful chance. I long to meet Mr Ling.'

'He may not be able to take you,' said Julius. But I thought he would. Then Julius said, 'I suppose your mother will miss you – but one has to make a life for oneself.'

In those minutes I had hardly thought of my mother. I stood, ashamed. Then I said, 'Well, thank you so much,' and left the room.

My mother was deeply upset at the prospect of my going to the Far East. I spent most weekends at Penterton and on the Friday evening following Julius's talk with me I told her how things lay. My grandmother had died in 1960 and my mother now had a little more money. She still worked part-time at the library – she enjoyed it and it occupied her. But she was, I realized, very dependent on my weekends. Since by now, and for unavowed reasons, I myself dreaded leaving England, her gentle pain made things even harder to bear.

'Perhaps,' said my mother, 'this Mr Ling won't want you to join him.'

'I think he will, Mum. I think Julius – Julius Wrench – will persuade him. He's keen on the idea, I know. And of course he's perfectly right. I ought to get some wider experience.'

'You've grown very close to the Wrench family. You owe them a lot, my darling, I see that. Mr Wrench's advice is obviously important. I'm rather surprised, though, that he's so anxious to send you off if he thinks so much of you, and I'm sure he does. They may never get you back.'

'I think he's looking at it from the point of view of my future, and of course his own son, Harry, is abroad for quite a bit, in America. It's quite a normal step for anybody of ambition. And I've got that, Mum, as you know.' It was true. The desire to succeed, to ascend, to prosper greatly, burned stronger within me every day. Without that success, that prosperity, I could imagine no chance of winning the great prizes life might offer. One such prize – and the only one which obsessed me at that moment – was Miranda. I might conquer her heart but I would be unlikely to win her for life without a penny but my earnings. I knew that. I knew the Wrench world by now.

'You say you saw Harry the other day, when he was over here,' said my mother. 'Of course, America is much nearer than Singapore or wherever it is you'd be working. And I expect he can afford to come whenever he likes – or the family to bring him. Besides, he's not the only child, is he?'

'No, there are two sisters. One's married.'

'The other's younger, isn't she?' my mother said. She was vaguely familiar with the Wrench establishment from my reports since Oxford and Zermatt days.

'Yes. Miranda's younger.'

An only son, his mother's principal prop and confidant, is unlikely to be able to disguise altogether his feelings. Yet I wanted to keep Miranda to myself for a little. My love was fresh, entirely without root or nourishment, and vulnerable to the lightest wind, the least exposure. My mother looked at me over her sewing and said, 'Is she at home?'

'Oh yes, some sort of artistic training.'

'Is she like Harry?'

'In a way.'

'Pretty?'

I acknowledged it. My mother sewed away. Then she

sighed. I think she felt clearer in her mind that my departure from Wrench Holdings was inevitable; that I was being propelled by strong forces, possibly beneficent, which the Marlows were unlikely to be able to withstand, and should not try.

Mrs Wrench and Miranda were both away in Scotland from early August. I several times telephoned before they went, to try to talk to Miranda. Each time Mrs Wrench answered. Once she said, 'Simon! How are you, my dear? I'm afraid Miranda's gone to Devonshire for a few days – she seems to treat her studies very independently, I must say!' for Miranda was studying art with the idea of gaining a diploma and working in the commercial world, rather than living by the pencil or brush. On the next occasion Mrs Wrench said, 'I'll see if she's about,'and after a long delay Miranda said, 'Hello, Simon,' in what sounded a rather unnatural voice.

'I wondered if you could have dinner with me later this week?'

'Oh dear, it's terribly difficult, Mother and I are going to Scotland together to get the house ready, then Daddy and a lot of friends are joining us in the middle of the month. I seem to be rushed off my feet.'

'Yes, I can imagine, and I know all that. But surely one evening – or a quick lunch perhaps . . . ?'

'Simon, I really don't think I can . . .'

'Miranda!'

'Yes?'

'I want to see you very badly.'

'Yes, well, we'll be back on the tenth of September.'

'Miranda, I may be going abroad for a long time. I really must talk to you about it.'

'In September, Simon,' said Miranda. I thought there was a quaver in the tone. She rang off immediately, and I meditated a number of courses of action. An immediate march to Eaton Square, confrontation, demands, declarations? Offhand silence, nonchalance, the appearance of invulnerability?

Next day, I rang again. Mrs Wrench answered, charming as ever.

'Simon, I'm afraid you've missed Miranda. She's out.'

'Will she be in later?'

'I'm not sure of her movements,' said Viola Wrench serenely. I thought she was, and that Miranda was in. Next day Jimmy Ling arrived in London.

Julius wasted no time in presenting me to Ling. He was a plump, smooth-faced man with a high-pitched crackling laugh which seemed to accompany almost every remark. He had made enormous sums of money in timber and had then diversified his business and, like Julius, had substantial property interests in Singapore and in various towns in Malaya. He owned a small airline, covering flights between Malaya, Borneo and the Philippines. He was also moving, a little late, into Hong Kong. His business was adversely affected by the war in Vietnam at this time. It was also damaged by the campaign Soekarno's Indonesia was conducting against 'East Malaysia', North Borneo and Sarawak. Ling, however, was always a man to turn circumstances to good account. Like many Chinese he was a gambler, but he never complained when the game seemed to run against him. He simply took stock, did his sums, thought hard and placed his bets, chuckling all the time. On this occasion he was betting – hard – that the Americans would sooner or later leave Vietnam to the tender mercies of the Communists; but that, with British assistance, the Malaysians would successfully resist the attempts of Indonesia. The Americans, of course, were at that time committed to Saigon only in a so-called advisory capacity; but even when, in 1965, they were launched by Kennedy on major and overt intervention, I know that Ling never wavered in his belief that political pressures would get them out before they could see off the North Vietnamese. As to Indonesia, Link reckoned, without doubt, that Soekarno wouldn't last for ever, and that his fall would put an end to the nonsense.

He was ultimately right on both counts. What he, rather surprisingly, failed to anticipate was something nearer home – the sudden secession of Singapore from Malaysia. This shook him when it occurred, which was a little time ahead – in 1965 – but he recovered, chuckling away. Anyway, his investments and dispositions were well covered by a system of, in effect, reinsurance and hedging (and a good deal of what may bluntly be called protection) so that it would have needed a remarkable cataclysm to overturn his empire. Julius had befriended him soon after the end of the Second World War, when his business was small. They recognized each other's talents. I had, and have, no idea of Jimmy Ling's age. His smooth, soft face appeared untouched by time. Perhaps he will one day be wrinkled and venerable in the Chinese manner. It is hard to envisage.

When Julius had brought us together in his office, Ling said, 'Ahhh – Mr Wrench says you might be interested to join us. He says you clever. I have a number of very interesting companies. You could have a position in one – a trading company. You would travel all over South-East Asia. It is very interesting.' He laughed loudly.

'It's very kind of you, Mr Ling.'

'Pay is good. Prospects are good.'

'Really very kind of you –'

'You start in Singapore. Then, after learning, travel.'

'Wonderful opportunity –'

'When you come?'

'Well I don't really know, you see, I've got this position in Mr Wrench's office at the moment and somebody will have to –'

'When you come? You can come in two weeks? I will be back in Singapore then.'

Julius came in wearing his usual disinterested expression. Ling laughed away and said, 'He comes to Singapore. Best in two weeks.'

'Well I should think that will be all right,' said Julius to me.

'I'll probably get Ralph Oldham' (a more experienced hand than I) 'to come into the office for a bit. He's had his holiday early and he can read himself in while I'm in Scotland. Well done, Simon, I think you've been very sensible. And well done, Jimmy, you've got quite a promising chap!"

Marlow did not relate much about his life in the Far East – John felt it was, in his mind, peripheral to the central story he was unfolding. He said that he had first of all suffered appallingly from the sense of separation from Miranda. He gave the impression that his mother took his departure bravely and that both he and she were regular correspondents. John interrupted at one point as Marlow was briefly filling in his career working for Ling Enterprises.

'Did you, if I may ask, write to Miranda?'

'Yes, I wrote once.'

John thought it best to be inquisitive, intrusive. Marlow felt he had to tell everything, so everything Tranter had better know.

'What sort of letter? A love letter?'

Marlow's extraordinarily, unnaturally even voice shook a little.

'Yes, it was – chiefly – a love letter.' Then he gave a long, sad sigh.

'She never answered. It was only later that I found she'd received it. I didn't write it until about December, 1963. You see, I realized I was being sent off because the Wrenches reckoned I had fallen for Miranda and they had other ideas for her. They may even – I liked to imagine this at least – have thought she'd fallen for me. They liked me. Their reasoning that it was much best for me to go, for my own career, was absolutely sincere. Julius had done me a very good turn. But he wanted to get me away from his daughter.'

John pursued it. 'Surely in these days they wouldn't have objected to you? You were intelligent, you had a future. Wrench could have helped you, I imagine, set you up. Why were they so opposed to you as a son-in-law, if they were? I don't get it. One's always reading in the papers of heiresses or whatever running off with impossible people, criminals, layabouts. Here were you, hard-working, promising, a friend of their son. I'd have thought you were very eligible.'

'I mustn't exaggerate this,' said Marlow. 'I think the Wrench motives were a bit mixed. But you must remember Julius Wrench had come up the hard way, and behind his relaxed manner was a man of great ambition and purpose, and he loved money. In a very old-fashioned way he wanted Miranda to make a 'good marriage'. I think – although he did, in his way, love her – he regarded her as a very promising asset on which he expected a better than ordinary return. He was a snob. Inwardly, secretly, he looked for a son-in-law with great possessions coming to him, or a distinguished name, or both. I was an agreeable, youthful nobody. His reactions were, I think, remarkably similar to those of a father of a century before. And perhaps fathers – anyway, fathers who are rich, successful men – change less, inwardly, than fashion suggests.'

'And Mrs Wrench?'

Marlow considered this carefully. 'I asked myself, often, what Viola's feelings about me might be. I felt perfectly sure she knew I'd fallen head over heels for Miranda. She, and all the family, were used to deferring to any strongly held view or sentiment of Julius, languidly though it might be conveyed. She was very proud of Miranda and very close to her. I think she probably just felt we were too young, and separation would cure youthful infatuation, if that was what it was. A perfectly sensible position, after all.'

'You're talking of the sixties. Everybody was breaking the conventions, knocking their parents' attitudes, doing their own thing. I can't understand why Miranda couldn't, if she felt like it, have put two fingers in the air to her parents and gone to you, if she really wanted to.'

'Well,' said Marlow, 'that wasn't what happened. And,

somehow, it couldn't have happened. Not to Miranda. Not to us. And, of course, the possibility I dreaded was that I was mistaken in supposing Miranda felt anything deep for me. I told myself I had no right to suppose she cared a rap. What had we done but sit and hold hands, gaze into each other's eyes, once? It was laughable, I said to myself, idiotic – and particularly so, as you've just implied, in an age when young people slept together at the drop of a hat. I'd never even taken her out! It was fantastic that I had built up this intense image, this white-hot certainty that I loved and was loved, as if the current which ran between us had been there, waiting for a switch to be turned on, since the beginning of time, as if we had known each other always. And yet, fantastic or not, I felt it to be true. I didn't mind – or mind so much – the idea that the Wrench parents did not favour me. Those were circumstances I might overcome. The only really destructive terror was that Miranda herself by now felt nothing.

This fear was, of course, fuelled by Miranda not answering my letter. I found, long, long afterwards, that she had kept it. Her mother, as I guessed, had spotted how things were with me. Viola had impressed on her with great force, when I had gone away, that it would be a cruelty to me to maintain any sort of contact. Miranda had taken that from her mother. So they indulged in another sort of cruelty and I had no reply to my letter.

1964 saw me becoming both engrossed and successful in Ling Enterprises. Jimmy Ling noticed me on occasions and chuckled happily. I had an excellent salary, and learned the business quickly. Even my few months in Wrench Holdings had given me a certain insight and a definite taste for the excitements and battles of a large diversified conglomerate of that kind, and it was in a strange part of the world with new sights to see and impressions to absorb. I may have been – I was – lovelorn, but I managed to have an extraordinarily interesting time. As at Wrench Holdings, too, I was fascinated by the amount of investment which flowed across frontiers. I was surprised to find that Ling Enterprises attracted considerable sums from European societies as well as from Japan, the Philippines and Taiwan and every corner of the capitalist world.

Then, one day in June, I opened the airmail copy of *The Times*. On the appropriate page the engagement was announced of Mr Alexander Bartholomew junior, eldest son of Mr and Mrs Alexander Bartholomew, with an address in New Jersey, USA, and Miranda, daughter of Mr and Mrs Julius Wrench of – and there followed a number in Cadogan Square. The Wrench family had, as Julius had said, moved from Eaton Square; I hadn't even known their new address. I didn't fool myself that Miranda would not have received my letter of the previous December for that reason, but not even to be able to envisage her surroundings emphasized my total separation.

There was nobody to whom I could talk who knew her or could imagine her. One couple called Prince – he was another British Ling employee, quite a senior man – had been particularly kind to me and welcomed me often to their home. I liked it and them. They had two small children and I found, to my surprise, that I was as easily fond of them. I had absolutely no experience of small children.

That same evening of reading *The Times* I had dinner with them. There were only the three of us. Mrs Prince said, 'You're looking rather done in, Simon.'

I told them I was heartbroken. I blurted it all out. It was a relief. They were sensible, sympathetic people and neither said, 'Oh, you'll get over it', or 'We must find another nice girl'. Perhaps something in my halting and inhibited account, something in the very brevity of my acquaintance with Miranda, the fact that 'nothing had happened', succeeded in conveying to them the sudden storm of love which had hit me. A year had gone by since I had left England, seen Miranda, and yet, I suppose, I felt and showed an emotion completely undimmed by the passing of that time. I was young. I had had a few casual sexual adventures in Singapore, but they had left my heart completely untouched and I was no hand at pretending otherwise. My host and hostess, I know, recognized 'the real thing'. They said little except, 'Do come again soon, and come often.' I will always be grateful to them. They had that rare and splendid quality of being able to deal with pain.

I couldn't avoid reading about Miranda's wedding three months later. It was at St Peter's, Eaton Square, and I imagined that large church full. My mother wrote with her usual good sense, 'I see your friend Miranda Wrench has married an American. Perhaps you will be a little sad, perhaps by now not so. I had a feeling your heart was touched in that quarter, but everything works out in the end. Your loving mother.' I thought Harry might write, but he did not. I sent a line to Miranda: 'I hope you will be very, very happy.' It was completely insincere. I found a nice piece of jade for her, and a friend travelling to London took it and delivered it to Cadogan Square before the awful wedding day. Life went on, to my surprise. I worked hard and quite intelligently. Jimmy Ling chuckled and gave me a rise in salary.

It was in October 1965 that four letters arrived one day by the same post. It was an extraordinary day. Except for my weekly letter from my mother I had few correspondents at home and I preferred to keep my thoughts away from England. I had recognized that something like two years ought to go by before I returned, if I ever did. Two of the letters were typewritten and I opened them first as likely to be less interesting. I was, on the whole, mistaken. One was on Wrench Holdings paper. It was from Bill Barnett.

Barnett wrote to say that it hardly seemed two years since I had left them; they had missed me. (Get to the point, Barnett! I thought. These courtesies to a one-time underling had purpose.) Julius had talked only recently about me – he had heard, to his delight, from Jimmy Ling that I was doing brilliantly. Now there happened to be a vacancy at home: Barnett was keen to 'sharpen up' business in the very section – property at home, investors overseas – where I had cut my teeth at Wrench Holdings three years ago. There followed some ambiguous, potentially disloyal hints about the present management of that part of the Wrench empire: perhaps by my old mentor, Baker, the stuttering solicitor. Barnett, clearly, had had orders from Julius. He was casting a fly. He implied that terms could be pretty good. It would mean being available as early as possible in the New Year. 'If you're interested, let me know. I gathered from Julius that Jimmy Ling wouldn't stand in the way. It would all be friendly. As you probably know, we've quite often sent people to each other in the past, to our mutual benefit.'

The second typewritten letter was from Mr Austin. I had, of course, left my address and occupation with him, but Austin, Boshy *et al.* had not been in my thoughts. I had been rather pleased with myself for managing to live, indeed to prosper, entirely by my own efforts. The cut-off of allowance on leaving Oxford had been amply counterbalanced by a modest starting salary with Wrench Holdings, and a very generous one from Ling Enterprises. Now even better times, perhaps, lay ahead. I felt independent, and whatever modest legacy might await me next year if I fulfilled Boshy's conditions played little part in my dreams. I was, also, happily enmeshed in the world of commerce and finance. I had no mind for the sort of academic distinction which, I was sure, would be Boshy's demand.

Mr Austin sent good wishes. Then . . .'

Marlow affected to refresh his memory, glancing at the letter he had drawn from the briefcase.

> 'You will, I know, recall the terms of the letter I signed to you about the late Henry Kinzel's will and testamentary trust. We, as you know, are to make you a beneficiary as to income on attaining the age of twenty-five, provided you

accept certain conditions; and we are to make trust capital yours absolutely on receiving from Mr Waldo Price at any time thereafter, but before you attain the age of thirty, a letter to the effect that you have fulfilled the late Mr Kinzel's wishes in their entirety.

I am sorry to say that I gather Mr Price has not been well. As you know, he has been living abroad for some time, and I tried and failed to contact him at intervals during last year. Recently, he has returned to this country and is living in London. He writes to me, however, that his health is not good and he does not feel up to a meeting with me – which I had suggested. He has, in spite of that, said that he is perfectly ready to play his part in respect of your business, and I have reminded him of the date of your twenty-fifth birthday.

Of course, certain arrangements – in law certain complex and, I'm afraid, protracted arrangements – will apply in the case of Mr Price being so indisposed as *not* to be able to do what Henry Kinzel requested. I need not anticipate these and I hope they will not arise.

What all this means is that the sooner you see Mr Price after 12 March next, the better. I do not know how long you propose to work in Singapore but you should be aware of this.

Yours sincerely,
Jacob Austin

Oddly enough, this communication now filled me not with reawakened curiosity, still less excitement, but with irritation. I was sure that all this was a wild-goose chase, not something to allow to disturb sensible decisions about a promising career. I was, of course, deeply grateful to Boshy, and touched by his having buried this crock of gold for my persistent search, to discover and to win. But I was sure that the prize would be unlikely to attract a potentially high-salaried man (as I was coming to think of myself) and I expected the conditions to be tedious and unacceptable. I noted that Mr Austin's letter referred to 'trust capital' – an ambiguous expression which could mean anything from a small part to the whole – and how large a whole? I was almost sorry that if I took up Bill Barnett's cautious proposition I should be back in England well before my twenty-fifth birthday and would have to see the ailing Price. As I read the Austin letter, with a touch of impatience, the picture evoked by Bill Barnett's offer blurred the page and took precedence of interest. Perhaps I had, I thought, been long enough in Singapore.

The third letter was from Harry. It reinforced my itch – if any reinforcement were needed. Harry was a desultory correspondent, but when he wrote, he wrote well. He told me that he was back in New York after a summer holiday in England and Scotland – his first visit home, I gathered, since Miranda's wedding. He was due to return, to a London merchant bank, in 1966. He was looking forward to it. Like me, he had been away long enough, I thought. My affection for him was untroubled by the appalling emotional turmoil I had suffered for Miranda. I had not recovered from that, but it seemed to have a little less violent power to disturb now.

> You might come back, too. My father always hoped you might come back to his little outfit, and the other day he apparently had such glowing reports from his old friend Ling that the cry throughout Wrench Holdings is 'Bring back Marlow. Marlow at all costs.' Have you heard from the arse-licking Barnett? I'm sure Father has given orders. Do obey them if they're passed on to you. Everybody wants you back.

All this was agreeable. I felt no animus against Julius for what I suspected (and it could not be certainty) was my exile – like Ovid's, for having ideas about the Emperor's daughter above my place in life. I thought I could see myself at Wrench Holdings again and I certainly knew far, far more about business. Harry's letter made no mention at all of Miranda.

The fourth letter was in an unknown and erratic hand, very blotched, very difficult to read. I'll read it to you.'

Marlow peered at what looked to be a rather flimsy and much creased piece of paper.

'Dear Mr Marlow,
As you know, we are due to meet next year, and I write to introduce myself. I am told you live in Singapore but I doubt if I can afford to visit you there so our appointed tryst next March may, I suppose, have to be postponed. I, myself, have only recently returned to England.

I have been in a pleasanter place than this, to wit Morocco, for three years. I intend to return there. I do not like England. I do not even like Wales, whence springs my blood. I find the climate here most disagreeable – especially what people call the summer' (it had been, I had read, a particularly damp English summer) 'I also find the people unsympathetic. They are given to alternate boasting and whining. They boast and strike attitudes as if they, alone, have defended liberty and the rights of man throughout our era, a most dubious claim. They whine whenever they are not repaid with ever-higher rewards for doing preposterously little, and that badly. My strictures apply to so-called rich and so-called poor alike. The rich are selfish and vulgar. The poor are stupid and obstinate. They hate each other and they're both right.

I plan to pass as short a while as I can on this revolting scene, but intend to discharge towards you, somehow, duties laid on me by one of the only truly good men I have ever known. I have been loaned a room at Flat G, No. 77 Shepherd Market, and that address will find me. I would be glad if you could tell me if there is any chance of our meeting in London. I intend, with reluctance, to stay here during most of 1966, at least the first half. But if you plan to spend many years in Asia I am at a loss what to propose.

Yours sincerely,
Waldo Price

There was not much to say to Mr Austin except that I would keep him informed of my movements. Mr Price sounded disagreeable in temper, but I liked his reference to Boshy and wrote back telling him that it was perfectly possible I would be in England in the New Year, and would keep him informed. To Harry I wrote a long letter of news and views. I, too, did not mention Miranda. His reference to Wrench Holdings I acknowledged non-committally. I replied pleasantly to Bill Barnett, avoiding any excessive enthusiasm but asking for as much detail as possible:

> . . . since I am becoming quite established here and it is financially, of course, very rewarding. Although I don't deny that in some ways a return to London would be agreeable, I must obviously think very hard before leaving Ling, who have done me well and with whom I have been happy.

I spoke to Jimmy Ling who was, of course, already informed of the probable tenor of Barnett-Marlow correspondence. He chuckled away, high-pitched as ever.

'We have a lot of business with Wrench, as you know. Many times I like people going from here to there, from there to here. I don't mind. You won't forget Ling.'

'I never could.'

'We are bigger than Wrench,' said Jimmy Ling, rather unexpectedly, 'much bigger. We have plenty of money in them. We hope they do well.'

'I'm sure they will.'

'Yes, I'm sure. Julius a great friend of mine. He's rich man now. He loves money – that's very good. To make it you have to love it. I know. Wrench ought to do well under Julius, bigger man each day. You tell them they do well or I'll come along like a crocodile, jaws going snappy-snappy,' said Jimmy Ling, chuckling so unrestrainedly that he almost fell off his chair. It was clear that he did not find my services indispensable, but he seemed full of good will. We left it that I would make a final decision in the light of further correspondence with Barnett, and at all events before Christmas. And by the end of November I had received a more definite and particularly attractive offer from Wrench Holdings. I had little difficulty in deciding, and planned to be home at Penterton for Christmas. Jimmy Ling said goodbye to me with added chuckling injunctions to make sure Wrench Holdings prospered so that the Ling Enterprises stake was secure. He said, 'You should make friends with Arthur Rivers. Very nice man Arthur. He will be useful to you.'

Arthur Rivers ran a Ling office in London, a particularly trusted ambassador. He had been often on men's lips at Wrench Holdings as well as in the office in Singapore. On Ling's original visit, when I had first met him, Rivers had been undergoing an operation in hospital so had not accompanied his master to see Julius. He was a name to me only, but a strong one. I told Jimmy Ling that I looked forward to meeting him.

'You keep in touch with Arthur,' said Jimmy Ling. 'He's a very nice man. Clever man.' I said that I would.'

Marlow said that he had returned to London and re-joined Wrench Holdings in January 1966. It was clear that he had gone back into a responsible and well-paid job. Although John found it hard to reach with the imagination, since he had absolutely no experience of the world of business, of offices, of organizations, Marlow successfully conveyed a rather changed atmosphere from that he had first sniffed as an apprentice at Covent Garden.

'Everything,' he said, 'was running in overdrive. Baker, my old boss, had left rather suddenly. People seemed more than ever nervous of Julius. I saw that we were doing well – very well. Julius was pleasant to me, but distant. 'Good to have you back, Simon. Come and see us soon. You know we've moved?' Harry was due back in the spring. I supposed Miranda was in America with her Alexander Bartholomew junior, and I kept my mind as clear of her as possible. I hunted for a flesh and blood replacement for this haunting insubstantial obsession – but found no girl who could, I thought, ever light a fire within me of the consuming kind I had felt in that one hour's language of the eyes with Miranda, long before. I took a flat and bought a few things. For a young bachelor I was prosperous. I was also moody and lonely.

I wrote in February to Waldo Price. His letter came by return of post.

> Your birthday is, I know, on 12 March. Will you name a Wednesday or Thursday after that when you could call here at six o'clock (he wrote from the same address, 77 Shepherd Market) and we could do our business? I have no telephone so please write a line and I shall be ready.

I named, of course, the earliest Wednesday. Wednesday, 16 March 1966.'

Marlow seemed more exhausted than usual and lay back in his chair. 'Do come next Friday,' he said with his gentle wave of dismissal. John said good night.

7

'Waldo Price's appearance gave me something of a shock,' said Marlow, as they sat over wine on the following Friday. 'I went to Shepherd Market and rang the bell of Flat G a few minutes after six o'clock. Quite soon I heard shuffling noises, doors banging, slow steps treading a creaky way from an upper landing to the front door. It was a tall house but there was no lift at No. 77. Waldo – I soon came to think of him only by his improbable first name – opened the door, turned saying, 'Do come in, Mr Marlow,' and led me up the stairs. He hardly looked at me until we reached his room. He was expecting me, of course. And nobody else called on him.

Waldo's room, loaned by his 'friend', was on the third floor, of decent size but with a low ceiling. The owner's furniture was unobtrusive, functional, undusted. The windows were grimy. Two things immediately struck a visitor. The first was Waldo himself.

He appeared to be about sixty, with high cheek-bones and a large nose. He was extremely shortsighted and his spectacles were generally in his hand if not on his nose. By some quirk of vanity, however – added to the fact that for reading he needed a different pair – he did not wear them permanently, so that they were often mislaid, and even the shortest journey, across the room, or down the stairs, was punctuated and delayed by exclamations of anger at not being able to lay his hands on these essential articles. Waldo was a tall man, his thinning hair white, his complexion pale and blotchy. He gazed at one with a peculiar fixity which owed something to the strangeness of his mind, and a good deal to the uncertain quality of his eyesight.

It also owed much to alcohol. For the second powerful impression made on a visitor to 77 Shepherd Market was of bottles. There were bottles – the great majority empty – everywhere. There were whisky bottles, beer bottles, and wine bottles, of many different shapes and sizes. Beer came more often in bottles than in tins at that time, but the latter were already in evidence and Waldo had, I noticed, constructed a rather charming pyramid of empty tins making a neat geometric shape rising some five feet from the floor against one wall. On Waldo's breath the stale aroma of mixed drinks hung heavy.

He was not unlike Boshy, as I remembered him, in his attire. He wore old nondescript trousers, a dirty, patched coat, a shirt and no tie. He had not shaved for some time. When he said, 'Come in, come in,' the years rolled away and there came to me that first visit to Potters. But I never saw Boshy other than perfectly sober, and even at twelve years old I would, I think, have detected drink in him. Waldo, on the other hand, I certainly never saw except mildly drunk. I don't think he had been sober for years. But although his speech suffered a little, his mind was not really blurred. He knew what he wanted to say. On this occasion he knew what he had to relate. I must record that Waldo, from first to last, repelled me. It was not only his dirt, but the general atmosphere of conspiratorial decrepitude. He seemed to pull me down to his level. I was fastidious; I had always been rather priggish. It was impossible to be either with Waldo. I could not – and I have still to make a difficult effort to – understand how Boshy, of kindly memory, could have liked this man. He must have done so. He had apparently made Waldo the arbiter of my fortune. On his word I would, or would not, inherit – something. Since Waldo's circumstances were so sordid – although there seemed plenty of money for drink – I fleetingly wondered whether he might be prepared to work the trick to his own advantage, to offer to go shares with me in return for a favourable testimony. I need not have thought thus. That was not Waldo's way.

He set me down – there were several chairs. 'Now *what*, Mr Marlow,' he said, 'would you like to drink? I can offer you whisky, brandy, a glass of wine?'

I like drinking gin and tonic, if anything, at six o'clock, and hesitated, eyeing the varied bottlescape for the familiar shapes.

'I suppose I couldn't have a gin and tonic?'

'You suppose right,' said Waldo, 'I like neither. I do not entertain and I fear you must be content with what I myself occasionally consume.'

'A glass of wine would be very good.'

'Ah,' said Waldo with satisfaction. He at once drew a cork. I squinted at the bottle and saw to my surprise that it ought to prove an excellent claret. I knew little of wine, but business life accustomed one to the perusal of expensive wine lists and I had learned something from more cultivated friends. Waldo was opening a good and costly bottle. He did it, furthermore, with the air of a man who drank bottles like that every day and at any time of day or night. As, indeed, he did.

He produced two wine glasses, of different types, undusted but adequate. We sipped claret and he watched me with his pale obsessive gaze. We sat in silence for a little.

'Mr Marlow, this is a curious job I have to do.'

'I suppose so.'

'I will come straight to the point. I have to tell you what my friend Henry Kinzel wished to happen – if it could be arranged. I must warn you that what I have to tell you is not pleasant. It will, I think, come as something of a shock.'

I said nothing, and Waldo began his story, talking fluently. He was a natural storyteller, relishing words, evoking scenes or people with artistry. Throughout his narrative I never doubted that he was enjoying himself, and he had the gifted narrator's talent for stillness, so that no irritating tricks or gestures disturbed my attention. When he interrupted himself to deal with bottles or glasses the timing was deliberate.

'First,' said Waldo, 'I must take you back in time to 1930 – thirty-six years ago, and eleven years before you were born. Henry Kinzel was undisputed master of his family business – investments, property, that sort of thing. He had managed it wisely since inheriting from his father. The slump in values and business activity which had already hit America was on its way here, of course, but by his wisdom he weathered that storm. He took one or two clever young men into the business. One, in particular, he took very much to his heart, and trusted absolutely – with excellent results because the company prospered exceedingly. In 1930 Henry, therefore, was riding high. He had every reason to feel satisfied with his success. He took pride in his personal achievements with his business, he felt profoundly involved with it, but it was a generous and never a miserly involvement. He was a very cultivated, kindly man, a most munificent host. I was much younger and became his friend about that time. He had a delightful house in Wilton Crescent, and entertained a lot. Anybody with what he thought might turn out to be talent – particularly with the pen – he encouraged and assisted. He was a genuine patron. As a rich man he could play Maecenas, but his taste was good and his protégés were generally deserving. A few even became distinguished. Of course, anyone like that attracts undeserving spongers, but Henry was pretty shrewd, and although warm-hearted he could generally distinguish the true from the false. He was a most amusing, attractive man, and dinner at Wilton Crescent was always fun. He had both wit and genuine goodness of heart. I myself had a certain poetic gift which Henry was good enough to admire. More claret?'

I had hardly sipped from my glass, and shook my head. Waldo refilled his own glass which he had, despite unbroken communication, been able to empty.

'It's a decent wine. Drink up, there are several bottles of this.'

'Thank you. It's delicious.' I hoped, perhaps uncharitably, that Waldo was not going to recite his poems to me. He never did, although given to quoting from brighter stars than himself.

'Well, that was Henry. A man of infinite charm. Of course, you knew him late in his life. It may be hard for you to picture the Henry of earlier days: good-looking, enthusiastic' – it was hard for me – 'and prosperous. Then – remember, we are in 1930 – he fell in love. He was, I think, forty-two and he fell passionately in love with a much younger girl.' Waldo sighed and did some bottle-work. 'She seemed fascinated by him. They got engaged. Everybody told her she was lucky to have caught such a popular, handsome, graceful and wealthy man. A few years' difference in age were unimportant, even desirable. Everybody told him he was clever and blessed to have caught such a lovely, intelligent and sympathetic girl. She was all of those things – I knew her well. She was much nearer my age, of course. She was beautiful. She hadn't a penny.

'Then it all went tragically wrong. Five days before the wedding she disappeared. Her father was dead, her mother went almost out of her mind. Everything was prepared of course – and everything was being paid for by Henry; and the girl disappeared. Nobody knew where she was. Her mother thought she might have been kidnapped. Henry was splendid – very calm, very dignified. I knew he suspected in his bones what the trouble was. Two days before the advertised wedding day a letter arrived. The girl wrote to Henry and her mother by the same post. She had been unable to go through with it. She was in love with somebody else. And she intended to marry that somebody else.

'Henry loved her and desperately wanted her – it was a frightful blow to him. It was also a blow, although of a different kind, to discover that the "somebody else" on whom she had set her heart was none other than the man – young, penniless, promising – whom Henry had taken into his business and who was making his way so well in it although without as yet money of his own.

'Henry behaved – I still don't know if one would call it well, but it certainly was generously. He told the young man that he would be absolutely right to marry the girl he loved and that he wished him every happiness. Of course the man in question – his name was Julius Wrench – had only met this girl because she was Henry's fiancée, so there was an element of treachery. But Henry didn't see it like that. He didn't blame Wrench. And he didn't blame the girl, Viola. He did, however, suggest that Wrench should seek his fortune elsewhere. He couldn't bear the reminder of pain which daily contact with Wrench would bring. But he helped him to make another start and after a bit Wrench began to prosper. Henry couldn't bring himself to meet Viola again for a long time, but he gave her an enormous wedding present. Of course she was right, and he recognized it. She didn't love him. I think he believed for a long time that he could have changed that – that she would have come to love him. It's not a thing one can ever know for certain. Now you really must have some more claret.'

My head was spinning from the impact of the name of Julius Wrench. Julius! Waldo had been wrong to describe him as 'penniless' – in spite of talk within the family of marrying 'without two sixpences'. In 1930 Julius must already have mounted several rungs of the ladder and started making money. But Julius! Waldo had said, 'There was an element of treachery.' So far he had described only the very natural, very human circumstance of a girl, engaged to one man, falling in love with another, nearer her own age. But I think I knew, at that moment, that there was a great deal more to come, and that, by some fearful process, my own life was to be involved in it. I already felt a certain trance-like sensation, as if overcome by the looming of a fate I could neither anticipate nor control. Waldo probably suspected a good deal of this. He was watching me. He replenished my glass, and his own.

'I like this wine. We'll open another bottle in a minute. I started, with Henry's help, a small poetry magazine in 1930, you know. He was extraordinarily good about it – took a huge interest. It didn't survive the slump.'

'I suppose he was very rich at that time. I imagine he was given a lot of sympathy over the broken engagement – that a lot of women were after him?' I put a great deal into keeping my voice steady.

'You bet they were! But he'd been hit very hard and he wasn't prepared to risk taking that sort of punishment again. He went on much as before. Then in 1939 the war came, of course. He hated it.'

'Were his German origins embarrassing at that time?'

'No. He had distant German cousins but he had never had much contact with them and his family had been naturalized for three generations – a very Anglicized, very cultivated family, producing, it always seemed to me, the best from two distinct if similar traditions. No, it wasn't that – although, as you shall hear, his blood was one day to be used against him. He just hated the ugliness, the destruction, the suffering. He was a gentle, affectionate man but with high standards of integrity and he hated, also, what he thought were ever-lower principles – when it came to people thinking rationally about what the war was about, where it would all end and so forth. Henry had fought in the First World War, you know. He had been an infantry officer on the Western Front, and I've been told a very good one. He won the Military Cross. He loved England. He was not at all a political animal but he had a great feeling for the unity of European culture, and as time went on the way the war went made him shudder. He was too old for the Services, of course – he was born in 1888, I think – but I believe he was extremely brave at his firewatching, his air-raid work and so forth. He had a quiet, old-fashioned sense of patriotic duty and, as I've said, he loved, loved deeply, the country of his family's adoption.

'He lived in London throughout the war. I saw a lot of him. I was in the RAF,' said Waldo, astonishingly. 'I was an Intelligence officer – first on a station, then with Air Staff Intelligence in London. I had a very interesting war. I wrote a good deal of poetry. A little of it is rather splendid. Henry was a delight to visit in the rather drab – but also frenetic – atmosphere of wartime London. He was so civilized, so sane. And I think that even more than most people he hated his friends – and he had so many – being killed.

'During the war, surprisingly, Henry took Julius Wrench back into the business. Julius had joined the Army in 1939, but had been extracted from it to work for the Ministry of Economic Warfare. I don't know what he did, but whatever it was apparently folded up in about 1944 and he arranged to return to the City. A good deal of business was stagnant during the war, of course, but far-sighted people could make plans for the period of recovery, and they laid foundations for great profit. Julius was one of them. He sought out Henry, made a great thing of how Viola and he still regarded Henry Kinzel as one of the central, formative influences in their lives; couldn't bear to feel that, after all these years, a gulf should exist for ever and so forth. And he talked to Henry about how he saw the future, and what the financial and property opportunities were.

'It was obvious that within a year the war against Germany would be over. People were tired, Henry among them. His mind, which was as shrewd as ever, told him that Julius was right in his commercial judgement. His energy to do much about it was, however, at a low ebb. He asked Julius to come back to his company, and he gave him a pretty free hand. He trusted him absolutely.'

My mind went back to Boshy, long ago. I could hear his voice, in the book-filled kitchen at Potters. 'The world,' he had said, 'is full of betrayers.'

'More claret? Good. I'll open the other bottle.' Waldo was apt, when opening bottles, to sing little songs. I got to know his repertoire. On this occasion he was carolling from *The Beggar's Opera.*

'*Women ruin*,' sang Waldo. 'Bugger this cork, *Others' wooing* . . . Simon, may I call you Simon? Give me that cloth from over there, will you? *Take no pleasure* . . . Here we are, where's your glass? Now, where was I? Henry and Wrench – yes, he trusted Julius Wrench absolutely, no question of it. And I know that he saw a lot of both Julius and Viola at this time, and the wound must, at least on the surface, have healed. He showed Julius real affection, treated him as a member of the family; and it had, of course, always been a family firm. He took Julius to his heart again. It must have given him happiness to feel he had purged the earlier bitterness, or at least could convincingly act as if he had.

'I didn't see Henry much just then. I got out of the Air Force soon after the end of the war against Japan. 'Forty-six saw me in Italy, doing a job for the British Council. I was mad keen to get abroad, preferably to the Mediterranean world I loved, and love. I'd had enough of England. And in the post-war atmosphere of envy and constraint there was too much meanness of spirit here. Still is, in my view. I came to England as little as possible. I sometimes wrote to Henry, and he to me. He was a marvellous letter-writer.

'But it was from other people I heard what happened, and I still don't fully understand it. It's not my world. Apparently, Henry was a bit inattentive, let too many things go through on the nod. He was, as I shall tell you in a moment, deeply involved in other matters – matters of humanity. Anyway, Julius Wrench beavered away and actually got complete control of Henry's business – his family business. His investment, property company, whatever it was. I gather it had grown enormously and was bursting with promise. And somehow, don't ask me how, Wrench had got majority control.'

'Did that matter? It sounds, from what you say, as if he did rather well by the company?'

'Certainly he did well,' said Waldo. 'Bloody well. But when he got possession he *at once* used the power of ownership to get Henry out. Right out. Of course, I suppose Henry still had a large share-holding, he was still rich, but as far as control or running the thing was concerned he was out on his ear. For it was at this point that Henry's foreign origins, remote though they were, were made to help betray him. It was 1946. Everywhere Europe was shattered by recent experiences. The culture which Henry adored seemed near-obliterated by destruction, hatred, barbarism, the wounds of war. In Germany itself, of course, people were starving. Henry tried to use his considerable financial resources – his company's resources – to help them. He was active in the matter. He was passionate.

'His feelings and his actions were, in the contemptible mood of the times, misunderstood. A movement against him was started, on his own Board, I believe. His origins were referred to with winks and sneers. He was represented as pro-German. He – who had fought for our country in the mud and blood of France and Flanders thirty years before and been decorated for it by his sovereign – was represented as pro-German by a bunch of greedy, skulking buggers who'd never, I dare say, heard a shot fired in anger,' said Waldo, lapsing, unusually, into cliché. 'Henry was simply on the side of humanity. Unfortunately, however, in his keenness to cut through the laborious mechanisms of official "aid" he had tried to get something done, to use funds charitably but drastically; and he had, unwittingly and innocently, made contact with some pretty undesirable people. These were the sort – both German and British – who were feeding like carrion crows on the corpse of a defeated nation. They saw in Henry, with his generous purse, an opportunity. He did not see in them the rascality that was there. All this, of course, came out. It was used against Henry. It was hinted – as usual in such affairs, rumour and nods were the agents of malice – that Henry had, from family association, been pro-German; and that this was now manifest in his desire to use company money for purposes of ostensible charity, but in reality to help some dubious people in Germany re-establish themselves. And he had, I am told, indeed been unwise – ill-advised about associates, naïve about their past and about their credentials. It undermined his position in his own business, and when he tried to fight back against Wrench's usurpation he had hardly a friend to support him. Smear had done its work. Wrench, I imagine, had seen to that.

'A mutual friend wrote a long letter to me about it. Apparently Henry took it terribly hard. He hadn't seen it coming. He saw Julius Wrench and asked him what on earth possessed him. How could he play cuckoo in the nest like this? How could he, in any case, not support Henry in his charitable endeavours? Wrench, of course, said that it was all for the best, Henry getting on in age, still a valued father-figure, major shareholder, deeply respected, all that stuff. And Henry later told me Wrench said, "I, for one, always knew that your motives have been honourable in all you've tried to do" – or some such humbug. I bet he'd been fomenting the suspicions about Henry, originating them as like as not. Even such good men as Kinzel can attract envy in meaner spirits who feel shamed by a generosity so superior to their own.

'Something snapped in Henry. It's obvious, when one thinks about it, that underneath all his generosity of act and heart, and in spite of recent rapprochement, a lot of resentment at Julius's getting Viola sixteen years before was still pent up. It now escaped. They had a murderous row. It ended, I believe, in Henry calling Julius a dishonest, grasping traitor– and Julius describing Henry as an incompetent dabbler who'd been able to keep neither a woman nor a business, and had lost both to one who could. Charming.'

At this point Waldo broke off his narrative and said, 'Of course, you work for Wrench, don't you.'

'I do. And his family are great friends of mine.'

'It's rather a coincidence, isn't it.'

'It's an appalling coincidence.' I spoke levelly, calmly.

'Yes,' nodded Waldo, pouring more claret into his glass and waving the bottle rather unsteadily in my direction, 'an appalling, appalling coincidence. Let me continue. By the way, do you recognize Henry Kinzel in the – I suppose old – man you knew as a boy? Do I explain him to you?'

Hardly. But I remembered Boshy's sweetness of smile, his readiness to listen, his shafts of sympathy, his power of quotation. Yes, I had known Henry Kinzel all right.

'And Julius Wrench? Do you recognize your employer in my account?'

This was easier. I remembered now not the casual kindness but the coldness of Julius's calculations, the ruthlessness of his march to any objective, the hardness of his heart, the awful character of his ambition.

'Please go on,' I said. By now, of course, I knew something of the plot from my conversations at Lincoln's Inn Fields.

'There's no doubt,' said Waldo, using similar words to those of Mr Austin on a previous occasion, 'that Henry at this time went somewhat off his head. He was convinced – in my view rightly – that he'd been subjected to an act of evil treachery. He was determined to fight back. He set out to prove Wrench had behaved improperly in obtaining control – that he'd broken the rules. He tried to build up information which he thought proved Wrench was mis-using his position. He tried to work on one or two previous employees with access to the workings of the company – a few were devoted to him – and he once muttered to me that he was getting somewhere. It didn't work, of course. Wrench soon found out and got rid of them. Henry also embarked on litigation. He spent a fortune, and then some, on the most expensive counsel in London, in action after action. He rejected advice. He hadn't an earthly – or so I'm told. Wrench had been far too clever. Henry ruined himself. He went a bit crazy in the process. He forfeited people's sympathy. You must have met him about that time. He sold everything in London, of course, house, everything. Finally, he went bankrupt. He financed various unsound operations which he thought could turn the tables on Wrench and he ultimately went bankrupt. He couldn't meet his obligations. And he did Wrench not one scrap of harm. Worse still, people sympathized with him – with Wrench – for apparently being persecuted by a lunatic – a lunatic with a German name. Wrench was able to appear generous. He played his hand cleverly. I heard that she – Viola – was rather upset by it all but I expect she deferred to him.'

I expected so, too.

'Boshy – I'm sorry, Henry Kinzel – wasn't crazy when I knew him,' I said. 'He was eccentric and had gone to seed and people thought he was mad – ignorant, malicious people. Of course he had been in our village for some years before I met him – I think he must have come to Penterton first in about 1948, and I didn't speak to him until 1953. But when I knew him he was as sane and as charming as you say. That's how I remember him.'

'I'm delighted to hear you say that,' said Waldo. 'Of course I, too, saw him shortly before he died when he – gave me certain instructions. He was by then in touch with no others of his old friends and protégés. He'd cut himself off. He saw his lawyer, Austin, a boring man. And he found me. By then he wasn't, as you say, crazy. He'd recovered a bit of equilibrium, I think. He'd inherited, quite out of the blue, another fortune. I expect that helped! He wanted to talk to me about that and what he proposed to do with it. He wanted to talk about his plans. I had another room, not far from here; I was in England for a bit. He came to me. He told me about you – about what a promising person of real quality you were, a boy who would become a man of spirit. He told me of the arrangements he'd made for your education. It was the old Henry – the patron of youth and talent. I know he really enjoyed that. You've already given him pleasure.'

'I can never repay him.'

'Well, perhaps you can,' said Waldo, 'because, you see, he wanted you to have the rest of his money, that's in a trust now. He wanted you to have a certain income now you're twenty-five – not before – if you agree specific conditions; if you agree to attempt a certain task. And to have the capital, on termination of trust, if you fulfil those conditions, complete that task. But you have to do it within five years. First, you've got to agree to take something on; and, for a while, you get income. Next, if you successfully do a job he wanted done, you get Henry's money. In each case I have to sign a letter to Austin saying you've satisfied the conditions laid down by the late Henry Kinzel. That unlocks the safe and out comes the loot. Do you know how much? Has Austin told you?'

I muttered, 'No. I've no idea.'

'I've done some sums and used some guesswork. I know what Henry left and I expect that it would have been well if conservatively invested. I read in the papers how much duty was paid. I know what money's done since 1954. If you do what Henry hoped, you'll get about one and a half million pounds, I reckon. Assuming values in the next five years do something like they've done in the last. That's for the trustees, of course. Austin and his colleague. But I thought you'd be interested in that, because it tells you what there is to go for, if, of course, you decide to go for it. Have some more claret.'

I accepted the claret. I was very silent. My head was spinning. Waldo drank contentedly and eyed me. He clearly felt he'd described things rather well. After a bit I said, quietly, 'Are you going to tell me what I have to do?'

'Oh, that's quite simple,' said Waldo, enjoying himself greatly. 'Simple to tell, at least. You've got to ruin Julius Wrench.'

'To get this money you've got to avenge Henry,' said Waldo. 'It seems very fair to me. And I also think it would be justice.'

I suppose that some extraordinary proposition of this kind had been taking shape in my mind as Waldo unfolded his tale of Julius's infamy, as he clearly felt it to be. And, surely, it was? Betrayal of a good, generous patron who had shown to him nothing but friendship.

Betrayal of Boshy, who was my own benefactor – the founder of my fortunes in life, the educator of my youth. A civilized, sweet-hearted man robbed by one he had taken to his heart. Driven into exile as an old, poor, ill, tormented scarecrow, mocked by the ignorant villagers of Penterton. Surely so gross a treason called for retribution?

One and a half million pounds.

Waldo was watching me in his fuddled but acute way. He had had a successful spectacle-hunt after completing his story and propounding my outrageous task. Now he sat, awaiting my reactions with what I recognized as half-malicious amusement. My heart was beating fast, but my head was cool. I tried to keep my voice entirely steady. I think I succeeded.

'Mr Price, may I put certain points and questions to you?'

'Let's make it "Waldo",' said Waldo. 'Fire away.'

'To start with – and I must thank you for telling me all this so clearly. I see it all, and of course it's a tragic story – to start with, Julius Wrench is my employer. There is what we've already called the "appalling coincidence" that the man whom I'm supposed to try to do down is my own boss. And he's never been other than kind to me. I don't doubt all you've told me about his behaviour to Mr Kinzel – and I think it's in character. But to me, of course, he's been a friend. And his son is a great friend.'

'I don't think,' said Waldo, 'that you should make too much of the "coincidence" bit. I didn't dissent when you used the word before, but I'm not sure it's entirely a coincidence you're working where you are. I've got no proof, of course, but I suspect Wrench knows you're – let's say a beneficiary – of

Henry Kinzel. And I also suspect that he'd rather, in that case, have you locked into his own organization than foot-loose elsewhere.'

'That's a bit far-fetched, isn't it? How could he have discovered?'

'Easily. He must know you came from the same village. A few enquiries would quickly show that you'd been helped a good deal from outside your family. At about the time Henry died. Wrench would have put two and two together. He lives by information, after all. To succeed he has to know.'

'Why would it have mattered to him?'

'Because he knew that Henry never forgave him, he knew he had an enemy. An enemy can strike from beyond the grave, if he has the weapons. What did the Yorkist leader say to his fallen enemy in the Wars of the Roses – battle of Towton, was it? "Thy father slew my father: thus will I do to thee and all thy kin!" That sort of thing. We're not talking of slaying. Still, Wrench would have guessed that Henry had befriended you and he would have heard that ultimately Henry inherited another fortune. He could have wanted to keep tabs on you. How better than employ you – or see that his friends employed you? Perhaps he was wrong.' Waldo chuckled.

I digested this and matched it against Julius's casual take-it-or-leave-it way of offering me a job both originally and now. It was – just – credible. Waldo was watching me.

'You've got to remember, too, Simon, that buccaneers like Wrench may put on an act of being aloof and secure but they're always haunted by the ghosts of men they destroy. They're not always as rational as they like to appear. Next point?'

'It's the same one. Whether or not his employment of me was calculated, I'm now invited to conspire against a man who –'

'Who ruined a man who gave you much. Including his trust.'

'Who, with his family, has been something of a friend.'

'Well,' said Waldo with a show of indifference, 'that's up to you, isn't it? You've heard it all, you've got to make up your own mind.'

We sat in silence again and Waldo did some work with the claret bottle. He was having a good time. He spoke next, quietly and reflectively.

'Yes – I reckon one and a half million.'

'My next question,' I said, a little more loudly than necessary, 'is how anybody – Henry Kinzel, you, anybody – could suppose that a young man of twenty-five can do anything to upset, let alone ruin, a strong, rich, successful man like Julius Wrench. It's to demand the impossible. It might be a just thing to do. I think that would depend on how it was done. But it's an absurd idea. I'm not some rival tycoon. It's impracticable. Didn't he see that, when he – described this condition to you?'

Waldo was expecting this. 'I don't think Henry thought it would be easy. You've got to realize, Simon,' he said, suddenly rather stern, 'that although Henry wished you well, his chief concern was not for your own future. He wanted vengeance – retribution. He thought, rightly, that he was dying and had no time to exact revenge himself. He was not trying simply to give you a virility test. He was entrusting you with an act of justice which he wanted performed. He thought that with intelligence, with – shall we say incentive? – it might conceivably be performed.'

'But by the age of *thirty*! It's an incredible idea.'

'Of course it must be as soon as that,' said Waldo impatiently. 'It must be while I'm around to testify, for one thing. You don't seriously think this sort of arrangement could be confided to a bank's trustee department, or to a lawyer like Austin, do you? He'd have a fit.'

'Of course.'

'And then there's Wrench. He's not getting younger. He mustn't fade out gracefully. Henry worked it all out.

Wrench must be toppled from a high seat. There's another condition, too. If you bring it off, Wrench must be told on whose behalf it's been done. I expect we'd better leave that until the time, don't you?' Waldo was in confident, exuberant form.

I said, 'But I still don't see how on earth such a thing could be managed, it's – it's bizarre. I can't believe this conversation has ever happened.'

'It's happened all right. As a matter of fact Henry realized you'd react as you have done; at first, anyone would. He didn't anticipate, of course, that you'd be working for Wrench Holdings – I think that means you've got over several fences already, but you may see it differently. Henry said to me, "He may not be able to do it, even if he's willing to try. But I'm sure Julius Wrench is vulnerable somewhere, and a good man as Simon will grow up to be" (he'd very much taken to you) "will find that vulnerability, and exploit it." And Henry gave me something for you. He said, "Give him this. It might help him. I haven't time myself." I've studied it but I'm buggered if I understand it. I've got an idea, but I'm not going to muddle you with it. Henry once told me something that gave me a notion – but the only thing I can do for you is to show you what he gave me. It might help, as Henry said.'

'Can I see whatever this is?'

'Only,' said Waldo, 'if you accept the conditions. If you say you're going to have a go. It wouldn't be reasonable for you to see what Henry left behind him otherwise. It was deposited with me,' said Waldo, lapsing into alcoholic pomposity and belching, 'deposited with me to help me to help the task my dear friend Henry Kinzel wished discharged. It is not right to show it except to one who is prepared to attempt that task. And so I have to ask you, Simon Marlow, do you accept the conditions I have described? Will you make the attempt?'

There was another long silence. In the distance and through

the closed window, I heard the uneven, pulsating blare of a fire engine racing through Piccadilly traffic. It was very stuffy in Waldo's room. I stood up. My heart was pounding.

'Yes,' I said. 'I accept.'

8

Waldo gave me the "something" which Henry Kinzel had left with him to be some sort of torch to help light me through the impenetrable dusk of my mission. It was a piece of paper, with figures. I glanced at it, and put it in my pocket. I felt an overwhelming need to get away from Waldo's presence and the suffocating atmosphere of his lair. It was a strange, conspiratorial parting. I had one last question for him.

'I may not be able to achieve this, of course. I may try and fail.'

'Naturally,' said Waldo, 'very probably, I imagine. I will write this evening to that stuffy old creature Austin and tell him that you have accepted the conditions laid down by the late Henry Kinzel. Austin will then pay you some income – I understand that exactly how much lies with the trustees, but it's bound to be something reasonable – and will await a further letter from me, at some time in the next five years, or never. If "never", the capital goes somewhere else and your income stops. On your thirtieth birthday. You've plenty of incentive to try, my boy!'

Waldo was giggling away happily. I left. Six days later I got a curt letter from Mr Austin saying that he had heard from Mr Waldo Price and that I would be paid, for a period of five years, an allowance of four thousand pounds per annum from trusts established under the will of the late Mr Henry Kinzel. The letter said nothing more about the capital of the trust – nor its size.

I considered whether I had a right, as a potential beneficiary, to ask. Probably not. My only information came from

Waldo. If he was right about the value of the trust, then four thousand pounds a year couldn't represent more than a tiny fraction of the trust income, which I reckoned could hardly be less than seventy thousand a year, gross. Most of it, I thought resignedly, no doubt went in tax, legal expenses, or to some other money-box out of Marlow's reach. I recognized, however, that with such uncertainty about the ultimate destination of Boshy's money, Mr Austin could hardly be expected to dish it out with generous hands to one who might be excluded for ever in five years' time. Meanwhile, four thousand a year was most agreeable. I thanked Boshy in my heart; but overshadowing those thanks was the extraordinary task he had set me. Probably impossible, certainly terrible. One and a half million pounds!

I studied Boshy's piece of paper, his clue to me, my talisman.

On one side was scrawled a list of names with substantial sterling figures marked against them. On the other side was typed another list of names and more figures. I didn't have much difficulty in recognizing the typed list, which had more figures in pencil scrawled against each serial. It was an extract from the accounts of Redvers Associates, the property company, the member of Wrench Holdings in which I worked. It was, I presumed, extracted in the early days of the company, about the time of the Boshy/Julius row, soon after the end of the Second World War. In those days the company had had a more independent existence. As I had noticed, when first serving Wrench Holdings as an apprentice to Vivien Baker in that same company, overseas investors had, from the start, placed considerable sums of money in British property, hoping, presumably, for long-term recovery and capital gain. Nor had they been disappointed. By now, however, these investors were more numerous – in 1946 there was little risk capital around for such adventures except in the Americas – and now investments were, inevitably, made in the holding company, Wrench Holdings. I examined the list, which looked to me as if it were a summary of some of our foreign investors and their deposits, wondering what on earth Boshy had seen in it which made him suspect Julius of malpractice – for that was presumably the implication. I feared, with good reason, that his mind might have been unhinged, so that where Julius was concerned he saw evil everywhere. Of course I resolved to go through those earlier records when back in the office, with the greatest assiduity. I must be careful. If there were something wrong Julius's internal intelligence system would alert him to my probing. He might get worried, make a false move. Somebody would say to him, "You know Simon Marlow's going through all the early company books of Redvers Associates with a fine toothcomb, Julius? Going right back to 1946. God knows why. Thought I'd better mention it,' and Julius would, one day, say to me, 'Everything all right, Simon?' and would watch me. And I would watch him.

My imagination was running too fast for my reason. I scanned the list until I knew it by heart. There were substantial purchases of company loan stock made by overseas institutions, largely banks, several South American banks, a Chinese bank (now Taiwanese I noted), the Moscow bank, a number from the Commonwealth. Some of the figures were very large – I was familiar with that. There were no surprises here. Nothing illegal or suspect. The list had, as I knew well, greatly expanded since that time. Foreign investment in British property was a Wrench speciality, and Redvers Associates had blazed the trail. I could learn nothing from this. Had Boshy, I wondered, conceived the notion that Julius was somehow 'lining his pocket' from these foreign investments, in some undiscovered way using them to personal advantage? I doubted the possibility. I was, by now, sufficiently experienced to know how difficult it was to defeat the auditors in a large concern like ours by calculated fraud. Still, something – rational or not – had aroused Boshy's suspicions in those foreign investors' lists and deposits. I would work until I had justified or refuted those suspicions. I felt, with what I already recognized as disappointment, that refutation was the more likely.

On the other side of the paper, in Boshy's own hand (I at first supposed), was what looked like an extract from the company list of recipients of donations. Our 'charitable list', loosely so-called, was, as I have already said, Julius's very personal concern. He controlled it now. He probably had quite a hand in it from the start of his association with the company, long before he became its master, long before it became Wrench Holdings. And yet – I doubted whether Henry Kinzel, from what I had heard of him, would have failed to take a personal interest in so significant an item of company expenditure. Kinzel was a patron, an idealist, something of a philanthropist. It was unlikely, I thought, that he would have been content to let that slip entirely into Julius's grasp, whatever he let go on the commercial side. Some of the charities listed had enjoyed support from the Kinzel family – and firm – for many years. I could not imagine what there could be suspicious here.

Then I thought I saw light. This list must be supposed more certainly important to me than the typed entries on the other side, since this had actually been copied out by hand; in fact, it was conceivable that it was the *only* important clue, and that it was simply written on the reverse of accounts which Boshy had anyway had to hand, simply a convenient piece of paper. This would have been haphazard, but by then Boshy was haphazard. And it might be, I thought, that he suspected Julius of somehow juggling with this list *after* he, Boshy, had left the company, *after* he had lost control, *after* their appalling confrontation. At some time thereafter (and it would be possible to date both lists by reference to the company's books, which I would now undertake, I said to myself), perhaps Henry had reason to suspect that Julius was somehow perpetrating fraud and covering it under the charity list. I looked at the entries which Boshy (I imagined) had copied.

Most were familiar to me from my own apprenticeship. I remembered how I had first asked Julius about them, and his reply. Although this list clearly came from long ago, the sums were already considerable. There were the same number of institutions, societies, cultural appeals, vaguely 'liberal' causes. It was puzzling. I could not imagine how Julius had worked the trick, if trick there were. But if there were something amiss I would find it. I had to start somewhere. I would discover if those innocent recipients of Wrench Holdings charity had indeed benefited, and to the extent shown. And if Julius had defrauded them – and his shareholders – I would expose the fact, however long ago. Other, sensible, questions intruded, of course. Why on earth should Julius, a hugely successful man, risk this jiggery-pokery, if he had done? He made enough money by honest means, one would suppose, not to need the sort of fiddling with the books that Boshy's suspicions (or my interpretation of them) seemed to imply. But I told myself that Boshy had been on to *something*. I told myself, from my reading of many such cases, that bigger men than Julius had found it impossible to resist the temptation of an illicit turn. If the man were flawed, he would have been driven not simply by greed but by the desire to outwit. Now, perhaps, from beyond the grave, the wronged Henry Kinzel could bring his malpractices home to him.

But as I looked at that paper for the thousandth time I thought I perceived one other thing. The scrawl was, I felt sure, not in Boshy's but in Julius's own hand – with which I was very familiar from my time in his outer office. Julius himself had, for some extraordinary reason, extracted and scribbled lists and figures from those accounts of long ago.

I knew my way around Wrench Holdings by now. If Julius was vulnerable I would find the spot. I would bring him down!'

It was obvious to John that this part of his narrative cost Marlow a good deal, and soon after telling of his compact with Waldo Price he brought the evening to an end. He had been talking jerkily and with frequent pauses, unlike his usual cool, factual flow. He said, 'I would bring him down!' with a strong, remembered emotion. Whether he was, at that moment, hating himself or others was impossible for John to say, but Marlow showed no sign of wanting to break off his story. John could guess that parts of it sickened him as he contemplated them, but he seemed as determined as ever to purge himself by confession to a stranger, for that was how John now thought of their evenings.

Next time they met, Marlow said that he had followed up such leads as Kinzel's paper suggested and could find absolutely nothing. He had identified the year in which the figures of deposits and investments by foreign banks corresponded to the list he held: 1949. Marlow explained that he had, as far as was possible some seventeen years later, followed the figures through into the bloodstream of the company and they had shown in audited balance sheets where it was proper. He said that he couldn't, at that stage, understand all the figures scribbled down. John didn't understand all his jargon at this point, having no sort of comprehension of business or finance, but he had obviously discovered not the faintest trace of malpractice. Then he had, he said, attacked what he called the 'charity list' – and found, unsurprisingly, that it was from the same year. And here, again, he could find nothing, no scent of corruption, no suspicion of a rat. Marlow had, at random, telephoned one or two of the recipient institutions – he had to be careful, as he wanted to avoid word coming back to Julius Wrench. To these he had explained he was 'checking on a few back figures' and asked them to confirm the size of a donation from Wrench Holdings, or Redvers Associates, or any other part of the group, past or present. In each of these few cases, apparently, he received confirmation. He told John that his enquiries were received politely but coolly – he obviously did his best to play down any suggestion of its being an important matter, but it was inevitable that he caused surprise with his probing and some, at least, must have asked themselves the reason for it. Anyway, he drew a blank. Completely, unmistakably, and – as he admitted – disappointingly blank. The sums recorded had been received. In one case he'd found, to his surprise, that the person he was talking to had been an Oxford acquaintance; a nervous, enthusiastic idealist, as Marlow described him. He remembered their conversation.

'I didn't know you were working for those people!'

'I am, indeed. And a very remarkable cause it is, Simon, though I'm not sure you'd see the point.'

'Well, I think my firm sees the point . . .' and he had expressed, casually, the purpose of his call: to check the size and timing of previous donations from Wrench Holdings. His friend was enthusiastic.

'Your boss, Julius Wrench, is a wonderful man. Of course, he's helped our committee as a consultant for years. Without him we would have made all sorts of financial mistakes, I expect. I don't approve of his line of business, of course, but his advice has been superb – worth the little we pay.'

It all seemed very above board. Marlow didn't work the whole way down the list. He reckoned he had enough evidence to demonstrate defeat.

Marlow said that all this took a few weeks of the early summer of 1966, and that he then felt, on reflection, that he had committed himself to an impossible task. He was clearly watching Julius Wrench with new eyes. Rightly or wrongly, he now saw him as a proper object of investigation and, probably, retribution. He did not explicitly disentangle his motives – he left John to deduce, without explanation or apology. Gratitude to his 'Boshy', zeal for justice, and greed for one and a half million pounds seemed mixed up for him in an indissoluble cocktail. He tried, he said frankly, to have it both ways – to manage it so that if he failed to discover anything against Wrench he would not personally profit from making the attempt. He wrote again to Mr Austin.

'I wrote to Austin,' said Marlow, 'I said that, in the event of Waldo Price not being able to produce a second letter, in confirmation that I had fulfilled Henry Kinzel's wishes, I had decided the honourable thing to do would be to repay all the sums received in the next five years. I told myself that by those means my conscience would be to some extent cleared. If Julius had done enough to deserve ruin and I could encompass it, God knows how, I would have done my duty by Boshy. Meanwhile, I wouldn't take money from somebody else to help me do down my employer undeservedly; I would pay it back. I could, that way, think of it as a loan. I removed from it, in my rather equivocal perception, the stain of blood money. Austin wrote back rather coldly that such an arrangement was certainly up to me. It was in no way obligatory and would be unusual. He would communicate my remarks to the trustees, and advised me to defer such a decision until the day. Letters like mine no doubt made him increasingly feel that the Kinzel trust was a most undesirable business. We left it there. And, curious as it may seem, I worked away during the next years conscientiously and I think successfully in Wrench Holdings, without incessant brooding on what might be beneath the surface of Julius's apparent invulnerability. I almost reconciled myself to the expectation that my task of retribution was impossible. I made certain elementary plans to be able to repay twenty thousand pounds in 1971 – while, in my innermost heart, knowing that this would not be bound to do so. But it helped my state of mind. I found a flat in Pimlico, and could now comfortably afford to live in it alone. I reanimated a few friendships in London from earlier days at Wrench Holdings. I did not throw Boshy's piece of paper away. I had five years in which – just – something might happen. I watched and read and calculated and pondered. I was not at peace.

In the winter of 1966 Harry at last returned from the United States for good. I had not been consistently in his company since we both went down from Oxford in 1962. Five years is an eternity when one is in one's early twenties. I told myself that we must both have changed; that easy, devoted friendship of the old sort would be impossible. I realized that he would have a host of friends, of impressions, of experiences I could neither share nor imagine. I ought, I reflected, to have the same – we could be on equal terms in the trading of memories; but I knew it would not be so. Harry's years would have been glittering, packed with anecdote, rich in laughter and success. He must, I was sure, have been a devastating success in New York.

There were, of course, two other shadows lying over our friendship, if it were to be renewed. The first was the circumstance that I was now pledged to bring ruin, somehow, some time, to the father he adored and admired. The whole situation sometimes made me feel physically sick. I suffered already and frequently from what felt like chronic indigestion, the sort of sharp pains that excess of food and wine can produce; although I was generally abstemious these seemed to increase at this time. I occasionally asked myself how I could possibly endure the falseness of my position. I would then answer that, admired or not, Julius Wrench had done wrong, that he deserved justice. If, conceivably, I could be the instrument of that justice, I was discharging a duty. The nature of that duty inevitably meant that action must be covert, concealed – a disagreeable necessity. To that extent, I reflected, deception of a friend was inevitable; but I knew that it meant our old, confiding affection, sharing and discussing all things, could never be recovered. I had a secret. Most of the time, however, I simply didn't think about it.

The second shadow was Miranda.

Miranda had gone to America with her Bartholomew husband. Harry must have seen her. Might they have spoken of me? He had already been away when I had fallen in love, he might have no idea, no sense that I still ached for news of her, still saw her face, her eyes holding mine. Harry was bound to talk of Miranda when we met – it would come up naturally in our conversation. He would say, 'It was great fun having Miranda and her husband over there, of course. He's a charming chap, they've got a lovely house, I could always get away to them, meet different people, have a marvellous time. They were wonderful to me, it made all the difference.' And I would say, 'Yes, that must have been excellent. I wish I knew him.' Then perhaps – or perhaps not – there would be a moment of silence. I should see. But although I longed for Harry's company I dreaded it too. And, more prosaically, I feared he would simply have grown out of me, that we would find the lines of communication between us corroded with time and disuse.

Harry and I made an arrangement soon after his return, and met at his club. I had no club. He had, as it were, inherited membership from a host of connexions. It was a beautiful house I had not visited before that day. We lunched together. I found, first with incredulity, then with joy, that all the constraint was on my side. I need have worried not at all. As far as Harry was concerned, there was no difference, no fading of memories, no blurring of affection. We were back at Eton, at Oxford, nothing had changed, remembered people were as absurd as ever. We laughed louder than I had laughed since I saw him last. There is nothing more moving,' said Marlow, with more emphasis than he had put into any part of his chronicle so far, 'than when a friendship shows itself absolutely unaltered by the passage of time. Nothing at all. And I did not expect this. I had steeled myself for the reverse. I was extraordinarily happy.

When we were drinking coffee, Harry said, 'Miranda's coming over this summer. She's not been here since she married, you know.' It was his first mention of her. The conversation I had anticipated had not – or not yet – occurred. I was very calm.

'I suppose you saw a lot of her in the States?'

'Not much. They live a long way from New York. I stayed

with them two or three times, and Miranda came to New York once without him and I saw her there.'

It would have seemed unnatural to change the subject. 'Do you get on well with her husband?'

'Her husband,' said Harry, 'is hell!'

I was silent, trying to look politely interested, amused and detached. I don't think I did it very well.

'Hell!' Harry said again. He poured us both some more coffee. He seemed to be awaiting some reaction. I said, 'In what way?'

'Every way. He's very rich, of course, but he's unbelievably thick. He's insensitive. He's vulgar. He hasn't got a generous impulse anywhere, and he's unkind.'

'To Miranda?'

'I expect so. She's certainly unhappy, I know that.'

'But she must have thought she was in love with him – she must have seen different aspects, different –'

'Oh, he's a very *handsome* man,' said Harry, 'and at a completely superficial level he's good company. He's full of rather gushing friendliness. But he's got a mean spirit. His judgements of people – and things – are so selfish and so arrogant you curl right up to hear them. And he hasn't the faintest idea what anybody except himself is feeling or could feel. Not the faintest idea. You say Miranda must have fancied herself in love with him – I doubt it. He was attractive, attentive; she was restless at home, brooding a bit. She deceived herself, I think.'

'Why do you say he's unkind?'

Harry was silent for a moment, and then said, rather impatiently, 'The stories he tells, the things he thinks funny or "smart" all mean that somebody's done down. And the way he talks to people he thinks don't matter is unkindness itself. Cruelty, really, except that I think to be cruel one may need a certain amount of intelligence.'

Harry was talking with considerable vigour. I said, 'Do your parents like him? Do they know what you feel?'

'No, they don't know. Rightly or wrongly I've said very little. It's for Miranda to put a brave face on it or not. And they'd be distressed of course – not only for her, but they were very much in favour of him and of the marriage. His father – and now he, himself – does a great deal of business with Wrench Holdings. In fact, I rather think –' Harry broke off. 'You must know more about that than me, Simon. You're in the firm, after all.'

'I don't know much. I look after my own little corner, you know. What's the Bartholomew company called?'

'American Land Incorporated.'

Of course I knew! I had never had occasion to make the connexion but I knew indeed. ALI. Pronounced 'Ali', as before Baba. They were enormous shareholders.

'Yes – of course, how stupid of me. I didn't connect them with Miranda.'

'Well, I rather think they've got what one might call the upper hand of the relationship.'

Julius was, I judged, pretty impregnable. Or so it seemed to us underlings. 'I don't think so, not to any degree that could cause concern.'

'I'm glad,' said Harry. 'Anyway, Miranda plans soon to come over here on her own. Let's all meet.'

He and I arranged to have dinner together at an early opportunity. Before we parted Harry said, 'I wasn't quite truthful when I said I "expected" Alec Bartholomew was unkind to Miranda. I bloody well know he is. She was in New York without him once, as I told you, and she broke down. I got it all out of her.'

I said, as neutrally as I could, 'What sort of thing?'

'He has,' said Harry, 'habits and tastes which Miranda finds – very unpleasant. He drinks far too much and it makes him a pretty disagreeable companion. For a wife. He's like a stranger to her, I could see that. And he feels inadequate with her so he tries to humiliate her in front of other people. She tried to be loyal – she still *does* try to be loyal at times – but

I got it all. Brother and sister. I got it all. She hates her marriage and she hates him, though she can't put it like that, even to herself. It's all – and I mean absolutely all, Simon – gone disastrously wrong.'

This was 1967, when there were already few bars to frankness of disclosure. Still, I didn't want to probe. I didn't want this conversation to go further.

'I suppose I always thought,' said Harry with a stronger note of loathing than I'd ever heard from him, 'that whatever mistakes Miranda might make she must choose a chap with some sort of sensibility. I was wrong. That's my sister's charming husband.'

I felt my face aflame. I couldn't control it.

I returned to Covent Garden with disturbed heart.'

When Marlow took up his tale again a new and, as John suspected, more central character came on stage, and his voice implied a certain heightening of tension within himself.

'That same spring, 1967, I met Arthur Rivers, Jimmy Ling's "man in London". I had made a tentative call after return from Singapore, but Rivers had been away and the months had gone by. One day his secretary telephoned. Rivers was, I knew, a man of power. He might be a "front man" for Jimmy Ling, but the front was an imposing one, involving chairmanship of a large London-based trading company. Now he asked me to have a drink at his flat in the Boltons.

Arthur Rivers immediately struck me as formidable. He was a man of, I suppose, about fifty at that time. He was tall and rather military in appearance, with a clipped moustache, pale blue eyes and a very soft, incisive voice. He had a habit of holding one with his eyes after one made a remark, as if making up his mind whether his companion was telling the truth, being intolerably frivolous, lying, or merely stupid. He would then respond very briefly and exactly. If making a suggestion or advancing an idea himself his eye would also fix one for a moment of silence beforehand, as if to impress with the importance of what he was about to say. I once saw him annoyed. A (quite senior and experienced) subordinate had misunderstood Arthur Rivers's request for a particular document. There was an implication that the request had been imprecise. Rivers fixed him with his implacable gaze and started talking, very softly.

'Explain to me the words I used which gave you a misleading impression.'

'No, it's not that, Arthur, sorry, my fault, I'll get hold of it, I thought, you know, that you were after –'

'But what did you think? I cannot follow your process of mind. Can you recall my exact words?'

'Oh, I think so, I –'

'Repeat them.'

The man was rapidly going to pieces. He eventually escaped. Arthur Rivers continued with me as if nothing had occurred. His voice had never been raised. When the man returned with the correct document Rivers gazed at him as at an unwanted intruder, eventually extended his hand to take the paper without looking at it, and continued to regard his victim with unblinking, unwavering eyes until he turned and fled. Rivers gave a low, menacing grunt. That was all.

On this first meeting he was most affable. In his low, clipped voice he said, 'You had an interesting time with us in the Far East?'

'Oh, very.'

He raised his eyebrows, inclined his head, and said, 'Very?' It was another disconcerting habit of his to repeat one's last word, as if with incredulity.

'Yes. Very.'

'But you left us. You came back to London.' He poured a gin and tonic for me. I told him that I had gone into the matter, gratefully, with Jimmy Ling who was most understanding. I had felt that, after the invaluable experience gained at Ling Enterprises, I would be well placed to start again in London; that my love of home and family dissuaded me from ambition for a lifetime in the Far East; that the offer from Wrench Holdings was a generous one. I found myself telling him what I was doing at Covent Garden and how it was going. He knew perfectly well, of course, but he listened, silent, immobile, sipping whisky, watching me.

'You will know that we have been great believers in Julius Wrench. I think one could say that we have helped, very materially, in his success.'

'I know. And, of course, Jimmy Ling talked to me –'

'Mr Ling,' said Rivers, reproving my youthful familiarity, 'has a high opinion of Julius Wrench – of your boss, your employer, your chairman. A high opinion. He would, quite obviously, not maintain his – our – considerable stake if he had not. You know our proportionate shareholding?'

I didn't, and he told me, very exactly. I was startled, although I don't think I showed it. Ling owned a very great deal of Wrench.

'A number of our own – foreign – investors and supporters accept our view of Julius Wrench. That is why so much of your company's equity belongs to us. Our customers have faith in us and we have faith in you. We are the means of channelling very substantial sums into investment in this country. We are the means; you are the recipients. I am glad to have the chance to meet you, Simon.' He gave me the penetrating stare. 'Mr Ling told me that you learned our business well and were very useful. I hope we can keep in touch, here in London. Whatever is good for Wrench Holdings is good for Ling.' He smiled, an inward smile.

'And vice versa, naturally,' I said with an answering smile. Arthur Rivers considered this carefully.

'Yes, I think so. In all circumstances, of course, we would have to protect our investment. By whatever means.' We chatted on a few other topics. Arthur Rivers was fanatically keen on winter sports. To him the two weeks he permitted himself in the Alps were the crowning glory of the year. I never discovered whether he went with a party; it seemed inconceivable. Or with a companion of some kind? I assumed he was unmarried. It was impossible to ask.

He told me that he hoped I would come to dinner 'on some future occasion'. 'We'll be in touch, I'm sure,' he said as he saw me to the door. I was not sure that I welcomed the connexion, but I knew it would be difficult to dissolve. 'I must look up your friend, young Henry Wrench, now he's back,' he said. 'I saw a good deal of both those children a few years ago. They are children no longer, but I'm sure their quality is as it promised to be. The girl married an American, did she not?' I said that was so. I still did not know how to think about Harry's revelations: Miranda married to a selfish, odious, unkind, boorish pervert – for surely Harry had hinted as much? – but a pervert, naturally, with oodles of money. A dreadful thing to contemplate, unbearable to allow the mind to dwell on it.

Or was it?

'An excellent family. Their father is a fortunate man, don't you agree?'

I said I did, and left.

9

'I drove down to Penterton most weekends. One Saturday evening, probably in May or June 1967, my mother said to me, 'I'm going to be very indiscreet. I'm going to break a confidence.'

I couldn't imagine what was coming. 'Do, Mum!' We had been talking about my work a little, and I had been speaking with enthusiasm of Harry's return.

'I have met Harry's father, your Mr Wrench. I met him once, and promised I wouldn't talk to you about it.'

'Mum, why on *earth* . . .?'

'Well, you see,' said my mother, 'he was perfectly charming and had your interests very much at heart and was so exceptionally thoughtful that I promised I wouldn't mention it. So I didn't. It wasn't important. I've smiled to myself at the memory. But it's so many years ago now it can't matter. Don't tell him I've talked about it, though.'

My mother told me that when I was at Oxford she'd been in the house one afternoon and a large car had parked outside. A very charming man had come to the door and asked if she was Mrs Marlow. He'd introduced himself as Julius Wrench, and said that he happened to be passing through Penterton and that he knew she lived there because his son and hers were close friends. He had then talked in very flattering terms about me. 'He said,' my mother recalled complacently, 'that he knew from his son and others that you were what he called "a star"; and that you were exactly the sort of young man he hoped to attract to his business.' Julius had asked my mother not to pass this on – he'd said that nothing so repelled the young as any sense that their elders were conspiring, even for their benefit. It might put me off if I were to imagine that he, Wrench, had been seeking to recruit me by using my mother's good will. 'Let all this happen, if it's meant to happen,' he had said. 'I hope it does, but one never knows.'

My mother said that Julius also spoke briefly about Boshy. He had apparently talked to one or two people in the village. He said, 'I believe you knew a dear, unhappy friend of ours, Henry Kinzel.' My mother said she found herself confiding that Boshy had been a friend indeed to me. Julius had been all interested understanding. 'How like him!' he had said. My mother had found Julius a sympathetic person and had, I suspect, hoped that in some way my friendship with Harry would provide occasion for further meetings. But, somehow, it had not happened.

'Anyway,' my mother concluded, 'it's all worked out. You're back now with Wrench Holdings, back near your home, my darling boy, and working for someone who obviously took to you from the start. I'm so glad.'

It looked as if Waldo Price had not been far out in his conjectures. I said little in response to my mother. 'You must meet Harry,' I said at last.

'The daughter's in America, isn't she?'

'Yes, Miranda married an American.'

'I expect they miss her. But perhaps she comes over often?'

'Not often,' I said, 'although I think she's coming over this summer.' I sounded vague and uninterested. My mother looked at me sharply. 'I may,' said Marlow reflectively, 'have overdone it.'

'I had a new friend in Wrench Holdings – indeed, in Julius's own office, in the holy of holies. By a pleasant coincidence James Todd, the young barrister with whom I had shared a flat as a fledgling, had been enrolled while I was in Singapore. He had been called to the Bar, and practised for a while. Then he had succumbed to a Wrench offer and had quickly prospered and come to Julius's attention. We had a good leavening of accountants, lawyers and other qualified people on our strength. James had married a charming girl. I saw a good deal of them both.

James was a useful friend, a sounding board for Julius's views and whims. One day he said to me, 'I gather you've been really getting down to historical research in the Redvers books!'

So my discreet hours of probing after first leaving Waldo had not passed unnoticed. Few things did, in any part of Wrench Holdings, but it was disconcerting – or perhaps illuminating? – to find my cautious examination had reached the ears at least of those closest to the top.

'Oh – I suppose you mean my poring over old accounts. That was last year. Yes, I wanted to soak myself a bit in the earlier transactions – background knowledge. I find it helps to be better informed about the past when I'm dealing with the present.'

'Well, don't do a Baker!' laughed James. I looked enquiring, and he said, 'Old Vivien Baker thought it would be useful to try to analyse exactly what our foreign investors have meant to us in terms of profit, over the years. Not very easy; so much depends on the conventions used, so much has gone across the exchanges and so forth. But he thought it would be interesting to try. He wanted to be able to say to the Board, "The following run of figures shows exactly what the custom of the Bank of Iran, or the Government of Bulgaria, or whatever, has meant to Redvers – has meant to Wrench Holdings – over the last fifteen years." He thought it worth while to try to analyse and quantify. He thought people were talking of "our overseas investors" too glibly and inexactly. He thought Julius would be fascinated. That he'd be pleased.'

'And wasn't he?'

'He certainly wasn't! Poor old Baker came out remarkably quickly, without his paper, and looking very shaken. Bill Barnett went in soon afterwards. And not much later Vivien

Baker was looking for fresh employment. Whether that was cause and effect I don't know, but it must have been about that time that Barnett wrote to you in Singapore.'

On another occasion, James said to me, 'You know Arthur Rivers well, I believe.'

'Not well at all. I've met him once – he was, of course, quite a name on people's lips in Ling Enterprises.'

'I gather he's going to have a dinner party in three weeks' time, 28 July. He's asked Polly and me. He's going to ask you. I hope you'll be able to come. I find him rather alarming, and Polly isn't looking forward to it. Do come.'

I said I saw no reason to refuse the invitation if it materialized.

'Is there a Mrs Rivers? Absurdly, I don't know.'

'No, I think not.'

Arthur Rivers was not married, but a Mrs Puxley acted as hostess whenever he entertained. The exact nature of their relationship was not self-evident. To say that Mrs Puxley was quiet would be inadequate. She not only seldom spoke but appeared almost dumb, although perfectly agreeable. If one were sitting next to her at dinner and launched some question or observation she would look fascinated. If the conversational gambit absolutely demanded an answer, she would sometimes say, 'Difficult!' with a little smile. Mrs Puxley had fair hair, always perfectly arranged, and was a little below middle height. She had a most expressive (and rather pretty) face, and if one's remark were a comment, say, on some topical disaster she would cast her eyes heavenwards and sigh, implying recognition of one's profundity. If one had essayed a flippancy she would laugh softly and pleasantly and look at one, in an absorbed way, with half-parted lips, inviting more. She would very occasionally utter a sentence showing perfectly sensible cognizance of what one had been saying, as a sort of reluctantly applied lubricant to get the social machine going again. But in any ordinary sense of the word she did not talk;

and if one's taste during some phase of the meal were for silent mastication – or for a little cross-table conversational intrusion or eavesdropping – she never showed, and I am sure did not feel, the slightest injury. Men, therefore, found her a soothing if unexciting dinner companion. She was probably about forty-five.

Since she, as I say, played hostess for Rivers, her remarkably limited powers of speech might have been thought a handicap – not well fitted for a role often thought to demand sparkle. Mrs Puxley was certainly no latter-day Madame de Staël, no presiding genius of a salon. But I soon discovered that her part was indispensable. She organized the dinners (I imagine an imported cook dealt with these occasions, but there was certainly supervision, and Mrs Puxley's eyes were watchful over the – I think also imported – servitor) and she organized supremely well. Everything was delicious. She also moved quietly among the ladies after dinner, seeing that they were happy. Unobtrusively, she made every evening a success by seeing that Rivers's guests' enjoyment of good food and drink was not spoiled by the smallest discomfort or inconvenience. What lay or had lain between her and Rivers none dared speculate. When one arrived, he said, 'You know Mrs Puxley.' On the first occasion – in my case on 28 July – he said, 'I don't think you know Simon Marlow. Mrs Puxley.' She was dressed simply and well, I thought; whether expensively I had not the experience to say. Her dress showed pretty shoulders and very white skin. She was a little plump, attractively so.

I was first to arrive on that evening. After the introduction to Mrs Puxley, Arthur Rivers gave me a dry martini, made by himself with skill and firm views on method, explained on request. He said, 'I'm afraid you'll find your office pretty well represented here this evening. The Wrenches are coming.'

'Ah!' I was surprised. Julius had been in Sweden. 'I didn't realize Julius was coming back this evening.'

'Not Julius. The younger generation. Your friend, Harry, and his sister. She's here without her husband.'

So the moment had come which I feared and longed for. My heart pounded. I thought Rivers was watching me, but he generally watched anybody to whom he was speaking, with that unwavering, menacing gaze.

'Oh, good!' I said feebly.

Soon afterwards another guest arrived, by some way the oldest of the party. He was a tall man of perhaps sixty. He was greeted by Rivers as a familiar; one who had a manifest role to play and needed no explanation. He was introduced as Desmond Dillon. Rivers must have told him more about me than vice versa, giving him instantly some sort of privileged status at the Boltons, one with a right to expect a preliminary briefing on his companions. He said to me, 'You've just come back from Singapore, haven't you? How's Jimmy Ling?'

'Very well. Are you in our sort of business?'

'Lord, no! I'm a journalist.'

'With what paper?' I asked.

'Freelance,' said Dillon without further elaboration. Irritated a little, I probed.

'And what are your particular interests? Finance? Foreign affairs?'

He looked at me with disturbing concentration; rather like our host. There was, however, something extraordinarily attractive in Dillon's personality. He had an ageless quality. He was still extremely good-looking, and he had a liveliness, a restlessness, which was both youthful and stimulating. His smile, too, was delightful.

'Oh, I've done a lot of stories in my time. I'm what's now called, with varying degrees of mistrust or contempt, an investigative journalist, I suppose! I've got an itch to get to the bottom of things. I really ought to give up, but I don't think I ever will!'

'And you write about things when you've reached the bottom of them?'

'If the story's printable!' said Dillon with his enormously friendly smile.

I heard the front doorbell ring and footsteps in the hall. It was James Todd and his wife, Polly. We all drank and chatted. Rivers was, as often, content to listen, preside, fill our glasses and yet somehow dominate the room. The doorbell rang again. It was Harry. He came in laughing. He knew everybody (except Dillon) and had clearly been before, perhaps several times. He embraced Mrs Puxley and Polly Todd. Rivers looked on tolerantly.

'I thought you might be bringing your sister.'

'Good Lord, I didn't know Miranda was coming. I could have picked her up, she's staying with my parents.' Harry now shared with two friends a rather sumptuous flat in Montagu Square. I felt slightly jealous – excluded; but the arrangement depended on one of the others, the master-partner so to speak, and he and I did not find each other particularly congenial. Their rents, too, were high. Pimlico sufficed.

We all drank our martinis and Rivers replenished them. He looked at his watch. Mrs Puxley murmured two reassuring words to him. Dinner, I guessed, would tolerate a little delay. I was feeling under considerable strain. I realized I had been standing talking to Harry and had not taken in a word he had said. When the bell rang at last I could not, for all my determination, keep my eyes easily averted, my tone detached, my expression calm. Instead I caught my breath and looked at the door: Miranda came in.

She apologized for lateness, a few murmured conventional words on scarcity of taxis. She shook hands with apparent affection with Mrs Puxley, kissed Harry, met the Todds and Dillon for the first time. To me she said, 'Simon, how lovely!' and moved her eyes away at once, exchanging merely a friendly smile. The extraordinary thing is that I cannot at all remember her appearance that evening, what she was wearing and so forth. I suppose the impression she made was so much greater than visual that I could not later form a picture of her on that occasion. Yet the evening transformed my life.

At dinner, I sat on Mrs Puxley's left, with Polly Todd on my other side. We were at a round table, and Miranda was opposite me, with James Todd on her left and Arthur Rivers next to Desmond Dillon on her right. Harry sat between James and Mrs Puxley. I remember little of what went on. We were a small enough party for much of our talk to be general, for Mrs Puxley's passivity and Dillon's quiet, rather unnerving concentration to be subsumed in the general conversational pool. The Todds were lively and agreeable but, to nobody's surprise I think, the conversation was dominated by Harry. Rivers fed him a question or two about America and my friend was in fine form in responding to it, as entertaining as ever.

Only once did my eyes meet Miranda's, but it was enough. Harry told a New York story, finishing with some unfair and outrageous generalization. Polly Todd countered across the table with a riposte – her mother was American and she knew the United States well. This animated crossfire, which amused us all, had the effect of making other conversation redundant for a little, and Miranda and I happened to look up and at each other at the same minute. And for that moment we did not look away. We looked, unsmiling, serious'

'And on the instant,' said Marlow, 'I knew that nothing whatsoever had changed and that the insubstantial bonds that held us, that had never been soldered by love-making nor admitted by spoken words, were as real and powerful as they had surely been since the dawn of the world.

We chatted to each other for a little after dinner. I tried to keep my voice steady. I asked how long she planned to be in England, and she said that everything was uncertain. She seemed almost relieved when Harry joined us. He was quieter than he had been at dinner, rather thoughtful. I wondered whether, in the course of his cross-table rallies with Polly Todd, he had observed the look between Miranda and myself.

I also wondered whether Rivers had remarked it; he missed little. I cared not at all.

Everybody started to leave, except Dillon who accepted a whisky in response to a quiet 'Don't go, Des,' from his host. The rest of us thanked and left together. The Todds lived in north London and had agreed to take Harry to Montagu Square. I had a car. I said, 'I'll drop you, Miranda. Cadogan Square is on my way.'

We said not a word. I drove into a quiet crescent off the Old Brompton Road and switched off the engine. I turned to her and said, 'Oh, Miranda!'

'Simon!'

Then I took her in my arms.

Next day, I was a different human being. I cared nothing for Wrench Holdings, for Boshy's money, for all the world. I would make Miranda mine. She loved me. The odious Bartholomew must be discarded by some means. There might be hurdles to leap, cliffs to climb, dangers to outface, but I, Simon Marlow, simply laughed at the idea that any of them would bring me down. Love is supremely strong, I said cockily to myself. I walked around the office in a golden haze, mind dominated only by the thought of when I would see Miranda again.

I had said to her as we got to Cadogan Square, 'When?'

'Stay in the car. Don't come in, Simon, darling.'

'When? I'll telephone tomorrow.'

'No,' she said, 'I'll telephone you.' Impatient, I gave her the number of my flat. I whispered, 'Promise!'

'I promise.'

'Tomorrow.'

'I'll try!'

'I'll be at that number all evening. I won't go out. I shall sit waiting.'

'Simon, my dearest –'

'Waiting!'

During the latter part of the morning, James Todd put his head round the door. He said that the evening before had been fun, hadn't it?

'And what an attractive girl Julius's daughter is. I believe her husband's a charming chap, but they must miss her a lot.'

I made no reply to this.

'Shall we have lunch together today, Simon?'

It would pass the time. I had absolutely no appetite but assented.

During lunch at a nearby pub, James dropped his voice and said, 'You know, I wouldn't be entirely surprised if our beloved master didn't receive some sort of recognition next year. He's on a lot of national boards and committees. He's done some remarkable things for British commerce.' He started to list them.

'What sort of recognition?'

'Well,' said James, 'I would imagine he must be on pretty well anyone's short list for a knighthood. And there's no doubt he'd like one. No doubt at all.'

Sir Julius Wrench. It sounded very suitable. I could not summon great interest, nor, indeed, enthusiasm. Sir Julius Wrench, destroyer of lives, cheater of friends, biter of the feeding hand. Sir Julius, father of Miranda.

The day dragged on. I went home to my flat as early as I decently could. Miranda might well have difficulty getting certain and secluded access to the telephone in Cadogan Square. I doubted if there were an instrument in her bedroom. Miranda would not, I hoped, wish to call me with anybody else in the room. I sat and waited. At half-past six the telephone rang. I fell upon it with a strangled 'Hello.'

A strange, rather musical male voice said, 'This is Desmond Dillon. It was nice meeting you last night.'

'Yes, indeed.'

'Would you have lunch with me, one day? I was very interested in what you said about Malaya.'

I told him I would be delighted, and he said he would telephone me at Wrench Holdings after returning from some trip abroad. I slammed down the receiver. For what precious moments had Miranda been attempting to contact me and getting the engaged tone? The telephone now remained silent.

At seven-thirty my control snapped. I telephoned the Wrench household. I recognized the voice at the far end as that of Viola Wrench.

'Mrs Wrench, it's Simon. Simon Marlow.'

'Simon, my dear, we never see you now! It's because Harry has this flat of his own. How are you?'

'Very well. As a matter of fact I was trying to get Harry. I couldn't get an answer from his flat so I thought I'd try Cadogan Square.'

'How odd!' said Viola Wrench. 'I've just been talking to him and I'm sure he was in his flat.'

'Oh well,' I said lightly, 'I suppose I just picked the wrong moments. You're not expecting him, are you?'

'Not this evening. Miranda's over here, you know, but Harry's not coming round this evening as far as I know.'

'Miranda's here! Oh, good, is she? I hope she's well, could I have a word with her perhaps if she's in, how splendid she's with you –'

'Of course, I'll get Miranda,' said Viola. 'I think she's in her room. She's perfectly well. But I imagine you know that. Harry told me that you were at a dinner party he and Miranda both went to last night.'

I waited. I had not done well. After a long time I heard Miranda's voice.

'Hello, Simon?'

I guessed Viola was in the room. I spoke softly.

'Listen, Miranda, lunch tomorrow. I'm getting Harry to come too. I mean, I'm trying to get Harry. I mean, *say* I mean I'm trying to get Harry. Just for God's sake say you'll come.' Was it possible, I thought, that Viola had said, 'Simon

Marlow, darling. Take it in my bedroom,' and was now sitting in the drawing room, ear glued to instrument? My boats were almost burned. This thing simply could not be managed discreetly.

'Quarter past one –' I named a restaurant and described its whereabouts. '*Say you'll be there!*'

'Yes,' said Miranda very calmly, in a most ordinary voice, 'that would be very nice. And you'll contact Harry? Excellent. What fun! Thank you so much, Simon. Goodbye.' And she put the receiver down.

I did not sleep at all that night. Much could go wrong. First, of course, Harry himself could upset the apple cart. At some time his mother would say to him, 'Simon Marlow was trying to get you, I gather it was about lunch with Miranda, the three of you.' And Harry would say, 'Oh, he hasn't been in touch today or yesterday.' Then he would think of my eyes and Miranda's eyes at the Rivers dinner table.

I tried to telephone Harry. No reply.

Then there was the office. Although I was doing well and in a fairly independent situation, Wrench Holding employees were expected to work rigorous hours. Long lunchtime absences were for the Board. In the morning I saw a colleague, and explained some urgent personal business. I would need longer than the usual lunch hour. He agreed to cover a few matters for me. I telephoned the restaurant. I had used it once or twice. It was a decent distance from Wrench Holdings, unfrequented by anybody I knew. Some of the tables were charmingly secluded. It was expensive. I had by now ingratiated myself with the head waiter, an Italian.

'Good morning, Mr Marlow. Very sorry, sir. We're absolutely full up. No table at all.'

'Look, Cesare, this is *really* important, somebody is meeting me at the restaurant, I can't contact them to change it.'

'I'm sorry, sir. There's really nothing.'

'There'll be a cancellation, I'm sure. Somebody won't turn up.'

'I can't say, sir. Of course you can come in the hope, but I'm afraid you may be disappointed.'

'I'll do that,' I said. At one o'clock I was in the restaurant. Cesare met me with raised eyebrows.

'As I said, Mr Marlow, sorry, sir. No table at all. We haven't been so full for a long time.'

'Oh God! I'll hang about in the hope. I'll be waiting on the pavement anyway. I must meet my guest and if I can't get in take a – go elsewhere.' I went out of the swing doors just as it started to rain heavily.

I stood, getting what cover I could from the overhang of the door. I could not stand inside – I had no table, customers were arriving and the place was small and crowded. I had no umbrella. I got wetter and wetter. It was, I thought, perfectly possible that Miranda would not come. Harry would have telephoned, Viola would have said, 'I gather you're seeing Miranda at lunch today?' He would have denied it, Miranda would have had to say, 'Oh, Simon's obviously made a mistake, I'll contact him some time.'

At twenty-five minutes past one Miranda got out of a taxi and started to pay it. I was soaking wet, seized her arm, propelled her back into the taxi, and gave the resentful driver my address in Pimlico.

'No table! We'll go somewhere else, but I must get dry. I'll change.'

'Simon, I'm not sure –'

'It won't take me a minute.'

'I don't mind about lunch. I don't really want lunch.'

I looked at her. I was bedraggled, dripping. She was well waterproofed, headscarfed, moist, her eyes unbelievable.

'Miranda, I don't want lunch either. Please don't say anything.'

I was shaking, and so was my voice. We sat beside each other in the taxi in total silence. We didn't dare look at each other. At last we arrived – it was still pouring with rain.

Together we ascended the unadorned stairs that led to my flat.

'And so,' said Marlow in a quiet, reflective voice, 'we became lovers. I learned, that afternoon, of her wretched marriage; her abominable husband; her mistakes, her regrets, her sense of both guilt and outrage, and, above all, of failure. I was so overjoyed, so bursting with achievement, that I brushed aside her anxieties. We became lovers. For me, for a little, that was enough. I had – it seemed for ever – been in love with Miranda, dreamed of her, possessed her in my imagination. The reality was overpowering, stunning! That is rare, I think, rare to be obsessed by desire for a woman and not to be secretly disappointed when the dream becomes substance! I can only say that with Miranda no shadow, no regret, no disillusion arose to mar my joy. Ever.

And for the first time, too, I began to know her as a person. I came not only to be in love but to love. Miranda had an enchanting serenity, a cool good sense which blended delightfully and often surprisingly with a passionate nature and a tender heart. She would go straight to the heart of a matter, uncompromisingly, always her own woman, indifferent to the conventional wisdom of the day on any subject. In this she reminded me often of Harry, and I loved it. I saw Harry, too, in her warmth, her quickness of perception and her emphatic declarations – 'No, there's *nothing* to be said for that! Nothing at all!' But in spite of Miranda's dislike of equivocation, she was less impetuous than her brother. She could, I thought, be strong in action but her heart would never completely dominate her head. Strong and true, Miranda was, nevertheless, prudent. And though I girded sometimes at this, I loved it too. It was sublime simultaneously to adore, to enjoy and to admire.

Of course our situation held much pain as well as huge delight. When away from her – and for most of the time, after all, I was away from her – I could all too easily remember the tone of her voice, calm, gentle, and torment myself with the thought that she was too controlled to be suffering as greatly as I from the pangs of love. Then we would meet again, make love again, and I would be reassured, sustained, would drown in delight. For an hour or two. At each of our meetings Miranda would say, 'I don't think we can go on,' and I would press for openness, for declaration, for Simon and Miranda against the world. They were wonderful weeks, those late summer weeks of 1967.

'You must never go back to America, now,' I said.

Miranda said she had to. She had to make the break – and it was no longer in question that there must be a break – face to face. She was not prepared simply to tell Bartholomew by letter that she had decided to leave him. Sometimes, appallingly, she used to say, 'He's not all bad. He's got a nice side.' I didn't believe it and hated to hear it.

We made love in my flat, in snatched and secret minutes. Sometimes it would be a lunchtime, sometimes the hour between six and seven. Miranda was determined that her family, even Harry, should know nothing of our affair. I told her that I was perfectly ready to leave Wrench Holdings if it disturbed her to be in the arms of her father's employee – that I would gladly tell her entire family that we loved each other, that she was proposing to leave her husband and come to me. She wouldn't hear of it. I said that I, by now, had a good many contacts. I would make a life for both of us. Miranda smiled and shook her head.

'Simon, dearest, you must be patient. You see, my father was very keen on my marriage. He had a lot to do with the Bartholomews, in business. They still mean a lot to him. And he knows they can be awfully tough. He knows that my walking out on Alec would be taken out on all of us.'

'But, darling love, your father and mother must know perfectly well you're unhappy! They wouldn't want to sacrifice you to some business deals, however large. And they can't imagine you're content just to sit at home for a little and then go back to that frightful man as if you'd never been away. This is 1967!'

'I know it's 1967, and it's true they know things aren't all that good, but they both hope that a few weeks apart, a few weeks of "thinking things over" will help. They remind me, too, of the practical benefits, as they call them. And it's true – I *do* enjoy a lot of what money brings. It's nothing compared to love, I know that. But . . .'

'But?'

Miranda sighed. I knew she was in no way of the spoiled rich, but she had grown up among pleasant and expensive objects. Frugality had not been bred in her. She said, 'I've very little money of my own, you know. Daddy made a trust but it only works while I'm with Alec. It was for our children if we had any. Apart from that I've never had anything but my dividends on Daddy's companies. I don't understand, but I don't think I can touch any capital. If I left Alec for good – don't worry, darling, of course I will, you know that, but it's a question of how and when – there might be alimony. The Bartholomews certainly wouldn't be generous.'

'I imagine not.'

'It would be one of those ghastly American divorces, with expensive lawyers thinking up beastly suggestions to make, to get huge sums of money for me – and fought by the other side all the way, of course. And I'd have to say – and prove – awful things. In public court. Darling, you must see that it's going to take some doing.'

Miranda told me she knew Julius would be bitterly opposed to any divorce, but if he were persuaded that there were no hope for her marriage he would come round to it in time. 'But,' she said, 'if Daddy knew about us, if he reckoned that you'd helped break up my marriage, he'd be implacable. And, you know, he can be very ruthless.'

I did know. But to my reminders that her parents were aware of her misery with her husband – for she had made little secret of it – she returned the same answer. We must, for the present, be utterly discreet. Our meetings must be clandestine, carefully plotted – and, inevitably, infrequent. I longed for her, every minute of every day and night. She lay in my arms for precious, occasional hours, the clock moving inexorably to the moment of parting. Then we would make another tentative appointment.

It was true that Miranda held a substantial number of shares in Wrench Holdings. On paper she was a wealthy woman. 'But,' she said, 'I could never dispose of them, unbeknown to Daddy. They give me a good income, but as far as capital goes they're untouchable. We haven't really got much freedom of action, darling.'

I resented the apparent weakness, the dependence of our situation. I resented it the more because Miranda did not seem to me to resent it enough.

'Your father would take a different view of it all if I were a rich man,' I said once, bitterly and angrily.

Miranda considered.

'I don't think it would reconcile him to my breaking with the Bartholomews. But, of course, it would make a lot of things easier, wouldn't it.'

'Would it?'

'Yes, my sweet,' said Miranda, 'I'm afraid it would.' Later she said, 'You resent the fact terribly, don't you – that our actions, without money, aren't as free as if we had some – or had more. You are a real romantic. You're like one of the charming young men in a Restoration comedy who aspires to the girl but hasn't a penny. Don't worry, he always gets his beloved in the last act.'

'I'm glad to hear it.'

'Still,' said Miranda, 'he's generally shown to be a rightful heir to a fortune or something like that. I don't remember any of them where he got the girl *and* stayed penniless.' She gave a small sigh, but the hands of the clock were moving and we turned to other things.

'It can only be a few weeks, my darling,' Miranda whispered several times. 'Then, for a little, I must go back. And nobody must know. But you must be patient. I won't shirk the issue. But I must have a little time. It will come right. In the end.'

'In the end?'

'In the end.'

'You'll write,' I said flatly. I faced a dreary and uncertain future. Miranda was flying back to America next day – it was the end of October. She said she'd write. She promised to send me an address, where I could write without the letter arousing suspicion. It was a question of arrangements, a question of trust, by no means easy. I was forbidden to telephone.

'But you'll write. Oh, my darling, you'll write and you'll come back.'

'Yes, I'll come back. At the right time. Not a minute later than I have to, but at the right time. I'll come back and in my heart I am with you always.''

10

The morning before John's next dinner appointment with Marlow, Mme Blanchard caught him.

'They telephoned from the Auberge last night, John. I did not leave a note since I knew I would see you this morning. Your friend is ill.'

'Oh dear! How ill?'

'Well, as we know, you and I, he is always ill, but it seems he has had a little attack of some kind, I believe quite a small affair, and Dr Pelegrin has said he must rest and see nobody for a few days. He is not in hospital but they have telephoned to postpone your next visit to him.'

Mme Blanchard was, naturally, curious about their exchanges. She eyed John.

'I hope you do not allow the poor man to exhaust himself.'

'He needs to talk. I think I do a little for him simply by listening. Simply by hearing.'

It was, therefore, a full fortnight after Marlow's passionate recollections of Miranda that they again dined, in the same way, at the same table, and sat afterwards at the same spot in the garden. Marlow apologized for any inconvenience. He did not refer to his 'attack' except to say, 'It comes and goes. That doctor, Pelegrin, is rather a nice man.' John thought that Marlow looked a particularly bad colour and said, hesitantly, that he was worried that these sessions were unduly tiring. John was sure by now that his silent attention was the greatest kindness he could do this man; and was intrigued, and oddly moved. But he heeded the justice of Mme Blanchard's warning.

'You mustn't let me exhaust you.'

'No, no,' he said, 'you must believe that it helps me. It helps me very greatly. I am grateful. It is a real blessing, a wonderful service.' He ate even less than usual.

'I don't know how I got through that autumn and winter,' he said. 'Being passionately in love is always delight and pain mingled, of course, but when separated physically and when there is a huge question mark hanging over the future, pain is ever-present. I found it difficult to eat, impossible to enjoy other company, and hard to sleep. Because of Miranda's absolute determination to keep our relations hidden I had not even the lover's relief of confiding in friends. I was scrupulous; I talked to nobody. I avoided Harry; it would have been happiness to be able to share the secret with him, but Miranda – who thought he suspected nothing – was adamant on the subject. I was less sure, but I didn't intend to find out. I passed a solitary, frustrated sort of existence. I was morose. I was not particularly companionable to my mother when I went to Penterton at weekends. People in love are generally bad company and I was no exception.

I was, however, able to work. I used work as an anaesthetic. I worked late. I soaked myself in the past, present and future of Redvers Associates. One evening in November I was alone in the office, secretaries having fled to catch commuter tubes, buses and trains as the clock struck five-thirty. My telephone rang. It was Desmond Dillon. He asked me to lunch on a day the following week.

Desmond Dillon had rightly described himself as one who liked to get to the bottom of things. He had an obsession about being well informed, about being 'in the know'. His character was such that, although happy (or so it seemed) to impart information, he appeared almost to resent receiving it. He should, he implied, have known that before. This suited me, who had, I thought, little information to give, but the trait could obviously be irritating. In Dillon it was not so, because irritation was at once dispelled by his hugely attractive qualities. He was extremely kind. He was a sensitive man. He, at sixty, was one of those who treated all people the same, as contemporaries. He had a sense of beauty, and a sound scale of moral values, as I increasingly understood. He loved his country too, with an old-fashioned, simple-hearted love. He deplored, loudly, many facets of modern Britain, but to him the country was a great deal more than its current obsessions, feeblenesses or vulgarities. Desmond was one to whom betrayal of country was the ultimate sin, the breaking of the taboo, the unthinkable, and he spoke of this with a sort of fervour which made me fancy he had some experience of the matter; painful, memorable. Desmond could speak of 'England' with poetic force. He meant, furthermore, no offence to Scots nor Welsh (he was himself in origin Irish) by this inexactitude. It was, simply, that the strength of his feeling needed, for its object, a symbol of ancient, historic power; the word 'Britain', for him, did not have that power. Desmond was a patriot. He hated his country's enemies, within or without. He was thirty-four years older than I and I soon felt as if we had grown up together.

He gave me a good lunch. I wondered whether he had noticed anything between Miranda and myself at the Rivers dinner party. I didn't want to go over that ground – Desmond was too alert, too shrewd. He said, 'Impressive, single-minded man, Arthur Rivers,' and I said, 'Obviously. I don't know him well but he had a great name in Ling Enterprises,' and I shifted the conversation to the unmined territory of Singapore.

We talked a little about politics, in which I had taken and still take little interest. I have small taste for it, and my study of history never, perhaps oddly, bred the slightest desire for involvement in the current political scene. Desmond talked about subversion – about the periodic alarms of Soviet-Communist infiltration and control of institutions in Western countries, including our own. He told me about Communist 'front' organizations, innocent in apparent purpose, then taken over, financed and used for party – and Moscow's – purposes.

'It is,' Desmond said, 'very much a syndrome of what Lenin called the useful idiots. You know' (I didn't know) 'good-hearted people who want peace or universal brotherhood or whatever. It sounds good. It *is* good, in the sense that virtue's good, niceness is nice. But the tactic – and Lenin said this clearly and prescribed it – is to encourage such people and such organizations to agitate in a particular direction consistent with one's own strategy. If that can be done, then one supports them. Covertly, of course – one doesn't want to seem too close to them.'

'"One" being the Soviet Union.'

'Of course. And support generally involves some degree of infiltration into these apparently innocuous organizations. Then any counter-subversive moves by the authorities will be denounced as the persecution of genuine and idealistic opponents of government. It's a very old game. It hasn't changed in essentials since 1917. You're dealing, Simon, with people who take the long view, you see. They claim, after all, to be on the side of an inevitable tide of history.'

I said, 'And the immediate object?'

'That will change from time to time. But the strongest single purpose, in our present era, is probably to drive a good thick wedge between the United States and the countries of Western Europe, including ours. Anything that makes trouble between the two sides of the Atlantic is good, from the Soviet point of view. Very good – and for obvious reasons.'

'And does one deduce from that the need to support America always and everywhere?'

'No,' said Desmond, sighing. 'One doesn't. But one should at least take one's decisions knowing what the game is all about.'

I had little experience of such things, although it was inevitable that anybody at university during the sixties had witnessed the antics of the extreme left – and the successes. I was inclined to take Desmond's tales with a certain pinch of salt. He was an 'investigative journalist', and he tended, without conscious dishonesty, to fit facts into the conspiratorial pattern which suited his story. Or so I thought. Developing his theme, he told me that he was sure a number of institutions received money from the East – respectable-sounding institutions, not demonstrably pro-Soviet. He was working on it.

'Which,' I asked, a little sceptically, 'and how? It's not entirely easy to hide that sort of thing. Accounts have to be published.' I felt wordly-wise.

Desmond would not be drawn much further. He mentioned, with a shrug, one or two names. They were familiar to me.

Later, however, he got round to what I suspected was the real purpose of the lunch.

'Simon,' he said, 'I'm not in business, as you know, but there's a rumour going round that your Wrench Holdings is vulnerable. That someone's out to get it.'

'You mean take it over?'

'I do.'

Now this was not absolutely news. There had been no comment in the press of the kind which always accompanies and generally precedes moves of that kind, but in a business like Wrench, words, hints, suspicions move through the passages like electricity. It only took one man of medium seniority to say, 'One can't exclude a bid for us all, some time, I suppose,' in today's climate for the alarm bells to start ringing.

I had, however, done some private research on the capital structure of the holding company. I doubted the possibility of any such move ever succeeding. I had, by now, views about Julius Wrench which could be described as ambivalent. With one part of me I had, however improbably, vowed to ruin him; and a successful take-over bid would, arguably, do so, for he was emotionally as well as practically involved in the company, and loss of control would, to him, be insupportable.

But another, more rational, part of me remarked, with self-mockery, that Simon Marlow was most unlikely to assist a take-over of Wrench Holdings, even if he thought it could be passed off as an achievement in terms of Boshy's task.

I had to remind myself that I had found absolutely nothing connected to Boshy's piece of paper, my talisman, which lent substance to the idea that Julius had indulged in malpractices deserving exposure and ruin. I had pretty well discarded that idea. I had, indeed, by now largely abandoned the idea of satisfying Boshy's conditions. I was trying to reconcile myself to the belief that a fortune, intended for me, was beyond my reach. I sometimes told myself, miserably, that it might make the crucial difference to my prospects with Miranda, to our future together. But then I thought of the precondition – her father's destruction – and my imagination found it impossible to travel further down that road. All this, for the hundredth time, went through my mind as I heard Desmond Dillon talk about the vulnerability of Wrench Holdings.

I said, in a discreet sort of way, 'Of course, the family shareholding is pretty large, as you know.' (This showed in the accounts. It was public knowledge.)

'Large but not impregnable. There are one or two very big shareholders who might be persuaded. Oh, of course, anybody prepared to go for you would reckon he'd need to pay a good price,' said Desmond, 'but we'd be talking of somebody pretty big, wouldn't we.'

The names of several such potential crocodiles had been canvassed in office gossip. For various reasons, each had been dismissed. I said, with a certain complacency, 'I don't think this is going to happen. I can say one thing – it would be fought tooth and nail. And Julius Wrench may seem languid but he's a fighter. There isn't a tougher fighter in London.'

'I don't doubt it. Well, we'll see, won't we?' said Desmond. He had paid the bill and made as if to move. He put his hands on the tablecloth and smiled at me. I said, 'Thank you so much. A very nice lunch.'

He said, 'I imagine you suspect who's after Wrench, don't you? In fact you, of all people, must.'

I looked as inscrutable as I could. I felt obscurely flattered as well as excited. He must, he could only, mean one thing. I got up. I preferred to say and hear no more. I had a good deal to digest.

So Ling was after Wrench.

This had not been rumoured as one of the possibilities. I considered what I had learned of Ling Enterprises in Singapore and had to face the fact that it wasn't much. I had worked in my own small patch of Jimmy Ling's huge empire and I had taken an intelligent interest in all of it. But it was so complex – a complexity which the management had little desire to simplify – that I found I knew very little about the overall capital structure, liquidity or, I had to admit, real size and power. It was too rambling and amorphous to grasp.

I assumed, however, that for any successful bid to be raised for Wrench, the instrument would be the company called Eastern Trading Incorporated which Arthur Rivers chaired, directed and most certainly ran. ETI, as it was called, was a wholly owned subsidiary of Ling, registered in London. It was Arthur Rivers who must be charged, if Desmond Dillon was right, with the stalking of Julius Wrench.

They were two heavyweights, I reflected. Julius obviously kept a pretty close eye on the company's register of shareholders. If there were any major move in the market he would spot it at once. I wondered how many shares in Wrench ETI already held. A good many, I supposed. I would find out. I also thought I would – 'purely for interest' I said to myself, half-convincingly – discover and remember the principal institutional shareholders and their holdings.

I always saw a good deal of James Todd. He was, within the limits of loyalty, often prepared for a little gossip about how matters looked at court. I thought that I would go out of my way to see more of James and Polly. I decided, too, to make contact with a City friend, an acquaintance from Oxford days I had recently met again with the usual 'let's lunch some time' on parting. He was genial and indiscreet, allegedly 'doing well' in a merchant bank. I would put out one or two personal listening posts. I wondered what had reached Harry – he was himself working hard and successfully in the City now. He was the obvious person to talk to, but I was not anxious for a heart-to-heart with Harry.

Miranda's first letter didn't arrive until the middle of November. We had been apart for two weeks. I found it on my return from the office in the evening, one Thursday.

I sat in my flat looking at the envelope. I felt sick. Would it – it must – confirm all we had last said to each other, whatever the difficulties, whatever the passage of time? 'I am with you always,' she had said. Would it tell me that matters had moved with her husband, that she had realized she could no longer postpone telling him she could not bear him? Or would Miranda's letter explain, gently, tenderly, that she had decided she must, after all, stay in America? That Alexander Bartholomew junior was not, really, too bad? I had considered every such possibility in long, tormented hours. I had not been able to write. I could not telephone. Now I sat and gazed at the envelope. Then, trembling, I opened it.

I first quickly looked at each page and at the end for clues. My heart immediately lightened. It finished, 'I love you as ever, Miranda'. It was not long – not nearly long enough, a mere three sides – but on the second page was an address. Good! That could only mean she had sent me the address to which I could write. I now settled down to read from the beginning, tension slightly relaxed.

Miranda's letter was in one way reassuring, in another remarkably unhelpful. She seemed still to love me – so far, so good. She was no great hand at self-expression but I could not detect any evidence of cooling off or of second thoughts. On the other hand, there was absolutely no sign that she had tried – or even contemplated – yet bringing matters to any sort of conclusion with her husband. The letter seemed to mix incompatible elements. In one place she recalled our times together – 'How I wish I could again *lunch* at (my address in Pimlico) – whenever every day comes to that point I feel myself there –' Excellent. I re-read that six times. On the other hand there were almost prosaic and certainly most unwelcome news items. 'Alec's sister and I went together on a business trip to Texas – lots of rather uncongenial people on the Bartholomew business contact side, but a rather fascinating, stimulating place, all the same. I'd never been down to the Gulf of Mexico before.' Fascinating? Stimulating? What on earth could she mean? *All* Bartholomews, awful in New York, must, I hoped and supposed, be trebly so in Texas. Could there have been some all-conquering Texan? I could almost face that possibility as easily as the impression that life with her husband's family was *tolerable.*

There was, however, one bit of which I had to make what I could and which contained a small, ambivalent promise.

'Alec has to go to Europe on a business trip around the New Year, January, February, he's not sure which. He'll be going all over the place, Frankfurt, Athens, Stockholm, the lot. We've not decided on what I'll do but I'll probably spend some of the time in London while he's travelling around. I might come over earlier than him.'

Still – 'I love you as ever, Miranda'. I held on to that. And there was a postscript – a wonderful postscript as far as it went: 'Thank you for understanding, darling, and giving me a little time, and January isn't far away.'

But there had been no crunch, no showdown with Alec Bartholomew.

I drank two large whiskies in succession. I then sat down to write my vital letter to Miranda. It was very long. When I had finished it, I re-read it, tore it up, and started again. The letter went through three drafts, and I then, sensibly but with pain, decided to leave it until the next morning to be re-read a final time and posted. I would, I thought, sleep on it.

I told Miranda in the best language I could find, using every flight of imagery I could extract from my own heart or from the recorded talents of others in like case, how much I loved her. I poured my love on to the page. I told her how I missed her every minute of every day. There was no contriving in my letter – no guile, no attempts to 'win' her heart. I made myself deliberately and entirely vulnerable. I concealed nothing of the strength or anguish of my love. I treated her as won already. If there was to be a rebuff, I courted it, breast bared to the dagger.

I wrote that I must have some hope, some assurance from her, that she would one day, very soon, come to me. I could understand and sadly accept, I said, that the timing of this must lie with her. She had said it would come 'in the end'. But in her letter – which I had loved and cherished as having been touched by her own hands – she gave little indication that 'the end' was any nearer than when she had last left America. I knew how unhappy she was. I believed in how happy we could be. Life was passing.

Golden lads and girls all must,
As chimney-sweepers, come to dust.

'Please, my own darling,' I wrote, 'believe that the present situation *cannot* be allowed to last and to destroy at least two lives. It can be fair to nobody. Give me some sign that you, too, see things in that light and I can and will be as brave and patient as you. But I must, in love, ask for that sign.' Although I prayed daily that the post would bring another letter from Miranda, I almost hoped that her next would be deferred until she had received mine.

This hope was satisfied since Miranda's next letter did not come until the first week in December. In some ways it was worse than the first, and for the same reasons. The earlier part of the letter, clearly found easier to compose, dealt with practical matters. She wrote that the Europe trip was postponed at least until February but that she planned to come over to London a little earlier. (My heart leapt. Six weeks was a lifetime but at least I had a date.) And, 'Alec has agreed to come over a bit later and we'll meet in London. Thereafter plans are uncertain.' What the hell did that mean? She told me that she had started painting again and that it was a joy – 'one can lose oneself in it'. Horror! The second part of the letter attempted to do something to respond to my own. My 'wonderful letter', Miranda called it. Excellent!

'You ask for a sign, darling, that it will all come right in the end. I don't think I can give you any sign at the moment, but I can only tell you, once more, that I know it will. I have to work things out for myself and to a large extent by myself. I know how hard patience is, but its opposite could be very wrong.' She had scratched out a word which I thought I could decipher as 'unsuccessful' and substituted 'wrong'.

I thought it best to seem to assume more from her letter than it had explicitly conveyed. I wrote, in my next, of how happy she had made me by reassuring me that all was, and would be, well. I told her that I understood fully how difficult life was for her, how agonizing decisions – 'and confrontations', I added, hopefully – could be. I was, I said, unchanged, adoring and living only for the month of January, or February at worst. A brief, I thought reassuringly loving, letter in response (but I was miserably aware of the dangers of wishful thinking) asked me not to write until I heard again: 'Things are difficult,' Miranda said. It was Christmas 1967.

'It was just before Christmas,' Marlow said, 'that I was made to realize how delicate was my – and Miranda's – situation. Lovers often over-estimate their powers of dissimulation and we were no exception. I received a note in the office: 'Julius would be glad if you would call at Cadogan Square this evening. He will be there between six-thirty and seven.' This was from James Todd. It was peremptory.

I had, of course, avoided any occasion for intimacy with the Wrenches since the previous summer. Still, I had once been a more intimate protégé and if Julius wanted to talk to me, and didn't choose simply to send for me to his office, it would in the old days have been likely that I would have received from Viola a more gracious invitation. Perhaps she was away. I never knew. Certainly when I arrived at their sumptuous flat in Cadogan Square that evening Julius was alone. He poured me a drink and remained standing, as I did also.I am a big man but Julius was a good deal bigger. He towered. He meant to dominate physically as well as morally. His voice was as languid as ever but his eyes were hard. He didn't intend to waste time.

'Simon, I've got an idea, and so has Viola, that you've rather fallen for Miranda. I'm not asking you a question. If you want to comment later you can. I simply want to tell you that I'm not going to watch Miranda's marriage being broken up, by you or anybody else. No – don't interrupt, if you don't mind,' he said, as I tried to blurt something. 'If we're wrong I'm delighted, but you'd better know how we feel.

'You don't know Miranda's husband. He's basically a very good fellow. I wouldn't be in the least surprised if there are periodic troubles in their marriage, but I know one thing – those troubles, if they exist, mustn't be made worse by anybody else trying to exploit them, turning Miranda's head. That would be unforgivable. If it were happening – if it happened when she was over here – and if the person were you, it would be trebly unforgivable. It would be rotten behaviour, it would be betrayal by so close a friend of my family, and it would, frankly, be absolutely inconsistent for a trusted employee. One can't separate the various parts of one's life tidily, beyond a certain point. If this isn't nonsense – and I hope it is – you've got no future with us – ever – and I expect you've got the sense to know it.'

Julius's tone was quiet, cold and unfriendly. It was clear that I had to say something. I had to decide very quickly indeed. It wasn't easy. I hated the idea of disowning Miranda's love. I didn't know whether words like: 'It's all nonsense, Julius. God knows where you got it', would pass my lips or whether they'd choke me. Perhaps, in fact, a bold, honest front and to hell with Wrench would force the matter so much into the open that when we'd swept away the smashed pieces Miranda would be mine. On the other hand, I remembered her agonized insistence on secrecy, especially from her father.

'It's all nonsense, Julius. God knows where you got it.' I didn't do it badly. He didn't believe me. Somehow he knew too much. But he hadn't obtained an admission and he had still to behave to Miranda, and to me, as if his suspicions might be unfounded. I put everything I knew into meeting his eyes levelly.

I sipped my drink and went ahead. If this was to be done it must be done well. 'I can understand what you say, and how you feel, Julius. But I'd like to say that I'm not upset – I'm flattered! I think Miranda is a wonderful person, and whoever has put about a story that I've fallen for her, let alone she for me, is doing me too much honour. But it doesn't happen to be true.'

Julius looked at me, silent.

'And I'd not be human,' I said, 'if I didn't wonder where in hell you got the idea.'

Julius said, 'No, you'd not be, would you.' He gave a small, unpleasant smile. Then he said, 'All right, Simon, I've said enough, let's leave it. Thanks for coming. I've got to push you out now. I'm changing and picking up Viola.'

I left. I had got the message.

As I moved to the lift outside their flat door I found a fat, elderly man fumbling in his pockets, as if for a key. He looked up. 'I know who you are! You're Simon Marlow! Friend of Harry's and so forth. Funny thing we've never met, I'm always hearing about you – Charlie Branson.'

We had, as he said, never met but I knew exactly who he

was. My mind went back to Eton conversations with Harry long ago. This was Charlie Branson, who hadn't a penny and had once used the Wrench household as home. Perhaps he did again.

'That's right,' I said. 'I'm Simon Marlow. Sorry, I'm just leaving.'

'I was talking to an old friend of mine about you the other day. He seemed to have a very soft spot for you. It was old Waldo. Waldo Price.'

'Oh yes,' I said neutrally and courteously. The lift made its appearance, having answered another call during my exchanges with Branson.

'I'd better take it this time,' I said, smiling. Charlie Branson stood, looking at me. It may have been something in his eye, it may have been the mention of Waldo Price, that made me think him a little drunk. He didn't move as I entered the lift and pressed the ground-floor button. I decided to walk home. I needed air and time.

11

'The battle for Wrench Holdings began on 21 January 1968,' said Marlow. 'A Wednesday. In the office we had the word in the middle of the morning.

'Ling's making an offer for WH! Half in cash! Values us at eight points above last night's WH share quotation!'

This was a terrifying amount of money, but nobody doubted that Jimmy Ling, with Arthur Rivers riding shotgun, as they say, could produce it.

'Borrowdale Kemp are acting for Ling.' This was less than exact. The bid was in the name of Eastern Trading Incorporation, ETI, Arthur Rivers's domain. Ling owned them, of course. Borrowdale Kemp were vigorous merchant bankers, looked on with some suspicion as buccaneers by the older stagers.

I don't know to this day whether Julius Wrench was surprised. Even the sharpest and most experienced of men can be taken unawares by something near their noses, something rumoured by lesser fry but disdained or ignored by themselves. I don't know whether it was like that with Julius. We hardly saw him during the early stages of the campaign. James Todd scurried about a good deal. I passed him in the passage on the first afternoon and he looked euphoric. Confidence must be the watchword at the top. He winked.

'You've actually *worked* with these people, Simon?'

'With Ling. Not ETI.'

'Same thing as far as personalities go. They've bitten off more than they can chew.'

'I suppose so.'

'When our defence document goes out it'll hurt them. It tells our shareholders a few things about Eastern Trading that *their* shareholders will be none too pleased to read! And as for the cash –'

'Yes?'

'Julius's assessment of our real value and of the future of our property – in the inflationary age we're heading for, especially – is going to be a masterpiece! You wait – personally drafted by His Majesty!' James sped happily on his way.

And it was indeed true that, as far as my still inexperienced eye could discern, the Wrench response to the takeover bid was highly convincing. It was trenchant, clear, and unequivocal. 'Stay with us,' Julius said to his shareholders. 'Reject the chance of a quick short-term gain for which you will receive some very over-valued shares in this Oriental concern and some cash whose value is anyway sliding. Stay with us and believe in me; it is I who have made your shares grow inexorably in value in bad times as well as good. Then you will see your investment many times more highly valued than the price – tempting today as it may be – which this bunch of adventurers are offering you.' Wrench was represented, as to bankers, by Vinings; but the defence and the style were those of Julius, and we admired them.

Nevertheless, it was known that ETI had picked up a large number of shares in the market, and their overtures were certainly not going to be rejected by all. But Julius's contacts throughout the City world were excellent. Men who would be advising major shareholders knew him well; and he knew, or reckoned he knew, just what weight each broker's, each banker's advice would carry. The arithmetic of the matter was simple, and the press reported it accurately. The Wrench family, through individuals, family trusts and so forth, owned fifteen per cent of the company (Miranda and Harry, incidentally, each possessing two and a half per cent). Arthur Rivers had acquired no less than thirty-three per cent. The battle was for the minds of those fifty-two per cent-worth of shareholders committed to neither Ling nor Wrench; and to win one third of them would give ETI control. As each day passed after the issue of the ETI document we saw a number of shareholdings pass to the enemy.

'Small fry,' reported James Todd accurately. 'The big boys are sitting back. And they know Julius.' There were, indeed, four or five very large institutional shareholders; and everybody appreciated their power. There was much murmuring in corners, many unreported meetings, some lunches well away from the usual clubs and restaurants. But as the days passed it looked as if the line was holding. Ling had been active among our overseas shareholders but it was noteworthy that ALI – the Bartholomews – were holding firm for Julius. 'Of course,' people said, 'they're very shrewd. And, after all, there's the family connection.'

The line had held for exactly ten days from the issue of the first offer document when two things happened to me which set my pulse racing. First, the morning post brought a brief letter from Miranda. She was not a gifted correspondent, but I was by now, if only to nourish some sort of hope, skilled at reading emotion and affection into neutral words, equivocal phrases. In this letter Miranda thanked me for my 'wonderful, patient understanding' (excellent) and said that she was now definitely coming to London in the second week in February, probably arriving on 12 February. She was planning to stay at Cadogan Square – 'I must, of course, stay with Mummy and Daddy' – and 'I'll try to be in touch.' 'Try!' I didn't care for that. It sounded pathetically lacking in purpose, in resolution. Furthermore, Miranda (since I had scrupulously observed the recent embargo on writing; perhaps her letters were subject to interception? Espionage? My 'patient understanding' gave me a fever) was, of course, unaware of the interview I had had with her father. I reckoned that this last communication and the general situation made it permissible to write, if only in guarded terms. I wrote that I was 'exactly the same as ever – but perhaps more so'. I wrote that I had

had a 'difficult' session with her father – 'on the subject nearest to my heart. I admitted nothing and we parted on non-committal terms.' I also wrote, 'It is very important that you get word to me *within twenty-four hours of return* as to where I can make contact with you. I shall be here, in the flat, alone, every evening from 11 February.'

I knew what a ghastly nail-biting series of hours I was in for, but I had to protect Miranda and it seemed extraordinarily hard for two free adults to arrange to meet privately in London. I posted the letter immediately. It should, without question, reach her well before departure.

The second letter by the same post was in an unfamiliar hand, large, feminine and London postmarked. Overcome by getting one from Miranda, I had already drafted the first version of my reply to my beloved before I opened the second envelope. The letter was signed 'Anthea Puxley'.

> Dear Mr Marlow,
> I wonder if you could lunch next Thursday, 5 February? It would be nice to see you again. We shall hope to see you, and will expect you unless you call me on – (she gave an unfamiliar telephone number). May we say one o'clock at 29 Manners Court?

I looked up Manners Court. It was a block of flats in Bayswater.

So Arthur Rivers was opening up a diversion, a line into the enemy camp; or so I supposed. I had every intention of going. The terms of the invitation made it clear that he thought I would. And when I rang the bell of 29 Manners Court on that Thursday, Rivers opened the door to me. Mrs Puxley had done her stuff, which included being somewhere else. Rivers said, 'Come in, Simon.' He gave me a glass of sherry. The flat was, I guessed, Mrs Puxley's principal abode, used for such purposes by Rivers. Lunch was cold, simple and excellently prepared. Arthur Rivers wasted little time.

'You probably think this surprising. Irregular. I'm going to be very frank with you. The fact is, we think we can do Wrench Holdings – the people who own the business – a lot of good.'

'That's not,' I said pleasantly, 'what the people who own fifteen per cent of it think.'

He nodded. He was as direct as ever.

'Probably not. You may like to know how it is going. We've got forty-four per cent. Julius Wrench has made clear he won't concede. Of course, with forty-four per cent we'll have a lot of influence – directors and so forth. We haven't the slightest interest in that. We want control. We want to have a majority shareholding.'

So much had been clear from the start.

'Getting seven per cent more,' said Rivers, 'is not going to be easy. You know that. Response to our improved offer has been . . . inadequate so far.' They had raised their bid by a number of points, after Julius's first defence; and had accompanied it with a lengthy statistical analysis of the future glories of Eastern Trading Incorporated for anybody lucky enough to be blessed with ETI shares.

Everybody at Wrench, of course, knew the state of battle. Looking Arthur Rivers in the eye was not an easy matter since he was so very expert, himself, at facing down all and sundry with his cold blue gaze. I did my best. I said, 'Why have you asked me to lunch?'

He looked at the smoked salmon on his plate and grunted.

'I don't want to intrude, but there is a rumour going around that you and Miranda Wrench are interested in each other.'

I said nothing, and went on looking at him.

'I expect, if that is so, that you know all about her position. She's been badly treated – I'm talking about money, of course, I know nothing of other things – by her husband's family. Very badly, in my opinion. She's got nothing – nothing except her Wrench shares.'

I hated hearing Miranda discussed in this way by her father's enemy – even if I was, secretly, her father's enemy too – but I had to hear more. I think I kept my face impassive.

'Obviously, she would not, in the ordinary course of events, plan to dispose of those shares. Were she to do so – a two and a half per cent holding is, after all, worth a considerable sum – she would be very rich and entirely independent. She could do as she pleased. Regardless of her father. Regardless of her husband. She might regard this as desirable.'

I still said nothing.

'So might you,' said Arthur Rivers. Nobody could ever have accused him of avoiding the point.

We ate in silence. He sipped a glass of Moselle. He looked at me again. His eyes were, I am sure, hypnotic.

'Of course, it goes without saying that if Miranda sold her shares –'

'I don't expect she's even had the offer document,' I broke in. I betrayed myself, of course, with the interjection. Rivers now knew that I was not Julius's man. He had probably always known.

'That sort of thing can be arranged. No problem. *If* she were to sell her shares, however, you would, I imagine, be blamed. Your position would be challenged, if it had not been already. You might find it easier to resign – at once.'

I looked at him.

'We would look after you – very well. Immediately.'

I played it lightly. But seriously underneath.

'Would you,' I asked with a smile, 'consider sending me to America on a short – attachment?'

'No problem. At once. Duties undefined, stay for up to three months, salary by arrangement. And a good future when you return.' He drank more wine. 'That's not simply a "thank you" for delivering Miranda's shares, by the way. We know you're good.'

'Thank you. Of course, all this has been – entirely hypothetical. I confirm nothing of what you have said. Nor – if things were as you have suggested – do I rate highly my chances of persuading Miranda. She loves her father.'

'Her father is going to lose. It won't make the difference in the longer run. And by – easing – the process she will make herself independent. Give herself a good life. And, of course, anybody she – cares for.'

'Well,' I said, 'I hear you. I hear you. But you're going to need a great deal more than Miranda's shares. And we think you've now got all that you'll get. Even when you go higher. There's great personal confidence in Julius Wrench. In his ability. In his energy. In his integrity. He's trusted as a man. If that were different I've no doubt you'd get what you want.'

'Yes,' said Arthur Rivers, 'if that were different I dare say that we would. Quicker. Of course, ALI might – in certain circumstances – not act out of loyalty to the Wrench connexion. There is also that point.'

But he looked disappointed. He must have hoped for more from me. It was a strange meeting. The quest for treachery on his part, the seething temptation blandly concealed on mine.

The weather was bitterly cold with much fog; February at its early worst. As I walked home from the office that evening, my mind cautiously pawing over Arthur Rivers's remarks, my heart and flesh dominated by pictures of Miranda, due in England so soon, I heard my name called as I started to cross the road at Trafalgar Square. I looked round. At first I could not put a name to the familiar face, clear under the street lights.

'Simon!'

Then I remembered. It was Vivien Baker – my first mentor at Wrench Holdings. Baker, who had crossed Julius and left quickly, whose place I'd filled. Baker who stuttered. Baker who had done such enthusiastic, such unpopular research and analysis into some of the Wrench accounts. I shook his hand. We stood on the busy pavement being jostled.

'How are you? How is WH? You're in the news, aren't you!'

He looked less prosperous but more relaxed than I had known him. I told him that all at the office was 'much as he remembered it', and that it was an exciting time, of course. He seemed surprisingly pleased to see me. Perhaps he simply suffered, still, from curiosity and welcomed the chance to hear a little Wrench gossip in the middle of the takeover battle. He said, 'Why don't we have a drink?' and I found myself walking with him towards a pub in Maiden Lane.

Over several drinks – for Baker seemed in no hurry and something made me feel the contact was ordained – I asked how he thought the Wrench battle was going. After leaving us he had joined a medium-sized firm of stockbrokers.

'Well for Julius Wrench, we think. We can't see Rivers and Ling picking up more than another one or two per cent of the shares.' He cited four huge institutions, one of whose holdings it would be necessary for Ling to acquire. 'And they,' said Baker, 'are pretty solid for Wrench. His financial record is good, and his public image is good. That's important to them – they're that sort of animal. There's never been anything phoney about Julius, none of the sorts of suspicion which could hit the shares or make people change sides. He's a hard, successful man, but he's trusted and he's done a lot for charity. For the country, come to that. People say he'll get a knighthood – you probably know.'

I didn't, but the rumour was widely believed. It was, I knew, true that Julius's reputation was his trump card. It was holding his troops in line. Baker must, surely, resent his own cavalier, even brutal treatment by Wrench, but he clearly still admired him. He went on.

'If Julius's name had any marks against it you can be sure Arthur Rivers, by now, would have seen they were widely known. It's what Ling needs and what he won't get. Your remaining shareholders aren't going to give. We're advising clients accordingly.'

'I suppose Rivers and Ling can raise the bid again. They've got time.'

Baker doubted it. He ordered more drinks. I said, casually, 'I gather before you left us you were doing some historical research.'

'Oh that,' he said with well-disguised bitterness. 'Yes, I thought it would help. I still do. Julius was so confident about our foreign investors – I wasn't so sure. It hadn't been properly analysed. He may feel rather differently now.' Baker laughed sourly. 'Ling!' he said.

'You put in a lot of work on it, didn't you?'

'I did indeed – and what did I find but that Julius himself had done exactly the same sums. I found some scrappy workings in his very evident hand – they'd somehow got lodged in one of the files and he'd made the same analysis as I had – assessment of exactly what each overseas investor had meant to us in terms of profit. Rather a difficult thing to define and assess, but worth it, I thought. And he must have thought so too, once. But instead of saying, "Interesting, Vivien, I had the same idea once," he froze me out.'

We talked again of how the battle was going.

'Well,' I said, smiling, 'I'm not sure I'd give your clients exactly the same advice as you.' I left him with his drink, looking puzzled.

That same evening I telephoned Desmond Dillon, and arranged to meet him next day. I wanted to keep every available minute free after Miranda's arrival, and I wanted to see Desmond. I spent the day thinking once again of what Baker had told me, and for the hundredth time looking at figures noted from my earlier researches in the accounts of long ago. Desmond and I had a drink together in the same pub. Once again I marvelled at how I regarded him, effortlessly, as a contemporary. He had unique charm, for all ages and both sexes. It was quite near the office so there was always a chance of seeing a colleague there, but Baker had been a 'natural', an unsuspicious contact from old days, and Desmond, I was certain, had a sort of magic which enabled him to fit quietly into any background. I had fixed a later hour, after the time when people from nearby offices sometimes had a drink before going home. The pub wasn't crowded and we found a quiet corner. I reminded Desmond of earlier conversations we'd had. I asked him certain questions. He answered, as usual, with a smile, with caution, without drama; but he was explicit and I committed what he said to memory.

'And at that moment,' said Marlow, 'I began to see it all.'

Most unusually, he attracted the attention of the Auberge waiter and ordered a cognac for himself as well as another for John. His voice was even quieter than usual. 'Yes,' he said, 'I began to see it all.'

Marlow suggested another dinner the very next evening, and John, with pleasure, agreed. He had reached a point in his narration, he seemed to imply, when the sequence must be interrupted as little as possible. John guessed, too, that he was to hear of Miranda's visit and that it would not be entirely easy to describe.

But when Marlow resumed his account he said at once that Miranda had not arrived for several days. He had, of course, lived on tenterhooks, and ultimately had had word that she would be in London from about 15 February. He made it clear how feverishly he was longing for her presence, but he also remarked, in a matter-of-fact sort of way, that after his talks with Baker and Dillon (of whose exact import he was, deliberately it seemed, keeping John somewhat in the dark) there had been 'a good deal to do'.

'I had to see Arthur Rivers again,' said Marlow, perhaps – despite his resolutely neutral, objective monotone – finding it pleasurable to mystify a little, 'I had to see him and keep in touch.

I told Arthur that there might be ways in which I could be useful, and that if this were so it would mean that I could be very useful indeed. He broke in to remind me of Miranda's shareholding. I said, again, that I doubted anybody's power to influence that matter. 'But,' I said, 'I will do what I can,' and he nodded, pleased. By the time that we parted (Marlow did not explain where this particular meeting with Rivers took place. It must have been clandestine and John could not envisage it) 'by that time, without matters being made too tastelessly explicit, we understood each other. I was a fully paid-up traitor to Wrench Holdings. I was in the camp of Arthur Rivers and Jimmy Ling. If they failed, I was likely to fall with them. If I did nothing to deliver, they would have no compunction in betraying my betrayal. Apart from them I had, probably, nowhere else to go.

When I left Rivers, that time, I said, 'Miranda is due here in a few days.'

'I have heard so.'

'I've got to resign from Wrench. You can see that. For more than one – or two – reasons.'

He acknowledged it. 'Timing will matter.' We discussed that also.

Miranda arrived in London on 15 February. A Sunday. I knew that for certain from Harry, whom I met walking through the City two days before. He seemed less at ease to see me than hitherto, his smile a little clouded and unsure. He must obviously, I realized, have been told by his parents of their suspicions in respect of Miranda and myself. I could not believe that he would feel about it as they did, but I was certainly not going to explore that. My line with Julius had been flat denial and so it must be, for the while, even with my dearest friend. Harry said, 'Well! How's my father? At home he's simply marvellous. I had dinner at Cadogan Square last night. He was completely relaxed. You'd never think he had a battle like this on his hands. And when I said a word about it after dinner, you never heard anyone so cool. He talked about it, absolutely frank, as if it were all happening to third parties. Objective. Dispassionate. What's more, he didn't talk as if I was his son. I've never admired him more.'

'He's very well in command of events, I think.'

'He certainly is! Most of the City – to say nothing of his family and his personal friends, who between them tot up a lot of shares – are right behind him. And Ling is hell. So is Rivers. I know he's a tough, able man but I think he's pretty beastly.'

I said nothing. Harry said, in a slightly embarrassed way, 'You probably know Miranda's due here any minute. Day after tomorrow, in fact. Breakfast time.'

'I didn't know.'

'Staying at Cadogan Square,' said Harry rapidly, 'lovely to see her again.' We said goodbye.

That Sunday I sat throughout the evening by my telephone. It did not ring. The following day – 16 February – I thought it reasonable to hope for some word. It did not come. I spent the whole evening at home, hour after tormenting hour, waiting for a telephone call which did not come. Tuesday was similar. I decided I could stand this no longer. Next morning I telephoned Harry at his office. After all, I reflected, it was the natural, the innocent thing to do.

'Harry,' I said, 'you told me Miranda was coming over. I can't remember when –'

'She's here.'

'I thought it would be rather nice if the three of us lunched somewhere together. I've not seen her for ages.'

'Well,' said Harry, uncertain, 'I'm sure she'd – like – to see you, Simon. She's lunching with me today.' He named a City restaurant.

'Could you join us?' he said.

I lied. I said, 'No – not today.' I sounded casual. Then I said, 'Just a minute – I'm lunching near there – and early. Could I look in and have a cup of coffee with you? After your lunch? It would be lovely.' I was unemphatic, relaxed. I did it well. Harry sounded relieved, and we left it like that.

I went into a pub where I felt tolerably sure of not seeing

a soul I knew. I could not eat, but drank a double whisky. I timed my arrival at Harry's restaurant exactly – two-twenty. I went through swing doors looking around me vaguely. I saw them, not far from the door, waved, went over, and said, 'Miranda!' pecking her cheek; and turned to Harry saying, 'Sorry I couldn't lunch, I'd have loved it and have had a bad and boring one instead. When did you arrive, Miranda?'

She didn't look at me as she said, 'On Sunday.' Harry was fussing about getting their bill. Unbelievably – providentially – he said, 'Have some coffee with us. But I've got to leave in a minute. I've got a two-forty-five meeting.'

'I must be on my way, too, I suppose,' said Miranda. 'Hair appointment.'

'I'll walk you to a taxi after we've had a cup of coffee,' I said lightly. Harry said to her, 'I'm coming round to Cadogan Square this evening.' He looked less than happy, but he left.

I looked at Miranda. I had made arrangements for the afternoon. For once my presence at Wrench Holdings would not be missed.

'Miranda, we must talk.'

'Yes, of course, soon – soon but not here.'

'No, not here. We will find a taxi.'

'Darling, Harry reckons we're – like, perhaps, we are to each other. He asked me. I said I wasn't sure, but that I'm unhappy, as he knows. He told me –'

'What?'

'That of course he hopes I leave Alec. Mummy and Daddy will be upset but they'll get over it. He hates to see me miserable.'

'Bless him! Of course he feels like that.'

'But, darling Simon, he – I hate saying this –'

'Out with it.'

'He thinks it would be an awful mistake – you and me –'

'Why?'

'He reckons Daddy – and Mummy, I suppose – will always think of it as a betrayal. And they'll say, it's utterly awful, of course, but they'll say you've got nothing, you're after my money, you're on the make.'

'Harry must know that's not true.'

Miranda sighed. 'I suppose so. But – Harry's one of us, you know, devoted though he is to you. He can't help seeing things with a sort of – cynicism – when it comes to money. He just said, "It would be a mistake, you know. A mistake."' She sighed again.

I repeated, 'We will find a taxi.'

'Darling, I must go, I've an appointment –'

'We will cancel the appointment.'

'Oh dear, that will look very odd! Darling, very soon, I promise –'

'You will not keep your hair appointment. There's a lot to say and to do. And it will not wait.' I felt calm and totally in command. I was unsurprised when, after a second's hesitation, Miranda said, 'All right.'

We walked along the crowded City pavement. It was, I remember, beginning to rain. Somebody said, 'Hello, Miranda, been looking up Harry, have you?' and she said, 'Oh, hello, Charlie.' It was, I recognized, Charlie Branson, the Wrench intimate and toady. I could not avoid being involved. Miranda had taken my arm. She said, 'Harry told Simon, here, to have coffee with us, and, thank heaven, he's going to find a taxi for me. You know Simon Marlow, don't you?'

Branson said he did. He looked at me, then at Miranda, then back again with what can only be described as a leer. Most disagreeable.

'Don't get wet, Charlie!' Miranda's tone was light. She did it well. 'Come on, Simon, find me a taxi or a tube station or something.' We went on our way.

Two hours later we looked at each other very steadily and I took her hands. We were naked, in my flat. She was sitting on my bed, murmuring that she must go. Nothing had changed. I knew that nothing ever would.

'Miranda, if you are sufficiently serious, if you care, then you simply must have the guts to see this through, to make the break. And, just at the moment, that is the most important thing in both our lives.'

'I know. But Simon, my beloved, you will be out of the firm, out of a job, you will have ruined yourself –'

'Nonsense. I shall get another job. And, anyway, I intend to leave Wrench Holdings quite soon. Perhaps not quite immediately, but soon.'

She shrugged her shoulders. 'I shall have no money. We might manage, of course, but you have nothing but what you earn, they'd stop –'

'Listen, Miranda, darling, that is all nonsense too. You say you have "no money". You are, in fact, a very rich woman. You own a large number of shares in your father's company.'

'You know I couldn't sell them. Especially now!'

'Especially now you could. Those shares could be disposed of immediately – and very profitably.'

'But Daddy would go mad – it would completely let him down – it would stab him in the back –'

'Miranda, my sweet love, I know that is your first thought, but believe me your father isn't going to win this battle he's in. Whatever you do with your shares, he's going to *lose* it. Your making yourself independent won't affect the issue.'

'If he's going to lose,' said Miranda slowly, 'presumably it comes to the same in the end. If his company is taken over we can all sell our shares anyway!'

'Probably for a great deal less. And that is going to take time. If you want to be independent, to snap your fingers at your beastly husband and at the world – including your father, who will oppose you coming to me with every breath in his body – if you want that, then you have a way of getting it. You can say the word and sell your shares. The whole thing can be done in a flash.'

'Darling – it's not only money –'

'Of course it's not. That's a tiny part of it. I am just telling you that it's not a problem.'

'I can't understand – even about the money – I'm pretty hopeless, I don't know what I've got . . .' I told her. I told her the size of her shareholding, and the price ETI would pay. Immediately. I wrote it down for her on a piece of paper and she looked at the figures disbelievingly.

'Take that piece of paper away and look at it again. It may strengthen you, my love. Only decide when you are sure. You are rich. You can do what you wish.' At the bottom of the paper I wrote, 'I adore you. These ridiculous figures are nothing. You, flesh and blood, are all.'

She laughed and put the paper in her bag. She was almost restored. 'It's as Harry says, they will be sure you wanted me for my money, Simon. They will never forgive you.'

I felt strong, exultant, victorious. 'Let them say!' I quoted. 'I don't believe you need go quite yet,' I added. I took her in my arms again.

Later, Miranda said, 'I've got some terribly hard thinking to do in a very short time.'

'You've got several weeks.'

'Less than I thought; Alec's European trip' (I loathed hearing her mention his name but it was unavoidable) 'is now only going to last a few days. He's coming over on 23 February – under a week away. He even talks about me going to Frankfurt with him –'

'You can't! Unthinkable!'

'Of course not. But after this trip's over – before he flies home – I think I must go back to America.'

'Miranda, you're mad! Why go back to the States? Why not make the break here?'

She stroked my face. 'I've made the break, my love. But I've some things to tidy up over there. I've got some support, believe me. Alec's sister is a wonderful person. She understands. I've got some splendid friends over there. But I can't send Alec back, just having sort of made the break, as you call it, while we're both on our travels, living out of suitcases. And in a way I don't want to do it from my parents' home here. In a way, you see, I'm making a break with them too. It's got to be, and be seen, as my own, unforced decision. It's got to be deliberate, independent. Believe me.' She promised, as she left me, that within weeks, when both had returned to America, she would make it utterly clear to her husband that she was leaving him for ever. She would explain to her parents that her marriage was a sham. She would come, then, to me. And, meanwhile, we made another delicious assignation. She was, after all, leaving London again in about a week.

That evening I telephoned Mrs Puxley, at the number she had given on her luncheon invitation. I recognized her answering voice.

'Mrs Puxley, this is Simon Marlow. I wonder if you have any idea where I could contact Arthur Rivers? I'm not sure –'

She said, 'Please hold on a minute.' One minute later, Arthur Rivers said, 'Well, Simon, what can I do for you?'

I felt light-hearted. 'I think, Arthur,' I said, 'it's more a question of what I can do for you.'

12

'I will always,' said Marlow, 'remember 23 February 1968. It was when I made my own break. Miranda had stolen an hour with me the previous day. She reiterated her promise. We were, she said, now within weeks of the storm which would, ultimately, blow us together. She was nervous, determined to return to America in a few days' time as arranged. Bartholomew was flying direct from Frankfurt on the last day of the month, she said. She promised to bear in mind what I'd said about her shares in Wrench Holdings, her ability to become independent; not only rich (she was already that on paper), but able to use her riches to help us both towards happiness. 'Give me a few days away from Father,' she said. 'I can't see it straight while I'm here in London. I've lost that little piece of paper you wrote it all out on but I think I've got it clear in my mind. And if I decide to sell – to take the plunge – you mean *you* can fix it? Without Father stopping you?'

'Certainly. Your share certificate is at your bank here in London. You told me so. Send me a telegram and I will at once post this letter.' She had signed a letter already, telling the bank to send the share certificate to me. I would do the rest.

'I trust you completely, darling. I want to think it out a few days longer, away from London.'

'I understand. And if you decide the other way it will make not the smallest difference. I will destroy this letter, and in the end, as you said yourself, your shares will turn into money without any revolution against your father having been necessary!' I laughed. 'It's not very important,' I said. 'All that matters is that you leave Bartholomew and come to me.'

'Bless you for being so understanding.'

Later she said, 'Simon, why do you have to leave Wrench Holdings? After all, the decision will be mine. I'll make it clear you've been absolutely –'

I cut in. 'Miranda, my love, I can have no future there now. When you first tell your parents you're leaving your husband and asking for a divorce, and that you intend to marry me, they are bound to regard it as a betrayal by me. Your father, too, will look on me not only as a traitor but a liar. I told him there was nothing between us.'

'Well, you had to! Anybody would understand that!'

'No. Believe me, I must leave, my position would be impossible.'

'I feel I've burned your boats,' she said. 'When are you going to tell them?'

'Next Thursday. I want you to have left England. Then I shall resign from Wrench Holdings.' She was flying on the Wednesday.

And the following Thursday I asked for an interview with Julius. I was determined on it. A chapter must end. I saw him at four o'clock. I intended to tell him that I wanted new experience, fresh fields; that I'd always be grateful for what the Wrench companies had done for me. I knew my resignation would be greeted with suspicion but the important thing was to break clear. I couldn't breathe in the Wrench building any more. My understanding with Miranda made it impossible.

To say nothing of Rivers.

Julius Wrench was standing up looking out of the window when I came in. He turned round, stood and stared at me, no languid smile, no 'Well, Simon?' No word. I said, inanely, 'Thank you for seeing me at a time when you've got so much on, Julius.'

He still said nothing. I plunged in.

'I want to say that I feel I must leave Wrench Holdings,

Julius. You've always been enormously helpful to me, you got me started, but I feel the need for a change, for new –'

He said softly, 'So that's it.'

I gave a poor attempt at an interrogative smile. Julius said, 'So that's it! You try to get her to sell her father down the river. You see her safely off to America. I suppose you're fixed up with Rivers. And now you clear your messy little book by getting out of here.'

'I don't understand you.'

'Of course you do. You need more practice at lying, that's all. I knew perfectly well how you lied to me about Miranda the other evening. I didn't, of course, then know the depths little jumped-up paupers like you can reach.' He suddenly threw a crumpled ball of paper at me and said, 'Catch,' with a sort of snarl. I caught it instinctively and straightened it out. It was the piece of paper I had given Miranda. She must have left it in her room or on a table where it had caught some malicious eye (I suspected Charlie Branson).

I felt short of breath. 'Julius, Miranda asked me about her shareholding. I tried to explain it. She asked me what could be realized by a sale, during this take-over battle. I explained that too. That's hardly a crime.'

'"These ridiculous figures are nothing,"' quoted Julius, '"I adore you". Don't treat me as a fool, you bloody little swine.' He spoke very quietly. 'Get out!' he said.

I shrugged my shoulders. The deed was done, and from his point of view nothing he had said or thought was unfair. Inside, I longed to fight back at him. I would have loved, at that moment, to ask him if he remembered his own treatment of Henry Kinzel, to inspect some other parts of his conscience. But it was not yet time for that. I had done what I had entered the room to do. I had severed my connexion with Wrench Holdings. For ever.

I only had to wait ten days for Miranda's first letter. She told me that her husband had 'taken it very badly, I'm afraid'. She was staying with a friend in Virginia – as long as she liked – and it was necessary to stay for a few more weeks, at least, in America while she dealt with lawyers and the hideous preliminaries of an acrimonious and expensive matrimonial case.

'As to the money,' she wrote, 'I really don't think I can, at the same time, do what you suggested. I haven't finally decided yet, but you see, I think *in the end* Daddy and Mummy will come round to see I've had to do what I've done. And I'm sure *in the end* they'll come round to you – to us – as well. But if I seem to Daddy to have turned against him in this take-over business *as well* it will make it many times harder to make peace.'

She had, she said, written to her parents, trying to explain. I, of course, knew that it would come to them as no surprise. I wrote back to her address in Virginia. I said that her letter made me entirely happy, and that I understood it all. I would, I said, next see her in America! I told her I had left her father's company, as promised, and that my new job would probably take me soon to the United States. I told her that things between Julius and myself were, at the moment, bad. I felt supremely happy at this time. Some of the road I had to tread was rough, but I enjoyed the direction and I was confident of the goal. I was, of course, rather wretched at the thought that Harry, inevitably, would take the Wrench line against me. But Miranda's love made up for that and he would, I was sure, come round in the end.

Arthur Rivers had acknowledged my message sent on the evening of 26 February – 'I have resigned from Wrench Holdings and would be grateful for a talk' – but he had to be away from London for several days and it was not until 8 March, when I had already received Miranda's letter, that he asked me to have dinner with him. I had been busy in the meantime. I had dinner and a very long conversation with Desmond Dillon. I went once to Shepherd Market and spent two hours there. I went for a weekend to Penterton.

Rivers's invitation was not conveyed in a way which suggested he thought I might have a prior engagement. I was, it was clear, already a dependent, an employee. It was a Monday.

'Dinner tonight, Simon. Half-past eight.' He mentioned a good restaurant in Chelsea. He had, I reflected, no particular reason now to refrain from advertising our meetings. The restaurant was popular and it was not impossible that somebody there might recognize both of us. By now I was quite widely known in the world with which Wrench Holdings dealt, and a lot of it dined in expensive places like this.

Rivers's general manner, although quietly courteous as ever, was authoritative. He said softly, 'I said we'd look after you. We will – on conditions, of course. But we haven't yet got Miranda's shares.'

'I don't think you will.' I told him how that matter stood. He stared at me.

'You implied, on the telephone, that you might – in spite of that or as well as that – have some, shall we say useful, suggestions to make? I think they're going to be – necessary.'

'Yes,' I said, 'I think I have.' And then we talked, quietly and with complete understanding, for a long time. Near the end of our conversation he said,

'I'm not sure we need that last – intervention. I can't see it's necessary. The effect will be produced without it.'

'It's necessary to me,' I said. 'I've got a job to do.'

I took a taxi home afterwards feeling exhausted. I was drained of power. Rivers now knew what I knew. That night, I felt really appalling pain in the chest; an attack, I supposed, of my usual indigestion, but as cruel as can be imagined. I slept little.

The battle for the body of Wrench Holdings was reaching its climax.

ETI had improved their offer on 1 March. Within days it was clear that the Wrench shareholders who had withstood earlier approaches were still unsatisfied. The financial pages of the newspapers, without exception, regarded the Wrench defence as brilliant and justified. The major shareholding institutions who now held the only key to a Ling victory (apart, of course, from the family) were praised by City correspondents for their shrewdness in staying with Julius Wrench and preferring his proven skill, his assurances about the company's future, which had so often been justified in the past, to the meretricious attractions of some potentially volatile shares drawing both sparkle and vulnerability from the Far East market – accompanied though the latter would be by a good deal of cash. I discovered afterwards that Julius had persuaded the Bartholomews to hold all their ALI shares, in spite of the family's fury with Miranda and, it might be presumed, disenchantment with the Wrench connexion. Julius rang Bartholomew senior in New York often. On this occasion he spoke to reinforce his confidence that the Wrench defence made it good business to hold on – he knew Bartholomew believed in him. 'And as to our family troubles,' I gathered he said, or something like it, 'I'm sure she'll see sense. I've sacked the wretched little pipsqueak who caused the trouble. She's being a fool, Alex, but give her time. Give it time.' ALI, so far, was not succumbing to the Ling approach.

One paper headlined, 'KING JULIUS THE INVINCIBLE'. A gossip columnist in one of the Sundays revived speculation about a Wrench knighthood in the next Birthday Honours, suggesting that this might have happened already except for the take-over battle; an honour at such a time would suggest government partiality, for rumours had abounded before the formal opening of Ling's campaign. The mood at Covent Garden was, I gathered from friends, euphoric. I saw, of course, nothing of Harry. I lay very low.

On 15 March, I reported to the ETI offices in Moorgate. That same afternoon Arthur Rivers and I appeared at Wrench Holdings at Covent Garden. The appointment had been made by Arthur with great skill as to security, and although we went there openly in an ETI car at four o'clock there were no press men around and we were met by a discreet James Todd at the front entrance. He smiled politely and, I thought, complacently at Arthur Rivers. He clearly thought he was receiving the negotiators of a surrender. He then looked further and saw me and appeared so astonished that he could not at first make the connexion.

'Simon, I'm afraid . . .'

Rivers marched into the lift. 'Marlow's with me,' was all he said. We ascended in silence to Julius's office. James avoided my eye, which was just as well. Julius's principal secretary, an efficient, pretty girl called Helen Vigor, also gave me raised eyebrows and an expression of well-registered mock dismay. All she said was, 'One moment, Mr Rivers,' and disappeared inside. Arthur stood, impassive. It was quarter past four exactly.

After slightly longer than protocol would normally dictate, Helen emerged.

'Mr Rivers, Mr Wrench would like to see you alone for a moment. He didn't realize you would have anybody with you.'

'He couldn't have,' said Arthur. 'I didn't tell him.' He said it very quietly and without emphasis; but with such confident force that one felt the ripples through the office. If this were capitulation, I imagined James Todd thinking, it was beginning in a curious way.

Arthur told me afterwards what went on, and I could without difficulty reconstruct the scene. He walked into Julius's office and found him obviously angry – so angry that he was, Arthur said, less controlled than he had ever seen him. This first, predictable, reaction to my own presence with Arthur was welcome to the latter. Julius said, 'Arthur, I was happy to have a very private meeting, as you suggested. I would never have agreed, and I decline now, to have a meeting attended by an ex-employee of mine, a very disloyal ex-employee of mine, young, treacherous and despicable. He has nothing to do with the level of business you and I are concerned with. I don't know what he does for you and I don't care. I'm not having him in this room.'

Arthur said, 'I have two people whose contributions I think it essential you hear. One is Simon Marlow. The other is not an employee of mine, but you must be told what he, too, has to say. Believe me, I want you to have that chance. If you won't I shall go away and events can take their course.' They glared at each other for a long minute.

'Very well,' said Julius at last, 'let them!' But there was a note of uncertainty in his voice. Arthur just looked at him and shook his head gently once or twice.

'I only ask you to listen. These men have something it is in your interest to hear. I assure you that's true.'

Julius made a shrugging gesture. Without waiting for him to speak to his secretary, Arthur moved to the door, opened it and said, 'Will you come in, Simon?' He was a round ahead. I felt a distinct sinking of the stomach as I walked into that room. Arthur let me go past and spoke directly to Helen Vigor, telling her that he was expecting somebody else at half past four, and would she inform us at once when he arrived. The Rivers authority was working well. Helen nodded quite amicably, although I doubt if she'd accepted an instruction from anyone but Julius since she first came to work at Wrench Holdings.

Julius was sitting in a large fawn-coloured leather armchair. Other, matching, armchairs were grouped symmetrically round a low, rectangular glass-topped table. Julius made no gesture and ignored me. Arthur and I took chairs next to each other on Julius's right.

Arthur sat silent, looking attentively at Julius. After a little Julius said, 'You asked for this meeting. You said you wanted it to be confidential, personal. What do you suggest we talk about?' His old languid, half-mocking manner was almost restored.

Arthur said in a very quiet voice, 'I've got a request. It's a very simple one. As you know, we have secured a large holding in Wrench. About forty-six per cent.'

'Forty-five and a half. You've picked up virtually nothing from your latest bid.'

'Forty-five and a half. My suggestion is that you advise shareholders now to accept our terms. That you concede defeat.'

Julius stared at him. Nobody ever under-estimated Arthur Rivers.

'And why do you suggest I should do that? I have every confidence that my shareholders – quite apart from my own family – entirely support my resolve to keep control of this company. If you think I'm wrong you'd better offer them more, hadn't you?'

'No,' said Arthur, 'we don't propose to do that. But I have certain information which, if made public, must so affect confidence in your company that large numbers of shares would, I am sure you will soon agree, be bought very easily. Our present offer will, in such circumstances, look remarkably generous.'

'Oh, it's blackmail of some sort, is it?' said Julius, his drawl exaggerated, his eyes narrow. 'Blackmail! Is that why we've brought the servants along, to produce some sort of scurrilous nonsense ferreted out which can be made to sound damaging?' He shot me a look of hatred. 'I begin to see, Arthur,' said Julius, 'but I would hardly have thought it of you. And it won't work.'

'I would like Marlow to talk for a bit now, Julius.'

'All right,' said Julius. 'Let's hear him. Provided you let me kick him out afterwards, and then change my shoes.'

Arthur ignored this and nodded to me. I started to talk. I had prepared myself well. As I talked, Julius's expression changed from sneering contempt to incredulity. Then incredulity gave way to intense, concentrated attention.

*

'It all began,' I said, 'when foreign investors first started to put money into Wrench Holdings in a big way. Certain profit was directly – and perfectly legally – attributable to the company on account of these transactions. Such profit fluctuated, of course. But it was, over the years, perfectly possible for a foreign investor to say, "We have placed such and such funds in Wrench Holdings. We have earned a return on our money. Additionally, our money has benefited yourselves, your company, Wrench Holdings."

'This benefit to the company, this part of the company profits attributable to overseas investors, can be broken down. Any particular investor has been responsible, in a given year, for a certain element of your profits. To calculate that is not easy, but it is perfectly possible. Vivien Baker did it. Investors themselves, given the data, could do it.'

Julius made an impatient gesture.

'The other person who did it was you, and the calculation had to be made and accepted. Because the object of certain investors – beside making a perfectly proper return on their capital – was to support, through you, certain institutions in this country without being known to do so.

'It was, really, very simple. It still is. The Soviet Union – and certain Warsaw Pact countries co-ordinated and directed, in this respect, by the Soviet Union – made large investments in Wrench Holdings, through the medium of their state banks. The condition of making these investments – which were, of course, wholly attractive to your company in simple, overt, commercial terms – was that exactly half the profit accruing to the company arising from the investments should be given to certain causes, certain organizations. All heavily, therefore, subsidized by the Soviet Union because their line of conduct, or pressure, however apparently innocent or idealistic, could be guided towards objects which were, or are, currently, tactical objects of Soviet policy.' All this could have sounded laboured, but I had rehearsed it, briefed Rivers exactly. The third man in the room, Julius Wrench, understood all right.

I added, 'And all these organizations, of course, being supported by numbers of innocent and well-meaning people ignorant of this fact of Soviet backing, and ignoring or choosing to ignore the reasons for it.

'The medium you used was the list of charities and causes supported by the company. A number of these were entirely orthodox. But a certain number – ranging between fifteen and eleven to be exact, depending on the year – were of the kind I've just mentioned. The contributions to them from Wrench Holdings have surprised a few of your shareholders, but you've said you support the Board in an even-handed, broad-minded approach to these matters. They've surprised a few of your colleagues, but you've told them the same; and you've kept the list entirely in your hands. Nobody challenges you on your Board.'

Julius sat as if turned to stone.

'These latter contributions can be shown, over many years, to correspond exactly to fifty per cent of the profit attributable to the company by reason of the investments made by the state banks of the four Warsaw Pact countries who have invested in you: the Soviet Union, East Germany, Romania and Czechoslovakia. What you have done, in effect, has been, for a very long time, to launder Eastern Bloc money and pass it to "front" organizations here. For their source of funds to be known destroys the credibility of a "front" organization. That is why they need to find a laundryman. They found one in you.

'All this needs, of course, no ideological commitment. It is perfectly good business. It has expanded the company to much greater size. It was of personal advantage to you – not only because of the immense expansion in your company from which you benefited both directly and indirectly, but because you were able to come to very profitable terms. You went on the payroll of all these organizations as a consultant. You drew – I don't know exactly how much; in today's money, I guess it's about four thousand a year, from some fifteen organizations. It was absurdly easy. Each of them has a lot of employees. Each of them received from Wrench Holdings on average, say, twenty thousand pounds yearly; this represented, in aggregate, fifty per cent of the profit you made from their paymaster. You got your cut by way of consultancy fee. Probably sixty thousand a year – earned income. Not much by your standards, but very useful petty cash even after tax. The real commercial motive, however, was the expansion of your company which these investments helped to happen. Still, the personal *douceur* must have been welcome. Especially in your early days, and you were always greedy. It looks absolutely undetectable. After all, one could construct all sorts of odd relationships between two runs of figures. The fact that you gave to a particular bunch of nominated organizations exactly half the profit you made out of Eastern Bloc investors – no more, no less, each year – could be coincidence. And you calculated on even that coincidence never striking the eye, since the profits were so hard to isolate and quantify.

'But you were let down by three things. First, the extraordinary quality of the bureaucratic mind in Communist countries. Your Eastern-Bloc investors didn't trust you. They were getting a perfectly good return on their money, but they still didn't trust you. They wanted proof – proof that exactly half the profit *you* were making out of them would, in fact, go to the people they wanted. They were terrified that you might make some small uncovenanted benefit. And although these sums weren't large in terms of the whole balance sheet of Wrench Holdings, they were determined to have an accounting – each year. You gave them that yourself. You did that homework. You managed to convince them – each year. But you didn't always destroy your homework with enough care, and one or two people, in the early days, were not entirely loyal to you and thought others should see certain pieces of paper they couldn't understand.

'Then, one day, Vivien Baker started on the same track.

But his motives were pure, of course. He wanted to help the company with a useful piece of analysis. He found your workings. He didn't put two and two together. He was nowhere near the truth, and, of course, you quickly sacked him.

'The second thing you ought to know – and I have it on the authority of an acquaintance who works with them that I may say this, indeed should say this – is that the security services have, for some time, been taking a very keen interest in this business of how money reaches its planned destination from the Soviet Bloc without people knowing. They think they're on to something. They're approaching it, of course, from a different end. But I don't think your own operations will escape official investigation for ever.' (I knew this, of course, from Desmond Dillon.)

'Red gold!' said Julius Wrench with a sneer. 'This is cheap melodrama with a vengeance! And where the hell is there any proof of anything except the extraordinary imaginings of this vicious little twerp?' He was shaking all over, convulsed with a mixture of emotions I could not dissect. Rage was certainly one. But I thought and hoped fear was another.

Arthur Rivers looked at him. Then he looked at me. I resumed as if there had been no interruption.

'The third factor which let you down –' At that moment the buzzer went on Julius's desk. He looked at it. It went again. He crossed to the desk and grunted 'No' at the machine. Helen Vigor's voice said something. Arthur Rivers inclined an ear. I had heard what I wanted to hear.

'The third factor,' I said, 'is waiting now outside your door.'

Waldo Price's entrance into Julius's office was not as startling as I feared it might be, but it had its own drama. I did not want the tension which my denunciation had by now created to be reduced by any element of farce. I had had a very long talk with Waldo, and impressed upon him the nature of his part. And I had put my conclusions together with his own.

He did not let me down, although I could not suppress the repulsion he always aroused in me. He was dressed respectably in an old flannel suit. He wore a tie. He had shaved. I caught, inevitably, a strong whiff of alcohol, probably brandy, as he passed my chair and moved on Julius with outstretched hand, but his voice and walk were steady and he carried himself with dignity. His Welsh blood rejoiced in the drama of the occasion, the sense of tragedy. He was, without doubt, enjoying himself a great deal.

'How do you do, Mr Wrench? How do you do? Mr Rivers asked me to come here, to bear witness, I think one might say.'

Julius took his hand in a stupefied way. I could see that his nostrils had caught the brandy fumes, and he looked disbelieving and puzzled.

'I don't know who you are,' he said.

'My name is Waldo Price,' said Waldo. 'I know, of course, who *you* are, Mr Wrench, although we have never met. At one time you were the trusted associate of the man I loved best in the world, Henry Kinzel.'

Julius was standing, as was Waldo. He said, 'Henry Kinzel! Well – what has that got to do with this business? Rivers, why have you asked this person here?'

'Let me speak for Mr Rivers,' said Waldo, happily taking the floor, so to speak. 'Let me justify my own presence. May I sit?' He settled himself in an armchair and gazed at Julius.

'Mr Wrench, before Henry Kinzel died he entrusted me with certain confidences. He explained to me, in particular, what had passed between you in the world of commerce, of which I know little.'

'I'm sure of it,' said Julius disagreeably, 'and I doubt whether you understand a word. I doubt, furthermore, whether you had anything but a one-sided account. But it's of no consequence now, and I don't know why you're here.'

'Henry Kinzel believed that you cheated him of what was rightly his.'

'Nonsense! There are laws in this country, and if a man feels defrauded he can invoke them.'

'I am only telling you what Henry believed. He believed that you intrigued and lied to obtain control of that which he had created. He knew that you were the source of unfounded rumours and vile whisperings that brought even his patriotism into question.

'This latter conspiracy of yours against Henry Kinzel has a peculiar irony. For he also, although only seeing part and guessing part, was discovering what you were, yourself, about – what you were, in part, doing with the power you had secured. You were attracting investment from Communist governments in return for passing funds to certain wretched organizations in this country, innocent in name, malign in purpose, which these enemies of ours – for such they are – had penetrated, mastered, and wished financially to support.' Waldo was having a splendid time.

'We have heard this unfounded accusation already this afternoon,' said Julius. His voice was by now again steady, 'and do you think that from the start I didn't know that this little rat,' he stabbed a finger at me, 'was poking about in the past, to see how he could put his trumped-up case together?'

I had to intervene. 'I'm sure you knew.' I said. 'Of course, it would have been their duty to tell you, wouldn't it.' I had worked that one out, and realized that Julius had decided – perhaps been instructed – that it was nevertheless better to keep me on. For a while. But my early enquiries from particular 'charities' must immediately have been reported, although he may have been simply puzzled by them at first. Julius looked levelly at Waldo. 'Have you anything else to say? If not, I suggest you go.'

'I was asked simply to bear witness,' replied Waldo, 'to the fact that your late employer, Henry Kinzel, had guessed what you were up to – besides cheating him of his life's work. Some people were still loyal to that good man. He was on your scent. He learned of your devious calculations. And it was his guess which led, I understand, to the charges which have been made against you, chapter and verse, in this room today.'

Julius was putting up an excellent performance. Waldo, of course, had contributed nothing which I had not already thrown at Julius, and his contribution might have been useless, even an anti-climax. But I was watching the handsome Wrench face closely and had seen what I wanted – the flicker of panic as well as puzzlement which had moved behind his eyes when Henry Kinzel's name was first introduced: that was the new element, that was the spear that Waldo had carried to plunge into the wounded beast. It might be a small spear, but I felt an exalted certainty, a certainty owing little to logic, that Julius could find it the final, lethal prick: to know that the man he had wronged had found him and exposed him from beyond the grave. I was satisfied that we had been right to bring in Waldo.

Arthur Rivers now spoke. 'The rest of this is likely to be a business talk. I think, Mr Price, it would be right for you to leave us. Marlow works with me and I want him to stay.'

Waldo got up, rather disappointed, and said, 'Thank you!' He left, and we heard some loud farewells and laughter from the outer office. I don't expect he reached the lift before a flask or bottle touched his lips.

Then Arthur stood up. He looked straight at Julius.

'You've heard what's been said of you. That story is going to reach the press on Monday next, 22 March. It will, I know you'll agree, attract headlines. You'll also agree that it will destroy confidence in you. Your shareholders will greatly regret they ever believed in you. They'll run for cover. We shall provide it.'

'No paper will print this,' said Julius. 'There are libel laws in Britain.'

'As to that,' said Arthur, 'we are advised that there is a perfectly good defence to any action you might bring. Of course, the allegations will be printed with care, but the story will break. I am suggesting to you that it is true.'

Julius said nothing.

'There is also the foreign press. Both Americans and Europeans have, after all, a considerable interest. They tend to be uninhibited. You must believe me when I say that this story – of your original obtaining of control, of your dealings with Communist authorities, of the laundering of their money – this story will be printed. Supported by a great deal of detail.'

'If I've done what you say,' said Julius very quietly, 'I should have thought the police would be interested in me. If I haven't, I think they'll be interested in those who utter a criminal libel.'

But Arthur continued imperturbably.

'I'm advised that any case against you may be difficult. Technically, you probably haven't broken the law. But that's for the Director of Public Prosecutions. I've already told you we don't believe the press will be deterred by fear of a libel action. We have, of course, paved the way.'

'I'm sure you have!'

Arthur's voice became rougher, brutal. 'You talk about the law. You know perfectly well that's not the point. You've been playing with what most people these days consider the other side for money, but you may well have broken no law. But two things are finished. First, your usefulness to – those particular investors. Secrecy was the name of the game. Secrecy alone could preserve the respectability of the organizations to which you channelled funds. And the second thing that's ended, I think you'll see, is the reputation of Julius Wrench, patriot, public-spirited man of integrity. I'm sure I don't have to tell you not to fool yourself. One can't live two lives simultaneously for ever. And you mind about your public image. You care. You don't only want money. You want esteem.'

Julius gazed out of the window. He appeared unmoved.

'It comes to this,' said Arthur, in a very matter-of-fact way. 'None of this unpleasant story need come to light at all. We want, before next Monday, control of Wrench Holdings. Our price is generous. You have six days. Your secretary will know how to reach me at any time and we can agree a press release. If I hear nothing, you know now what to expect.'

He nodded at Julius and walked out of the office. My flight to the United States as an employee of ETI was booked. I didn't know whether I would ever be in a room with Julius Wrench again. Perhaps, unimaginably, as a son-in-law, breach healed, time passed. I followed Arthur from the room.'

That evening, back at Les Manottes, John thought that he could see it all – Wrench, Rivers, Price, Marlow – and could imagine the tension it still created in Simon Marlow to recall it. Marlow had said, abruptly, 'We'd better leave it there for now,' after describing how he left Julius Wrench's office, left with Arthur Rivers, no backward glances. Marlow was particularly tired that evening; John knew it and felt contrition. Should he make excuses to end this emotional and demanding narrative? Should he say, 'I'm afraid I've got a lot of commitments – perhaps one evening next month –' knowing that Marlow would probably be gone? He could not. He felt entirely involved with them all – with Simon, with Miranda, with Harry, with Julius. He had agreed, humanely or not, perhaps simply out of inquisitiveness, to another dinner, another evening, another unbaring of Simon Marlow's past: in three days' time.

13

'Those who know it,' Marlow began with something like nostalgia in his voice, 'say that Virginia is beautiful always, but especially so in the spring and in the autumn – the fall. Spring came early that year, and already before March was out the buds were opening and the trees showing signs of awakening. I flew to Washington on the Sunday after our confrontation with Julius Wrench. On the Friday, I went for two nights to Penterton, to say goodbye to my mother before an absence of what might be several weeks. She looked tired. She was worried by my change of jobs.

'Darling, I do hope you've not quarrelled with the Wrenches. They've been so good to you.'

'I need the change, Mother. And there are a lot of big shifts coming in Wrench Holdings, you know.'

'Well, of course, I've read the papers, though I don't understand them, but I always read anything about Wrench Holdings. Your boss, Julius Wrench, must be a marvellous man. They say he's going to win this battle against these Chinese people, whoever they are. They aren't exactly the ones you worked for –'

'Pretty well.'

'It seems an odd time to be leaving . . .' My mother knew nothing of business, but she knew her son very well and her antennae were as sharp as ever. 'Won't it look like desertion, your leaving now?'

'Mother, I have to tell you that in my view Julius Wrench is going to lose this battle.'

'Nobody else seems to think so.'

'I know. Anyway, that's my view. But I'm not leaving because I think he's going to lose. I'm afraid I'm leaving because I think he deserves to lose.'

My mother said, 'You've changed sides, Simon!'

'You could say that. But for good reasons.'

'I thought he was charming.'

'He *is* charming. But, Mother, this is business. And there are a lot of things I can't say, even to you.'

'Do you see his children now? Harry, you were so fond of –'

'Sometimes.'

'And the daughter – the one who married an American?'

'Oh, Miranda,' I said. 'Well, she's in America.' My mother said nothing more.

Miranda was lucky in her friends, and especially lucky in her hostess in Virginia. The house was a long, low, white clapboarded piece of heaven set in sweet-scented woods, whose foliage promised a hundred different shades of green. A number of railed paddocks grazed by friendly horses surrounded the place. The nights were cold but it was already warm by day. It was in the south-west corner of the state and from the porch one could see the Blue Ridge Mountains on a clear morning. Miranda's friend, Joan Witheridge, had not only asked her to stay as long as she wished but had herself gone for a fortnight to New York. When I arrived, by air and hired car, Miranda had the place to herself; to ourselves.

When we were at last alone together, I took her in my arms.

'Please never leave me now.'

'I never will.'

Those few days in Virginia were, in a way, my introduction to happiness. I was insecure, an uncertain rather than a melancholy person, and no delights, especially none arising from human relationships, had hitherto seemed anything but transient to me. My moments of fleeting joy with Miranda in

London had always been overshadowed by her imminent departure – within the hour, within the minute – and by my sense of the impermanence of it all. She swore she loved me, and I needed to believe her; she shared her body with me, and I took it hungrily; but hitherto I had possessed her not at all. Now, when she said, 'I never will; I never will leave you,' I made myself throw away a lifetime's habit of emotional caution; I made myself believe it and trust it. Thus I came to happiness and peace. It was Monday. It must have been 22 March.

Later that day she said, out of the blue, 'I hope you're not angry that I held on to those shares!'

I was existing in a drowsy love-sated paradise, far from thoughts of Wrench, Ling, ETI and all their damnable contrivances. I said, 'Of course not. We'll manage perfectly well. I expect there'll be some way of getting funds for the divorce.'

'You see, I think Daddy *will* come round. He's very fond of me, and I'll really explain what hell life is with Alec. There are things I hate talking about to them – but I'll get it across somehow. Mummy will be harder. And in time they'll accept you. But if I'd run out on him during this take-over business – that's how he'd have seen it – it would have been doubly hard.'

'I understand you, my love.'

'How's all that going, by the way? I've seen no English newspapers for days, and although the local ones have quite good foreign news coverage it doesn't extend to a story about control of Wrench Holdings, believe it or not! I don't feel very involved. I suppose Daddy's winning, isn't he? As far as I can see, it might suit me, personally, better if he didn't but I can't help feeling on his side, poor love.'

I had decided that I would say nothing to Miranda about the confrontation with Julius and what passed at it. She knew I had left the firm, but for the rest we had made clear to Julius that if he conceded defeat in the take-over battle his dark story was safe from publicity. As far as I was concerned, that meant I would speak of it to nobody. I couldn't answer for Arthur Rivers, but it was not in his character to tell tales unless there was profit in it. As to whether Julius had surrendered, I knew nothing. There had been no move up to the Sunday night when I left England. Julius had one more day and he'd look for any weapons that lay to hand. Arthur had been categoric that he wanted to give him a week. He had calculated, very carefully, the disadvantages of Julius having more time in which to set up a libel case, starting, presumably, with an injunction. He'd had the best counsel's opinion London could produce. He was confident that every editor worth his salt – and he knew them all – would publish, backed by the advice Arthur had obtained – and funded – in advance. On the other side, he didn't want to rush Julius too much. He wanted to give him time to digest the logic of the situation – to learn to live with defeat.

'He's still going to be a rich man,' said Arthur. 'He's going to be perfectly all right. Everybody goes at some time. We'll have a press release which saves his face. "After mature consideration, he believes shareholders will do well to accept our offer." No problem. He will have a seat on our Board – that sort of thing.'

'Will he really have a seat on your Board? After a showdown like we've had?'

'Why not?'

'And after what you know about him laundering money to Communist front organizations?'

Arthur had looked at me. 'Listen, Simon,' he said, his penetrating eyes holding mine, 'don't imagine you told me – or told him – much I didn't know already. What you did was show sufficient proof. You knew how it was done because you'd done your digging. Your detail is vital to the story – if there has to be a story. But of course we knew what went on. Do you think we invested a lot of money – and a lot of Communist Chinese money, over the years – in Wrench without understanding that part of his game? Why, some of our clients played it too – in a small way, of course.'

'But in that case –'

'The Soviet Union and its protégés aren't popular with the Chinese any more. Remember?'

I remembered. Arthur said, 'They're called the hegemonists. Knocking this particular little game on the head will do us nothing but good with our chief client out east. Commercially speaking, I mean,' Arthur explained patiently. I understood. Whether I would spend a lifetime working for ETI, Ling Enterprises or anyone else, I doubted.

I said, 'His only object was money. He played their game for money, only for money.'

To my considerable surprise Arthur said, 'There's a story that he was recruited when quite young. I don't know whether it's true and it doesn't matter, but it might explain why they chose him in the first place.'

'Recruited?' Even Desmond Dillon the all-knowing, the friend of security people, the specialist reporter of espionage and subversion, had not mentioned this. What is more, I remembered that Desmond had been at Cambridge only a year or two after Julius, and had the recruitment been there I was confident that Desmond, with his nose and his opinions, would have ferreted it out, anyway by now. I believed, and I still believe, that Julius Wrench's motives were mercenary from first to last. Suddenly the old Julius, Julius the host, Julius the benefactor, Julius, Harry's father, stood in front of my eyes. Recruited as an ideologically motivated agent? Julius Wrench, capitalist? Never!

'Well, it's a story,' said Arthur, 'talked about at that time, the twenties. He was making his way fast. He'd travelled in Germany, worked in America. The story was that, like plenty of others, he'd been recruited, told to succeed in life, get a position of influence, lie low till wanted. It used to be muttered around. I've no idea if it's true. It might be. Equally surprising things in that line have happened, haven't they.'

I could not think of Julius as an ideologue of any kind, overt or disguised. I said so. Arthur nodded, by now regarding all this as fairly irrelevant. He said, 'He likes intrigue, doesn't he. Likes the sense that he's manipulating people unbeknown to them. Perhaps he enjoyed the feeling of belonging to something entirely secret? As well – in his case – as profitable, of course.'

'Personal gain and emotional satisfaction.'

'Maybe.'

'But not idealism. Not conviction.'

'I dare say not,' said Arthur, looking at his watch. These were not words he often employed. I remembered that I had said to Julius, during my terrible speech of accusation, 'All this needs no ideological commitment.' I thought I would still say that; but who can ever disentangle motive so confidently as to be entirely sure?

Arthur promised to keep me informed about what we now thought of as the Wrench capitulation. Miranda had sent me a telephone number in Virginia and Arthur had it. Nobody wanted to see me until the end of April, when I had arranged to report to the ETI office in New York and see how matters stood. Meanwhile, I was expected to do nothing and to lie comparatively low.

'I suppose Daddy's winning, isn't he?' Miranda said again. I didn't answer. It was many, many hours since I had left England on what had been Sunday evening there. I was sleepy, disorientated by time changes, stunned by the impact of a continent entirely new to me, tired by travel, and emotionally exhausted by the dramas of the previous week. None of this signified compared with the fact that I was, at last, alone, unhurried, undisturbed with my beloved. We were sitting stretched in basket chairs on the terrace of Joan Witheridge's house. The sun was up, already producing a foretaste of spring, and Miranda had put on for the first time a pair of shorts and was extending her superb legs in its just perceptible warmth. She stretched herself beside me, brown skin like satin; huge grey eyes searching my own; very slender limbs. There seemed no cloud. I had never known peace like that peace in South Virginia. We were near the borders of North Carolina. We might have been on the moon. We made our own world. We made love, we slept, we murmured recollections to each other, we ate and drank when we felt like it, we drowned ourselves in each other. We could not believe it.

There were, inevitably, moments when caution and the exterior world broke in. Miranda said, 'You're staying here as Joan's guest, of course. And nobody knows she's away. I don't think Alec will be having me watched yet but I suppose that sort of dreary thing will come.'

I supposed so. 'Isn't all that, perhaps, something we'll just have to go through? You want a divorce.'

'My beloved,' said Miranda, 'there's a thing called alimony. And the circumstances of the matrimonial breakdown will affect it. I'm likely to need it.'

'I don't think so.'

As always, she got confused and a little impatient if we spoke of money. 'Oh, I'd be happy to be poor with you, my darling, don't worry about that! But I am so hemmed in, either by Bartholomews or Wrenches, so dependent!'

I did not want yet to speak of my own circumstances. Miranda did not even know that I was 'working' for ETI (and I was by no means sure I would continue to do so). She knew I had been given a few weeks off in the United States and my new employers then wanted to see me in New York. In her world, none of that was particularly surprising or worthy of remark. She took it for granted that I would return to London and continue to do the same sort of things I had been doing before. And I was, myself, uncertain. I turned my mind away from the insistent picture of one and a half million pounds or thereabouts, waiting to be collected by Simon Marlow, destroyer of Julius Wrench.

No word came from Arthur Rivers. Tuesday drifted into

Wednesday. Swimming, whispering, love-making, basking in the warmth of the spring sun, luxuriating all the time in the ever-present scented texture of Miranda.'

'It couldn't last, of course,' said Marlow. John was expecting that. Marlow was his usual self, quiet, controlled, impersonally talking of very personal experiences and emotions as if they had occurred to another, long dead, whose character and reactions he knew intimately and could exactly describe. In their evening sessions in the Auberge garden, now, he sometimes poured a glass of wine for himself; this had seldom happened at the beginning. On the night he told John of his final facing of Julius Wrench, he actually ordered a second bottle. John had drunk no more than his moderate norm.

'Good Lord, there's no more in this! I'm sorry.'

'It's all right. I've done very well.'

'No, no, we must have another. I've got a good deal to say yet.If you can stay.'

And John had stayed.

'On the Thursday morning,' Marlow continued, 'I thought I must ring Arthur Rivers. His ultimatum had expired. I had a right to know how things stood. I chose a time when I knew he'd be in his office. I told Miranda I had a business call. I was alone – very early morning in Virginia.

I got Arthur.

'I've not heard from you, Arthur. How's it going?'

Arthur tended to use veiled speech on the telephone. No doubt rightly, he had an obsession with security. He could, in consequence, sometimes be obscure. I knew from his opening remark that we had not yet won, but it was less clear exactly how matters stood.

'I have agreed a limited extension.'

'Can you say why?'

'Er – there are certain legal complications. Our – er – friend has received some advice inconsistent with what we received.'

Presumably Julius had been told he could get an injunction to prevent publication.

'So where do we stand?'

'It's unlikely that anything could affect the matter in the longer term,' said Arthur.

I found this harder, being unskilled in the law. Wasn't there, I thought, a thing called an interlocutory injunction, which stopped somebody doing something for a limited time but which then had to be substantiated or contested in court at the end of the period? Something like that – but I couldn't remember how long the period was. I had a ghastly feeling it was something like a month. In which case it was likely to be a pretty uneasy month, and I didn't expect that Miranda and I would entirely escape the fall-out.

'That's a set-back, isn't it, Arthur?'

'Not necessarily. As I said he has received this – er – contrary advice. Our men think differently. It would, of course, be up to, to –'

'Editors.'

Arthur didn't care for such explicitness. 'Up to others than ourselves. There are also, you understand, foreign interests.'

The foreign press. Uninhibited by the peculiar libel laws of the island race.

'That must be almost as strong a pressure? You made that clear from the start – to JW, I mean?'

'Yes,' said Arthur, 'I think so. Anyway, I have agreed with all concerned that nothing shall happen before the middle of next week. There is a certain amount of impatience, of course, but I have obtained agreement. The – er – gentleman concerned has also, I know, investigated very urgently the question of whether we ourselves may be said to be acting improperly in any way . . .'

We had gone into this obvious point pretty thoroughly. Inducements. Menaces. Arthur reckoned that his modus operandi was proof against such counter-attack.

'There is, I'm assured, no worry there,' Arthur said. 'Thank you for ringing, Simon. I still think he will – er – see the light within forty-eight hours. Goodbye.'

On the whole this sounded good rather than bad from ETI's point of view. I hardly knew, by now, what I thought or what I wanted. I was undisturbed by the conversation, although it would have been good to hear that the end had been reached. Certainly nothing in my talk with Arthur Rivers prepared me for Monday morning. It was 29 March.

I had, for several days, taken to driving to the nearest town eight miles away and buying the local paper while Miranda did something about a midday meal. On Monday I did this. The paper was dominated, very reasonably, by the activities and the politics of Virginia. There was a front page carrying any bigger United States stories, and some international coverage on the back. Limited international stock market news also appeared in the financial columns inside. There had not so far been any reference to ETI and Wrench, and by the standards applied there was little likelihood that the battle in London, whether by virtue of drama or scale, would rate a mention. On that Monday I didn't open the paper until I got back to Joan Witheridge's house. Miranda was mixing a salad. I got us both drinks and put my arm round her as she stood at the kitchen table. I shook the paper open with a disengaged hand to the page where I knew any foreign news appeared. Then I took my arm away from Miranda's waist and walked to the window with the paper. After a moment or two I said, 'Darling –'

She took one look at me. My voice had said it all. She snatched the paper, and took a second, brows knitted, searching, to see what I had read:

'BRITISH PROPERTY TYCOON SHOT DEAD IN LONDON.'

There was not much in that paper about Julius – just enough to make clear that he'd done it himself. On Sunday, it appeared.

The rest of that appalling day was dominated by telephoning. Miranda at first, of course, needed to reach her mother. Viola had been trying, herself, to make contact. She had no number for Miranda except that of Alec Bartholomew and his parents and from neither could she obtain certain news of where Miranda was. There had been, I gathered, perfunctory expressions of condolence – the Bartholomew–Wrench connexion was, after all, of long standing – but Miranda's defection had created outrage, and it was not simply to be purged by death in spite of Julius's temporary concordat over ALI's shares during the take-over battle. Viola herself had only just learned of Miranda's flight from her Bartholomew husband. She had barely had time to digest this unwelcome news when blinding tragedy had hit her.

For Miranda, rightly, all that mattered now was to go home to London. She had a long talk with Viola on what I knew was an indifferent line, affected no doubt by one of Virginia's thunderstorms whose crackling imminence had been felt since before dawn. I heard her voice, sobs half suppressed, as she shouted to Viola. I mooned wretchedly about. There was no place in this for me. I had been, I supposed, a principal cause of the grief these people were feeling. One day they would discover that. Perhaps Viola had already done so. I had my own sorrow. Something more precious than I had ever before known was slipping away from me, slipping because of a process I had myself started.

At such times,' said Marlow, in his quiet, exhausted voice, 'one may sympathize with a beloved's suffering, but one's own predicament, like it or not, dominates one's mind and feeling. I wondered, stunned, whether or not I would hold Miranda through this. This, and what would probably ensue.

When she finished talking to her mother I saw, at least, a chance to be useful.

'Darling, you're going to London, of course. I'll get on to someone about flights.'

'Thank you,' she said, dully. People had always done that sort of thing for her and now it had better be me. I expected there was a perfectly efficient local agent, but I wanted to do it my way. I had my reasons.

'Leave it to me.'

She went to do some repair to a tear-ravaged face and I rang the ETI office in New York. They knew my name. They were expecting me in a few weeks' time. I talked to the top man's secretary.

'What can we do for you, Mr Marlow?'

'I'm afraid I've got to fly, quite unexpectedly, to London. I'm in Virginia. Could you fix it? It's urgent.'

'Of course. I'll ring you. When do you want your ticket for? It'd best be from Washington and I'll get a connecting internal flight for you.'

'As soon as possible.' I told her how far we were from the small local airport.

'Two tickets.'

An hour later she rang back.

'Mr Marlow, I have your tickets. You need to fly at three o'clock tomorrow afternoon to Washington DC. You'll have three hours to wait there and are booked on the nineteen-fifty hour flight to Heathrow, London. Reaching London very early next morning, English time. Is that all right?'

'I imagine there's nothing earlier.'

'There is not. Mr Marlow, I have to tell you, too, that there is some kind of difficulty at the London end. The airline office said it was some sort of threatened strike action. Flights are subject to delay. And they're heavily subscribed.'

'Oh hell! Well, thank you so much.'

'Your tickets will be at the airline desks in each case. Have a pleasant journey, Mr Marlow.'

I sought Miranda. She was sitting looking out of the window. The storm had broken, the rain was torrential.

'I've got tickets. We fly from here tomorrow afternoon. We reach London early Wednesday morning.'

'We?'

'Darling, I'm not going to intrude, but I just want to do

everything necessary for you at this grim time. Don't worry, I'm unobtrusive. But I can't see you go alone.'

She looked at me puzzled – was I wrong in thinking even a little irritated? God destroy the thought!

'I thought you had to be here to go to New York?'

'Not yet. There's no reason on earth why I can't go to London, and I'm going to. And Miranda . . .'

She smiled at me, tired.

'Miranda, my love, all I want is to be of use to you. Believe that.'

She nodded.

'Well, I'll write a line to Joan,' she said. 'She's been very kind, and I'd better tidy things up a bit. I know we've got till tomorrow afternoon but I must do something.' I made myself as helpful as I could, which was not much. Miranda developed a blinding headache. I slept alone that night.

Next morning Miranda answered the telephone. We were moving about aimlessly, waiting to drive to the airport. She spoke little, and when she did it was always tearing, worrying at the agonizing business of Julius.

'He couldn't bear defeat,' she said. 'He must have thought he was losing this business about control of the company. Poor, poor, darling Daddy, as if it mattered! But he couldn't bear defeat, he had to win.'

Then the telephone rang. I heard her say, 'Hold on please.' She turned without interest. 'It's for you.'

It was Arthur Rivers. I said at once, 'Arthur, I'm coming back to England. I'll get in touch at once. I get to London tomorrow morning.'

'There's no need for you to do that, Simon.' Arthur was trumpeting as if to carry the Atlantic.

I didn't want to start justifying my return in the hearing of Miranda. I said again, 'I'll be in touch, Arthur. There's been a lot happened.' That sounded all right, whoever I was talking to. I was sure Miranda would not have recognized the Rivers voice. I did not wish her to do so.

'Simon, this is an unfortunate business, but I'm afraid he had it coming to him. The whole story's breaking in Europe tonight. It's a big scandal, of course. Top British businessman acts as Communist paymaster, that sort of stuff.' Arthur's reticence had, for a little, departed.

'I thought that – all that – wasn't being released, used, whatever you like, until mid-week.'

I looked at Miranda. She didn't appear to be paying the slightest attention to my conversation.

'There have been some premature initiatives. It is regrettably clear that the – er – story was in any case to be used. Abroad. The – er – person in question appreciated that. Or so I understand.'

'He was owed silence, Arthur. At least for a few more days.'

'Certainly. Now, however, our – contacts – feel that this lamentable occurrence has freed them from any earlier undertakings.'

'Bloody hell! I see. Well . . .'

'Anyway,' said Arthur, 'I wanted to tell you that there's no question about difficulty in – buying what we wanted. Those shareholders are only too glad to take real money. As you'd expect. Only too glad. I promised to keep you informed. The party's over.'

'I see,' I said, non-committally.

'One more thing,' shouted Arthur. 'I saw that rather odd fellow Price, this morning. In fact, he came to see me here.' It was, of course, late afternoon in London. Waldo must have discovered Arthur's whereabouts with some determination.

'What did he want?'

'He was a bit sozzled.'

'He always is.'

'Of course we had an – er – an understanding with him, as you know, and I think he wanted to cash in early, or make sure he was going to be able to do so without misunderstandings. I expect his habits come expensive.'

'Certainly.'

'He wanted to get a message to you. Something about that you'd discharged your duty and could rely on him.'

I could imagine. Although why the hell Waldo couldn't have waited until I returned for that sort of benediction I didn't know. I didn't know, either, how wide Waldo was opening his mouth about the strange circumstance which bound together himself, Henry Kinzel, Julius Wrench and Simon Marlow. I didn't know, but I felt uneasy. Arthur Rivers had said goodbye and rung off. He had sounded his assured, confident, implacable self.

We reached Washington airport at last. Miranda said little during the journey. She looked exhausted, and I was glad to have the chance to support her, to save her minor trouble. I know, and I think I knew at the time, that this wasn't really unselfish on my part. In fact, bereavement is sometimes well served by having minor tasks which have to be undertaken; my bustle was of assistance primarily to myself. I needed to have the illusion I was needed. Terror stalked my soul that the moment would return, despite all our loving assurances to each other, when I would be needed no more.

But the situation at the airport was damnable for both of us. The girl's voice over the announcer system hit us as we moved into what seemed an unusually crowded hall.

'You will be kept informed. We regret inconvenience to passengers to London. You will be kept informed.'

I muttered to Miranda and ploughed towards the airline desk, taking my turn in an irritable queue of enquirers. Miranda stayed close to me.

'We've just arrived. I didn't get that about London flights. I'm booked in – my name's Marlow.'

'All flights to London subject to delay,' said the girl, no doubt for the thousandth time. 'There are labour difficulties in handling at London airport, we understand. The service is intermittent. Some airlines are being successfully processed, others not. Some aircraft are being diverted to other British airports not affected.'

I found out all I could. Our flight was delayed. 'Indefinitely.' Seats to other British destinations were being bid for by London travellers and aircraft were, it appeared, all full. I turned to Miranda, who had moved out of the crush.

'Darling, it's hell; it's a strike at Heathrow. Some flights are going, but much delayed and no certainty. There are no places on UK flights. They can't guarantee anything. We could try and get to somewhere like Paris or Brussels, and then go by train and boat.'

'How long would that take?'

'A long time, but at least we'd be moving. Trouble with London is they just can't say when we might fly – or whether.' We were talking among a large, sullen crowd of fellow aspirants to reach the British capital. Everyone listened eagerly for a word of hope overheard, a suggestion to follow.

'Typical!' said a furious Englishman to his wife. 'Typical!'

Miranda looked drained of feeling. 'I don't mind, as long as I don't have to stand here for ever.' It looked as if that were indeed a possibility. I knew that any decisions must be taken by me. It cheered me. The girl announcer repeated her depressing statement.

I took Miranda's arm. We still had our bags with us.

'Come on, darling,' I said with a brave show of proprietorial confidence. 'I'm going to find you a table to sit at and have something to drink, and I'll come back here and make a plan. I'll fly us to somewhere.' I had in mind another call to the wonder-working girl of ETI in New York. One never knew.

'I think I must get something to read,' said Miranda. 'I'll go to the bookstall.' I had found a chair for her at a buffet. I said, 'Sit here, darling, then I'll know where you are. I'll get you a – a what? English paper?'

'Yes, thank you.'

She was submissive. I bought her a double scotch and raced to a bookstall. The morning's *Times*, miraculously, had arrived and not been sold out. I bought it, and the *Guardian*, to give plenty of pages in which her saddened, uninterested eyes could find distraction. As I moved away I saw a French side headline in another paper on the stall.

'SUICIDE D'UN TRESORIER COMMUNISTE.' Phrases, words – 'LONDRES', 'SCANDALE', 'VIE SECRETE D'UN MONDAIN' – jigged before my eyes. I supposed this would be in the American papers too. Would it be in the British? Had it been yesterday? I took sixty seconds off and flipped through the pages of *The Times* and *Guardian*.

I could see nothing. Of course it was going to come out; nothing that I could do would save my beloved from knowledge of what her father had done; but it was better that she should be among her own people when she learned it.

And better that she should not learn that I had been the principal means of its disclosure. Not, anyway, for a very, very long time.

I gave her the newspapers. 'Now, my darling,' I said, 'I'll make the best arrangements I can. It may take a little time.'

She managed a smile.

'I know whatever you decide will be best.'

I was warmed. Then Miranda said, 'It's evening in London. I'm going to try to ring Harry. There's a call box over there.' There was. Miraculously vacant. She moved towards it in a dreamy sort of way. Then she came back and collected her small piece of luggage.

'We'd best keep these with us. I'll come back to this spot, darling, even though the table will probably have been bagged!'

An airport at any time is one of earth's most disorientating places. When flights are delayed at best, and may never take off at all at worst; when incomprehensible announcements of a vaguely menacing kind disturb the air; when private grief and wracking uncertainties over other things dominate the mind, an airport must be as near to hell as can be imagined outside a concentration camp. Yet sometimes, even in that inferno, a sudden shaft of relief penetrates. Before telephoning ETI I thought I would return once to the airline enquiry desk to see whether the situation was unchanged. The same very charming girl looked up. For a moment the crush around her had dissolved, unsatisfied.

'It's Mr Marlow, isn't it? You wanted two places to London? I've this instant had two seats on an airplane to Manchester, England, surrendered by an American gentleman. The flight leaves in approximately two hours from now. Is that any use to you, Mr Marlow?'

'It is indeed!' I said. Miranda and I could get a train to London. Anything was better than hanging about. I thanked the girl effusively.

'These things are real bad, aren't they,' she said. 'And your wife looked kind of tired. She'll be glad to have a sleep on the plane. It's due at Manchester around nine o'clock tomorrow morning.'

'Bless you!' I said.

'There are a few formalities.' She busied herself with lists and tickets. I left her with them, triumphant, to find Miranda and have a drink. We had more than ninety minutes before needing to check in, but time was now passing and the sense of aimless uncertainty had gone. I felt in control again. I would care for her, put her ultimately into a taxi at Euston or wherever Manchester trains arrive in London, and disappear – for a little. It was going to be as it had so wonderfully been. An airline ticket, a firm place on a scheduled flight had restored my morale.

I went back to the buffet. Miranda was where I had left her. Her chair had, it appeared, not been grabbed by another traveller. With something like cheerfulness I called, 'Better news, darling,' as I approached.

'Better news!' I sat down and smiled tenderly. 'We're flying to Manchester. In just over the hour. We'll easily get a morning train to London. Much better than hanging about here until God knows when.'

Miranda remained very still. I remember that she had not looked up as I approached and sat down. Her next words were entirely unexpected.

'Give me my ticket, please.'

'Of course. But if you like I'll keep them both –'

'Give it to me.'

I did, and she put it in her bag. She was not looking at me.

'I got through to Harry.'

'I'm so glad,' I said.

'He told me something I needed to know. He told me that our father shot himself because there were terrible, wicked, stories being put about – that he was disloyal, treacherous in some way, to England I mean. So everybody was losing confidence in him – and in his company. It broke him.'

I said nothing.

'It wasn't just losing control of his company. It was his good name – the evil lies being said about him. Apparently it's in some papers. And hinted at in others.'

I remained silent. Miranda continued very softly, without emphasis or change of tone.

'Harry told me that it was you who have done this to us. He told me that you had been offered a great reward to blacken my father. There's a man called Price –'

The whole world was collapsing. I never took my eyes off her face. She never looked at me.

'This man Price must have had a guilty conscience. He knew about you. He's an old friend of our friend, Charlie Branson.'

So that was the link. But it would have come out somehow if Waldo was as indiscreet as he manifestly was.

'Price told Branson all about it – you. You've been offered a fortune by someone to tell ghastly lies about my father. And you've done it very well. I told Harry I couldn't believe it of you. He swore it was absolutely true.'

'Miranda, it's not like that –'

She stood up. 'I don't mind where you fly or where you go to,' she said, 'as long as it's not to Manchester with me. Nor anywhere else. Ever again.'

I heard a flight being called for last check-in. I looked, without being conscious of much, at the closed-circuit television screen which showed which aircraft was boarding its passengers. It was, I remember, a flight to Frankfurt. Much too early for Manchester. When I looked back again Miranda had gone.'

14

There was so long a pause after Marlow described that scene at Washington airport that John thought he'd collapsed. Normally, Marlow talked with few breaks – with extraordinary fluency. He always made it clear when he'd said enough for the evening. 'I'm tired, I think it's late enough.' 'I do hope you'll come again – shall we say . . . ?' He called the tune. On this occasion he sat silent and unmoving. At last John thought he'd best make a move.

'I should be going. You've reached a very dramatic point in your story –'

He looked up. 'There's not much more. But, as you say, it's late. I hope you'll come again.'

'Of course.'

He nodded. 'Thank you. As I always told you, and meant, you have helped me. I'll be in touch.' He made no attempt at naming a day. John sensed that he wanted to prepare his own mind a little before a resumption of his tale. It could hardly be cheerful.

As it happened, John was well content to have both days and evenings uninterrupted for a few weeks. Things had, unexpectedly, gone well for him. A small gallery was to put on a show of his pictures, and the prospect was enormously exciting. He had sometimes dreamed of having an exhibition in Avignon, the nearest city of note, with its jostling crowds and occasional collectors. That was not to be. Instead, a charming man rang up one day from Apt, a small, attractive town some twenty miles east of Les Manottes.

'You showed me two of your pictures last summer, remember?'

John did. 'I'm glad you remember them, Monsieur Lambert.'

'I think we might discuss a project.'

And so the first Tranter show was born. Lambert's gallery was in an excellent position and he planned the timing to coincide with the maximum influx of tourists. He said, with delicacy but, John had ruefully to admit, with truth, that the Tranter Provençal landscapes were attractive to lovers of the obvious rather than connoisseurs of the subtle or the rare. He put it with more tact than proprietors of galleries always display towards artists. He flattered.

'*L'allure de vos peintures – c'est exactement ce que cherchent nos visiteurs . . .*'

John knew what he meant and didn't mind. Tranter's work was going to be on general display in Apt for two weeks! Lambert settled terms and John was delighted. The show was arranged for a date in August, not long after he listened to Marlow's sad story of his own lost love.

The weeks before the show opened, John was working day and night. The heat was intense, but Lambert assured him that '*les visiteurs*' still patronized Provence notwithstanding. Furthermore, Lambert said, they were drawn to the shaded quiet of his gallery (which was well arranged) and were happy to admire therein sunlit scenes while themselves cooling off. They could thus enjoy heat vicariously, and buy a little of it to take home to some northern winter. He was funny about it, and John laughed and made himself believe. There was much to do. John had one picture still to finish which both were keen to include; and he cared a great deal about the hanging. He spent as much time as he could with Lambert in Apt, generally helping, checking catalogues, and doing the physical work inseparable from exhibition. It was a splendid time, but John was glad that it included no evenings at the Auberge de Varnas. He needed every minute.

The exhibition went astonishingly well. Lambert was a delightful patron – shrewd in business and exacting his pound of flesh, but with great feeling for the pains and uncertainties that beset anybody who tries to express something on canvas. He was, too, an excellent salesman. He made every visitor to his gallery feel a friend with whom he was, as host, sharing a private pleasure. He was an example of how such things should be done. He sold, in the first week, more pictures than he had prophesied to John even in optimistic moments and was already muttering about a repeat performance in the spring.

One evening in the gallery – they stayed open late – John heard a very musical, slightly American voice saying in English something pleasant about one of the Vaucluse landscapes. He was hovering, as usual, marking possible sales and avid for any hint of praise. The voice belonged to a tall, good-looking woman, accompanied by a man with horn-rimmed glasses and receding hair; a man who also looked agreeable, though not, John decided, as agreeable as his companion. John reserved judgement: the man had not yet commented.

'I like that, James. I like that *very* much.' They went on looking, silent and – surely – appreciative? Intelligent faces both, John thought happily. He decided to introduce himself. There was a small flattering photograph and account of the artist in the brochure, but he was generally unrecognized despite it.

'Good afternoon. I'm John Tranter. I was so glad I heard you say you like that one. It was fun to do . . .' He told them where the picture was conceived, the problems he'd had with it, a little about it. They responded sensibly and without embarrassment. John didn't talk as a salesman, and they didn't treat him as one. They chatted about painting, and they were, it was clear, sensitive and well educated in the subject. The man was English. The woman appeared American, and attractively so. John found himself enjoying the conversation. They were his own kind.

'Would you like to go on talking for a bit over a drink?'
'That's an excellent idea!' said the woman.
The man said, 'My name's James Todd.'
'And I'm Polly Todd,' she said. The names were vaguely familiar, but John was sure he'd never met them before. They went to a café and sat at a shaded table in the narrow street. John ordered drinks.
'You've come to Provence at a pretty hot time of year! It's too much for a lot of English people. Next month, September, is better – really lovely.'
'I know,' said Polly Todd. 'I've always wanted to come later – or earlier, in the spring. But we neither of us mind heat. I'm half English but I was brought up in Louisiana, so I'm no stranger to the sun!'
Her voice, thought John, was heavenly.
James Todd said, 'August is a pretty awful month in which to travel, but one's often not one's own master. One must get away when one can.'
'What do you do?'
'I'm a lawyer.' He opened up a little, an engaging, alert man of about John's age with an infectious smile. 'I was in business for quite a while, then there was a shake-up and I returned to the law. It's a hard taskmaster, but I enjoy it.'
The Todds were staying in a little hilltop town between Apt and Aix. 'But we're leaving tomorrow, alas,' said Polly. 'We're on the road north, early. You live here always?'
'Always. I have for about three years. And my parents lived in France – further south, in Roussillon – before that.' John told them a little of how it had come about.
'You don't regret it? You don't miss England?'
'Not much.' But he did a little, of course. Even Simon Marlow's unevocative account of childhood brought to the eyes different landscapes, green Gloucestershire hills, grey stones, grey skies and ever-changing light. At such moments, Provence became harsh and obvious, but the moments never lasted long.

They talked about the expatriate community in France – British, Americans, living lives curiously embalmed in that moment of time that they had chosen for emigration; not thereafter responsive to changes in their native lands, firmly rejecting any evolution they disliked in the country of their adoption. Peter Pans. And perhaps, like him, ever less in touch with reality. Or so the Todds, delicately, charmingly, implied.

'It may be so,' John said happily. He didn't mind – or dispute – any of this. 'It may be so. I just like the sun and the colour and the wine, and I like to paint and to get up when I like, eat and drink when I like, and spend time doing what I enjoy, not what bores me.'

James Todd had been reflecting. He said to his wife, 'You know, I heard, somewhere in London this summer, that Simon Marlow had decided to spend some months in Provence.'

'You didn't tell me that, James. Simon Marlow! Good heavens, we should really – after all these years . . .'

'They're probably his last months, poor old Simon, from all I hear,' said Todd. He said to John, 'Someone we used to know well. Got a very serious heart condition. Angina, I rather think. I hear he's been given a *very* short time by the doctors. We never see him now. I heard he'd come to Provence.' He looked at his wife. 'Darling, we've got an early start tomorrow, I think . . .' He had offered more drinks already and been declined. She nodded.

John said quietly, 'Simon Marlow is indeed in Provence. I have been seeing a great deal of him.' He felt a peculiar sensation of excitement, for no reason whatsoever.

'Really? How extraordinary! Is he near here?'

'Not very. He is staying near where I myself live. About twenty-five miles away.' John told them the address.

The Todds said nothing and John could see that something made it less than easy for them to say, 'Let's ring him up. Let's drive home that way.' Something additional, perhaps, to the simple fact that it was in the other direction from where they were staying. And now it had come back to him. James Todd! A flatmate of Marlow's long ago! Julius Wrench's confidential assistant! Married to an American.

The Todds were not now re-emphasizing their impatience to depart. They were both looking at John.

'And how is Simon?' James Todd said at last, rather lamely.

'I gathered from him that he is, as you said, dying. He seems to have no doubt about that. He has been very generous to me. I have dined with him often. He seems to accept everything in an uncomplaining sort of way.'

'I used to work in the same outfit. Before I returned to the law.'

'In Wrench Holdings.'

'Ah, you knew that!'

'I knew that.' John rather enjoyed this game. He knew, after all, a good deal about them. Or thought he did.

Polly said, 'It's extraordinary meeting someone who knows Simon – one in a thousand chance. James, I've an idea. Don't you think we three might have some dinner here together? I'd like to hear more and it's been so nice meeting you, Mr Tranter.'

James said, 'It's an excellent idea. I do hope you can. As our guest.'

They wanted, clearly, to talk about Marlow, and within strict limits John was prepared to do so, indeed wanted to do so, but had no intention of betraying how much of Marlow's life – both his exterior and his inner life – had already been disclosed to him, John Tranter. Although Marlow had never imposed any sort of commitment to confidence – indeed, could hardly have done so, in what he had himself described as a cathartic exercise, a helpful essay in self-expression – nevertheless, John felt absolutely bound. This man had told him an appalling amount. He wasn't sure what he thought of it, or of the narrator, but he felt that to hear such things from a man automatically created inhibitions. John could not gossip about Marlow.

On the other hand, Marlow's story had only reached a point about, John reckoned, ten years before. Yet he had said, 'There's not much more.' Had he, as had been his goal, become rich, earned his reward? Had he ever been accepted by the Wrenches again – or, perhaps, by their associates and employees? Had he married, had he worked at a new profession, had he lost his fortune, or made another? John needed to know these things, but Marlow had not indicated that there was a saga yet to come.

They found a table in a small restaurant, and when they had ordered, James Todd said, 'Of course, we've seen nothing of Simon since the bust-up at Wrench Holdings. Did he tell you about that?'

John played for time, raising eyebrows and looking interrogative. James Todd went on.

'It was one hell of a business. We were taken over, and our chairman, Julius Wrench, shot himself. Which was ghastly. I was his confidential assistant. In fact, I found him. It wasn't – very nice.'

'How perfectly beastly!'

'The take-over went sour on him. But there was a lot more to it than that. The papers were full of stories that he'd been bribed by the Russians to use our books to pass money to some of their protégés – innocent-sounding organizations in England. That and other things.'

'Was that true?'

'Unfortunately, I'm afraid it was. We'd all been entirely in the dark. I was fond of him. The whole thing was a terrible shock, coming on top of his death. The family were knocked endways, of course.'

Explaining, Polly said, 'Simon Marlow worked with James, but he'd left the firm by that time, and it appears he'd had quite a hand in exposing the whole business. To the press.'

John nodded, saying nothing. He could see that James was looking back on it all, with unspeakable pictures in the mind's eye. Polly said, 'And, of course, we've not known Simon since he became rich.'

'Did he become rich?' This was safe ground. And John didn't know the answer.

'Oh yes. He became very rich – just about then –'

'And people said,' James took up the tale, 'that he was bribed. That he sold his information to the bidders in this take-over business – people called ETI – and that they used the information to blacken Julius Wrench's name, depress his shares of course, bring him down. In which process he shot himself!'

'I've *never* thought,' said Polly, 'that Simon did that. Not just like that. It wasn't in his character. And I do *not* believe that ETI or anyone else would have paid the sort of money one gathers Simon Marlow now has, to get a story. It's disproportionate.'

'It might not be,' said her husband. 'After all, it got them Wrench Holdings. Rather cheap as it's turned out. Men like Arthur Rivers are shrewd investors. They know when to cast bread on the waters, and how much.'

'It's disproportionate,' she repeated.

John said, 'He's very rich, is he?'

'Oh, you could say that! You ought to get him interested in your pictures, John!' They were on christian name terms by now.

'Simon is thought to be worth at least three million. I know a man who's worked closely with him in a particular show he's concerned in, a charity. At least three million. That's not what it was, but it's a reasonable fortune for a man who started with absolutely nothing.'

'What does he do with it?'

James said that in 1969, as far as anyone knew, Marlow

had left ETI. He had, it was generally supposed, little to do there and seemed to have no taste for the business. And at about that time he became known as rich. Privately, John supposed that the wheels in Mr Austin's office had turned by then, that the coffers of Boshy's treasure had been unlocked and that Simon Marlow had entered into his inheritance at last. A wretched man.

Polly took up the story.

'He became quite a recluse. He never married –'

'There was a story there,' said James. 'He was after Julius Wrench's daughter, of all people!'

'– never married, and the next thing we heard was that he was living by himself, somewhere in the West Country, and had started a home for down and outs in Bristol!'

'I gather that's right,' said James. 'He started this place – sort of high-class dosshouse for tramps – then improved it, expanded it, gave a lot of destitute old people a home and some hope. A man I know with a business down there said he'd done an incredible job. All financed by him, of course; he's raised a bit from others here and there, but it's his baby.'

'And there's another thing,' said Polly. 'He doesn't just sign cheques. He works there. He's there most of the time. He shares his life with them, as well as his money. That's what we've heard. I think that's very fine.'

'He *did* share his life with them! We've also heard, as you know, and as you've born out, John, that there's not much of life left.'

They talked about other things, and soon the evening had passed and they prepared to depart. John thanked them.

'It was delightful.'

'And we never bought one of your pictures!'

'Never mind. You gave me much more than that.' They exchanged addresses. James shook John's hand and Polly said, 'Will you see Simon again?'

'I think it's likely.'

'Tell him we think of him and would have liked to see him but hadn't the address in time. Tell him friendly things.'

'I will,' John said, meaning it.

Several weeks passed. The picture show closed. Lambert was pleased.

'Perhaps another in the spring!'

There was no word to John from Marlow. Mme Blanchard said, 'Your friend at the Auberge is not well – not well at all.'

'Indeed he is not, madame.'

'He is worse. I hear it. You have not seen him for some weeks.'

'He will get in touch with me when he wishes to. I'm sure of that.'

'John, I think you should make the contact. It is not always wise to wait. Sometimes one regrets.'

Perhaps she was right, thought John as another week went by. It was September. The weather was perfect and he was painting furiously. He had received great stimulus from the show in Apt. Not only could he paint, he now felt, with a surge of joy, there were people who actually wanted to buy what he painted, and go on looking at it. Mme Blanchard looked on him with approval. She liked energy, respected enterprise, had a high regard for success. But one morning she murmured again, 'You should make the contact. He is still at the Varnas, your friend. You should not wait. One can regret these things.'

And that afternoon John walked to Varnas and left a note at the Auberge, inviting Marlow to dinner. The following day he got a message of acceptance.

They dined in a small restaurant, also in Varnas, less spacious (and less expensive) than the Auberge, but with pleasant food, quiet and friendly. John knew that if Marlow had a mind to continue his story he could do so there without too much clatter or interruption. As at the Auberge, there was a garden where guests drank their coffee. John hoped the atmosphere would not be too dissimilar. He found, a little to his surprise, that he had missed Simon Marlow. He was intrigued by what he had learned from the Todds of Marlow's more recent life. In a sense, John was ahead of the Marlow story, but he wanted to hear how much Marlow would himself say, and also owed him messages from the Todds.

John got over the latter task as soon as they met. He told Marlow that he had met old friends of his.

'They were asking after you. They were sorry to have missed you.'

'They were charming people. I knew them well. Do you recall I mentioned them in – in what I told you one evening?'

'I think I do.'

John felt Marlow might suspect they had talked more fully of him and his confidences than was the case. 'They wanted to hear how you were, of course. I didn't say much. You know.'

Marlow nodded. He understood and believed, and didn't greatly care. After dinner he said, 'Perhaps I'd better round the story off. Do you remember what I described last time we dined?'

'Vividly.'

'I stayed for another week in America, miserable, forlorn. I went through the motions of learning how the ETI office in New York worked. They made it clear that it didn't much matter whether I learned or didn't, but I supposed I must have some occupation and at the moment it was the only thing on offer. Arthur Rivers was busy digesting Wrench, and although he made clear that I would be, if I wished, a valued employee, I had served my main purpose. It was up to me.

I felt sickened by the thought of London, and particularly by the idea of Waldo Price. I returned to England like a wanted man. I felt that in every street, at every turn, eyes would recognize me and fingers point – Look at that man! He murdered the father of the girl he loved, and sold his employer to enemies! I told myself that I had acted throughout in good faith. I had shown up a rogue; the fact that that rogue had once befriended me counted little. He had had his reasons. I had executed a little posthumous vengeance on behalf of a man Julius Wrench had grievously wronged. That, surely, was justice. I had let the cat out of the bag about the finances of a number of unsavoury organizations. That, without question, was a patriotic duty, a public service. But I could not get rid of a feeling of sickness all the time. The sickness was with myself. And if I thought about Miranda I approached, quite certainly, a state of madness. I wanted her so terribly, missed her so desperately, was caused such unspeakable anguish by her rejection, her contempt, probably by now her hatred. And the best to hope for in that direction was that these emotions might just, one day, soften into indifference. Or was that not even worse? I lived in hell.

It did not help that Mr Austin told me that all the conditions of Boshy's testament were satisfied, that he could and must now make available to me a fortune. Nor did it help to find that it was substantially larger than Waldo Price had estimated. This fortune, which once was to be my passport to the favours of such as the Wrenches, make smooth my life with Miranda, erase lingering memories of childhood impoverishment, give me standing in the world – this fortune was tainted. It was purchased with the soul's blood. It was Faust's reward. I gave directions for its investment without joy. My only gleam of genuine pleasure derived from the thought that at least I could now do something tangible for my mother.'

'But even this thought,' said Marlow, 'was a mirage.' He was silent some time and John could see he was finding it hard to relate this part.

'I visited my mother at Penterton a few days after my return. She told me that she had cancer. A very malignant, rapidly developing cancer. She had known for some weeks but had not wanted to put a burden of worry on me before going to America. It was curious that she had sensed I might have burdens already to bear. I had not indicated it – far from it. But she was always shrewd.

I told her I now had money. We would solve this if money could do anything for it; medicine these days had made great strides; get the best man – I gabbled on. She shook her head.

'No, Simon, Dr Heathcote is very sensible, and I've seen good people down here. I know what's what.'

'And all I want is to stay here,' she added.

As we sat together in sadness and recollection that evening my mother said, 'That was a terrible, an extraordinary business about Julius Wrench. Then all those stories in the papers. It was on television too.'

'Awful.'

'Simon,' said my mother rather sternly, 'you ought to know something, and I must ask you something. I wrote to Mrs Wrench. I told her how distressed I was for her. How I'd met her husband once and how nice he'd been. How good they'd been to you. How devoted you were to her son. How much I felt for her in her sorrow.'

'I'm glad you did, Mother.'

'She wrote back after only a few days although she must have had a lot of letters. What she wrote, poor thing, upset me very much.'

My mother worked away at her interminable needlework and did not look up at me.

'Viola Wrench said, in her letter back, that I probably didn't know what you'd done. She said that you, personally, had put around the terrible stories about her husband which broke his heart and caused him to destroy himself. She wrote a long letter. She said she knew this would cause me pain, but that she could never forgive the part you'd played. That's what she said.'

I sat in silence. My mother said, 'What I want to know, Simon, is what she meant. What am I to believe?' She raised her eyes and held mine. And I knew that she had the right to know. Before she left me, as soon she would, she had the right to know.'

15

'That evening at Penterton,' said Marlow, 'I told my mother everything.

I told her that I had agreed to right a wrong by bringing down Julius Wrench – with the inward reservation that I would and could try to do this only if I discovered he had genuinely been guilty of some malpractice. He had and I did. I told her, without equivocation, that to succeed in this had been the condition of receiving a substantial legacy. I had succeeded. I had received. I had avenged Boshy. I was rich.

I told her that Julius Wrench had, without question, betrayed Boshy and – in my view – betrayed his country. She questioned this, quietly.

'Is it against the law, what he did? Is it actually illegal for these people – I don't hold any brief for them, of course – for them to receive foreign money like that? Did he connive at a crime?'

'I'm not sure. Technically perhaps, yes. But the real point is that these really are subversive organizations, Mother. They're out to destroy Britain as we know it, while pretending to hold a "liberal" point of view – or even to be non-political. Now, people may sympathize with that. But Julius didn't. Far from it. He just acted as a Soviet paymaster. Secretly. I think that's appalling. It's just possible that once, when young, he was recruited by the Communists and had some sort of conviction, a young man's conviction – but I've thought about it endlessly and I don't think so. He did it for profit. And all the time he posed as a pillar of what people call "the Establishment".'

My mother went on with her needlework. Then I told her

about Miranda. Not quite all, but a good deal. It was hard to do; the wound was raw. My mother sighed. There was a long silence between us. After a little she murmured, 'Poor Simon.'

I tried, out of my misery, to summon a touch of bravado.

'I'm not the first man to lose a woman . . .'

There was silence again. Then she said, very softly, 'Did you want money so terribly badly, my poor darling? When you were young?'

I didn't answer. I couldn't speak. I shook my head.

'My poor, dear boy! You should never have agreed to those extraordinary conditions. Maybe poor Julius Wrench deserved retribution. I rather think he did. But by bringing it about for money you poisoned the whole business. Don't you see that?'

I sat there, numb.

'You loved these people – not Julius, but the rest of his family. You loved them, yet you set out on a road which could only earn their hatred. What you did was self-defeating. It had to be.'

I mumbled something about justice. My mother said sharply, 'Justice is one thing – a clean thing. Even revenge may be a clean thing. Maybe wrong, maybe cruel, but a clean, genuine emotion. What you did was quite different. It was mercenary. Your only genuine emotion, Simon, was greed. Not revenge, not justice, not hatred even. Just greed. And look what it's brought.'

We sat silently again, and again after a little she sighed and said, 'My poor, poor darling. But all that matters is that you should see it.'

I left for London next morning. Before she died, four months later, my mother at least had the satisfaction of knowing that I did see it.

I wrote to Miranda. Although I had little hope of a reply, I wrote. I sent my letter to Cadogan Square, typing the address on the envelope to avert the possibility that my familiar writing would be sufficient to bring about its destruction, unread. Then I lived with sick anxiety for several weeks, during which time she could receive it, forwarded, wherever she was. There was no reply, of course.

People come to one's help, find one, even in the darkest and most lonely times. It's curious – it's as if certain helping spirits really are guided towards one at critical moments, turning out to be exactly the people one needs. That happened to me in Singapore with the Princes, as I've told you, when I first learned of Miranda's engagement to Bartholomew. It happened even more traumatically now. I met the Rudbergs again – Toni and Marcia Rudberg. They live, or lived then, at Bargate in Sussex. You've told me you know it – some relationship, you said . . . ?'

'Yes,' John said. 'The Marvell house. You mentioned it in connexion with your friend Franzi Langenbach and I said the Marvells are cousins of mine and I used to stay at Bargate when I was a child.'

'Quite so. Marcia Marvell married this Austrian, Toni Rudberg. When her brother was killed in that accident in 1958, she inherited Bargate – I mean she inherited it when her father died a few years later. About the same time as her brother's death she left her first husband and ran off with Toni Rudberg. They'd known each other in the war, you see. I think, from the way they were together, they'd been lovers in the war. But, as a relation, I expect you know all that.'

John remembered, from childhood, his parents, scandalized, in the post-war years. 'Poor Hilda,' they said, lips pursed. 'That girl of hers has made a real mess of things! Spent the war in Germany, got mixed up with heaven knows what young men! Lucky not to be in prison! Poor Hilda.' For the youthful John, unknown Cousin Marcia Marvell, or whatever she became, had a certain fascination. He said, 'How do these Marvells – Rudbergs, rather – come into your story? I remember how, weeks ago, you said Bargate once meant quite a lot to you.'

'I met them again about that time,' Marlow said. 'In 1970,

I think – anyway, it was after my mother died. I was still working in London. They'd been married about ten years and weren't exactly young – Toni must have been in his late fifties at least, Marcia a good deal younger and still delightful to look at. I can't remember where I ran into them – I drifted about London when I wasn't in the office. I saw a few people and I suppose I found myself talking to the Rudbergs. They asked me to Bargate. I will always remember the sense of peace, of comfort. Toni and Marcia were extraordinary – middle-aged people, they were like newly-weds. It was rather touching, and it was good for me to see the possibility of happiness even though it was incredibly painful. On the whole, I think that when one's unhappy one prefers the company of other unhappy people. They are in harmony with one's own suffering and like exercises a certain gravitational pull on like, depressing though it is to say it. But one can be helped, too, by the exact opposite, by being shown that although one may be slithering about in the mud at the bottom of the hill there are mountain peaks still. And the sun touches them,' added Marlow, with an unaccustomed glint of imagery.

'They knew the Wrenches. I knew about them from Franzi Langenbach long ago. They –'

John interrupted.

'You confirmed to me earlier that it was Miranda – who was the one mixed up in that Langenbach kidnapping.'

'Certainly. In 1972. It was much reported. Miranda herself was also kidnapped.'

'That's it! Headlines everywhere, some sort of hostage . . .'

Marlow nodded.

'Naturally, the story stunned me. I only knew what we read in the papers, watched or heard on the news. Miranda was demanded by terrorists – by name – as hostage. They intended to hold her while one of their number was operated on for a dangerous condition by Franzi Langenbach, this surgeon they'd kidnapped and would release for the operation. It was a bizarre episode. Miranda agreed to do it.'

'Why?'

'Perhaps,' said Marlow, 'she was in love with Franzi, whose life, I suppose, was at stake. I've told you about Franzi, I've described him earlier. He was a charmer.'

'You have indeed.'

'It was a peculiar business. But I must continue a little about the Rudbergs. They gave me at that time, God knows why, understanding and relief. They knew Miranda a little. I stayed with them several times. I could, you see, talk about Miranda. That was the relief – I could talk about Miranda to someone who knew what she looked like, sometimes even saw her. For a little while I thought we might be brought together – or tried to think it. I used to hatch plans and put them to the Rudbergs – couldn't they ask Miranda to stay and then I'd turn up? That sort of thing. We'd meet conventionally – and then, perhaps, the old magic would work, would be at least given a chance to work. In the end I remember Marcia saying, 'My dear, I have to tell you this. The bitterness against you is much too strong for that sort of arrangement to be a success. One hears things, you see. They are *really* bitter.'

'Including Miranda, I suppose.'

'Very much including Miranda.'

I didn't tell the Rudbergs everything. In fact I didn't really tell them very much – just that I had discovered Julius Wrench was playing a dirty game and I exposed it, which led to his suicide. I didn't tell them about Boshy. Or Waldo Price. Marcia said to me once, 'The story going about is that you did all this for money.'

'Not true.'

I said that. I still tell myself there's something in it – in spite of what my mother had said and I had conceded to her. I don't think the Rudbergs believed me entirely. I expect they reckoned I'd had a sizeable *douceur* from ETI, something like that. Whatever they believed, they were unfailingly affectionate and understanding to me. I know Toni Rudberg thought I was rather neurotic, and should simply shrug my shoulders and find another girl, but he didn't say much. Marcia understood me perfectly. Once she said, 'One lives through situations, one just keeps going. Don't plan too much. Things happen. Even you will be surprised one day.'

Marlow was silent for a minute, and then remarked with an unusual, indeed unprecedented, note of bitterness, 'The only surprise, to tell the truth, has been the discovery of the nearness of death!'

They sat in the warm Provençal darkness for a long time. Marlow did not make a move to go. Nor did he speak. At last John said, 'You've said perhaps Miranda was in love with Franzi Langenbach. When she went through all she did for him – I remember something of the story.'

'I have to consider that possibility. Why not? I can't tell.' He was holding his voice very steady. He added, 'I don't think they've married or anything like that.'

'She got away safe?' John had forgotten how the Langenbach story ended.

'Yes. Miranda got away safe. That I know, and she was pretty brave. That I would always have known.'

'You've never seen her again?'

'I saw her once. I saw her last year – by accident. I seldom go to London now. I sometimes have business there – once every few months at the most. I live in the West Country, very quietly, and if I go to London, I go by train. I hate driving in the place. I go by train and I walk everywhere. I sometimes take taxis, occasionally the underground. I spend the minimum of time, and I get away as fast as I can. I rarely pass a night there.

In November last year, 1977, I had to go up. As a matter of fact, it was to see a specialist. Things got much worse very soon after all the business I've described to you. Pain – I'm not going to talk about that. Anyway, my doctor in Bristol, a most intelligent and delightful man, wanted me to see someone in London. When I came out into Harley Street there was little doubt in my mind. The news, as far as survival went, was a good deal worse than even I had hitherto expected. I told you about that at the beginning. My only hope, if you can call it hope, might have been an operation on an artery that's so well tucked away that they almost certainly would kill me trying to get at it! And for what purpose? It was better to thank this particular specialist, say I'd think it over and leave. I knew perfectly well there was nothing that could be done for me, in spite of the way he hedged his opinion. I was, anyway, reconciled to the fact that I'd got a short time. Now it was a year, perhaps two. Not more.

It was raining on that November afternoon. There wasn't a taxi to be had. I walked, not feeling nor caring much, towards Oxford Street. The rain came down heavier. Still no sign of a taxi. I know what you're thinking – with a lot of money, why don't I hire a driven car on these occasions? Well, I didn't, and I don't. I like solitude – and anonymity, I suppose. I reached Oxford Circus.

I dived into the underground. I was very wet, I'd had my death sentence. I bought a ticket to Paddington and got on to the downward escalator.

Then I saw Miranda. She was on the escalator going up. I looked across in the sort of uninterested way one does when propelled by an impersonal machine like that, beyond one's control to stop or reverse – and there she was! I spotted her, looking upwards, a little way below me. She had a headscarf, a raincoat, her face was flushed from the cold and damp. She looked the same as ever – glorious! She was nearly ten years older than when we'd broken for ever – thirty-five, I reckoned. Glorious! In the second before we came level I remember feeling surprise at her being on the Oxford Circus underground at all – it wasn't exactly her style in earlier days! But the extraordinary thing was the way the years dissolved and I was seeing her as I first did, as in our snatched, secret times in London. I went scarlet – I hadn't blushed for years. My heart raced. I called out, very loudly, 'Miranda!'

She looked across. I don't think I'd greatly changed in appearance in those years –'

John wondered. He suspected the great, pale man sitting opposite, with the attractive, haunted face, had had lines which were never there in 1968.

'– She looked across. Her eyes were exactly the same. They held mine, and opened very wide. She seemed to be saying something. She didn't look away, didn't cut me. As her escalator continued upwards I saw her turn her head and look downwards. I shouted, 'Wait at the top, Miranda!' and when I reached the bottom I pushed into the crowd and ascended, heart pounding. I didn't climb – I knew my limitations by now, and I didn't want to pass out. But when I reached the top she was not there.

I considered writing – writing, after all those years. I didn't know if she was still Mrs Bartholomew, if she'd married again, if she lived in England, America or anywhere else. From that kidnapping incident I remembered references to her working somewhere in London, but I'd not tormented myself again with details and anyway that was five years ago. I'd cut myself off, absolutely, in recent years. I'd avoided any circles where talk of the Wrenches might have been heard. I never saw the Rudbergs these days.

And I didn't write. I never saw Miranda again.'

Marlow said nothing of his activities, his charitable enterprises in Bristol. After a while he told John he must be going. There was no mention of another evening together. He obviously felt some word of valediction, of signing off, was necessary, but didn't know how to express it, and John realized that this articulate man of extraordinary memory, given to describing scenes as if they had occurred yesterday, capable of total recall, could not find the words to show that his story was at an end. Perhaps, thought John, in this like most of us, he could not, even now, quite believe that it was. John tried to help him. He said, as lightly as he could, that he'd been moved and fascinated by the whole account, honoured by Marlow's confidence. Marlow looked at him, as ever, impersonally. Polite as always, he was looking, John knew, at a listening machine.

'Thank you. I'm afraid I've not been a cheerful companion, but your attention has been a great help to me. As I have several times told you, I needed to say all this aloud. I have not done so before. I had no desire, nor energy, to write it down. It is not an agreeable story. I told myself from the start that I had been appointed an instrument of justice. What does that mean? There was no question of deterring other people from doing the sort of thing Wrench had done to Henry Kinzel. And nobody was thinking of reforming him, making him see the error of his ways! No, what was needed was vengeance – retribution. Is that justice? I think that often it has to be.'

His voice was a little stronger than it had been, but whether from inner conviction or from the effort to feel it John knew not. Marlow went on more quietly.

'My story is not heroic. It is certainly not a story of success. I earned, if you can call it that, a great deal of money. I also earned the contempt of the only persons I loved – for my mother despised me too, although she loved and forgave. I betrayed – whether that is the fair word I am still unsure. Does betrayal involve motive? Mine were mixed. Doesn't most betrayal come from a good deal of confusion, self-deception, as well as greed, revenge or whatever? My mother said greed was my only clear emotion. In that, I think, even she was less than fair.

Betrayal – I have read, somewhere, of a theory that when Judas betrayed Christ he acted from good motives. He wanted to force the issue, to make Him and others defend themselves, come out into the open, raise the standard of revolt. The thirty pieces of silver were simply a cover to make his action credible. He didn't need them personally. I haven't the faintest idea whether there's anything in that. If there is, he is a most unfortunate man. Anyway,' said Marlow without particular bitterness, 'I didn't go and hang myself. I didn't need to.'

John asked if he planned to stay longer in Provence.

'I like it here,' Marlow said. 'I've got things organized at home now, I shall like the autumn here, I know. I'm going away for a few weeks next Sunday. I've got a whim to go to Rome, a city I've never visited, and I've arranged it. It will be good for them here to get rid of me for a little. Of course,' he said in his matter-of-fact and unaffected way, 'I may not get back. I suppose the clock might strike at any time now and even the flurry of a comfortable journey might move its hands on. Dr Pelegrin has shrugged his shoulders – he's armed me with all sorts of medicines and letters of explanation to Italian doctors if I collapse on the way. Then I plan to come back. They're decent people at the Auberge de Varnas, and I suppose the place has become somehow woven into my life because I have been able to relive it here, in telling it to your patient ears.' He smiled, as he did infrequently, with very great charm. 'I hope we meet again – John,' he said, using the name as he had only rarely, almost establishing another human link than that between chronicler and audience. 'I hope we meet again, I'm so glad your show of pictures went well. I know I should have gone to see them but I felt rather done in, that week.'

'I hope there'll be another in the spring.'

'Perhaps then,' he said, 'perhaps in the spring.' He rose to walk back to the Auberge and John knew he wanted to walk alone. They shook hands and Marlow turned as he left the garden, raising a hand in a half-wave, a rather more decisive gesture than his usual goodnight. It was a dismissal. To John's surprise he found his eyes wet with tears.

It was exactly three weeks after that last dinner with Simon Marlow that John returned to Les Manottes one evening to find Mme Blanchard eager to impart news.

'John, you have had a visitor. If you had been at home painting you would have been here to receive –'

John had been in Aix all day. 'What sort of visitor, madame?'

'It was a lady. She will probably call again tomorrow morning. I said you would be working – painting – here in your *atelier.*'

'Did she,' John said hopefully, 'look as if she wanted to buy a picture?' There had been one or two enquiries since the exhibition at Apt, and one American had arrived with great enthusiasm only to find, disappointingly, that John had not been the painter of the pictures he had apparently seen and coveted.

Mme Blanchard was unsure. On the one hand the visitor had arrived (she was either English or American, Mme Blanchard had not exactly distinguished) in a smart car, exuding a certain aura of wealth. Mme Blanchard was as perceptive as any Frenchwoman in noting particulars, observation of which did credit to an artist's widow while deductions therefrom would not have disgraced Sherlock Holmes. On the other hand, Mme Blanchard (who appeared to have 'taken to' this vistor) had asked if she wished to make an appointment to see M. Tranter 'in the *atelier*', and the unknown lady had seemed disappointingly vague. She would 'try' to return in the morning. It did not sound very promising.

'It doesn't sound as if she's after a Tranter creation, Madame Blanchard.'

'Only God creates,' said Mme Blanchard sternly. 'Some of you interpret.' This, thought John, might well be so.

However, he planned nothing for the following day, and at about midday was pushing some paint tubes round his working table when a middle-sized BMW drove up to Mme Blanchard's door. He looked out of the 'studio' window whence he could observe and get some warning. He had never seen the woman before. She walked to Mme Blanchard's front porch, adjusting some dark glasses which she must have removed for driving. As far as John could see in the few seconds available before he heard Mme Blanchard at the door and a lot of '*Bonjour, madame*' and '*Bien sûr, bien sûr*', his visitor was a woman of great elegance. Dark hair was straight and gathered at the nape of the neck, skin was olive but not, it seemed, excessively bronzed by life in a southern climate. She was wearing blue linen trousers and a loose coral-coloured shirt. So much John saw – and noted with appreciation a slim, superb figure – before she vanished into the interior with La Blanchard. The latter was right, John thought. There was, here, a chic which implied money. Might she also have with it taste which had led her to seek an original Tranter or two?

There was commotion outside and John moved to the door as if taken by surprise. Mme Blanchard hovered enthusiastically.

'I'm John Tranter. You came yesterday – I'm sorry I wasn't here. Do come in – it's rather a muddle I'm afraid . . .'

She came into the studio. Mme Blanchard withdrew, making genial observations addressed to nobody in particular.

John's visitor said, 'My name is Miranda Wrench.'

So this was Miranda! Not Miranda Bartholomew, either. And not Miranda something else. Divorced but not remarried probably. Miranda Wrench! John looked at her.

His first reaction was that Simon Marlow had by no means exaggerated. This was a delicious woman. She had lively eyes – the dark glasses had been taken off again on coming into the studio – flawless skin, and a figure with which John could find no fault at all. She had a serious expression – tragedienne rather than comedienne, he thought. She did not look radiant or happy, and John supposed, knowing all he did, that it would have jarred upon him had she done so. But of her beauty there could be no doubt, and it made him catch his breath. She must have been used to producing this effect but she showed it not at all. She was as unselfconscious as she was exquisite.

'I'm sorry to break in on you. Your address was given to me by the Todds – friends of mine, James and Polly Todd.'

'Of course. They were out here last month.'

'They much liked your pictures. I run a small gallery in London and I'd love to see some of your work if I may?'

'Delighted!'

'But that's not really, or primarily, why I'm here,' she said, with a smile which removed any slight from the words. 'The thing is that the Todds understood you have been seeing a good deal of someone I used to know, someone called Simon Marlow.'

'That's true! Do you want his address? He's been staying at the Auberge de Varnas, which is a short way from here, but I happen to know he's away at the moment. He should be back quite soon. We had dinner together a few days before he left. He went to Rome.'

'No,' she said, 'I have his address – Varnas. You gave that to the Todds. I just wanted, if I may, to ask one or two things. You see . . .' She was hesitant, in difficulties. It was a curious situation. John knew – or thought he knew – a great deal about this woman and he certainly knew a great deal (assuming Marlow to be truthful) about her and Marlow. What her life had been in the last ten years he could not guess, but of those passionate and tragic events of 1968 he was more fully informed than anybody has a right to be of someone else's affairs. He could not let her talk, the usual commonplace half-concealments of life, while all the time knowing so much. Yet he could not, surely, make free with Marlow's confidence. Simon Marlow had come to terms with the past in his own way. He had now accustomed himself to the idea of meeting death soon, and uncomplaining. John knew that he should do nothing to disturb him, but must neglect nothing which could, conceivably, help or comfort him. Even now. Even when the hour was so late. The whole situation was complicated by the fact that within the three minutes which had passed since John first saw her he had discovered in Miranda a powerful, an outrageous attraction for himself. It is dangerous to step into a dream.

'Do please,' John said, 'ask away. But wouldn't it be better to ask over a drink? Even over an omelette? There's a little café I frequent. And it's the right time.'

'Thank you. I'd like that.'

And as they walked to the café John knew, with a good deal of regret, what he had to do.

'So you see,' John said, 'I know how Simon feels. And I know, at least from his point of view, how it all happened.'

Miranda had heard him in silence as he told her, in the merest outline, that he had learned from a heartbroken Marlow the story of Wrench Holdings, the fate of Julius Wrench, the eclipse of his own love. John told her what he knew of Marlow's physical condition, of a near-inaccessible artery behind the heart, of his indifference to the possibilities of operation or cure and his scepticism about them.

'One thing is certain. He loved you desperately, he loves you still, he will love you always. But always isn't going to be very long.'

Miranda thanked him; a reserved enchantress, whose serene personality John could all too easily imagine complementing the inner force, the clarity of mind of Marlow himself. She wanted to think about all that had been said. Meanwhile, she said, she wanted John to know certain things. Her words helped complete a picture in John's mind, brought to bear a crossbeam on people and events.

Miranda told how both she and her brother, 'whom Simon perhaps talked about', had taken a long time to come to terms with the fact that their father had, indeed, done evil things. 'We loved him,' she said, 'and always will. We've seen it all now, Harry and I – we're very close. My father was very ambitious. He was impatient of anybody who stood in his way. He was obviously impatient with this man I didn't know

– Simon's friend, Kinzel. Then, he obviously despised these various organizations he was made to give Communist money to; he thought that they were futile people, that their power for harm was grossly exaggerated, that if he could make money out of the Communists simply by directing some funds in particular, useless directions, why not? I'm sure he calculated it could do no real harm to the country, and it could do a lot of good to his company, which was of real benefit to Britain – to the economy and so forth. I don't say that's right, but I'm sure it's how he saw it. Can you understand that?'

John said he thought so. He felt scepticism. Somehow Simon Marlow's portrait of Julius Wrench – ruthless, unscrupulous; perhaps tempted not only by gain but by the atmosphere of secrecy, of influence exercised unseen; merciless to opponents – this portrait was more compelling than the flawed but beloved father of Miranda's description. Yet both, thought John, doubtless have validity. It depends where one's standing. And Miranda, thought John, could not possibly see Boshy clearly; as Simon Marlow saw him; as John, too, now thought he saw him.

'But of course it was wrong, and of course it was defensible to expose it. It looked like treachery, corruption – any name you like to give. And I've come to think Simon had a – a right to do what he did.

'Then there's the business of him doing it for money. Of course, I now see it wasn't quite like that. This old man, Kinzel, wanted my father shown up – thought he deserved it. Simon agreed. It's understandable. Kinzel was his patron. Simon thought he owed it to him to be a – a champion. I couldn't accept such a thing at first but I do now. It must have set up some terrible conflicts of loyalty. In a way I suppose it was rather heroic of Simon.'

This was moving extremely fast. John said, 'I don't think he now looks on it like that, himself.'

'Of course not. He's still, I expect, eaten with guilt – because of what happened to Daddy. But I understand it all now. And of course he couldn't foresee what was obviously a mental breakdown; leading to suicide.'

'I'm sure he didn't. Not that.'

'Now,' said Miranda, 'I want to talk to Simon. I want to see him. I want to heal something that I think is healable. One can't drag these misunderstandings to –'

'One could say to the grave.'

'Right,' she said fiercely, 'right, one could. And there's more to it than just a sort of reconciliation. You see, I think I can help him. I happen to know about his heart condition. At least, I can guess, and what you've told me confirms the guess. I expect his condition was largely brought on by the strains and stresses through which he lived – the awful inner distraction – and I'm sure it's as serious and complicated as you say. He went to see a specialist in London, a friend of my brother's, it happens, though Simon didn't know that. Of course, they don't talk about cases, but this man let drop to my brother last November that he'd seen, recently, a previous friend of Harry's, who was mixed up in what they call the "sad business of 'sixty-eight": Simon Marlow. Nothing more, but he's a very great heart specialist and it wasn't hard to put two and two together. Harry mentioned it to me. I was in London at the time, I live there now.'

You were, John thought, on the Oxford Circus underground.

'Last month when the Todds told me about meeting you and hearing about Simon I went to see Dr Rathbone – the man I'm talking about. I said I was interested in open-heart surgery. It's been developed in the States a lot more than in Europe and I knew a number of Americans who experienced – or witnessed in their friends – some really extraordinary cures. There's an amazing man in Boston – I suppose Simon told you I was once married to an American and lived in the States – yes, of course he did, he told you a good deal about us. That was all over – divorce – long ago.

'I said to Dr Rathbone I wasn't asking anything I shouldn't, but that I had a friend who'd consulted him. I named Simon. I said that I just wanted him to know that *if* there was any hope for Simon, in his opinion, in open-heart surgery, I wanted to make funds available. I went to America a lot, I told him, and I knew the expense – but also the possibilities. I wanted no answer, no comment. I just wanted him to know, in case at some future date he found the information useful.'

'But Miranda,' John said quietly, 'Simon Marlow is a very rich man.'

'Naturally I knew that. That was what Dr Rathbone said, at once. He said, "I don't think money would be his impediment. Will-power perhaps, but not money." Of course, that told me what I wanted to know. Simon can't be bothered with an operation that's maybe dangerous and difficult, not because he fears it but because he's decided to die. He's under forty and he's decided to die. He has no will to live. But he *could* live! Even now he could make a fresh start! I could take him to America. I could make him have these operations. I'd be with him all the time.'

Her energy was infectious. It might be done. Yes, John thought, as he looked at her, by now jealous and certainly enthralled, it might be done.

Miranda said, with determination, 'And, of course, there is Franzi Langenbach. He's working in New York, there's nobody better, and there's a particular connexion –'

She seemed to hesitate, and John said, 'To save whom you agreed to be a hostage. Six years ago, was it?'

'You know about that?'

'It was in all the English papers – and some of the French ones. And Simon read it. And mentioned it in his story. He talked quite often about Franzi Lagenbach.'

Miranda nodded.

'Franzi Langenbach is the most brilliant heart surgeon of his generation. And a dear friend. What's more, he once knew Simon. When we were all young. He'd do it, naturally. In New York.'

'Naturally. Miranda, may I ask you something – something personal to me? When Simon first mentioned the name Franzi Langenbach it struck a chord of memory. He had some sort of – connexion – with a family called Marvell, a house in Sussex called Bargate.'

'Yes,' said Miranda, 'he did. How odd that you should know that. And know about Bargate. Franzi – well, there's a close relationship. It's a strange story – he's really the son of Anthony Marvell, you know. Anthony died – a car crash with Franzi driving. The sister, Marcia Rudberg as she now is, inherited Bargate. She's Franzi's aunt, in fact if not publicly. And she's a dear friend of mine. She went through hell at the time of the kidnap.'

'She's a cousin of mine. Her mother was a Paterson. So was mine.'

'You know Bargate? I love it dearly.'

'I remember it, visiting it when I was young. It was an enchanted place. One felt the generations whispering to one in that great panelled room, the inner hall.'

'Yes, one did. But no more. Marcia's husband died last year, you know. She can't manage. She's sold Bargate – some Arabian embassy has bought it, as an out-of-London residence, I believe. Marcia's kept the land, of course.'

John felt a great sense of desolation. It had, like all childhood memories of beauty, been a part of his own inheritance. We do not only possess what is ours in law. So the Marvells had left Bargate at last! We disappear, leaves drift in the wind, what seemed almost permanent lasts only for a little while.

Miranda had finished, it seemed. An enchanted hour for John was over and there was melancholy in the warm Provençal air.

She said that she had booked into an hotel in Avignon, that she would descend on the Auberge de Varnas immediately Simon returned to it, and that she proposed to keep in touch with it every day.

John stood up. The business was over.

'May I ask you a very personal question?'

'Go ahead.'

'Do you suppose you still love Simon?'

She looked at John, that steady look of which Simon himself had spoken. There was a moment's silence.

'Yes. I know that perfectly well. I've tried to make myself believe I was – fond – of other people. Without success. There was about Simon something – his inner vulnerability, perhaps, his voice, his – oh, I don't know –'

There was a break in her voice now, the strength and certainty discomposed.

'May I ask you another question?'

'Of course.'

'Did you ever see Simon after you parted from him in anger immediately after your father's death?'

'I saw him once. In a crowd. We caught each other's eye – we couldn't meet or talk.'

So one passing moment on a London escalator had been enough to reawaken ancient magic, or remind of an unextinguished flame. John marvelled. They had, it seemed, fallen in love and known it instantly when both were young. One long look had then sufficed. Some years apart, and her indifferent marriage, had done nothing to change the hearts of Simon and Miranda. They had met again in London. A secret, intoxicating affair, short-lived, was followed by her disgusted rejection of him as the man who, deliberately, destroyed her father. Ten years later – years of which she had hardly spoken, years John could not envisage apart from the peculiar incident of the Langenbach kidnap – they had seen each other for a flash, an absurd situation reminiscent of ancient cinema. It had apparently been enough to confirm what Simon Marlow had said – the current which passed between them was a natural force, something that had existed, waiting for discovery, since the beginning of time. Something which had the strength to transcend misunderstandings and hostility.

Something which could not be altered, was destined, written in the stars. These people really were made for each other, in that unbelievable phrase. They inhabited a world apart and to them all else was illusion. Or so it might be, John thought, watching Miranda's grave face. She thanked him 'for a great deal, John', and drove away. John walked home, feeling extraordinarily lonely.

16

John never saw Simon Marlow again. Five days later Mme Blanchard grabbed him in the evening in high excitement.

'Your friend – your friend at the Auberge de Varnas –'

'Yes, Monsieur Marlow. Is he returned?'

'He returned two days ago. And now, suddenly, he has gone. They thought he was staying for another month. He told them so. He paid that woman for the inconvenience his change of plans had caused her. *Inconvenience*! Can you conceive of such a thing? When they have been robbing him for months!'

'I think he was happy there,' John said mildly. He was startled. He supposed that this was Miranda's doing and that he must rejoice. Mme Blanchard snorted.

Later John learned a little of what had happened. Miranda was 'that visitor of yours' to Mme Blanchard, disapproving now, who somehow resented Marlow's departure (and even more the largess he had apparently heaped upon the management of the Auberge de Varnas) and associated Miranda with its occasion. 'That visitor of yours,' she said, 'appeared at the Auberge the very evening your friend returned from Italy. He was very tired. He was probably not himself. We know he is extremely ill in any case – not long for this world. She sat with him *until midnight*! Imagine! A sick, exhausted man, and a woman imposes herself on him when he has not the strength to push her out! Well, he is rich, everybody knows that, but to be pursued in that way, it's disgraceful.

'And next day she returned – to lunch. At the Auberge. After lunch he told them he was going to leave next day. She collected him in her car. He telephoned England several times. They've gone to America together. Just like that!'

'Yes, madame,' John said. He smiled at her, and she looked at him, puzzled. 'Just like that.'

It was December when the envelope arrived with an English stamp, addressed in an unfamiliar hand. A letter and a newspaper cutting. From Polly Todd.

Dear John,

I don't know whether you have seen the enclosed? I gather all is going extraordinarily well – from every point of view. I have the feeling that you may know a good deal of the background to all this – from S.'s point of view at least. We're delighted. And Harry Wrench, Miranda's brother, who was once very fond of S., has entirely come round, I'm glad to say. It's an astonishing outcome. The last we heard was of an amazingly successful open-heart operation. They're still in the States. The operation was done by the Dr Langenbach who was kidnapped some years ago, and for whom Miranda was demanded as a hostage.

James says he always felt S. was driven on by demons. They once shared an apartment. Well, they drove him to some funny places but I reckon they've got him to the winning post now! Or something has! We'll come to Provence again one day. We promised – !

Love from us both,
Polly

'The enclosed' was a notice from *The Times* saying that Mr Simon Marlow and Mrs Miranda Wrench had been married quietly in Richmond, Virginia.

John was in Varnas that afternoon and some impulse made him enter the church where he had first seen Simon Marlow. The same curé was rustling about in a side-chapel. John put coins noisily into an alms box and approached him. They were alone. The curé looked up without enthusiasm.

'Father, I remember coming in here once in a very bad thunderstorm last July. You were in the church then, I recall.'

The priest grunted.

'There are many thunderstorms in July.'

'On this occasion I saw an Englishman, a stranger, in here. I happened to overhear him make a remark to you.'

'If you will excuse me, monsieur –'

'He said something about the time having perhaps come for some charity to be shown to Judas Iscariot, some pity for that unfortunate, even a candle lit. I wonder if you remember that peculiar conversation?'

'Something comes to my mind, some inappropriate blasphemy of the kind you mention,' said the curé impatiently. 'What of it? What is this about? Was this man a Catholic? Was he a friend of yours? Why do you ask me?'

'I don't know,' John said. 'I don't know any of that. I just wondered if he lit a candle in the end. It doesn't matter.'

Treason in Arms

THE KILLING TIMES
THE DRAGON'S TEETH
A KISS FOR THE ENEMY
THE SEIZURE
A CANDLE FOR JUDAS

Treason in Arms spans the years from 1912 to 1978 in many countries. A list of some of the individuals who played a part in the story is given below.

Anderson, Robert
Friend of Anthony Marvell, 1930s and 1940s

André, Monsieur
Russian émigré; taxi driver in Paris, 1930s

von Arzfeld, Frido
Born 1917; second son of Kaspar von Arzfeld

von Arzfeld, Kaspar
Retired colonel, seriously wounded 1918

von Arzfeld, Klara
Widow of Kaspar von Arzfeld's cousin; mother of Anna Langenbach

von Arzfeld, Lise
Sister of Werner and Frido von Arzfeld

von Arzfeld, Werner
Born 1912; elder son of Kaspar von Arzfeld; Panzer officer

Austin, Jacob
Lawyer; family friend of Henry Kinzel

Baker, Vivien
Employee of Wrench Holdings; later stockbroker, 1970s

Barinski, Klaretta
German terrorist, 1970s

Barnett, Bill
Senior executive, Wrench Holdings, 1960s

Barnett, Freddie
Oxford undergraduate, 1930s; brother of Bill Barnett

Bartholomew, Alexander
Son of American millionaire financier

Bastico, Stefano
Young resident of Umbertide, Italy, 1970s

Bates, John
Chairman of a Sussex Constituency Conservative Association, 1920s and 1930s

Berckheim, Christoph
Captain in the Wehrmacht; friend of Toni Rudberg, 1940

Betteridge, Francis
Eton housemaster, 1950s

Blanchard, Madame
John Tranter's land-lady in Provence, 1970s

Branson, Charlie
Friend of Wrench family

Breitfall, Wieland
SS Sturmführer; nephew of Christoph Fischer

Brendthase, Gerhardt
Officer in Saxon Guards Regiment, 1912; later adopted mother's name, 'von Premnitz'

Brendthase, Wilhelm
Berlin businessman; father of Gerhardt

Brenndorf, Captain
Brother officer and friend of Toni Rudberg; wounded at Stalingrad, 1942

Bressler, Lt-Colonel
Commandant of Oflag VI, 1945

Brigitta, Sister
Ward Sister of hospital in Silesia, 1945

Briscoe, Mrs
English grandmother of Anna Langenbach

Carr, Francis
British diplomat, 1911–40; cousin of the Marvell family

Clandon, Bruce
London banker, 1972

Delac, Michel
French minister, 1934; friend of Adrian Winter

Dietrich, Sepp
SS Obergruppenführer

Dillon, Desmond
Born 1906; aspiring novelist and investigative journalist; son of Patsy Dillon

Dillon, Emma
Probation officer; twin sister of Desmond Dillon

Dillon, Patsy
Widow; mother of the Dillon twins

Drew, Dominic
Journalist and intriguer; known as 'Printer'

Fantini, Angelica
Young married woman in Perugia, 1972

Feely, Thomas
Groom to the Alan Marvells at Ballinslaggart, 1916

Fischer, Christoph
Distinguished German journalist, 1920s and 1930s; wounded in 1916 in France

Forrest, Angela
'Cousin Angie'; married Francis Carr

Frenzel, Rudolf
Official in Justice Department, Federal German Government, 1972

Gaisford, Henry
Businessman, London 1911

Gaisford, Veronica
Wife of Henry Gaisford

Gunther
Christoph Fischer's manservant in Berlin

Headley
Left-wing publicist, London, 1920s

Hermann
Guard at Oflag XXXIII

von Hochstein
Sturmführer SS, 1934

Hoffmann, Captain
Colleague of Frido von Arzfeld in the Bendlerstrasse, 1943–4

Josef
Austrian member of 'European Liberation Front', 1970s

Kinzel, Henry ('Boshy')
Businessman, patron of the arts, 1920s and 1930s; brother officer of John Marvell, 1917

von Kleist, Colonel-General
Werner von Arzfeld's commander, 1939

Krempe
Ex-Captain, member of the 'Black Reichswehr', 1923

Langenbach, Anna
née von Arzfeld; wife of Kurt Langenbach

Langenbach, Franzi
Son of Anna

Langenbach, Frau
Mother of Kurt Langenbach

Langenbach, Gottfried
Father of Kurt Langenbach

Langenbach, Captain Kurt
Distinguished Luftwaffe officer, 1930s

Ling Kuo Seng
'Jimmy Ling'; Chinese businessman in Singapore, 1960s

Marcus
Soviet Control officer in London, 1920s and 1930s

Marlow, Mrs
Simon Marlow's mother

Marlow, Simon
Employee of Wrench Holdings and also of Ling Kuo Seng, 1960s and 1970s

Marvell, Alan
Lieutenant-Colonel; Owner of Bargate

Marvell, Anthony
Son of John Marvell

Marvell, Helena
Widow, mother of Alan and John Marvell

Marvell, John
Publisher; younger son of Helena Marvell

Marvell, Marcia
Daughter of John Marvell

Meier, Ilse
Inmate of Tissendorf Concentration Camp, 1945

Muller, Herr
Gestapo officer, 1944–5

Oliphant, Charles
Captain, inmate of Oflag XXXIII

Oliphant, Robin
Charles Oliphant's younger brother

Parano, Vittorio
Petty crook in northern Italy, 1970s

Parham, Philip
Diplomat, British Embassy, Berlin 1912

Paterson, Cosmo
Adventurer, Intelligence officer, brother of Hilda Marvell

Paterson, Hilda
Wife of John Marvell

Paterson, Stephen
MP, 1930s; younger brother of Cosmo Paterson

Playfair, Alaric
Cambridge professor, 1920s, 'The Tapir'

Ponti, Battisto
Police Lieutenant, Perugia, 1970s

Price, Waldo
Friend and confidant of Henry Kinzel

Puxley, Anthea
Friend of Arthur Rivers and acted as hostess for him, 1960s

Reitz, Edle
Widow, friend of Sonja Vassar in Bamberg, 1933

Rivers, Arthur
Executive chairman of Eastern Trading Incorporated, 1960s and 1970s

Rodoski, Casimir
Known as 'Serge'; Polish journalist in Berlin, 1932

Rosio, Carla
Member of 'European Liberation Front', 1970s

Rudberg, Amalie
Countess; cousin of Toni Rudberg, chaperone of Marcia Marvell, 1939

Rudberg, Casimir
Count; husband of Amalie Rudberg

Rudberg, Toni
Count; Panzer and Staff officer, 1940s

Schwede, Egon
Kreisleiter of Langenbach; later SS Obersturmbannführer

von Seeckt, General Chief of the Reichswehr, 1920s

Starckheim, Clemens
Fiancé of Anna von Arzfeld

Tate, Theo
Discount broker in London; aspiring parliamentary candidate, 1930s

Todd, James
Barrister; employee of Wrench Holdings, 1960s

Todd, Polly
Half-American wife of James Todd

Tranter, John
English painter in Provence, 1970s

Vanetti, Reno
Member of 'European Liberation Front', 1970s

Vassar, Sonja
Journalist, Berlin, 1930s

Wendel, Maria
Schoolmistress of Kranenberg, Lower Saxony, 1940s

Winter, Adrian
MP; long-serving member for a Sussex constituency

Winter, Mary
Adrian Winter's first wife; lived at Faberdown

Withers, Colonel
On Staff, Dublin, 1916

Wrench, Harry
Merchant banker; son of Julius Wrench

Wrench, Julius
Entrepreneur; protégé of Adrian Winter; later chairman of Wrench Holdings

Wrench, Miranda
Daughter of Julius Wrench

Wrench, Viola
Wife of Julius Wrench

David Fraser

THE KILLING TIMES

Veronica Gaisford was an exceptional woman – beautiful, passionate, and utterly loyal to her native Ireland.

Amid the violence and bitterness of the First World War and the years that followed she bound together the lives of three very different men.

Francis Carr, a British Diplomat, desired her but doubted her apparent innocence. His cousin John Marvell loved her blindly, boundlessly, was prepared to perjure himself for her safety. More ambiguous was Veronica's relationship with Gerhardt, a young German officer in Berlin . . .

'David Fraser's story touches the pulse of history . . . in this enthralling good novel'

Daily Mail

David Fraser

THE DRAGON'S TEETH

The German Nazi movement of the 1920s and 30s attracted many a high-minded young patriot, as well as misfits and sadists. Wieland Breitfall, dedicated and idealistic, was one such rising star.

In England, Theo Tate, brilliant and ambitious, worked zealously for a different cause – as an undercover Communist.

Extremists like these – at either end of the political spectrum – are often portrayed as monsters. Yet they were sometimes people of great charm and character, and in that strange unsettled era they sometimes met.

This is the story of two who did.

'A rattling read' *The Times*

David Fraser

A KISS FOR THE ENEMY

Brought together by a drunken brawl in Oxford in 1937, Anthony Marvell and Frido von Arzfeld found friendship even as the threatening clouds of war were gathering over Europe. Then their families – sisters, cousins – found love against a background of growing hate and strident war cries.

From the false idyll of pre-war England and Germany, through the desperate fall of France in 1940, across the ravaged mountains of North Africa, to the savage carnage of Stalingrad, the Marvells and the von Arzfelds played their parts in the war and saw the bonds that had united their families put to the final test.

A KISS FOR THE ENEMY – an unforgettable story of a world at war.

'A constantly readable novel. His depiction of the battle scenes at Stalingrad and in the mountains of Tunisia are vivid and compelling.'

Yorkshire Post